Models of Musical Analysis

Series Editor Jonathan Dunsby

Early Twentieth-Century Music

Models of Musical Analysis
Series editor: Jonathan Dunsby
Professor of Music, University of Reading

Music Before 1600
Editor: Mark Everist
Lecturer in Music, King's College, London

Models of Musical Analysis

Early Twentieth-Century Music

edited by

Jonathan Dunsby

BLACKWELL
Reference

Copyright © Basil Blackwell Ltd

First published 1993
First published in USA 1993

Blackwell Publishers
108 Cowley Road
Oxford ox4 1JF
UK

238 Main Street
Cambridge, Massachusetts 02142
USA

British Library Cataloguing in Publication Data

A CIP catalogue record for this book is available from
the British Library.

Library of Congress Cataloging-in-Publication Data

Early twentieth-century music / edited by Jonathan Dunsby
    256 pp. 274 × 219 mm. – (Models of musical analysis)
    Includes bibliographical references
    ISBN 0-631-14335-1 (acid-free paper)
    1. Musical analysis. 2. Music—20th century—History and
criticism. I. Dunsby, Jonathan. II. Title: Early 20th-century
music. III. Series.
    MT90.E15 1993
    780'.9'04–dc20   93–20050
                                                          CIP
                                                          MN

ISBN 0-631-143-35-1

Typeset in 10 on 12 pt Baskerville
by Selwood Systems, Midsomer Norton

Printed and bound in Great Britain by
Alden Press, Oxford

This book is printed on acid-free paper

Contents

Acknowledgements

I am grateful above all to the contributors, for their diligence and forbearance: also to Cristle Collins Judd for her activity as research assistant in the early days of this project; to my supportive publishers John Davey and Sean Magee who were the inspiration behind it, and Alyn Shipton who has brought it to fruition; to the University of Reading and to the Warden and Fellows of New College, Oxford, for the time and opportunity to finish this work; and to Esther Cavett-Dunsby, for support beyond description.

Jonathan Dunsby
Reading, 1993

The editor and publisher would like to thank various publishers for permission to reproduce the following music extracts:

Béla Bartók, Sonata for Solo Violin. *Mikrokosmos* No. 133. Reproduced by kind permission of Boosey & Hawkes Music Publishers Ltd.

Alban Berg, *Sieben frühe Lieder*, No. 1. Copyright 1959 by Universal Edition A. G. Vienna.

Alban Berg, *Wozzeck*. Copyright 1931 by Universal Edition A. G. Vienna. Renewed copyright 1958 by Universal Edition A. G. Vienna. Act 3 copyright 1977, 1978 by Universal Edition A. G. Vienna.

Josef Hauer, Piano Etudes, Op. 22, No. 1. Copyright 1926, 1953 by Universal Edition A. G. Vienna.

Arnold Schoenberg, *Das Buch der Hängenden Gärten*, Op. 15, No. 5. Copyright 1914 by Universal Edition. Renewed copyright 1941 by Arnold Schoenberg.

Arnold Schoenberg, *Klavierstück*, Op. 33b. Copyright 1932 by Arnold Schoenberg. Renewed copyright 1952 by Gertrude Schoenberg.

Arnold Schoenberg, *Lockung*, Op. 6, No 7, from *Structural Functions of Harmony*. Reproduced by kind permission of Faber and Faber and of Lawrence Schoenberg.

Igor Stravinsky, Three Pieces for String Quartet, No. 3. Reproduced by kind permission of Boosey & Hawkes Music Publishers Ltd.

Introduction

The editor of this volume is far from being alone in his sense of awe at the achievement of the best composers in the early years of our century; and early twentieth-century music still conveys an effect of contemporaneity, confronting us with the mystery of what we are still learning to assimilate. There are analysts who believe that thinking about the music of this period is – apart from the special challenge of absorbing the music of our own age – the most important analytical thinking to be done. What the student needs is direct influence in the shaping of approaches to the repertory, 'models', if not of how it is essential to proceed, then at least of how others have proceeded with knowledge and conviction. Assimilation is one trend, but it is also true that composers are turning more and more towards a neo-Romantic, and certainly a neo-tonal attitude in their work. It cannot be long until the former pre-occupations will seem to represent a past age that we can begin to see much more clearly in its historical context than at the time when it was still possible to call the composers who figure here 'modern'. Some would claim that this is already the case. They will perhaps be fascinated to see how, to the extent that there is a consistent thread running through the arguments below of seven distinguished commentators, it is a concern with how music is organized, a concern that was kept alive in the early twentieth century as a lifeline between the late Romantic and the early 'postmodern' composer.

The format of the 'Aspects' in this volume is designed to enhance the student's appreciation of the complexity involved in any study of the early twentieth-century repertory. Orientation/Method/Model/Summary is the template, though each author treats it with flexibility in the interests of each topic. The common intention of the seven chapters is twofold: to provide a thorough exegesis which can satisfy the undergraduate that the essence of an analytical issue is learnable to a realistic depth; and to provide the framework – in ideas, repertory and bibliography – of further investigation for those who specialize in analysis or, indeed, in the history of the period. Although this is intended as a textbook on which teachers can base modules of courses in theory and analysis, it should also serve as an adjunct to the courses in the history of twentieth-century music that are now considered obligatory in virtually all tertiary music education – courses in which the question 'how do I actually deal with these scores?' is often articulated by students and, I suspect, well-nigh universally thought.

It can be argued that in modern Western music there is no period less amenable to the idea of analytical models than this one; no period in which the very criteria for understanding any one piece have been more entailed in that particular piece; no period which was marked by such diversity of compositional practice, to the extent that the possibility of generalized analytical explanation may be doubted. Yet this also argues strongly for the establishment of some touchstones in what most musicians seek: explanation, interpretation, comparison. It argues for informed help in musical assimilation.

Equally important, there are methods of analysis both established and pioneering of which a clear exposition is needed. These methods have their origin in theorizing at the extreme of musical and intellectual achievement – in the concepts of Arnold Schoenberg, Heinrich Schenker and other more recent figures discussed in the following pages – and it is hardly surprising that the student often finds it difficult to understand the questions which have stimulated new methods and the technicalities inherent in some of the answers. While few analysts can ever have actually intended, by gratuitous complication and jargon, to block access to their thinking, theory and analysis have gained a reputation for being among the more perplexing options in a student's development. As an awareness of analytical matters is becoming more often a requirement than an option – which is much to be welcomed – it is all the more important that studies are available which are as clear to the student as they are to the teacher, without diluting either the musical or the theoretical content.

In the years since this volume was first conceived there has been a change in the intellectual climate which makes it – or so it seems to me – particularly interesting to see the publication of a kind of 'introversive musicology' where the authors confine themselves rather strictly within the boundaries of a music-theoretical tradition, to which they add significant new findings. They will appear to be, on this showing, as indeed will the editor, the 'formalists' who are nowadays under considerable pressure from postmodern critics to defend the narrow view. I remain to be convinced that any thorough *apologia* is necessary, for the seductive debates – about intertextuality, the anxiety of influence, and at the heart of it a deconstructionist approach to criticism – are flurries from non-musical, philosophical and critical thinking, some of it twenty and more years old, that have some striking characteristics. First, they re-open the door to that kind of music-critical irresponsibility which seemed to some of the best musical commentators of the 1960s and 1970s to dog musicology. I can only agree with myself in the following conclusion from 'Music Analysis: Commentaries' in *Companion to Contemporary Musical Thought*, ed. John Paynter et al. (London: Routledge, 1992, pp. 634–49):

> Those who have contributed to analysis as a discipline conscious of its own developing history welcome it in no small measure because it forces criticism to be explicit in matters of musical structure and effect (pp. 647–8).

Secondly, these debates, when conducted at the highest level, are conducted by writers who have already absorbed the benefits of what they call formalism. Those brilliant 'new musicologists' such as Carolyn Abbate and Richard Taruskin show every sign of being well aware of the details, scope and intention of the practices they wish to supplant. It is not right to withhold that kind of knowledge from the eager student. Thirdly, and of course closely related to the second point, even if 'narrativity', indeed feminism and various other politically correct ideologies are not in play here overtly, I feel that the specialist reader will find some of the best impulses of the new musicology driving these acutely focused studies in any case. If that amounts to saying that the emperor's new clothes are suspiciously like his old ones, this is hardly a novel or controversial thought.

The limitations of a study such as this are so plain that they need not be celebrated in detail, but some must be recognized. First is the unintentional but inevitable implication of what constitutes an early twentieth-century repertory. Clearly, music is selected here on a somewhat fleeting basis. That said, there is a reasonable cross-section, with obvious perversion, in what follows. The emphasis is on music that is unlikely to be regarded, or come to be regarded in the near future, as peripheral, on a balance between the instrumental and vocal repertory (though there is no intention to try to cover the wide spectrum of topics which would fall under a 'music and text' heading), and on music which is simple enough for the student to be able to learn thoroughly within the constraints of time and attention that any educational programme involves. Secondly, the 'Aspects' in the title of this book should not be overlooked by student or teacher: the volume is not a statement about all that is important in the study of this repertory, but rather a statement about where and how such study might well begin. The reader who finishes the book thinking that 'there is so much more to be said' is, without doubt, quite right.

The book contains seven chapters grouped around three central considerations in the understanding of early twentieth-century music – extended tonality, twelve-tone tonality and post-tonality. And in this grouping the chapters fall into two types, those which offer the exposition of mainstream analytical methods (chapters 2, 4 and 6) and those which offer related approaches.

In 'Tonality and the Emancipated Dissonance', Arnold Whittall, without seeking to side-step the intricacies of chord classification (the history of which in the twentieth century is discussed by Bryan R. Simms in chapter 6), nevertheless recognizes the need for accessible procedures to help grasp harmonic constituents in some of the earliest music to challenge major-minor tonality (Stravinsky, No. 3 of Three Pieces for String Quartet; and Schoenberg 'Saget mir, auf welchem Pfade', op. 15, no. 5). Chapter 2 is a study of 'Post-Tonal Voice-Leading' in which James Baker guides the student through a double minefield: on the one hand, the ramified techniques (illustrated through Wolf) of voice-leading analysis, which was originally conceived if anything to subvert the music on which this book concentrates, and certainly not to lead to its better understanding, but which is now in widespread currency as an adapted technique; and on the other hand, the muscular but often seemingly imponderable tonal logic of pieces (an Ives song and piano music by Debussy and Bartók) which revel in the taut freedoms of the period. Chapter 3 provides an introduction to, as it were, dealing with the composer, showing how a close study of historical evidence, and especially of particular notations, stimulates analytical appreciation in various ways. The musical revolution which historians date informally but realistically from 1908 implied many forms of re-evaluation, and the composer considered by Malcolm Gillies in 'Pitch Notations and Tonality: Bartók' was exemplary in the deep thought he applied to the mechanics of how to write down new music.

It could be maintained that twelve-tone music is the least controversial aspect of our overall theme, so crucial and widely discussed has it been in the development of twentieth-century music. There is already an abundance of exegesis in this area – the reader is referred, among the most recent literature, to *A Guide to Musical Analysis* by Nicholas Cook (London: Dent, 1987) and *Music Analysis in Theory and Practice* by Jonathan Dunsby and Arnold Whittall (London: Faber and Faber, 1988). However, as Martha Hyde points out in chapter 4, 'Dodecaphony: Schoenberg', in the last decade there has in fact been an 'intense re-evaluation' of Schoenberg's music and it is only now that new contributions such as hers can begin to reflect fully the shifts in thought that are not to be found in most of the textbook literature that the student is likely to come upon. That dodecaphonic and tonal structures are not in fact opposites has been a claim of early dodecaphonic composers and, increasingly, of historians of twentieth-century music. Whether it will become a commonplace in the assumptions of analysts remains to be seen. Meanwhile, Craig Ayrey shows in chapter 5 how it may be investigated in what is called a 'tonal-serial' structure (Berg's second setting of the song 'Schliesse mir die Augen beide', which was that composer's first twelve-tone composition), revealing along the way the rich variety of factors which any analyst of early dodecaphonic composition should take into account.

The third mainstream method, after voice-leading and twelve-note approaches, is pitch-class set analysis, discussed by Bryan R. Simms in chapter 6, with reference to various extracts from the repertory culminating in an overview of Webern's song 'So ich traurig bin', op. 4, no. 4. There is a strong conceptual link here with chapter 1, since again the issue is access to procedures which yield harmonic description, though Simms does not hide the fact that pitch-class set theory rests on descriptive assumptions the intuitive relevance of which it is for each practitioner to determine. Chapter 7 is an exposition of the rhythmic characteristics of a Bartók *Bagatelle* for piano. Allen Forte suggests here that such close study as can emerge from the lead he presents may reveal considerable insights into the contour and phrasing of a wider repertory. If within the context of this volume 'Foreground Rhythm in Early Twentieth-Century Music' stimulates the student to examine the pitch structure of the repertory through the perspective of other musical domains, much will have been achieved beyond the overt pedagogical intention of what is said.

I

Tonality and the Emancipated Dissonance: Schoenberg and Stravinsky

ARNOLD WHITTALL

I ORIENTATION

i Schoenberg

Theories of musical structure and techniques of music analysis may both be expected to give the highest priority to elements that can be defined with the minimum of ambiguity. For this reason, the very idea of 'emancipation', with its implications of freedom from constraints and from all contextual consistency, may appear profoundly anti-theoretical – something that could have been conceived only by a composer concerned above all to subvert the predictable and to challenge convention, if not positively to ridicule the whole concept of musical discourse as a system-based phenomenon. Moreover, now that Schenker's theory of tonality has gained such widespread support, many theorists are quite prepared to move onto the offensive, arguing that the 'principle' of 'emancipated dissonance' is a contradiction in terms, given the ultimate subordination of all tonal elements and events to the consonant major or minor triad. Emancipated dissonance was, after all, the particular concern of a composer whose progressive disposition might be expected to embrace a zeal for the unclassifiable; a composer who, although capable of arguing that he 'could provide rules for almost everything' (Schoenberg, 1964: p. 104), also asserted that 'musical logic does not answer to "if-, then-", but enjoys making use of the possibilities excluded by if-then-' (p. 210). How, the Schenkerian may ask, can any worthwhile rules be provided for such 'logic'? And the Schenkerian answer is likely to involve the drawing of a very clear distinction between the tonal logic illuminated by Schenker's own theory and an atonal logic requiring very different analytical methods to elucidate its foundations.

One of the purposes of this chapter is to explore an alternative to that kind of very clear distinction. It was in his *Theory of Harmony*, first published in 1911, that Schoenberg used the expression 'emancipated dissonance' (Schoenberg, 1978: p. 323), and proclaimed the principle that 'dissonances are the more remote consonances of the overtone series' (p. 329). Schoenberg did not actually invent the expression (for a discussion of its provenance, see Falck, 1982), but he made it very much his own, with his passionately proclaimed belief that the terms 'consonance' and 'dissonance' represent a false antithesis: 'It all simply depends on the growing ability of the analyzing ear to familiarize itself with the remote overtones, thereby expanding the conception of what is euphonious, suitable for art, so that it embraces the whole natural phenomenon' (p. 21). In an essay of 1926, also using the specific phrase 'emancipation of the dissonance', Schoenberg underlined his claim that 'consonance and dissonance differ not as opposites do, but only in point of *degree*; that consonances are the sounds closer to the fundamental, dissonances those farther away; that their comprehensibility is graduated accordingly, since the nearer ones are easier to comprehend than those farther off' (Schoenberg, 1975: pp. 260–1). In a later essay Schoenberg stressed what he saw as the historical, evolutionary basis for this view: 'The ear had gradually become acquainted with a great number of dissonances and so had lost the features of their "sense-interrupting" effect. One no longer expected preparations of Wagner's dissonances or resolutions of Strauss's discords ... and Reger's more remote dissonances' (pp. 216–17).

In the *Theory of Harmony*, Schoenberg vehemently rejected the possibility that dissonance might be a purely melodic phenomenon: 'there are no non-harmonic tones, for harmony means tones sounding together' (Schoenberg, 1975: p. 322). Everything in Schoenberg's understanding of the evolution of music up to his own time, and his own work, encouraged him to follow those aspects of nineteenth-century Viennese theory that supported the right of each and every dissonance to an independent harmonic existence. (For a full discussion of this historical context, see Wason, 1985: pp. 131–43.) And in brief examples from Bach and Mozart to which Schenker took the greatest exception (see Kalib, 1973: II, p. 199) he claimed that unprepared vertical events which are, by any standards, highly dissonant, have as much right to be termed chords as do their resolutions (Schoenberg, 1978: p. 324). In Schoenberg's view, masters like Bach and Mozart used such chords as 'passing phenomena so that we can learn to use them freely'; they 'used a life-belt so that we learn to swim freely' (p. 328). The problem is not their right to exist as chords, but how they are to be defined: as Schoenberg admitted, 'I have not yet succeeded in finding a system nor in extending the old one to include these phenomena' (p. 329). A little later, however, he offered a clear indication of the difficulties of definition involved, when claiming that

> it would not in fact be too difficult to figure out all conceivable harmonies of from two to twelve tones in relation to a root, to connect them with one another, and to illustrate their potential use with examples. Even names could be found. For example, one could designate a C-major triad with a 'non-harmonic' D flat as a 'minor-two-one major triad', one with a non-harmonic D as a 'major-two-one major triad', one with E flat as a 'double-third triad', one with F as a 'minor-' and with F sharp as a 'major-four-three major triad'. One could apply the familiar rules of resolution to these chords and add to these rules the ones arising from the treatment of non-harmonic tones. But whether all that would amount to much is questionable, because without description and evaluation of effect we have no practical application. (p. 330)

At the very least, these cumbersome verbal designations indicate the importance of retaining the principle of root progression in Schoenberg's harmonic theory. Nevertheless, towards the end of the *Theory of Harmony* the author acknowledges the difficulties of interpreting complex chords with reference to the principles of fundamental bass and root designation.

> Modern music that uses chords of six or more parts seems to be at a stage corresponding to the first epoch of polyphonic music. Accordingly, one might reach conclusions concerning the constitution of chords through a procedure similar to figured bass more easily than one could clarify their function by the methods of reference to degrees. For it is apparent, and will probably become increasingly clear, that we are turning to a new epoch of polyphonic style, and as in the earlier epochs, harmonies will be a product of the voice-leading, justified solely by the melodic lines. (p. 389)

In his own, usually sketchy, analyses of music with complex harmony, Schoenberg nevertheless prefers to trace an outline of what he regards as essential progressions, using the plain and inflected Roman numerals of functional harmony, rather than to test the consequences of 'a procedure similar to figured bass'; that is, he illustrates the most appropriate context for emancipated dissonance – extended, floating or suspended tonality – rather than emancipated dissonance itself. For example, Schoenberg's analysis of the first two bars of his song *Lockung*, op. 6 no. 7, identifies only the dual or floating tonality of the basic harmony, as both altered mediant in E♭ major (T) and dominant of C minor (sm) (Schoenberg, 1969: p. 112; see example 1). The emancipated dissonances – the unprepared E♭, the unresolved C♯ (bar 1) – are not, with good reason, identified as explicitly harmonic events. And even when, later on, the dissonances do occur within chordal formations, Schoenberg regards those chords – for example, in bars 20–3 – not as a literal succession of increasingly chromatic dissonances which are called to order by the diatonic IV–V progression of bar 23, but as relating to a 'background', or implied statement of V, altered and inflected as his supplementary examples (see (c) and (d) in example 1) attempt to indicate.

It is indeed easier to identify the probably diatonic, consonant source for these chords than to describe, literally, their actual surface identity; and this very fact indicates a paradox in Schoenberg's position as theorist, proclaiming the emancipation of the dissonance while demonstrating, through the principles of extended or floating tonality, the ultimate subordination of all harmonic events to the minimum number of basic tonal regions. Of course, the essential creative consequence of the emancipation of the dissonance, as of ever-more-extended tonality, was atonality. But as long as tonal forces, however attenuated, continued to function, dissonances would either (eventually) resolve, or appear as substitutes for, or alterations of, triads or seventh chords on the diatonic scale degrees. And even though it would be mistaken to claim any great prescriptive force for examples like those in *Structural Functions of Harmony*, since their object is to illustrate particular compositional procedures, not to be part of 'complete' analyses, it appears that the possibility of any harmonic event being 'prolonged' – linearly extended in time by melodic processes not involving the establishment of new or different chords – is one that Schoenberg accepts. Indeed, his discussion of *Lockung* reinforces the sense of extended or floating tonality as, in effect, emancipated tonality (just as emancipated dissonance is extended consonance) – a tonality in which diatonic essentials need no longer occupy the central structural position in a work. Such music is inevitably ambiguous and elusive, and much more challenging to the analyst than music more explicitly diatonic, or atonal. The elusiveness also relates in no small measure to the sense in which, while Schoenberg's pedagogy remained faithful to chordal and harmonic factors, his compositional thinking gave linear, motivic elements the central role. This paradox may reinforce the reluctance of most theorists today to treat emancipated dissonance as a useful basis for analysis. And yet the fact remains that Schoenberg himself, with his comments about figured bass, has given a clue as to how such usefulness (or otherwise) may at least be tested.

Example 1.1 Schoenberg: *Lockung*, op.6, no. 7

ii Stravinsky

> For over a century music has provided repeated examples of
> a style in which dissonance has emancipated itself. It is no
> longer tied down to its former function. Having become an
> entity in itself, it frequently happens that dissonance neither
> prepares nor anticipates anything. Dissonance is thus no more
> an agent of disorder than consonance is a guarantee of security.
> The music of yesterday and of today unhesitatingly unites
> parallel dissonant chords that thereby lose their functional
> value, and our ear quite naturally accepts their juxtaposition
> (Stravinsky, 1947: pp. 36–7).

These remarks of Stravinsky's, or of his 'ghost' for the *Poetics* lectures, Roland-Manuel, could well be taken from any of the Schoenberg writings cited in Section 1. Yet Stravinsky, unlike Schoenberg, never taught composition and never compiled a theory text; nor did he ever feel it necessary to confront the specific analytical consequences, with respect to his own music, of this new freedom. For him, the results of the emancipation of the dissonance were perfectly capable of general definition: the traditional diatonic system was replaced by a music recognizing 'the polar attraction of sound, of an interval, or even a complex of tones. ... This general law of attraction is satisfied in only a limited way by the traditional diatonic system' (pp. 38–9). It follows that those sounds, intervals or complexes of tones with which a composition's pole or poles of attraction can be identified may not easily be definable in terms of 'the traditional diatonic system': that is, as a statement of, or substitute for, a tonic triad.

As a composer Stravinsky followed a broadly similar path to Schoenberg, from late Romantic tonality, through extended tonality, to atonal serialism. As is well known, however, the nature of those paths could hardly have been more different. Schoenberg, eight years Stravinsky's senior, had moved decisively beyond essential tonal procedures by 1909, at a time when Stravinsky had composed little of consequence. Schoenberg produced a significant number of non-twelve-tone atonal works between 1908 and the early 1920s, and then, during the last thirty years of his life, wrote mainly twelve-tone compositions, which can often plausibly be termed 'neo-classical' in their adaptations of traditional musical forms. For the first forty years or so of his composing career – up to the early 1950s – Stravinsky remained, in essence, a tonal composer, even though the nature of the tonality in his works from *Petrushka* to *The Rake's Progress* (that is, works from both his 'nationalist' and 'neo-classical' periods) is more extended than conventional – the kind of harmony to which the comments quoted earlier refer. For about the last fifteen years of his composing life, Stravinsky used a personal but systematic form of twelve-tone technique, and, at least from *Threni* (1957–8) onwards, his compositions are essentially atonal. With two such important and influential composers, it is scarcely surprising that a great deal of searching technical study of their music has been undertaken, exploring matters of pitch organization, rhythmic structure and formal procedures in great and varied detail. It

remains to be seen whether studies from the angle of emancipated dissonance can add much of substance to this technical exploration and understanding. Nevertheless, in view of the fact that the term itself was actually accepted by both composers, it is surely a valid exercise at least to outline what the elements of such a study might be.

2 METHOD

In exploring the possibilities inherent in Schoenberg's verbal description of emancipated dissonance for devising a means of describing dissonant formations with maximum consistency and completeness, it should be borne in mind throughout that any such descriptive method is itself very unlikely to be adequate for the 'complete' analysis of the chosen music. Nevertheless, if it can provide significant interpretations of particular passages not achievable in any other way, it may have some value.

Our starting point is Schoenberg's comment, already quoted, that 'one might reach conclusions concerning the constitution of chords through a procedure similar to figured bass more easily than one could clarify their function by the methods of reference to degrees'. It is indeed perfectly possible to translate his cumbersome verbal formulations into figures: a 'minor-two-one major triad' becomes, under 5, $\flat^3_2$, a 'major-two-one major triad' $^3_{\flat 2}$, a 'double-third triad' $^{\natural 3}_{\flat 3}$, a 'minor-four-three major triad' $^4_3$, and a 'major-four-three major triad' $^{\sharp 4}_3$. In general, however, the more extended or ambiguous the tonality of a composition, and the more dependent its harmony on non-traditional dissonances, the most difficult it becomes to use figured bass designations in the conventional manner. After all, the use of figures normally enables a performer and analyst to distinguish between consonance and dissonance with reference to the tonality in question: the '6' of a $^6_3$ or $^6_4$ will be major or minor, depending on whether the key at that point is major or minor (see Bach, 1974: p. 182). Figures can obviously be modified by accidentals, yet such modifications do not alter the fact that the interval above the bass is calculated with reference to the functions and terminology of tonality. '6' is not six times a single, uniform entity, but six degrees of the scale (containing both major and minor seconds) from which the bass note takes its own identity and function. It follows that, in music which touches, or straddles, the borderline between tonal and atonal, traditionally based scale-degree figuring may well oversimplify, if not positively misrepresent, the true nature of chord-identity. However, in music without key signatures, and a much greater degree of chromatic variety, it becomes essential to use a qualifying accidental for every figure, and to have an inflected figure available for every possible interval above a given bass note. The complete set of figures proposed here is given in figure 1.1. It will be noted at once that it is not ideally consistent: certain diminished intervals are represented by single flats, others by double. It is, however, comprehensive; other aspects of its design will be commented on in the context of examples of its use.

Figure 1.1

augmented unison	♯1
minor second	♭2
major second	♮2
augmented second	♯2
diminished third	♭♭3
minor third	♭3
major third	♮3
augmented third	♯3
diminished fourth	♭♭4
perfect fourth	♮4
augmented fourth	♯4
diminished fifth	♭5
perfect fifth	♮5
augmented fifth	♯5
diminished sixth	♭♭6
minor sixth	♭6
major sixth	♮6
augmented sixth	♯6
diminished seventh	♭♭7
minor seventh	♭7
major seventh	♮7
augmented seventh	♯7
diminished octave	♭8

First, let us take the last two bars of Schoenberg's song op. 15 no. 10 (see example 1.2). This cadence takes its character from the fact that what, from the bass alone, could support a full close on and in G is not confirmed diatonically by the upper voices. As a chordal analysis, therefore, a simple 'G: V – I' will not do, unless we have no interest whatever in the type of dissonant harmony involved, and the differences between this cadence and those which really do comprise the unadulterated dominant and tonic triads of G major or minor. The fact remains, however, that these bars do contain a D major triad, and a final chord on G which includes the augmented second above the bass, the enharmonic equivalent of the minor third. It is these diatonic features that are preserved alongside the less orthodox harmonic elements in the analysis below:

Figure 1.2

Bass				
	♮5	♮5	♭7	♭7
		♯4	♭6	♭6
	♮3	♮3	♯1	♯2
	D	D	G	G

(It will be noted that no distinction is made between simple and compound intervals – sharp 9 is shown as sharp 2 – with the exception, in later examples, of notes which are doubled as the result of independent voice-leading rather than textural filling-out.)

Example 1.2 Schoenberg: op.15, no. 10

Voice omitted

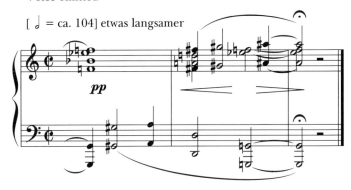

Of course, the mere possibility of translating one form of notation (staff) into another (figures) does not automatically or inevitably make the exercise worthwhile. Perhaps the most commonly recognized index of analytical value is the revelation of unexpected underlying similarities or even identities. Another Schoenberg piece from this period – the second piano piece from op. 11 – ends with a chordal motion whose voice-leading disguises the way in which the three upper parts may each be shown to descend by one whole step (see figure 1.3 and example 1.3).

Figure 1.3

♮7	♭♭6
♮4	♭3
♮3	♮2
E♭	E♭

Example 1.3 Schoenberg: op.11, no. 2

[Mässige ♪]

With this music, however, it is much more difficult to argue realistically for a still-surviving degree of association with a tonal background – of E♭, or of any other tonality – and I believe that there must always be an element of *progression* for such an association to be justified, not merely occasional, isolated, 'traditional-sounding' chords. If chords like those which end op. 11 no. 2 are atonal constructs whose identity is determined more by motivic or textural criteria (Schoenberg's 'product of the voice-leading justified solely by the melodic lines') than by any other, there may well be a case for representing them less as dissonances whose intervals above the bass can be compared and contrasted with the 'ideal' $\frac{5}{3}$ consonance, and more as selections from the total chromatic representable by figures which indicate the constituent pitches as pitch-classes in terms of the number of semitones between them and the bottom note. On this basis a major triad would appear as $\frac{7}{4}$, and the two final chords of op. 11 no. 2 as, under 11, $\frac{5}{4}$ and, under 9, $\frac{3}{2}$ respectively.

Such a procedure inevitably brings the figuring of atonal chords into the domain of pitch-class set theory, and it becomes increasingly important to reinforce the distinction between emancipated dissonance, whose ultimate point of reference is always consonance, and therefore tonality – diatonic, extended, floating, suspended – and atonal harmony, in which Schoenberg's ideal elimination of the distinction between consonance and dissonance is – ideally – attained. Another important factor is that, while the concept of a bass line, and the value of calculating entities upwards from that bass line, retain their relevance (if only intermittently) in music retaining some ultimate association with tonality, bottom-upwards calculations may well be misleading in atonal music, where the composer might be working with a 'centre-outwards' symmetrical scheme. It is for these reasons, in particular, that the method of figuring proposed here does not use a 0–11 scale, but one that inflects diatonic scale degrees *in such a way that no assumption need be made about the mode of tonality present*. Extended tonality may well be neither major nor minor, but a rich blend of both. As will emerge in subsequent sections, however, the use of these figures does not automatically confer on the bass note of any particular chord the identity of a scale degree within a particular tonality. The figures demonstrate the relative closeness to, or distance from, a basic triad or seventh chord: but there is no attempt to argue that it is possible to reveal a 'background' of such chords, forming a logical and consistent linear sequence, and 'against' which the music is actually composed and heard. What these analyses illustrate is not the prolongation of scale-degree rooted harmonies, but the succession (linearly motivated) of chords whose character resides in their degree of dissonance (relative to the bass note). It will nevertheless be possible to identify those occasional chords – the 'focused' dissonances – that are most strongly associated with a relevant functional harmony, and it is those chords that tend to give the composition such tonal character and identity as it has.

Some further general points should be made here. Since (unlike pitch-class sets) emancipated dissonances are 'ordered collections' – there is no inversional equivalence in this scheme – the total number of possible chords is very large: for example, there are 55 different three-note chords on any given pitch-class, as opposed to a mere 12 pitch-class sets of three elements. (For this reason I have not attempted to provide a single listing of all possible chords against which both the models discussed below, and all other suitable pieces, could be measured.) Of course, not all 55 are dissonances. But the

sheer variety of material provided by this method of chord identification emphasizes that its usefulness is likely to be most immediately evident in statistical, distributional areas of analysis – areas where subsequent interpretation of accumulated data is as essential as it is problematic. As with set theory, the analyst may well conclude that what this theory requires for its fullest justification is a compositional repertory created in the full knowledge of and admiration for the theory itself!

3 MODEL

i Stravinsky: No. 3 of Three Pieces for Sting Quartet (1914)

An analyst wishing to focus on the nature and function of emancipated dissonance may attempt one of two initial strategies: either the identification and interpretation of dissonant formations which are in themselves traditional, and only emancipated in their behaviour; or the identification and interpretation of dissonant formations which are emancipated in their own actual content, to the extent of escaping plausible codification by traditional criteria. The first strategy is not my prime concern in this study, but one brief example may serve to indicate that it is by no means necessarily an easier exercise than the second. For example, the 'dominant sevenths' of bars 2 and 3 of the first movement of the Symphony of Psalms (see example 1.4) may be deemed emancipated in that they are not prepared from within their parent tonalities of E♭ and C, nor do they resolve within those tonalities. There is a problem, nevertheless, affecting interpretation of function rather than the identity of the dissonances themselves, for although E♭ and C are both strongly tonicized later in the symphony, the first movement is more concerned with the centres, or poles, of E and G. Should these sevenths therefore be defined in terms of the scale degrees of what appears to be the tonality at the outset, E minor? That possibility must in turn be considered in the light of the increasing conviction among analysts that Stravinsky was not working with the traditional diatonic system but with an 'octatonic' scale of alternate half and whole steps: in this case, E, F, G, A♭, B♭, B, C♯, D (see van den Toorn, 1983). This scale, or mode, has the powerful effect of extending tonality in such a way that the E♭ and C dominant sevenths can be shown to express rather than disrupt the 'octatonic tonality' (E migrating to G) of the movement as a whole. The problem is whether the degrees of the octatonic scale can be regarded as providing a series of roots for functional triads and sevenths, just like the degrees of a major or minor scale. Clearly, the two sevenths can be regarded as the wholly linear result of a prolongation of the E minor chord itself, and not as chords at all, but the theoretical context of this chapter demands that the possible consequences of interpreting them chordally be seriously considered. Fortunately, perhaps, a discussion of the possible nature of an 'octatonic tonality' is beyond the scope of the present enquiry.

Example 1.4 Stravinsky: Symphony of Psalms

Example 1.5 Stravinsky: Piano Sonata

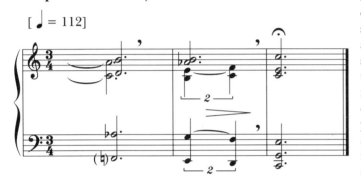

A simpler case of emancipated dissonance in a context of extended tonality, where the process of extension does not render identification of the basic tonality itself problematic, is the cadence ending the first movement of Stravinsky's Piano Sonata (see example 1.5). Here the dissonances are not only prepared, but resolve, ultimately, by stepwise motion, in keeping with the music's neo-classical (neo-baroque?) style. And even if common sense seems to dictate an interpretation which describes the passage as a plagal cadence, with the IV altered – emancipated – by the addition of non-harmonic tones, and with two passing chords connecting the IV to the I, the power and quality of emancipated dissonance can be precisely rendered in figures:

Figure 1.4

			♭7	
	♮6		♮6	
	♮5	♮5	♭5	♮5
	♯4	♭4		
	♭3	♭3	♭3	♮3
Bass:	F	E	D	C
C:	IV	III	II	I

As emphasized earlier, the closer to a background in traditional tonal harmony and progression, the more practicable it is for the analysis to retain references to concepts of scale degree, chord root, chord inversion and so on. Much of Stravinsky's

music is of this basic type. Nevertheless, for my principal model I have chosen an example of a more radical type, demonstrated in a composition where dissonances are consistently 'emancipated in their own actual content' and there are no conventional triads at all. It is of course rare for a single movement to be as consistently homophonic as this, the third of the pieces for string quartet. The example is therefore not a model in the sense of providing a 'typical' Stravinsky composition, if such a thing exists: rather it exemplifies in a particularly concentrated and consistent fashion the issues arising when chordal analysis is employed for music in which tonality, though not positively absent, is extended – possibly even to the point of seeming to be suspended.

The movement (see example 1.6) is in two principal parts: the first (bars 1–26) has a two-bar introduction followed by a succession of 'verses' and 'refrains' forming the sequence a – b – a¹ – b – a² – b – a³: a¹ and a² are variants of a; a³ is a partial restatement of a. The b sections recur unvaried. The second, shorter part subdivides into two sections: the first (bars 27–37) has material whose pitch structure evolves from, perhaps even develops, the introduction in ways which suggest points of contact with the 'verse' material (type 'a'). The closing section (bars 38–46) in turn alludes to the 'refrains' (type 'b'), and also confirms that the piece's principal tonal orientation is C. It is worth reiterating here that the ensuing chordal analysis in terms of emancipated dissonance ultimately derives its logic from the connection revealed by the figures and intervals with the extended tonality of C: but the figures themselves are concerned primarily with chord structure, not with tonal orientation, still less tonal function.

It should be obvious enough that no composition which, however homophonic, is also so plainly linear in the equality of its superimposed melodic lines can be fully 'explained' by a chordal analysis. What I believe such an approach can do (and here the relevance of this model to Stravinsky's music as a whole can be reinforced) is perform the usual, useful analytic task of revealing invariant features, the balance between similarity and variety which is perhaps the most basic of all compositional techniques in all styles and cultures. And I would also argue that those 'invariant features' gain from being described in ways which make comparison with conventional tonal, triadic harmony not just possible, but unavoidable. With this piece, however – as already suggested – the function of such comparison is not to claim that the music has a consistent 'background' of conventional harmony: it is simply to define with some degree of precision the distance between such harmony and what Stravinsky actually writes.

This composition comprises a succession of 123 chordal statements – a total arrived at by counting all immediate repetitions (as in bar 1) as *one*, but all separated repetitions (as when the first chord of bar 1 is repeated in bar 2) as one each. Even when all repetitions are grouped together, and all enharmonically equivalent intervals regarded as the same (for example, sharp 4 as flat 5), there remain 45 different types of vertical sonority – not totally different, of course – and it is through plotting the relationships between invariants and variants in this material that analysis can begin to interpret the harmonic character and structure of the music. Figure 1.6 lists the 45 chord-types in an order determined by the gradually increasing size of their constituent intervals, and also indicates which of the 123 chord statements are represented by each type.

As the formal analysis has already indicated, the first part of the piece, up to Chord 82, is dominated by exact and varied repetitions. Chord-type 3 (flat 2, natural 3, flat 6 and its enharmonic equivalent flat 2, flat 4, flat 6) accounts for 18 of the 82 statements, and chord-type 23 (flat 3, natural 3, flat 7) for 13. It is also these statements together which do most to orient the harmony towards an extended C minor. Indeed, Chord 7 in its first, predominant, form might be defined in scale-degree terms as the third inversion of a C minor tonic seventh, though such nomenclature is scarcely very illuminating, given the context. Chord-type 3 is particularly important, not just as a focused dissonance with strong C minor connections, but as the leading member of a family of chord-structures whose offshoots can be found in significant numbers throughout the piece. In particular, the fact that Chord 7 is an exact transposition of Chord 5, and the additional fact that both share the invariant flat 2, flat 6 element with Chord 4, point to the piece's most significant unifying features, chordally speaking. It will be noted that Chord 6 (Chord-type 23) does not share this feature, beyond the ubiquitous minor second between its flat 3/natural 3, and this distinction demonstrates a strong contrast between the present method of analysis and pitch-class set analysis: chord-type 3 is pitch-class set 4–19 [0, 1, 4, 8]; chord-type 23 is pitch-class set 4–Z15 [0, 1, 4, 6]. In pitch-class set terms, therefore, the invariant relationship is much closer than it is in the chordal analysis. The argument for a significant difference in structure between Chord 6 and the chords on either side of it centres on the fact that Stravinsky consistently uses it as a passing element between the two type-3 chords. And in the larger context of the piece as a whole chords built from the flat 2 interval are much more prominent, numerically and structurally, than other types.

Chords built from the flat 2 interval provide 54 out of 123 statements, including the first and last chords of both parts of the piece, and 16 out of the 45 types of sonority. Moreover, the flat-2 type chords are particularly important in linking the two parts of the piece. If the principal contrast is provided by the shift of pitch centre from C to C♯ (itself a flat-2 structure) in bars 27–37, just under half of the 30 chordal statements in this segment – 13 – are of the flat-2 type. More importantly still, chords containing the flat 2/flat 6 sub-collection (types 3, 6, 8, 9, 10 and 16) provide an even stronger invariant quality to the harmony throughout.

The most prominent intervallic invariant on the surface of the piece is provided by the perfect fourths between the two violins which persist through most of Part 1. Study of the chordal analysis reveals the extent to which something which recurs with almost monotonous regularity in one segment of texture may be constantly recontextualized by much freer movement in the other segment. Similarly, in the passage between bars 27 and 37, where pitch invariance centres on three bars of repeated Ds in the cello followed by seven bars of a D–A drone, the chordal analysis reveals that intervals common to successive chords may not be equivalent to shared pitches. Figure 1.5 shows a relatively simple case:

Figure 1.5

Chord 111: ♭4, ♭6, ♭8: A♯, D , F♯, A

             ♭4

             ♭6

             ♭8

Chord 112: ♭2, ♭4, ♮4, ♭6: C♯, D , F, F♯, A

             ♭2

             ♭4

             ♮4

Chords 111, 112: invariant pitches   invariant pitch-class F♯
            D, A: A♯/D(111)   C♯/F(112)
invariant intervals ♭4:
            ♭6:   A♯/F♯(111)   C♯/A(112)

It is also worth noting that the presence in the music of what may be generalized as a tendency for pitches to change their intervallic significance in successive chords represents a principle fundamental to tonal composition.

As with other types of analysis, however, the maximization of invariance through reduction to common interval patterns will override significant differences in actual chord layout in the piece. For example, the first and last chords, though of the flat-2 class, are distinctive sonorities because they are built upwards from perfect fifths, a property they share with the five representatives of chord-type 22. And the interpretation of Stravinsky's use of chord-types, as opposed to a mere description of them, will conclude that one of the piece's most essential features is the way in which what one might expect

Example 1.6 Stravinsky: No. 3 of *Three Pieces for String Quartet*

Example 1.6 contd.

Example 1.6 contd.

to be the more stable features of Chords 1 and 123 are rendered ambiguous by the fact that the main body of the piece gives more explicit attention to the dissonant flat-2 component. Chords 1 and 123 may be cited as evidence of Stravinsky's continued liking for 'bi-triadic' sonorities, four years after *Petrushka*; but, again, context suggests that ambiguity and tension are less a matter of superimposing D minor on C♯ major (Chord 1) or F major on C (Chord 123) than of the doubts cast on the significance of the bass note in the light of the strongly symmetrical cast of the chord's intervals – abstractly in the case of Chord 1, literally in that of Chord 123. (The final event of the piece is melodic rather than harmonic, of course, but it cannot be said to contradict the C-tendencies of the piece's final stages, nor to eliminate all sense of the music's invariants being dissonant rather than consonant.) It should perhaps also be noted that these fifth-based chords are significant for providing a degree of relative consonance against which the more decisive dissonances can be heard. Overall, 28 of the 45 chord-types have one or more triadic components, and these are marked M (major), m (minor), A (augmented), D (diminished) against the chord-type number in figure 1.6:

these 28 types account for 77 of the piece's 123 statements, and the only important component not to contain this feature is chord-type 23, from Part 1: flat 3, natural 3, flat 7. Once again, therefore, one is encouraged to view this type as more unstable and more dissonant than is usual for this piece, despite the fact that it accounts for 11 of the composition's 15 C-based chords!

ii   Schoenberg: Das Buch der hängenden Gärten, no. 5

As with the Stravinsky piece, this particular song (see example 1.7) has been chosen partly because its texture makes a comprehensive chordal analysis possible, and partly because it offers the consistent use of dissonances 'emancipated in their own actual content'. Many analysts today would probably prefer to describe the song as atonal, but I would argue that, on the evidence of the harmonic goal represented by the ending, and its clear anticipation in bars 3 and 4, the possibility of an extended G tonality makes good musical sense: the most

Figure 1.6

			Stravinsky		
Chord-type			Pitches in ascending order		Chord-number
1	♭2, ♭3, ♭7		D, E♭, C, F		50
2	♭2, ♮3, ♯4 (♯1)		A♭, C, A, D		29, 53
3 m	♭2, ♮3, ♭6 (♯1)	(i)	D♭, F, A, D		5, 8, 12, 18, 73, 76, 80
		(ii)	E, G♯, C, F		65
	♭2, ♭4, ♭6	(i)	B, E♭, G, C		7, 10, 14, 20, 44, 75, 78, 82
		(ii)	D, G♭, B♭, E♭		17
		(iii)	C♯, F, A, D		57
4	♭2, ♭4, ♭5	(i)	G♯, C, A, D		21, 45, 68
		(ii)	B, E♭, C, F		114, 118
5	♭2, ♭4, ♮4, ♭5		G♯, C♯, D, A, C		106
6 M, m, A	♭2, ♭4, ♮4, ♭6		C♯, F♯, D, F, A		112
7 M A	♭2, ♭4, ♮4, ♮6 (♭♭7)		E♯, A♯, D, F♯, A		97
8 M, m, A	♭2, ♭4, ♮5, ♭6		C♯, G♯, F, D, A		1, 3
9 M, m	♭2, ♮4, ♭6	(i)	B, E, G, C		43
		(ii)	C♯, F♯, D, A		83, 87, 91
10 M	♭2, ♮4, ♮5, ♭6		C♯, G♯, D, F♯, A		108
11 M, A	♭2, ♮4, ♮5, ♮6, ♮7, ♮8		C, G, D♭, B, F, A, C		123
12	♭2, ♯4, ♯11 (♯1)		D, G♯, D♯, G♯		92

13 m, D	♭2, ♯4, ♮6 (♯1) (♮7)	(i)	A̲♭, F, A, D G♯	24, 35, 48, 71
	♭2, ♭5, ♮6 (♮7)	(i)	A, G♭, B♭, E♭	52
		(ii)	E♯, B, D, F♯	93
14 M	♭2, ♯4, ♭7 (♯1)	(i) (ii)	D, G♯, C, E♭ D, C, D♯, G♯	63 84, 86, 88, 90
15 m	♭2, ♮5, ♮8̲		D, E♭, A, D	26
16	♭2, ♭6, ♭9̲		D, E♭, B♭, E♭	4, 25, 49, 72
17 M, m, D	♮2, ♭3, ♭4, ♭6 (♮3)		F♯, B, D, A, A♭	105
18 M, D	♮2, ♭3, ♭6, ♮6 (♮3) (♮7)		B♯, G♯, D, D♯, A	110
19	♮2, ♯4, ♮5, ♭6 (♯5)		D, A♯, E, G♯, A	2
20	♮2, ♮5, ♭6 (♯5)	(i) (ii) (iii)	G, E♭, A, D F, D♭, G, C A♭, E, B♭, E♭	32, 39 37 38
21 m	♮2, ♮5, ♭6, ♭7 (♯5) (♯6)		G, D, D♯, A, F̲ E♯	96, 104
22 M	♮2, ♮5, ♮7	(i) (ii)	B♭, F, A, C D♭, A♭, C, E♭	23, 47, 70 116, 121
23	♭3, ♮3, ♭7	(i) (ii)	C, E, B♭, E♭ D, F♯, C, F	6, 9, 11, 13, 15, 19, 56, 74, 77, 79, 81 58
	♭3, ♭4, ♭7		A, D♭, G, C	28
24 M, m	♭3, ♮5, ♭6		F♯, C♯, D, A	94
25 M, N, D	♭3, ♮5, ♭6, ♮6 (♮6)		F♯, D, D♯, A, D̲♭/C♯	95, 100, 103
26 M, m	♭3, ♮5, ♭6, ♮7 (♭8)		F♯, C♯, D, F, A	99, 102
27 M, D	♭3, ♭6, ♮6 (♮7)	(i) (ii)	G, E, B♭, E♭ B, A♭, D, G	30, 54 51, 120
28 M, m	♭3, ♭6, ♮7 (♭8)		D♯, B, D, F♯	89
29 D	♭3, ♮6, ♮7 (♮7) (♭8)	(i) (ii)	D♯, C, D, F♯ D♯, F♯, C, D	85 61
30	♮3, ♯4, ♮7		E♭, G, A, D	16
31 m, A	♮3, ♯5, ♮6 ♮3, ♭6, ♮6		G♭, D, B♭, E♭ F, D♭, A, D	33, 36, 40 34, 41
32 M, A	♮3, ♯5, ♭7, ♮7		C, B♭, G♯, E, B	113, 117, 122
33 M, A	♮3, ♯5, ♮7		A♭, E, G, C	31

34 M, m	♭4, ♮4, ♭6, ♮7 (♮♮7)(♭8)		E♯, A♯, D, A, E	107
35	♭4, ♭5, ♮7 (♭8)		D♯, G, A, D	59
36 M, A	♭4, ♭6, ♮7 (♭8)		A♯, A, D, F♯, A	111
37	♮4, ♯4		B♭, E, B♭, E♭	27
38, D	♮4, ♭5,♮6, ♮7 (♮♮7) (♭8)		D♯, G♯, D, A, C	98, 101
39 m, D	♮4, ♭6, ♮7 (♭8)		E, A, C, E♭	62
40	♮4, ♮7 (♭8)		C♯, F♯, C	55, 60, 67
41	♯4, ♮7, ♮14		F, E, B, E	22, 46, 69
42	♭5, ♭6, ♮7 (♭8)		E, C, B♭, E♭	42
43 D	♭5, ♮6, ♮7 (♮♮7) (♭8)	(i) (ii)	D♯, A, C, D / D♯, B♯, D, A	66 / 109
44	♭5, ♮7		A♭, G, D, G	115, 119
45	♭6,♮7 (♭8)		C♯, A, C	64

essential elements of that tonality are not excluded, but they are not allowed to function diatonically.

The initial process of identification and classification is shown in figure 1.7. The vocal line is not included (a pointed indication that this account is in no sense an analysis of the song as such), for while to include it would obviously increase the number of dissonant events still further, it does frequently double notes in the accompanying harmony. In the interests of methodological simplicity, and to ensure consistency with the Stravinsky analysis, I have again not included any octave doublings in my figures, using '2' rather than '9' even when the textural and harmonic context might present a case for the latter. I have, however, shown all the relevant enharmonic equivalents, and matters of textural and harmonic context are not ignored in the subsequent commentary.

Figure 1.7 shows that there are 61 chords in the piece: 6 have three pitch-classes, 8 have five, and the vast majority – 47 – have four. (The two three-note sonorities beginning bars 8 and 9 have not been registered separately.) The most urgent necessity is therefore to find ways of classifying the four-element chords in order to shed light on their nature and function. As with the Stravinsky, however, it is important not to minimize the significance of the sheer harmonic diversity that this composition reveals: such freedom and variety were of the essence in Schoenberg's early explorations of the 'no man's land' between tonality and atonality.

A survey of the 47 four-note chords soon shows that exact, transposed or texturally redistributed repetition within the 27 chord-types is rare: 5 are used three times each; 8 are used twice, and all the rest occur once only. Further types of classification are therefore clearly desirable, provided they bring to light properties of genuine musical significance. (As with the Stravinsky, I have chosen to group all the chords in figure 1.7 in terms of the first interval above the bass after the pitches have been arranged in ascending order within the octave.) The statistics are as follows: 6 have a minor second (or augmented unison), 11 have a major second, 9 a minor third (or augmented second), 8 a major third (or diminished fourth), and 3 a perfect fourth.

The relative rarity of chords built upwards from flat 2 is striking, especially when comparison is made with the Stravinsky model. Semitones are to be found in plenty in the higher positions of the other chords, but the emphasis is firmly on structures that, in context, often set up particular, if ambiguous, associations with the traditional consonant triads and sevenths, to such a degree that there is some justification for regarding at least some of them as altered triads or sevenths. The relatively consonant nature of chords in these categories is reinforced by the fact that 5 of the 11 natural-2 structures are whole-tone chords, as are 3 of the 8 major-third structures. Another important factor, though overriding the categories established by considering the first interval above the bass

Example 1.7 Schoenberg: op.15, no.5

Figure 1.7

Chord-type			Schoenberg Pitches in ascending order	Chord number
1 m	♭2, ♭3, ♮5 (♯1)		G, B♭, D, G♯	41
2 m	♭2, ♭3, ♮5, ♭7		A, E, G, B♭, C	27
3 D	♭2, ♭3, ♮6 (♯1) (♯2)		A♭, B, F, A	10
4	♭2, ♮3, ♭5, ♭7 M, D (♯4)		A, C♯, E♭, G, B♭	50
5	♭2, ♮3, ♮5, ♭7 M, D (♯1) (♭4) (♯6)	(i) (ii) (iii)	A, E, G, B♭, C♯ E♭, E, G, B♭, C♯ F♯, C♯, E, G, B♭	17, 26 25 49
6	♭2, ♮4, ♮5, ♭7 m		A, E, G, B♭, D	18
7 m	♮2, ♭3, ♮5		G, B♭, D, A	40
8 D	♮2, ♭3, ♮6 (♯2)		A♭, B, F, B♭	11
9	♮2, ♮3, ♭5, ♭7 A (♯4)		A, C♯, E♭, G, B (whole-tone)	51
10 A	♮2, ♭4, ♮6		F♯, B♭, D, G♯ (whole-tone)	34
11	♮2, ♮3, ♭7	(i) (ii)	E, G♯, D, F♯ G, B, F, A (whole-tone)	45 56, 59
12	♮2, ♯4, ♭6 (♯5)		C, G♯, D, F♯ (whole-tone)	13, 21
13 D	♮2, ♯4, ♮6		F, D, G, B	7, 53
14 A	♮2, ♯4, ♭7 ♯6		C, F♯, A♯, D (whole-tone)	4
15 m	♮2, ♯4, ♮7		B♭, C, E, A	15, 23
16 m	♮2, ♮5, ♭7		D, C, E, A	47
17	♮2, ♭6, ♮6 (♯5)		F, D, G, C♯	32
18 M, A	♭3, ♭4, ♭6		F♯, B♭, D, A	33, 39
19	♭3, ♮3, ♭7		G, B, F, B♭	9, 55, 58
20 M, D	♭3, ♮4, ♮6 (♯2)		F, B♭, D, G♯	35
21	♭3, ♮4, ♭7		E, D, G, A	30
22 m, D	♭3, ♯4, ♭7 (♯2) (♯6)		E♭, F♯, A, C♯	16, 24
	♭3, ♭5, ♭7		C, E♭, G♭, B♭	48
23 m, A	♭3, ♮5, ♮7		B, F♯, A♯, D	5

24 M D	♭3, ♭6, ♮6 (♯2) (♯5)	(i) (ii)	A♭, F, B, E D, B, E♯, A♯ F, B♭	3 8, 54
25 D	♭3, ♮6, ♭7	(i) (ii)	A, G, C, F♯ E, D, G, C♯	1 31
26	♭3, ♭7, ♭14		G♯, F♯, B, F♯	43
27	♮3, ♯4		D, G♯, D, F♯ (whole-tone)	46
28	♮3, ♯4, ♭7 (♯6)		D♭, G, B, F (whole-tone)	2
29	♮3, ♯4, ♮7		E♭, D, G, A	29
30 M, A	♮3, ♮5, ♭6, ♮8		G, E♭, G, B, D	61
31 A	♮3, ♭6, ♮6 m, (♮♭7)		D, C♭, G♭, B♭	57, 60
32 A	♮3, ♭6, ♭7 (♭4) (♯5) (♯6)	(i) (ii)	B♭, G♯, D, F♯ F♯, B♭, D, E (whole-tone)	14, 20, 22 36
33	♮3, ♭7, ♮7 (♯6)		E♭, D, G, C♯	28
34 m	♭4, ♮6, ♮13		G♯, E♯, C, E♯	42
35 M m	♮4, ♭6, ♮6 (♯3) (♯5)		F, D, A♯, C♯	6, 52
36 M	♮4, ♮6, ♮8		F, B♭, D, F (consonance)	38
37 M	♮4, ♮6, ♮7		F, B♭, D, E	37
38	♮4, ♮7, ♮8		B♭, B♭, E♭, A	12, 19, 44

alone, is the contrast between dissonances which contain a perfect fifth and those which do not: again, comparison with the Stravinsky piece is of interest. In the Schoenberg, only 10 of the 38 chord-types do not contain a triadic sub-component (see annotations on figure 1.7), and only 10 do not contain a whole-tone component (including augmented triads).

One of the features leading the analyst to regard the piece as ultimately relating to a G tonality is the way in which the cadential progression at the end of bar 3 and the beginning of bar 4 is taken up more decisively in the last four bars of the piece. And it is striking that, whereas the first cadence involves chords from the minor-third category, those at the end exploit the major-third category: it is also striking that the only one of these chords to include a perfect fifth is the very last, accepting vertically the linear promptings of the bass line.

It is the threefold bass motion from D to G at the end which does most to give the music an aura of G tonality, and other analysts may well be tempted to discuss the entire harmonic structure in terms of such a background. My own view is that the song enshrines a very subtle yet strong contrast between resistance to this 'background' and points where extended tonality comes into focus, for example, the progressions in bars 6, 8 and 14 where Schoenberg uses the song's only five-note chords to suggest V of V; this is clearest in bar 6, where the dominant ninth and eleventh of D can be detected. However, I see little point in using the fact that G: 'V⁷ d' can be heard on the second beat of bar 2 to justify an attempt to describe all the chords in the first four bars in terms of G tonality: in this music the extension of tonality has reached such a degree as to make interruption or suspension of tonality a more realistic interpretation – perhaps 'intermittent tonality' is an even better term. And I would also argue that the method propounded here of identifying chords as emancipated dissonances provides one way of illustrating harmonic consistency and variety – harmonic 'style' – in the absence of the use of scale degrees and functional relations to which a tonal interpretation must ultimately appeal.

As for the all-important matter of how these variously identified chords function – whether their behaviour has a rationale – it might seem that, with the absence of consistent tonality, there will also be an absence of consistent voice-leading. To take a simple example: chord-type 11, one of the whole-tone structures based on a major second, occurs three times in the piece. The second and third occurrences are chords 56 and 59, the incomplete G-tonics in bars 16 and 17 (G, B, F, A, with the voice adding another whole-tone, E♭), and both are approached with maximum possible preparation on the previous beats. The first occurrence (Chord 45), on the second beat of bar 13, could scarcely be more different. Given the context, the source for Chord 45 is Chord 13 (bar 5), another whole-tone member of the natural-2 group (chord-type 12). In bar 5 (and bar 7) Chord 13 is approached by half- or whole-step in all four voices, but in bar 13, perhaps because he had already assigned a C to the voice, Schoenberg replaces the major-second step in the bass with a tritone. Clearly, there are no 'rules' operative here which require the composer to prepare that particular whole-tone sonority in the same or even a similar fashion each time. Even more striking, perhaps, is the treatment of chord-type 24 which, as Chord 8 (bar 3) and Chord 54 (bar 15), has a crucial 'dominant' function. Yet the first occurrence of chord-type 24, on the first beat of bar 2 (as Chord 3) – with exactly the same vertical succession of intervals – is approached and quitted quite differently, its bass note apparently the outcome of a brief and hardly typical 'real sequence' (A–D♭; A♭–C).

Schoenberg's part-writing in this piece is free rather than arbitrary: common-tone and stepwise connections do much to prompt succession, the latter in keeping with that quality of leading-note tension to which Ernst Kurth drew particular attention. But the music's undoubted tension owes most to its consistent motion within its wide repertory of dissonant chords – chords which can be consistently described whether they are extended tonality or suspending it.

4   CONCLUSION

Given the enormous number of possible dissonant chords available under the present system, it may come as something of a relief to note that these two compositions, not selected with the intention of close comparison in mind, do actually share five chord-types:

Figure 1.8

Stravinsky	Schoenberg	Interval sequence
23	19	♭3, ♮3, ♭7
27	24	♭3, ♭6, ♮6
30	29	♮3, ♯4, ♮7
31	31	♮3, ♭6, ♮6
40	38	♮4, ♮7, (♮8)

Even so, it is the differences between the two compositions that are most striking. Perhaps understandably, the earlier, the

Schoenberg, is the more traditional in chord-structure, with a strong whole-tone presence (9 out of the 38 chord-types), and 9 other chord-types with quite close relationships to the 'ideal' 5/3 consonance. 30 out of the 61 chord-statements come into these categories: 14 are whole-tone, 14 have a perfect-fifth component alongside dissonances, and one is a consonance. Alongside the Schoenberg, Stravinsky's harmony may seem unremitting: that it is not, in practice, is perhaps best illustrated by the way the flat-2 component moves between 'fundamental' and higher positions as the chords succeed one another; its function is in its mobility. Here too, however, it might be concluded that the commonest chords are 'altered' consonances: chord-type 3 (minor triad with added seventh) and chord-type 23 (incomplete 'dominant' seventh with added minor third). Nevertheless, the whole point of the preceding discussion is to argue that a consistent analysis of the whole piece in similar or comparable terms to those just employed, even if possible, is highly misleading, suggesting approximations to a consistently traditional harmonic background which cannot be proved in practice.

In an earlier publication I questioned the extent to which the 'focused dissonances' of music such as I have discussed here can be shown to be 'part of coherent and connected harmonic progressions' – an extended tonality in which a post-Schenkerian background of 'I (dissonant) – V (dissonant) – I (dissonant)' can be shown to operate. And I further argued that, in music where the principal structural feature or event is perceived as 'dissonant' (whether because of less fundamental consonances elsewhere in the piece, or because of our wider response to the composer's style and techniques), 'analysis should surely be more closely concerned with the ways in which the complete dissonances themselves function' (Whittall, 1982: p. 51).

As the analyses here indicate, if only in outline, such dissonances may indeed function, and in the only ways possible to any established entities: by reproducing themselves, by being repeated literally or in varied guises; by reacting to other, though often still dissonant, entities; but ultimately by confirming the essential integrity of their own constitution. Carl Dahlhaus has argued that the best way to confront what he regards as the main problem with emancipated dissonance, 'harmonic lack of consequence', is to understand such chords as motifs – 'as individual, self-justifying constructs' that 'do not need to have any immediate consequences; it is enough that they fit meaningfully into a context of variants and contrasts' (Dahlhaus, 1987: p. 126). Whether emancipated dissonances are motifs or chords, the description of their constitution remains a challenge to music theory. Showing this constitution by means of figures is, all too clearly, only a beginning: we would rightly argue that a figured bass analysis of a Bach chorale, whatever its statistical precision, quite lacked the subtlety and sophistication of a Schenkerian, or even a functional, harmonic interpretation. But in music so full of tensions and ambiguities it seems to me particularly appropriate to propose an analytical strategy that brings the objectivity of figures into confrontation with interpretative prose. Perhaps other methods of analysis would benefit if such oppositions were encouraged within them?

BIBLIOGRAPHY

Bach, C. P. E., *Essay on the True Art of Playing Keyboard Instruments*, trans. and ed. William J. Mitchell (London: Eulenburg, 1974).

Dahlhaus, C., 'Emancipation of the Dissonance', in *Schoenberg and the New Music*, trans. Derrick Puffett and Alfred Clayton (Cambridge: Cambridge University Press, 1987).

Falck, R., 'Emancipation of the Dissonance', *Journal of the Arnold Schoenberg Institute*, 6, 1 (June 1982), pp. 106–11.

Kalib, S., *Thirteen Essays from the Three Yearbooks, Das Meisterwerk in der Musik* (dissertation, Northwestern University, 1973) [an annotated translation].

Schoenberg, A., *Letters*, selected and ed. Erwin Stein, trans. Eithne Wilkins and Ernst Kaiser (London: Faber and Faber, 1964).

——, *Structural Functions of Harmony*, ed. Leonard Stein (London: Faber and Faber, 1969).

——, *Style and Idea*, ed. Leonard Stein, trans. Leo Black (London: Faber and Faber, 1975).

——, *Theory of Harmony*, trans. Roy E. Carter (London: Faber and Faber, 1978).

Stravinsky, I., *Poetics of Music*, trans. Arthur Knodel and Ingolf Dahl (Cambridge, MA: Harvard University Press, 1947).

van den Toorn, P. C., *The Music of Igor Stravinsky* (New Haven, CT and London: Yale University Press, 1983).

Wason, R.W., *Viennese Harmonic Theory from Albrechtsberger to Schenker and Schoenberg* (Ann Arbor, MI: UMI Research Press, 1985).

Whittall, A. 'Music Analysis as Human Science? *Le Sacre du Printemps* in Theory and Practice', *Music Analysis*, 1, 1 (March 1982), pp. 33–53.

2

Post-Tonal Voice-Leading

JAMES M. BAKER

I ORIENTATION

The vague term 'post-tonal' was apparently coined in order to designate any and all Western art music written after the so-called common practice period (from Bach to Brahms). The term thus embraces a body of music of incredible breadth but says nothing with regard to the style or structure of individual works. As it is used in this chapter, however, 'post-tonal' refers to music in which structure is based on extensions or modifications of conventional tonal procedures. This more restrictive definition thus excludes music which is strictly atonal.

In order to discuss extended tonality in twentieth-century music, it is first necessary to have a clear understanding of the tonal system which governs structure in Western music of the eighteenth and nineteenth centuries. Because the present chapter focuses on voice-leading techniques, it is particularly appropriate that we adopt the model of the tonal system developed by the Austrian theorist Heinrich Schenker (1868–1935) in the early decades of this century. It has been primarily through Schenker's theories that we have come to understand and appreciate the critical role of voice-leading in determining the structural coherence of the musical artwork.

Schenker demonstrated that tonal coherence is based on the projection through time of a single consonant harmony, the tonic triad, which he believed originates in the natural phenomenon of the overtone series. He viewed the authentic cadential progression I–V–I as the essential means for composing out the tonic. This progression occurs most simply in conjunction with the stepwise descent in the melody from the third of the scale to the root, $\hat{3}$–$\hat{2}$–$\hat{1}$, although descents from $\hat{5}$ or $\hat{8}$ to $\hat{1}$ may also occur. Elaborations of the cadential progression, such as I–IV–V–I or I–II–V–I, are in essence further expansions, or *prolongations*, of the tonic. Schenker showed that voice-leading is intrinsic to prolongation, and further that harmony and voice-leading are dual aspects of a single process and do not function in isolation one from the other. Even in such a simple progression as I–I⁶–II⁶–V–I, for

instance, the bass is a contrapuntal expansion of the tonal axis I–V–I.

In the Schenkerian view, tonality is hierarchical in structure, since a prolongation is an elaboration either of a single harmony or the progression from one harmony to another at a more fundamental level of structure. The prolongations discussed above entail only a few structural levels, but there is virtually no limit to the number of levels through which the prolonging process may be extended. Through modulation, any harmony within a prolonging progression may itself be stabilized, or *tonicized*, serving temporarily as a tonic within a limited sphere. In spite of the fact that a tonicized harmony may be the focus of attention for a considerable portion of a composition, it nevertheless retains its original function relationship with the overall tonic. Schumann's 'Hör ich das Liedchen klingen' (no. 10 from the song cycle *Dichterliebe*, op. 48) provides a clear example of this phenomenon. The song opens in G minor but modulates to C minor in bars 9–12. A sequential passage then leads to a cadence returning to G minor in bar 20, which is prolonged thereafter for the remainder of the piece (bars 20–30). The key of C minor is not introduced simply for the sake of contrast. On the contrary, C minor functions as IV of G minor, preparing V in the conventional manner. Through the processes of modulation and sequence, the simple progression I–IV–V–I is expanded to govern the structure of an entire composition.

This chapter focuses on voice-leading in four works representative of innovations introduced by composers of various nationalities around the turn of the century. By that time, most younger composers had come to feel that the forms and methods of traditional music had been virtually exhausted by their late-romantic predecessors, and they were actively seeking new resources with which to refresh their art. Conventional wisdom holds that some of these innovators made a complete break with the practice of past music in the first decade of the twentieth century, yet many of the composers considered most radical – Arnold Schoenberg and Béla Bartók, for example – insisted that their work followed directly from the musical traditions in which they were raised. If in fact modern music evolved within a continuum, this process may most likely be observed through a comparative study of voice-leading techniques in tonal and post-tonal music. Certainly, if one is to come to grips with the overriding question of tonality in twentieth-century music, one must grasp its voice-leading procedures.

2 METHOD

In this chapter, Schenkerian analytical techniques will be extended to compositions which might well have elicited a strong negative response from Schenker himself, since his personal criteria for artistic unity and quality were quite conservative. Indeed, theorists have differed widely on the question of the applicability of Schenker's approach in the analysis of twentieth-century music, with the most orthodox Schenkerians rejecting the method for any music which does not clearly and strictly conform to the conventional model.[1] In dealing with music based on extended tonality, however, the Schenkerian approach appears to offer the most effective means for analysing expansions of harmonies through voice-leading and for evaluating the relation of modified tonal procedures to conventional tonal practice. The scope of this chapter precludes a complete exegesis of Schenker's theories.[2] Instead, by way of demonstrating the analytical method and illustrating the types of problems involved in analysing post-tonal music, we begin by examining a work from the late nineteenth century which lies on the borderline between conventional and extended tonality, a song by the Austrian composer Hugo Wolf (1860–1903). Table 2.1 explains briefly the analytical notations which are employed in the voice-leading sketches of the works discussed.

Table 2.1 Special Analytical Notations

	An overlapping is shown by a dotted arrow pointing to the pitch in the more important register.
[ ]	Brackets enclose an implicit harmony.
( )	Parentheses indicate a pitch crucial for strict voice-leading which is not explicitly stated.
	Dotted slurs indicate displacement of a pitch from its expected occurrence in strict voice-leading – either by anticipation or delay. Dotted slurs connecting octave equivalents indicate a coupling.
	A horizontal bracket between two notes indicates the tritone relation. In the bass, this relation prolongs a dominant function (either secondary or primary) at a given level of structure.
	A solid slur with arrows points to a motivic reference which is not technically a prolongation.

3 MODELS

i Hugo Wolf: 'Das verlassene Mägdlein' (1888)

Wolf's 'Das verlassene Mägdlein' features a number of elements of structure that are characteristic of a broad repertory of post-Wagnerian tonal compositions. He wrote the song on 24 March 1888 during a period of feverish creativity inspired by a passionate affair with Melanie Köchert, wife of a patron, and perhaps equally by his intense involvement with the poetry of Eduard Mörike. The song vividly depicts the atmosphere of early morning and even more remarkably the vacillating psychological state of a young girl abandoned by her lover. Mörike's poem consists of four stanzas, the outer verses dealing with the external scene of the maiden lighting the fire, the interiors ones depicting her fascination with the flames and the remembrances they kindle. This structure enables Wolf to employ the traditional ABA form to very moving effect.

Although it is based unquestionably in the key of A minor, the song contains no direct simple statement of the complete tonic triad. In a four-bar piano introduction, the composer provides just the minimal information by which the listener may infer the tonality. Rather than employ full chords, he uses only dyads (two-note combinations) as simultaneities, and strong bass support is absent. While both tonic and dominant notes occur as lower elements of dyads (bars 2 and 4 respectively), neither sounds in the register associated traditionally with strong cadential progression. One may look ahead to bars 47–8 to see that Wolf does conclude the song with a progression by descending fifth in a true bass register.

The pitches employed in the introduction constitute six of the seven notes of the A (harmonic) minor scale. The presentation of these elements as members of dyads placed alternately in high and middle registers weakens their connotations as scale degrees. The alternating registers create the effect of a sequence, defined by descending sevenths (first minor, then diminished) in the melody. These large intervals create a melodic disjunction which results in the phenomenon of compound melody. In a compound melody, elements in the same register – in particular those related by step – are associated with one another, even though they may be separated in time by intervening events. The most obvious non-consecutive relation in this passage is the linkage of the Fs heard in the same register in bars 1 and 3. More generally, one tends to hear the upper-register dyads of bars 1–3 (placed on the upper staff) as participating in upper-voice motion, while the lower-register dyads of bars 2–4 are involved with voice-leading of lower parts.

When the voice enters in bar 5, the progression in the accompaniment continues the material of the opening bars. The initial E of the vocal part, doubled in the same register in the piano, as scale-degree 5̂, resolves the tension inherent in F (6̂) in the preceding bars. At the same time, however, the dominant note in the lowest voice (bar 4) ascends in bar 6 to F, its upper auxiliary, which is then sustained until it resolves momentarily to E at the end of bar 8. The vocal line begins with the descent of the perfect fifth E–A, a contrast with the descending sevenths of the piano opening. This fifth initiates a sequence of descending fifths – D–G♯, C–F, B–E – by means of which one may trace an underlying stepwise descent from E. This line continues ostensibly as far as B in bar 11, but in fact would descend by implication to A in bar 13 in conjunction with the cadence to A. The unusual treatment of A in bar 11, left dangling unresolved in the vocal part in bar 12, strongly indicates that this note would complete the unfolding. Thus, spanning the initial section of the piece (bars 1–13), is the melodic unfolding of the descending fifth E–A, signified in the sketch (example 2.1) by the traditional symbol, beamed notes with stems in opposite directions.

Example 2.1 shows that the underlying bass motion of this section similarly alternates dominant and tonic notes, beginning with a′ (Helmholtz notation) in bar 2 and descending gradually until A is attained in the strong bass register in bar 13. This process is typical of larger-scale tonal progressions and is conventionally referred to as an *arpeggiation* of a basic harmony, in this case the A minor tonic. The bass arpeggiation in conjunction with the melodic unfolding from fifth to root is in effect a 'composing out' of the A minor tonic, serving to prolong this harmony throughout the first section of the song. This is not to say that other chords are of little importance in the progression. But they can be shown to be less essential in the sense that they serve only to flesh out the skeletal framework defined by the bass arpeggiation. For example, the chords in bars 10–11 are both dominant preparations (ii⁷ and the French sixth chord respectively) which modify and are thus structurally dependent upon the V⁴₋♯ in bar 12. In terms of voice-leading, they are based on a double auxiliary motion about the dominant, and accordingly these bass notes are each slurred to the E which they embellish. It is conventional in tonal analysis to slur non-essential elements to those elements upon which they depend.

Example 2.1 shows that the double auxiliary bass motion from D to F about E in bars 10–11 is accompanied by a contrary motion about the dominant from F to D♯ in an inner voice. The reciprocal relation between the parts is that of a *voice exchange*, demonstrated graphically by crossed diagonal lines connecting exchanged elements. (The cross-relation between D and D♯ is peculiar to the passage and not an essential feature of the voice exchange.) The voice exchange is a contrapuntal device which prolongs a harmony or harmonic progression, in this case expanding the preparation of the dominant.

Because of the phenomenon of octave equivalence, pitches in extreme registers are frequently understood to represent their equivalents in more normal registers. For example, *f ″* in the piano part in bar 10 might best be considered a displacement of *f ′* in the vocal part. Because it ascends above

the main melodic unfolding (involving the descent from *c″* to *b′* at this point), it may be said to *overlap* this more important voice. Similarly, *a″* in bar 1 might best be heard as overlapping the main unfolding beginning with *e″* in the vocal part in bar b4. An overlapping is indicated by a dotted line connecting octave equivalents, with an arrow indicating the more essential register.

Although the first section of the piece (bars 1–13) is based conventionally enough on a tonic prolongation, several aspects of voice-leading serve to weaken the tonic so that its presence is felt yet never strongly asserted. As mentioned, the fact that the register of genuine bass motion is approached only at the end of the section attenuates the effect of the prolongation. Moreover, at the moment the bass arpeggiation is completed in bar 13, an unexpected change of mode occurs, replacing the expected A minor chord with A major. The major harmony stated in widely spaced chords – a new sonority, and one which becomes characteristic of the middle section of the song – thus functions more as a point of initiation than of completion. Another factor in the dilution of the power of the tonic is the focus on F, which, as upper auxiliary to the fifth, E, displaces or interferes with the more fundamental element for an extraordinary proportion of the duration of the section. Except for bar 5, which contains the A minor tonic only implicitly, and the last quaver of bar 8, F is present until the arrival at V at the end of the section – the first strong presentation of V in the piece.

Finally, the harmonic vagueness of the initial section is attributable in part to the non-tonic beginning – a characteristic of many late-romantic compositions. As we have seen, the tonic octave is defined (in upper registers) in the first two bars, but in such a way that its significance is not immediately appreciated. This is because the F and B presented in middle voices in bars 1 and 2 respectively do not normally commence voice-leading motions within the context of a tonic prolongation. Their place in the voice-leading is readily apparent, however. As we have noted, F is technically an incomplete auxiliary, since it would ordinarily depart from an initial E. One may likewise posit an initial C, which would be connected by means of B (bar 2) to A (bar 6). This descending third span would normally be encountered in an A minor prolongation. We have thus posited points of initiation for several voice-leading spans which in the actual music are incomplete. It is no coincidence that the elements which we have inferred together comprise the tonic triad, and this implicit tonic is shown at the beginning of example 2.1 in square brackets. Wolf's technique of allowing voices to commence in midspan is a means of obtaining tonality by implication as opposed to direct statement. His experiments in 1888 represent the beginnings of an intensive effort by composers around the globe to explore the limits of implicit tonality.

The appearance of the parallel major in a new, wide spacing (the *c♯‴* is the highest pitch thus far in the piece) depicts the sparks of the newly lit fire. The glow of the fire is not enough,

Example 2.1 Hugo Wolf, 'Das verlassene Mägdlein' (1888)

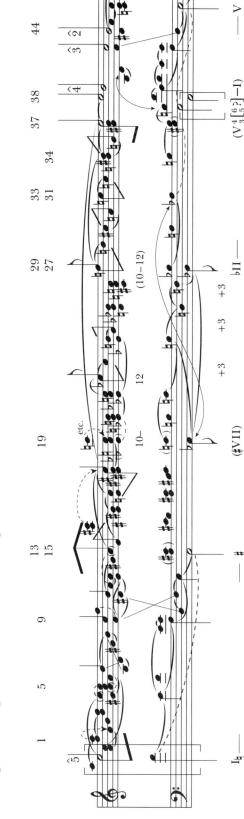

however, to distract the girl, who remains 'deep in sorrow'. The melodic shift from C♯ to C♮ in bars 18–19 perfectly conveys the fact that the beauty of the fire is hardly sufficient to lift the girl out of her depression. A lesser composer might have set the C♮ with the A minor tonic expected in bar 13. Wolf, however, allows the bass to slide chromatically in parallel with the melody, from A♮ (bar 17) to A♭, the lowest pitch of the entire piece. The pathetic character of the A♭ harmony, comparable in sonority with the A major chord in bar 13, is particularly poignant at the moment the fifth, e♭", is added in bar 20. Here, at the melodic high point of the second stanza, Wolf sets 'Leid' (sorrow) with the note a chromatic half-step lower than the initial e" (bar 5), thus far still the highest pitch of the vocal part. Having begun on e' (bar 15), the melody of the middle section spans an ascending major sixth to c♯" as the girl observes the flying sparks. The e♭" apex (bar 21) of the overall contour thus stands as a kind of false relation with the initial e'. From this moment of exquisite pain, the melody droops down, reflecting the girl's despondency. The melody of the second stanza entails a symmetry in the relation of antecedent and consequent phrases. The sixth-span of the first phrase ascends appropriately through adjacent major thirds: E–G♯/A–C♯. On the other hand, from the high E♭ the melody descends a minor sixth, through both minor and major thirds: E♭–C/B♮–G.

Whereas in the first phrase of the second stanza (bars 13–18) Wolf uses the familiar $\frac{4}{2}$ sonority as an auxiliary chord, in the second he introduces the less conventional augmented chord in bar 20 for the same purpose. As we approach the dramatic crux of stanza 3, the augmented triad becomes a basic component in a transitional passage for piano alone (bars 23–6). In this passage, which culminates in the startling arrival on B♭ major in bar 27, one finds an exhaustive patterning and chromatic saturation which are characteristic of much post-tonal voice-leading. From A♭ (bar 19), the bass progresses by ascending minor third through B♮ (bars 20 and 22) and D (bars 23 and 25), to F♮ (bars 24 and 26). In conjunction with this pattern (which, despite appearances, is in no real sense an arpeggiation of a diminished seventh chord but is rather a composing out of the A♭–F third), the melody descends chromatically from C♮ (bar 19) through B and B♭, to A (bars 24 and 26). After the initial A♭ harmony (itself ambiguous), each vertical component is a form of the augmented triad. In all, of the twelve pitches of the chromatic aggregate, only E♮ is missing in bars 19–26 – clearly indicative of a progression away from the focal melodic pitch of the initial A section.

With the sudden arrival of B♭ major in bar 27, it becomes apparent that the augmented triad on F♮ in bar 26 functions as an applied dominant. The harmonic progression of bars 27–30 is roughly equivalent to that of bars 19–22 transposed up two half-steps (henceforth, at T₂), and the initial B♭ chord is accorded the same distinctive registration as the A♭ chord in bar 19. The piano plays a much more active role here, however, continuing the melodic material of the preceding

transition. The voice is now quite agitated, leaping to f", the highest vocal pitch of the piece, and from there down a minor sixth to a', the widest leap of the vocal part. With the augmented chord on A in bar 27, the dynamic level reaches *forte*, the loudest point in the piece. It is no coincidence that, at this moment of crisis, the A–F interval of the first bar is the focus of attention, with special emphasis on F in the vocal part in the same register in which it first appeared. The girl's exclamation 'treuloser Knabe' (faithless boy) is a moment of true pathos, the singer's phrase beginning on the climactic f" and descending in parallel (at T₂) with the earlier phrase 'deep in sorrow' (bars 21–2). The moment of realization past, tension subsides and melody and bass descend chromatically to the pitch level of bar 19 (with the bass in bar 31 an octave higher). A crucial difference here, however, is that A♭ supports an augmented triad, whereas formerly we inferred a major chord. The augmented triad on A♭ is the last of the four available forms (with respect to pitch-class content) of the augmented chord to be used in the piece (the other three having occurred in bars 20–6), and thus also constitutes the completion of a process.

Absent since bar 17, E now returns, first with some subtlety in a middle voice, but then with poignant effect as the high point of the vocal phrase in bar 33. With the final phrase of the third stanza, a process is completed and a symmetry realized which effectively enclose the middle section of the composition. As mentioned, with the first line of stanza 2, the melody set forth an antecedent idea consisting of an ascending major sixth apportioned as successive adjacent major thirds (E–G♯/A–C♯), to which the interim response of a descending minor sixth was made in bars 21–2 (E♭–C/B♮–G). This consequent was repeated at T₂ in bars 29–30, but likewise outlined the minor sixth. Ultimately, however, the true consequent satisfying exactly the requirements for symmetry occurs as the final phrase of the section; for here (bars 33–4) the descending major sixth is spanned in adjacent major thirds, beginning with e": E♮–C/B♮–G. With this phrase it becomes apparent that E is the axis of symmetry for gestures both ascending and descending which entail the same intervallic sequence (M3–m2–M3), and that e" is the goal of a large-scale motion unfolding the E octave which spans the entire middle section (bars 15–33). In this regard, the melodic high points of e♭" (bar 21) and f" (bars 28–9) are only approximations of – in fact, chromatic auxiliary pitches to – the e". The pain associated with these chromatic neighbours is alleviated only in the girl's dreams, as Wolf indicates with devastating irony in arranging for the note of resolution, e", to coincide with 'geträumet habe' (dreamed). The vocal part of the middle section concludes with the augmented harmony on B♮ (bar 34), which is converted linearly in the subsequent piano extension to V$\frac{4}{3}$ of the overall A minor tonality.

The final stanza of the poem receives the same setting as the first, with only slight modifications. The resulting ABA form serves to maximize the contrast of the central section, which deals with the girl's distracted fantasies. The repetition of the A material signifies a return to reality: she stands at the fire as at the beginning of the song, crying now that the image of the faithless one has forced itself upon her memory, as it inevitably will many times more. In bars 44–6, the first part of the final phrase – involving the descent from B♮ to A – is reiterated three times in conjunction with the imitation between piano and voice. Ordinarily this descent might signify firm melodic closure as the second scale degree descends to the first. Here, however, this effect is pre-empted by the harmonic setting, still dominant in bar 46. In fact, A is actually a passing note here in a third-span, B–G♯, which is part of a prolongation of V. The dominant in bars 46–7 effects the main structural cadence of the piece, to the tonic supported by a low bass A. The basic melodic descent of the fifth from *e'* is completed with the arrival of *a'* coinciding with the cadence. This note does not occur in the vocal part, however, and in the piano codetta is concealed by the overlapping *e'* – thus producing closure only in the technical, not the dramatic, sense.

The final tonic chord is itself incomplete, consisting simply of the open fifth A–E, which defines the tonality unequivocally nonetheless. The minor mode is not actually in doubt either, since the half-diminished ($^6_5$) auxiliary chord heard in the latter half of bars 48 and 49, containing F, belongs clearly to A minor. Rather, the fifth contrasts with the ambiguous thirds of the beginning, signifying what for the maid in her present state is undeniable: the barrenness of existence. The tonic chord in the closing bars spans the registral extremes of the composition, *e'''* linking with its appearances in bars 31 and 33 and serving as the resolution of *f'''* in bars 27 and 29, the highest pitch of the piece.

The final cadence, despite the incompleteness of the ultimate tonic, is nevertheless relatively strong, especially owing to bass support in the lowest register. The weight of this cadence (and of the comparable cadence to the unexpected A major in bars 12–13) points to a comparative weakness in the overall structure at a point where in most conventional ABA pieces one would expect a strong dominant: the close of the B section. Here (bars 34–7), as described, the dominant evolves out of the augmented chord on B♮, appearing first in $^4_3$ form before fading with the even weaker $^4_2$ form. Had a strong dominant occurred in these bars, the underlying voice-leading of the middle section would likely have been understood as descending from the strong initial E through D (bar 27) and C (bar 31) to B (bars 32 and 34), after which the melodic descent towards the tonic root would have been interrupted with the repetition of the opening material. The effect in this piece of such a conventional 'interruption form' is considerably attenuated owing to lack of a suitable dominant supporting scale-degree 2̂, the harmony Schenker termed a 'divider' (*Teiler*).

The deliberate relegation of the dominant to the weaker middle register in the B section contrasts effectively with the registral emphasis accorded other, much less conventional

harmonies in this section – specifically the harmonies of A♭ major (bars 19 and 21) and B♭ major (bars 27 and 29). As described previously, the melodic notes E♭ and F♮ supported by each of these harmonies respectively are – by virtue of their distinctive registration – involved in long-range associations, functioning as chromatic auxiliaries of E. Correspondingly, the low bass A♭ and B♭ are in fact chromatic auxiliaries of the low–bass tonic root. The A♭ major chord might therefore be more appropriately spelt as G♯ major (♯VII), since it entails two lower auxiliaries – although in pictorial terms the use of flats better conveys the girl's sinking spirits. The B♭ major chord functions as the more conventional ♭II and in a sense is the most significant preparation for the dominant which closes the section.

The voice-leading of section B is thus built upon the progression from I(♯) through the auxiliary harmonies ♯VII and ♭II to V($^4_3$). (Parallels in the progression from ♯VII to ♭II are avoided by means of a 10–12/10–12 voice-leading pattern.) Because of their conspicuous presentation, the auxiliary chords appear to rival the weak dominant with regard to importance for overall tonal coherence. One senses here the intimation of twentieth-century structures in which the dominant of the conventional tonal axis (I–V–I) is replaced by other, linearly derived harmonies. (Felix Salzer has called these harmonies 'contrapuntal-structural chords'.) In 'Das verlassene Mägdlein', however, the ultimate appearance of the strong dominant (bars 46–7) with the return of section A renders the interpretation of ♯VII and ♭II as components of fundamental structure less feasible. It seems entirely possible and appropriate, however, to hear the relations of the large-scale structural auxiliaries of the B section in direct association with the ultimate tonic, even though in terms of overall coherence the intervening dominant supersedes these chords with regard to structural primacy. Because the lower registers have been broached in the middle section, one cannot hear the return of the initial material as a mere repetition. Having experienced the richness of the widely spaced major chords in section B – if only in a dream – the sonorities of the A section can only seem bleak and empty.

ii   Charles Ives: 'In Flanders Fields' (1917)

Shortly after the United States entered World War I in April 1917, Charles Ives set a text by Col. John McCrae, a medical examiner for an insurance company, on the occasion of a convention of Ives's fellow insurance executives. The song embodies the complex emotions felt by Americans, most particularly Ives himself, at that momentous time. Sung by baritone or male chorus, the words of fallen soldiers spoken from the grave appeal to the living (especially to Americans) to 'take up our quarrel with the foe'. Having overcome isolationist leanings out of sympathy for the English and the French, Americans now set out with heady idealism to 'make the world safe for democracy'. Each of these allies is fittingly

Example 2.2 Charles Ives, 'In Flanders Fields' (1917)

represented in the song: the French by 'La Marseillaise', the English by 'God Save the King', and the Americans by 'Columbia, Gem of the Ocean' (Ives's favourite motto), the 'Battle Cry of Freedom', and numerous other musical allusions. Although the music soars to heights of noble determination and patriotic fervour, Ives's tone is anything but blithely optimistic. With the guns of August 1914, Western civilization had lost its innocence irretrievably. The picture Ives paints of the fields of poppies at the beginning of the song is grim indeed, and at the conclusion one senses his anxiety at the prospect of failing to carry the torch of liberty on to victory.

The challenge in analysing this song (example 2.2) – or many other works by Ives – is to discern the basis for the structural unity underlying the pastiche of diverse motifs and themes that are its substance. After all, the coherence of the work could well be essentially poetic, residing in the extra-musical associations of the text and patriotic tunes. Generally, each cited tune clearly projects a key, and the keys thus defined may bear little obvious relation to one another. The 'Columbia, Gem' theme is stated in G major (bars 7–8), 'God Save the King' appears in A major (bars 14–15), and 'Reveille' is quoted in B minor (bars 19–20), for example. Other sections of the work, notably the opening and closing bars, are composed in a freer and more dissonant style. The crucial question is whether these discrete harmonic areas function within a single tonality – whether there is a fundamental tonic harmony which is prolonged through a large-scale cadential progression or analogous means.

The most prominent key in the song is G major, the basis for 'Columbia, Gem' with which the voice first enters (bars 8–9) as well as the climactic counterpoint of 'La Marseillaise' and 'God Save the King' beginning in bars 29–30. The piece neither begins nor ends with clear reference to this key, however. (This situation, commonly encountered in post-tonal music, in no way precludes the possibility of the composition being tonal in a conventional sense.) An overall view of the elaborate and highly dissonant piano introduction (bars 1–8) shows this section to be a thoroughly coherent preparation for the cadence to G major in bars 8–9. In this regard, as in all tonal music, the progression of the bass plays a particularly important role. The low bass D, which serves as a pedal from the end of bar 5 through bar 8, functions as dominant, even though no complete D major chord is presented before the cadence (compare, however, the latter half of bar 9). In retrospect, the climactic chord on A in bar 4 – a full dominant seventh containing additionally a minor third and a diminished fifth – functions as V/V; the bass A is also treated as a pedal note.

Although the bass motion preceding A is complicated and bears no ostensible relation to G major, the imitative entrances of 'La Marseillaise' in the right hand in bars 2–4 project this key, especially through the ascending fourth, D–G. (This theme could also be heard as 'Columbia, Gem', the incipits of the two being quite similar.) The chromatic bass is designed to provide maximum conflict with the melody, aptly depicting the climate of strife. The intervals formed by simultaneous attacks in the outer voices in bars 3–4 are especially strident: m9, M9, a4, m9, d5. On the downbeat of bar 3, the first appearance of G in the melody is marred by the clash with the leading-note in the bass. The dominant note in the melody on the downbeat of bar 4 receives comparable treatment. The bass $C\sharp$ here appears to belong to (or at least to anticipate) the harmony on A which follows directly. The high $E\flat$, supported by A, apparently a chromatic upper auxiliary to D, clashes not only with the bass but also with the regular fifth, E, which occurs in an inner voice. The A–$E\flat$ tritone seems particularly crucial, since Ives states the inversion of this interval on the upbeat to bar 4; these inversely related intervals may well be involved in a voice exchange.

The $E\flat$ in the bass in bar 4 is in fact identical with the initial pitch of the introduction. The whole-tone oscillation between $E\flat$ and $F\natural$ (neither elements of G major) ultimately appears to embellish $E\flat$, from which the bass finally descends through $C\sharp$ to A in bar 4. The deviation of the bass to $F\sharp$ in bar 3 hints at an upward resolution to G, a motion thwarted by the immediate return of $F\natural$. With the exception of $F\sharp$, all the pitches of the bass line in the first four bars belong to the whole-tone scale – a synthetic formation popular with post-tonal composers since the time of Liszt and the Russian nationalists. The conflict between right- and left-hand materials here could well be heard as the clash between diatonic and whole-tone constructions. It is apparent that the A–$E\flat$ interval defined by the registral extremes of the climax chord in bar 4 also spans the bass progression from the beginning to this point. The tritone bass progression is one associated in romantic harmony with the preparation of the dominant, in particular with the progression from $\flat$II to V as observed in the song by Wolf. The bass progression from $E\flat$ to A here is likewise one which prepares and thus prolongs a dominant – the applied dominant of D. The fact that the tritone is subsumed within the sonority supported by A in bar 4 confirms this interpretation. The harmonic progression of the introduction is thus essentially [$\flat$II–V]–V–I. The G major material in the right hand of the opening bars is simply out of synchrony with the bass progression but clearly anticipates the tonic in bar 9.

Following the climax on $e\flat'''$ in bar 4, the melody descends by whole step through the span of a seventh, from c''' to d'', paralleled by a middle voice a major ninth below. The whole-tone scale entailed in these spans is the complement of that involved in the bass of the first four bars. The melodic descent effects a transfer of register from d''' in bar 4 to d'' in bar 6. Between the parallel voices separated by a ninth, another voice descends chromatically but, significantly, avoids the pitches $G\natural$ and $D\natural$ emphasized in the melody of the first phrase. Over the dominant pedal, the melody of bar 6 foreshadows the tune treated at the same pitch level but over a G major tonic in bar 18 – with the critical difference that D is embellished here by the chromatic auxiliary $E\flat$ as opposed to the diatonic $E\natural$.

in the later passage. The melodic E♮ is transferred another octave lower (to e♭') and suspended over the dominant, along with other elements of V/V, resolving only at the upbeat to bar 9 to the simple dominant octave.

With the entry of the vocal part in bars 8–9, the listener settles into the simple, fairly consonant setting of 'Columbia, Gem' in G major, only to be jarred by the strange inflection of 'poppies blow' in bar 10. While in the accompaniment B♮ descends to the tonic root before moving on to the leading-note, the vocal part skirts G, moving directly to F♯ and then immediately on to F♮. (The latter motion is motivically associated with the bass motion of bar 3.). Accompanying this melodic motion, the harmonic progression proceeds from tonic through mediant to the minor dominant, which contains the tonic root as well. The material of bar 10 is presented in a varied repetition in bars 11–12, with the minor dominant receiving further chromatic inflection. While F♮ remains fixed in the melody into bar 14 (embellished by the motivic E♭ in bar 12 and reiterated in the tiny fanfare in the accompaniment), the bass descends by step to G♯ (bar 14) supporting a diminished seventh chord. (Do the parallel fifths and octaves in the progression from D minor to C minor in bar 12 depict the parallel rows of crosses?) The diminished seventh chord functions traditionally as a substitute for an implicit V_5^6, in this case applying to A major, the goal of the cadence in bar 15. Here the conventional descending stepwise resolution of the seventh is transferred to the bass, where F♮ descends to E♮. The F♮ supports a modified augmented sixth chord in A, while E♮ supports the A major $_4^6$ chord replacing the expected dominant. (Chopin had employed the identical substitution at the climactic cadence of the Polonaise-Fantaisie, op. 61.) In essence, the bass of bars 12–14 descends a seventh from D to E', a composing-out of the step relation.

The modulation from G to A major completed by bar 15 coincides with the introduction of 'God Save the King', setting a new line of text which directs our attention to larks flying overhead. Appropriately, the vocal line rises gradually in contours resembling arcs of flight, reaching d', the highest vocal pitch thus far, with 'singing fly'. The shift to the parallel minor with 'still' (bar 16) reminds us of the guns below, however. The bass moves from the tonicized A to E♭ (bar 16), recalling the use of this interval in the introduction. The E♭ supports an inverted half-diminished chord by means of which we pivot back into G major (bar 18), proving the modulation to A to have been but a momentary digression within the tonal area of G. From the melodic apex of d', the singer's line descends a seventh to e ('guns below'), perhaps echoing the same span in the bass in bars 12–14. At the same time, e'' occurs as upper auxiliary in the accompaniment to d'' (bar 18) which is based on 'The Battle Cry of Freedom', a song from the American Civil War (much more spirited in the original than in the present context).

The C major subdominant, a chord of special emphasis in bars 18–19, progresses by tritone in the bass to F♯, thereby serving as pivot into the area of B minor. As 'Reveille' is sounded in the highest register of the accompaniment (the uncharacteristic slow tempo and minor mode making this quotation especially poignant), the singer intones 'we are the dead', employing the short–short–short–long rhythm Ives often used in allusion to the 'fate motif' of Beethoven's Fifth Symphony. The ascending fourth here echoes that with which the voice entered in bars 8–9, but the specific pitches involved resonate with those used in the descending B–F♯ fourth setting 'poppies' in bar 10. Indeed, in tonicizing B minor at this point, Ives is expanding the harmony which occurred as mediant of G major in bars 10–11. Whether this functional relation obtains here remains to be investigated.

Immediately following the cadence to B minor in bar 21, the bass descends to G♯, recalling the progression of bars 13–14. Whereas the chromatic conflict between G♯ and G♮ which followed in bar 14 was resolved in favour of G♯ (which cadences to A), in bar 21 G♯ descends to G♮ supporting an applied dominant of C major, a function which might well be prolonged into bar 26. After sustaining G as a pedal note into bar 24, the bass ascends to B and then returns to G (bar 25), moving on to F supporting a G_2^4 harmony on the downbeat of bar 26. (The bass in bars 24–5 actually proceeds in imitation at the lower seventh of the first part of the obbligato tune in the upper register of the accompaniment: G–A–A♯–B–A–(G♯)–G = F–G–G♯–A–G♮–F, T_2.) The mood turns nostalgic in these bars; the vocal melody, tender and lyrical, arches to e' in bar 25 – the highest pitch of the vocal part – reached for the first time with 'loved', and accompanied by the touching, Schumannesque half-diminished chord. At the point where a resolution to the long-awaited C major harmony might be expected (bar 26), an E minor chord is substituted, focusing abruptly on the grim present ('now'). In retrospect, the harmony on B in bar 25 may be heard as pointing towards E minor, and one may observe a voice exchange between obbligato melody and the bass which would prolong the fifth of this key. Nonetheless, given the strong expectations of a progression to C major and a return to its dominant at the end of bar 25, one probably does not interpret the intervening bass progression to B as a modulation towards E minor. In fact, the stepwise bass descent which has carried the progression to E actually continues to D in bar 27 as the melody repeats the motif associated with poppies and crosses. As in bars 10–11, this chord is the (minor) dominant of G major, a function clearly realized as the bass descends to D' in bar 29 – the lowest note of the song, heard previously only in the ambiguous context of the introduction but now supporting a definite dominant seventh chord. In conjunction with the coupling of the D octave, the tempo accelerates to the steady pace of a march, and the music crescendos to a victorious arrival on G major in bar 30. We recognize on the large level a prolongation of G from bar 18 to bar 30 by a progression through the mediant (bar 21) and dominant (bar 29) – an expansion of the distinctive progression in bars 10–11.

The urgent appeal 'take up our quarrel with the foe' is set to the thrilling strains of 'La Marseillaise' accompanied by the heroically proportioned harmonies of 'God Save the King' in the piano, each anthem adhering to its own metre. The decisive character of this treatment of the British anthem in G major contrasts with its earlier, less stable appearance in A major (bars 14–17). As this theme modulates to C major in bar 34, the singer leaps to the climactic *e'* as the torch of liberty is tossed. Significantly, the melody is traded at this point for a phrase from the American 'Columbia, Gem of the Ocean', a staple in Ives's repertoire of patriotic tunes. The consonant setting of the singer's E with a C major chord sets in relief the only other occurrence of the highest vocal pitch in the earlier lyrical section in bars 21–6. There, as mentioned, E itself was part of a yearning dissonant chord occurring briefly on a weak beat, and the key of C major, while anticipated, was not attained. Together these features reinforce the image of the unfulfilled dreams of youth. By contrast, the ultimate arrival on the climactic C major harmony setting the high E in bar 34, while hardly signifying fulfilment, lends immediacy and urgency to the symbol of the torch, which embodies all of the aspirations of the fallen soldiers.

Since the phrase from the 'Columbia, Gem' remains in G major after the accompaniment has modulated to C, in bar 35 E is approached from above via F♯ in the voice and F♮ in the keyboard counter-melody, a chromatic duality no doubt derived from the melodic motif introduced in bar 10. The cross-relation creates a certain tension with regard to a melodic resolution to E, a tension heightened in the following bar as F♮ in the melody is attacked simultaneously with the bass E, resolving only with the last quaver of the bar. The increased dissonance coincides with the injection of the element of doubt in the text: 'if ye break faith with us who die ...' Befitting the more challenging tone of these words, the harmony shifts towards the relative minor of C, with E supporting the dominant seventh of A minor. Ives's unflagging determination on behalf of America is evident from his source for the melody of this phrase: 'Down the Field', a favourite fight song from his alma mater, Yale ('March, march on down the field/Fighting for Eli [Elihu Yale] ... Harvard's team may fight to the end/But Yale will win'). The tune introduces an element of irony, of course, for the original words conveying youthful high spirits have been replaced with a plea made in deadly earnest. The use of the minor mode highlights this change.

The final phrase of the song ('We shall not sleep ...') is symmetrical with the opening phrase in that it also cites 'Columbia, Gem of the Ocean'. Here, however, the full melodic phrase occurs in the vocal part as well as in the piano, and the key is A as opposed to G major at the beginning. A weak cadence by stepwise descent to A major occurs in bar 38, followed by a strong authentic cadence to the parallel minor in bar 39. With the shift to minor, coinciding with 'poppies', the diminished fifth E♭ sounds as the uppermost

element of the harmony (clashing with the perfect fifth in an inner voice), resonating with the comparable climax chord of the introduction (bar 4). Unexpectedly, in bar 39 the harmony slides from A minor down to G minor, presumably as a corrective to the setting of the 'Columbia, Gem' theme up a step from its original harmonization, whereupon the final line of text ('In Flanders fields') is set with the familiar bass arpeggiation, G–B–D. The descent from A to G in the bass is coupled with the ascent from E♭ to F in the obbligato – in fact an inversion (retrograde motions in switched registers) of the outer voices at the end of bar 3 in the introduction.

The approach to G in parallel chords (resembling the progression at the end of bar 12) does not permit its being heard as a focal harmony, even though its function would ostensibly parallel that of the G harmony in the corresponding passage in bars 10–11. (Moreover, it appears here as a dissonant minor seventh chord.) The appearance of G at this point in the composition, then, is no more than an allusion to its former occurrences as tonic (bars 10, 18, 30). The closing bass progression by ascending fifth (through B♮) to D may nonetheless be effective in asserting the final chord as an altered form of the dominant of G. This chord is in fact the same sonority as that associated with A in bar 39 – the minor triad with both perfect and diminished fifths, spelt in the latter case as the raised fourth, G♯. (The G♯ occurs as well in the preceding chord on B, thus setting 'Flanders' with the identical pitch-class collection associated formerly with 'dead' in bar 21.) The chords on A and D are of course themselves associated by fifth, in this case the descending fifth, which in the larger view continues the motion by descending fifth initiated with the bass progression from E to A in bars 36–8 (repeated in bars 38–9). The underlying E–A–D bass progression of the concluding measures closely resembles both the progression of the introduction, which leads to the cadence to G in bar 9, and even more closely the progression in bars 14–17, which is part of a circular progression prolonging G. These observations lead to the conclusion that the final progression may most reasonably be heard as functioning within the purview of G major, which is therefore the single prevailing tonic throughout the piece.

The basic melodic motion of the song conforms to the projection of G major as tonic overall. The fifth, D, is strongly indicated as the primary melodic note ($\hat{5}$) of the fundamental line, evident especially in the climactic passage in the tonic which begins in bars 29–30. Characteristically, D is embellished by its upper auxiliary – E♮, as in bars 18 and 34, or E♭, as in bar 4. Although anticipated in the piano introduction, $\hat{5}$ first occurs in a consonant setting in bar 18. In the preceding bars it is approached by a scalar ascent from the tonic root beginning in bar 9, in conformity with the conventional tonal procedure identified by Schenker as the *Anstieg*, the ascent to the main melodic element. The primary melodic note is recalled by the *d'''* in the obbligato at the end, in a manner typical of tonal compositions. The descent of the fundamental line begins as late as the final phrase, proceeding only as far as B♮ (3̂) – although A (2̂) would ideally be supported by the closing dominant. Ending the melody in midspan only adds to the effect of the seemingly indefinite close. The lack of final resolution – quite the norm in Ives's compositions – aptly reflects the uncertainty of the final lines of text and indeed of the situation of the Allies in 1917.

iii Claude Debussy: 'Canope' (1912–13)

If conflicting harmonic regions pose difficulties for the analysis of 'In Flanders Fields', problems of this sort can be even more complicated in the vague, impressionistic works of Claude Debussy (1862–1918). 'Canope', from Book II of Debussy's *Préludes*, will be discussed as a representative example of voice-leading in early twentieth-century French music. Debussy assembled two books of preludes for the piano (twelve in each), in 1910 and 1913 respectively. These works continue in a sense the romantic tradition of the character piece, although Debussy's designation of the collections as preludes invokes the more 'classical' models of Bach and Chopin as well. (Shortly after completing these collections, Debussy became involved in editing the works of Chopin and dedicated two books of Etudes [1915] to his memory.) In providing titles for his preludes, Debussy intended merely to suggest the sources of his inspirations, as is indicated by his having appended the titles in parentheses at the close of each piece. A number of the preludes evoke legendary times and faraway places – 'La Cathédral engloutie' and 'Danseuses de Delphes' from Book I, for example. 'Canope' refers to the ancient Egyptian city located on the Mediterranean near the mouth of the Nile. The city was named after Canopus, Spartan pilot during the Trojan War, whose body was supposedly buried near the site and who, according to mythology, was transformed into a star of the constellation Argo. The name is also associated with the canopic vase, a type of burial jar – typically with a cover in the form of a human head – in which the viscera of embalmed bodies were preserved. Little wonder, then, that the piece has an air of mystery, its subdued harmonies redolent of ancient ruins, its mournful, reed-like melodies tinged with eastern colour.

The tonality of 'Canope' is ambivalent, hovering between D minor and C major, the prevailing harmonies respectively at the opening and close. At times C and D are combined vertically, always featured conspicuously in the outer voices: see, for instance, the downbeat chord in bar 4, with C in the bass and D in the melody, or the sustained harmony in bars 7–9, in which these elements are inverted. Indeed, the final sonority is a C major ninth chord, with D sustained unresolved for the full duration of the chord. The key signature of D minor is effective throughout the piece.

The opening material of the prelude, characterized by the distinctive voice-leading of parallel triads, recurs at the close in somewhat modified form (bars 26–30), thus framing the structure. The main body of the composition is based on contrasting melodic material introduced in bars 7–8, which is highly chromatic and rhythmically much more active than the initial subject. This material is recalled in the final bars as a brief codetta. The parallel voice-leading of the opening phrase is of course a hallmark of Debussy's style, usually employed as an evocation of antiquity. The progression opens with triads seemingly drifting in the upper register without bass support. In bar 3 an independent line enters beneath the floating chords – at the very moment when the upper voice reaches its apex. There follows a gradual descent in the lower voices into the conventional register of structural support, while the chords in the right hand progress back to the original D minor. With the exception of the C major chords in bars 1 and 2, all the chords are pure minor triads until the major chords on E♭, A♭ and G♭, which effect a sort of cadence to D in bars 4–5. (The seemingly independent entry of the left-hand line in bars 3–4 of course clouds the pure chords which sound above.) Until these quasi-cadential chords, the harmony is strictly diatonic, the single exception being the B♮ in the downbeat chord of bar 2, an alteration necessary to retain the minor sonority. The major chords on E♭, G♭ and A♭ traverse a remote tonal region and exert a cadential effect in part because they provide the elements necessary to complete the chromatic aggregate within the phrase: D♭, E♭, G♭ and A♭.

The melody opens so as to emphasize symmetries about D. Thus C and E are lower and upper whole-tone auxiliaries in bars 1 and 2, while A and G are introduced respectively as lower and upper fourths. These five pitches, which comprise the pentatonic scale, constitute all of the melodic notes until the chromatic chords in bar 4. At this point the cadence is accomplished by means of a bass motion – A♭–G♭–D – which is inversely symmetrical with the melody – A♭–B♭–D. Within the cadential progression, D is also embellished by its chromatic auxiliaries E♭ and D♭ (though only E♭ is stated explicitly in the upper voice).

As shown in example 2.3, the unity and uniformity of the initial melodic subject is attributable in part to the fact that it is saturated with a limited number of types of trichords. Trichord *a* (set 3–7 in Allen Forte's nomenclature) may be formed by attaching an element to one of the pitches of a perfect fourth so that it forms a whole step inside the fourth; for example, C–D–F. Trichord *b* (3–9) is similarly structured, but with the whole step outside the fourth; for example, C–D–G. In fact, these two trichords are structurally similar in that they both maximize intervals of two and five half-steps. In Debussy's melody, the trichords are freely reordered, transposed and inverted, with trichord *a* more frequent at the beginning and trichord *b* predominant towards the close of the phrase. The theme closes with a distinctly different trichord (*c*) featured both in the melody and (inverted) in the bass. Trichord *c* (3–8) in a sense represents a compromise between trichords *a* and *b*, in that it features a whole step attached

Example 2.3 Claude Debussy, 'Canopé' (1912–13)

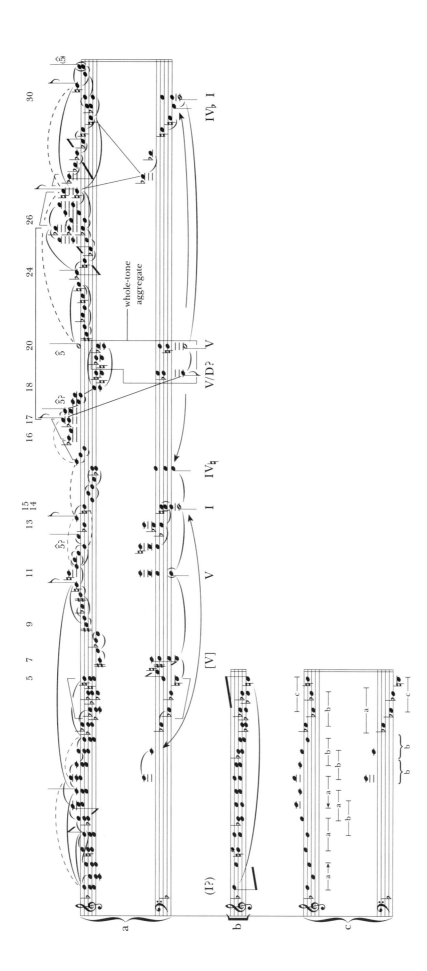

within the tritone, the interval midway between the perfect fourth of *a* and the perfect fifth of *b*.

In its contours, the opening theme strongly projects D minor as tonic. After leaping from tonic root to dominant, the melody circles about D before ascending by fourths to the upper C in bar 2. The seventh thus spanned represents an expansion of the relation between D and its lower auxiliary, and indeed, with the sequential repetition of the ascending fourth G–C up a step in bar 3, the melody attains the upper D, the apex of the phrase. (The slurring to the downbeat A in bar 3 renders the sequence less than obvious.) The arrival at the high D is in fact symmetrical with the departure from D an octave lower, since the trichord involved in its approach, C–A–D, is the retrograde of the initial trichord, D–A–C. The coupling of lower to upper D thus accomplished is then briefly reciprocated by a descent to the original D through another disposition of fourths: D–A/G–D. With the first motion by half-step, the melody ascends in bar 4 from D to its upper chromatic auxiliary, E♭, which ultimately resolves to the original D on the downbeat of bar 5.

The chromatic harmonies involved in the cadence to D may be analysed as lower chromatic equivalents of ordinary diatonic functions (all modified so as to yield major triads): ♭II–♭V–♭IV. The ♭II harmony is standard in late-romantic cadential progressions. The lowered dominant is more unusual, but extends the tritone relation directly to the tonic and has its advantages as well with regard to the symmetrical voice-leading between outer voices already demonstrated. The ♭IV comes about as a result of that symmetry, but in progressing to the tonic effects a modified plagal cadence. In conjunction with the circular progression prolonging D through the first phrase (bars 1–5), one may also observe voice-leading associated with the stepwise unfolding of the tonic octave. Finally, one discovers in the rhythmic and metrical organization of this material a subtle process which emphasizes the D minor tonal axis. The initial slur leads to the (minor) dominant on the downbeat of bar 3. Before this, the tonic is stated twice, but each time on the weak second beat. The tonic occurs on the second beat yet again in bar 3 (right hand only), but arrives as the goal of the descending octave coupling on the downbeat of bar 4. While the tonic function may be somewhat obscured by the presence of C in the lowest voice, its stability is in no doubt when reiterated – with full bass support – on the downbeat of bar 5.

While D is clearly the focal harmony for the opening material, one is obliged nonetheless to inspect closely the function of C in these bars, given the fact that C is comparably stabilized at the conclusion of the piece. And it does seem that C receives special treatment at the beginning. As mentioned, C is the only melodic element (before bar 4) to be set with a major triad, and it is conspicuous as the apex of the first melodic contour (as defined by the initial slur). The leap by ascending fourth to the high C receives a response immediately followed by the lower voice introduced in bar 3. This voice,

the first to assert a certain independence from the melody and its parallel voices, sounds the descending fifth, G–C, as if to cadence to C. This motion, coinciding as it does with the coupling of the octave Ds in the upper voice, cannot succeed in stabilizing C, especially because it does not occupy the register of the structural bass. Nonetheless, in this gesture the conflict between C and D is presented with a mysterious significance, an enigma not solved within the initial phrase itself.

As a transition to contrasting material, the initial melodic phrase (bars 1–2) is restated, doubled simply at the octave, in the lowest register of the piece. The main elements of this phrase – the D–A fifth defined by its endpoints as well as its apex, C – are then combined vertically with F♯ in a dominant seventh chord sustained throughout bars 7–9 (or 10). This harmony supports the presentation of the new chromatic melody in balanced two-bar phrases. The middle-register antecedent (bars 7–8) is based on the chromatic double auxiliary motion about D, a motion implicit in the voice-leading of bars 4–5, as mentioned. (The half-step clash between the harmonic C♮ and the melodic C♯ make the entrance of the new tune especially striking.) The consequent (bars 9–10) – doubled an octave higher – elaborates on the ascending arpeggiation of the D major triad. The chromaticism here derives directly from bar 4, the pitches D♭, A♭ and F♯ (G♭) having formed the bass line of that passage. At this point the melody has regained the upper register of the opening bars. The critical feature of the voice-leading in these bars is the employment of F♯, heard previously only momentarily as its enharmonic equivalent, G♭. This pitch, perhaps even more than the seventh formed with C, renders the harmony on D unstable, changing its quality to that of a dominant seventh of G, a function realized with the progression to G minor in bar 11. The arrival on G does not effect a strong cadence, however, owing to lack of strong bass support, as reflected in Debussy's notation of the lower notes on the middle staff. The harmony on G is not a simple consonance but rather is enriched by the major sixth, *e‴*, the highest pitch thus far.

The melodic motif introduced in bar 11 emphasizes the D–A fifth of D minor, at first descending in response to the ascent through the same interval in the preceding bars. One may in fact, consider the D–A fifth to be suspended from the phrase in bars 9–10; it certainly alludes as well to the identical fifth spanned in the opening melodic phrase. This fifth continues to define the melodic contours, as the harmony progresses through a variety of chords, at least through bar 16. The D–A fifth is reiterated at the close of the piece over a strong bass C as the melody from bars 11–13 is restated (with only a minimal, but critical, change at the end). Because it recurs as an *idée fixe* over a variety of harmonies, the D–A fifth has a special integrity which renders its pitches more stable than they might otherwise be. In each of the pertinent harmonic contexts, however – G (bars 11–12), E♭ (bar 13) and C (bars 30–3) – A would conventionally resolve to the harmonic element G, and indeed might well do so. (The slurring to G at the end of bar 12 bears out this interpretation.) In the case of D, on the other hand, in both bars 14 and 30–3 – where the same C major harmony prevails – no explicit melodic resolution is provided. It would seem entirely reasonable to hear the D–A fifth sustained without resolution at the close.

The next important harmonic goal is the C major ninth chord in bar 14, which is accorded the same broad registration and low bass support as the chord on D in bar 9. In retrospect, the shift from G minor to G major in bars 11–12 is important in preparing the progression to C, since the major chord functions as its dominant. The non-harmonic *e'''* supported by this dominant might well be understood as an anticipation of the third of C major. The E♭ harmony in bar 13 is a connecting chord, the bass note involved in the arpeggiation of the fifth descending from G to C. The subsidiary status of the harmonies on G and E♭ is indicated by their lack of strong bass support. The descent from G to E♭ is taken up as a melodic motif in a middle voice in bars 14–15, in conjunction with a plagal embellishment of C major by its subdominant, F – a harmony left dangling unresolved after bar 16. The pure D minor triad is arpeggiated in the upper part of these bars, reaching *d'''* in bar 16, a link with *e'''* in bars 11–12. (The *e♭'''* grave note might thus be considered a passing note connecting the two.)

The ensuing episode (*Animez un peu*) develops the fourths of the opening theme by restating them as verticalities with grace-note decorations alluding to the contrasting theme of bars 7–10. Underlying the obvious leaps are lines spanning significant intervals. One line spans a descending fourth beginning with the motion from the *a'''* grace note – the highest pitch thus far – to *g'''*; the *g'''* is then picked up an octave below as a grace note resolving to *f''*; finally, *f'* itself becomes a grace note moving to *e'*, the fifth of the harmony on A in bar 18. The other line descends similarly from the *e♭'''* grace note (bar 17) to *b*, the ninth of the A chord, which has the quality of a dominant. The A is taken up through several octaves to return to a repetition of the material of bar 17 in bar 19. In place of the A chord expected in bar 20, a harmony on *G'* occurs, supported by the lowest note of the composition. This chord comprises the entire whole-tone aggregate (if the grace notes are included). Correspondingly, the linear progressions underlying bars 19–20 span intervals of the same whole-tone scale, descending from *a'''* to *d♭'* and from *e♭'''* to *a*. With the substitution of the chord on G in bar 20, *g''* becomes prominent in the normal melodic register. In the course of this episode, a crucial resolution has taken place in several registers: the descent from A to G, hinted at in the grace-note figuration of bar 17. (It will be remembered that A has been suspended in the melodic register since bar 11, with the expected resolution to G postponed.) This descent is confirmed when, in the repetition of the contrasting theme from bars 7–10 over the G harmony, the consequent phrase ascends not to *a''* as before, but only as far as *g''* (bar 23).

The middle section of the piece closes with the ascent of *g''* to *a♭''* in the upper voices (without bass support), from which the melody ascends through the A♭ major triad to *e♭'''*, the highest pitch of the piece. The meaning of the A♭ harmony is not immediately clear, although at the very least it is an allusion to the chromaticism first encountered in bar 4. In fact, with the return of the main theme in bar 26, E♭ resolves to D, just as in bars 4–5. (The duplication of the parallel triads in the upper register takes the melody close to the high E♭ in bar 25.) The A♭ of bars 24–5 would ostensibly resolve to A of the D minor chord in bar 26, thus serving as a chromatic passing note from G in bars 20–3.

In bar 28, the repetition of the main material continues, but with an unexpected shift up a half-step from the original level of bars 3–4. This shift results in a reiteration of the A♭– E♭ fifth of bars 24–5, with the *a♭'* in precisely the same register as its earlier occurrence. On the downbeat of bar 29, the outer voices juxtapose E♭ and D♭, which served at the outset as chromatic auxiliaries to D♮, associated especially with the contrasting theme of bars 7–8. A continuation of the restatement at T_1 would result in a succession of major triads on E, A and G to complete bar 29. Instead, Debussy alters the chord on E to become a minor triad, which then progresses to the expected A major chord. These two harmonies are in fact diatonic II(♮5) and V♯ of D minor, functions which might have occurred in bar 4. Here, then, Debussy apparently corrects his chromatic deviations by returning to diatonic elements – a return especially evident in the melodic ascent from E♭ to E♮.

With the arrival of the A major chord, one might well expect a cadence to D minor. However, with the final chord of bar 29, Debussy thwarts expectations by employing an F minor chord in the context of a plagal cadence to C. The F minor chord is involved in several large-scale relations by virtue of which this ostensibly mystifying harmonic turn towards C proves to effect a fully satisfying harmonic close. Most important, the subdominant harmony is linked with the chord of the same function which dangled unresolved as an auxiliary harmony to C in bar 16. The plagal cadence to C resolves the tension remaining from that previously uncompleted progression. The use of the minor form of the subdominant in bar 29 focuses attention on A♭, a reference to the critical pitch at the close of the middle section. In the context of the final cadence, A♭ strongly indicates G as a fundamental element. The A♮ of the melody returning from bars 11–13 at the close is thereby more audibly an upper auxiliary to G. The melody continues to assert D, which is sustained as the ninth of the C major chord for the rest of the piece. In conjunction with the final fade-out, however, the phrase in bar 32, corresponding to that in bars 13–14, dies away before completing the expected descent to D. The effect of this closing gesture is to suggest a resolution of D to E, the third of the C major harmony.

Example 2.4 Béla Bartók, Scherzo from the *Suite* Op.14 (1916)

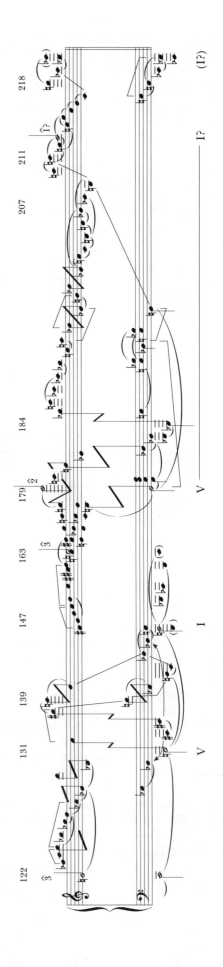

In the largest view, Debussy's 'Canope' is in the tonality of C major, in spite of the protracted focus on D minor. (In this regard, the key signature is a deception of Debussy's part.) Of critical importance in determining overall tonal coherence is the progression of the bass in the lowest register. The harmony on D is effectively supported at the beginning by the low bass D in bar 5, but it loses its quality of stability in bar 7, when it is converted to an applied dominant of G. Tonicized through the cadence from G and through subsequent plagal cadences, the harmony of C major (bars 14–15) appears to rival (if not supersede) D minor for structural primacy. In bar 18 the dominant of D is stated with strong bass support, apparently shifting weight back to its tonic. A cadence to D does not ensue, however. Instead, this dominant is transposed down a step, restated as the dominant of C. As with the dominant of D, a cadence to C does not follow directly, but no other strong dominant harmony intervenes before C major is restated firmly as the final chord. Thus the connection between C and its dominant (supported by the lowest pitch of the piece) not only is not disrupted but is in fact conspicuous. As mentioned, the recurrence of the strong subdominant of C in bar 29 reinforces the link between the statements of C in bars 14–15 and 30–3. Working against the relatively firm tonal definition by the bass is the lack of closure in the melody – not only at the surface but more importantly at the level of fundamental structure – responsible in large part for the allure of the piece.

In analysing works such as Ives's 'In Flanders Fields' and especially Debussy's 'Canope', one might be tempted to invoke the notion of polytonality as an explanation for the occurrence of conflicting harmonic regions – particularly in view of the use of contrasting harmonies in conjunction with discrete strata within a single timespan. The validity of the theory of polytonality as an explanation for musical structure as it is perceived by the listener has long been disputed, however, although it does seem to reflect the way certain composers put their music together. Composers from entirely different musical backgrounds – Paul Hindemith and Milton Babbitt, to name two – have held that it is impossible to perceive more than one harmonic root at a time, that is, to hear in two or more keys at once, regardless of the composer's method or intent. The theory of polytonality is impoverished, since it dispenses with the hierarchy of tonal relations so essential to tonality and to much music employing techniques of extended tonality as well. To state, for instance, that in 'Canope' the harmonies of C major and D minor are of equal structural weight would be to miss the tensions inherent in the pitch relations within the piece. The hierarchy among pitches, though expressed with the delicacy and nuance, is nonetheless real. To call the work a polytonal piece would be to say, in effect, that the close on C major is arbitrary, when, in view of the process of the composition as it unfolds, there is a rightness – even an inevitability – to the final cadence.

iv   *Béla Bartók: Scherzo from the Suite, op. 14 (1916)*

As a final, more problematic example of extended tonality, I shall analyse the Scherzo (second movement) of the *Suite*, op. 14, for piano by Béla Bartók (1881–1945). By the time Bartók composed the *Suite* in 1916, he had conducted a great deal of ethnomusicological research on the folk music of Hungary, Romania, Czechoslovakia and even North Africa. The *Suite* is one of a number of works composed at this time which deal overtly with ethnic materials; indeed, virtually every aspect of the music is touched by folk influences, including harmony, melody and rhythm. The Scherzo exhibits another feature characteristic of much of Bartók's music: a conscious, formalistic experimentation with non-tonal components, in this case the augmented triad.. It is important to recognize that Bartók himself regarded even his most systematically experimental works (which approach the style of the Viennese atonalists) as fundamentally tonal. The tonal methods which he developed, however, greatly modify or even replace conventional tonal procedures, thereby posing immense difficulties for the analyst.

From the beginning of the Scherzo, the importance of the augmented triad is evident (see example 2.4). The first 16-bar period is composed for the most part of sequences of arpeggiated augmented chords, one per bar, articulated every fourth bar by an octave leap followed by a rest. In the course of the period, all four possible forms of the augmented chord are used. If labelled a, b, c and d in order of appearance, their occurrences may be mapped as in figure 2.1 (with pitches of the punctuated octaves shown in parentheses):

Figure 2.1

bars   1 2 3 4   5 6 7   8   9 10 11 12   13 14 15 16
         a b c (B♭)   a b c (F♯)   b c d (E♭)   b c a (A♭)

It is evident that the first two four-bar phrases employ the same sequence of triads, but leading to different pitch goals. The last triad-form, d, is reserved for use in the second eight-bar phrase, and triad a is brought back in bar 15 at the close of the period.

In traditional usage, the augmented chord is a linear harmony embellishing a consonant triad. For example, in the introduction to the first movement of Liszt's *Faust Symphony* the augmented triad C–E–A♭, though it occupies a considerable timespan, resolves ultimately to the C major tonic (with A♭ acting as chromatic upper auxiliary to G). Bartók's treatment of the augmented triad is actually quite similar, with one element serving as a dissonant auxiliary requiring resolution. On the minutely local level, for instance, the initial B♮–E♭–G augmented chord, arpeggiated in descending fashion, would appear to resolve on the downbeat of bar 2 to an implicit C minor chord. In sequential fashion, the lowest elements of the augmented chords in bars 2 and 3 (each on the third beat) act as leading-notes to the downbeat note following. In the second four-bar phrase, the same sequence of augmented chords culminates with a different pitch, F$\sharp$, with the downbeat of the third chord, E$\sharp$, now serving as leading-note. In the second phrase (bars 9–16), the first six bars duplicate those of the first phrase, transposed to T_5. In bars 15–16, however, the level of transposition (of the material of bars 7–8) is shifted to T_2, thus leading to A$\flat$.

Because the melody leapfrogs across registers and has no explicit harmonic support, it is difficult to reach an unequivocal analysis of this material. One may trace a succession of descending fifths in the first four bars, defined by the downbeat pitches G–C–F–B$\flat$. In subsequent phrases, however, this pattern is not necessarily maintained. Because adjacent augmented triads are most often types related by half-step, it is possible to trace chromatic linear progressions underlying the arpeggiations. Thus, for example, the interval G–B$\flat$ defined by the endpoints of the first four-bar phrase is unfolded as a conventional third-span through A$\flat$ and A$\natural$ in bars 2 and 3 respectively. The rhythmic disposition of the elements of this span is particularly interesting: G (on the first beat), A$\flat$ (second), A$\natural$ (third), B$\flat$ (downbeat). This sort of connection across registers is typical of the voice-leading in the Scherzo and contributes to its acerbic humour. The third-spans E–C$\sharp$ (descending) and E$\sharp$–G$\sharp$ (ascending) in bars 57–64 are especially clear instances of this practice.

In the first period, the bass register is reserved for pitches which end the four-bar phrases. The first and last such pitches, B$\flat$ and A$\flat$, are related by step in the same register. The A$\flat$ is approached by descending fifth from E$\flat$ (bar 12), which is itself related by fifth to the initial bass B$\flat$. The bass F$\sharp$ in bar 8 might well be considered the midpoint (equivalent to G$\flat$) in an arpeggiation from B$\flat$ to E$\flat$. A cogent voice-leading motion underlying the upper voices of the first period is difficult to discern. Since the original augmented chord recurs an octave lower in bar 15, attention is focused on the downbeat pitch G, which resolves in bar 16 to A$\flat$. The melodic high point, C, is attained as a result of transposition up five half-steps, and is thus related to the initial G by fifth (ascending fourth). The C is at the same time related by tritone – always a significant interval in Bartók's music – to the preceding F$\sharp$, which concludes the first eight-bar phrase.

The first period is balanced symmetrically by a second 16-bar group (bars 17–32) whose phrases proceed, in motion contrary to that of the first, from low register to high, beginning with $B\flat'$, the lowest pitch thus far. The second period is also based on the augmented triad, but here triad forms are arranged so that pairs of adjacent chords form complete whole-tone aggregates. For example, chords a and c in bars 17–18 form a whole-tone scale which is the complement of that formed in bars 19–20 by chords d and b. The pairs are so arranged that the endpoints of the two-bar grouping define the tritone. This becomes particularly evident in bars 25–32, when the pairing a + c is repeated in several registers. The

period begins in bars 17–18 with a literal retrograde of the pitch-classes of bars 14–15. (This relation is itself a feature of transition or reciprocity and perhaps explains why Bartók chose to shift transposition level at bar 15, setting chords c and a as adjacencies for the first time.)

Because the progression is purely sequential in the second period, it is perceived primarily as a transition from the main material of the first period to the contrasting section beginning in bar 33. The sequence connects the bass B$\natural$ (bar 17) with E$\flat$ in bar 25, most clearly through the passing C$\sharp$ in the bass in bar 21. The endpoints of the four-bar phrases actually serve to fill in the B$\natural$–E$\flat$ span chromatically (the high B$\sharp$ and C$\times$ in bars 20 and 24 acting as passing notes). Finally, one can trace a progression by ascending fifth linking B$\natural$ with E$\flat$, through the downbeat notes of alternate measures: F$\sharp$ (bar 19)–C$\sharp$ (bar 21)–G$\sharp$ (or A$\flat$, bar 23). These bass notes are distinguished because each coincides with a change to the complementary whole-tone scale. On the largest level, the bass E$\flat$ – which carries over into bar 33 to become the harmonic foundation at the beginning of the contrasting section – is related by fifth both to the initial bass B$\flat$ and to A$\flat$, the goal of the bass progression in the first period (bar 16). The bass B$\natural$ in bar 17 might well be interpreted as the midpoint (the equivalent of C$\flat$) in an arpeggiation from A$\flat$ to E$\flat$.

The second period climaxes with the first simultaneity of the piece (with the exception of the octave doublings in bars 28 and 30) – the strident G$\sharp$–A half-step, which is also the registral high point of the period. Repeated without accompaniment in bars 31–2, this minor second carries over into the contrasting *Tranquillo* section, where it becomes part of an ostinato figure in the right hand. As mentioned, E$\flat$ is the harmonic foundation for the beginning of the new material, although the bass register is abandoned for most of the section. The G$\sharp$ and A of the ostinato form respectively the perfect fourth (spelt as augmented third) and the tritone with E$\flat$ (comparable with the relations among G, F$\sharp$ and C in the opening bars of the piece). The high D of the upper semitone dyad introduced in the right hand in bar 35 is also related by tritone and perfect fourth with G$\sharp$ and A (in fact is inversionally symmetrical with E$\flat$ about the G$\sharp$–A semitone).

In bars 41–8, the first eight-bar phrase of the *Tranquillo* section is repeated transposed down five half-steps, effectively carrying the bass to B$\flat$. At this point the bass has returned to its point of origin, having descended by fifth from B$\flat$ to A$\flat$ (bar 16) and returned by ascending fifth through E$\flat$ (bars 25 and 33). In conjunction with the transposition the main semitone of the ostinato becomes D$\sharp$–E, while G$\sharp$–A occurs as the higher dyad (bars 43 and 45). In bars 49–56, an eight-bar period is appended as a transition returning to the main subject of the Scherzo. At this point the bass oscillates chromatically within the span from A$\sharp$ (equivalent to B$\flat$ in the preceding phrase) to C$\sharp$. The endpoints of the reiterated two-bar phrase in the bass are B$\natural$ and B$\sharp$, which might indicate a chromatic ascent from B$\flat$. In this transitional phrase, the melody ascends several times to A♯ before ascending by whole step to *e'''* which coincides with the resumption of Tempo I. This *e'''* is the highest pitch thus far, a goal of long-range motion from *c'''* (bar 9) through *d'''* (bar 37) – a motion summarized in the melody of bar 56. The *e'''* is coupled with *e''* in bars 41–9, through the symmetrical division of *a♯''* in the transitional phrase.

The *marcatissimo* passage in bars 57–72 is in itself transitional, leading to the bass note C which governs harmonic structure for the next hundred bars. The C in bars 75–6 links with the bass B♯ of bars 48–56. More locally, two ascending-fifth bass progressions are evident: from C♯ (bar 60) to G♯ (bar 68) and from F♮ (bar 69) to C♮ (bar 71). The latter fifth is filled in chromatically, with elements of this motion spread across a wide range. In fact, *e'''* of bar 57 leads to *e♯'''* – the highest pitch thus far – in bar 61 (recurring in the same register in bar 69 as *f'''*). Thus the C–E major third is prolonged throughout this passage. The bass notes C♯ (bar 60) and B♮ (bar 65) are chromatic auxiliaries to C, which occurs in the same low register in bar 73. The low-register B♮, which before the appearance of the low F has been the lowest pitch of the piece, links with its earlier appearance in bar 17. The motion from the bass C♯ (bar 60) to B♮ (bar 65) may also be seen to stand in reciprocal relation with the motion ascending from B♮ to E♭ in bars 17–25 – especially since in the interim no low bass note has intervened between E♭ and C♯ in bar 60. Within this section one important tension remains unresolved: F♮ has been set up conspicuously in both registral extremes and receives no effective resolution in either register.

The bass C is now sustained as a pedal note through bar 122. Against the bass in bars 73–81 the tritone-related G♭ is conspicuous as a grace note in the right-hand melody and as the point of initiation for whole-tone slides in the left hand. Beginning in bar 81, the left hand arpeggiates augmented trichords d and b, forming the complete whole-tone aggregate with the bass C. The melodic material of bars 73–80 derives from the chromatic bass progression of bars 49–56, emphasizing upper and lower chromatic auxiliaries to C – D♭, and C♮, the latter approached from B♭. In bars 81–96, the music is restricted to a central register corresponding almost exactly to the range of the opening phrase. The main melodic elements here belong to the underlying whole-tone scale, with non-whole-tone elements E♭ and F♮ occurring as grace notes. The elements of the E–G♯ third are prominent in the lower register of the melody, while those of D–F♯ are important in the upper. Beginning in bar 97, a climactic phrase is heard (thereafter repeated) whose contours are defined by these four pitches. The *f♯''* remains the highest pitch through bar 122, possibly linking with *f'''* in bar 69. In bars 108–17, the D–F♯ third is brought down an octave to function apparently in an auxiliary capacity to E. At this point Bartók uses A♮ in association with D and F♯, suggesting an opposing D major harmony. The greater significance of this pitch, however, is

that it completes the twelve-tone aggregate within the section that began in bar 73.

In bar 118, the right hand doubles the left-hand ostinato as a transition to a new section beginning in bar 122, which closely resembles the opening subject. Looking ahead to the *leggiero* episode beginning in bar 147 and especially to the *Meno mosso* section beginning in bar 163 – both of which are based harmonically on C – it seems reasonable to interpret the extreme chromaticism of the passage linking bar 122 and bar 147 as an expansion or elaboration of the region of C. Most noticeable with the return of the original subject is the bass progression from E♭ to B♭ (bars 126 and 130), perhaps a response to the opening bass progression from B♭ to E♭ (bars 4 and 12). A less obvious reciprocal relation is achieved in bars 123–5, where the augmented triads of bars 9–11 are presented in reverse order: d–c–b. (One result of the reversal is that the leading-note effect in moving from upbeat to downbeat is inverted, so that G♭ in bar 123, for instance, descends by half-step to the downbeat F♮ of the next bar.) The third four-bar phrase of the section climaxes with the F♯–C tritone, the inversion of the interval which was stressed in the preceding section (bars 97 and 103) and which defined the registral extremes of that section. The bass *F♯'* in bar 134 occurs in the same lowest register as the lowest note thus far – *F'* in bar 65. It is connected with *G'* (bar 131), which begins the phrase. The phrase involves a compound motion of an ascending fourth from G to C combined with a descending semitone from G to F♯. These three pitches are identical to those underlying the spans of the opening phrases (bars 1–9).

The phrase beginning in bar 135 is equivalent to its predecessor transposed up six half-steps, and is thus expected to climax on the C–F♯ tritone (the inversion of the interval in bar 134). The phrase breaks off unexpectedly, however, and F♯ occurs only as the point of departure for a slide (an allusion to bars 73–81) up to B♮ (bar 139). As the phrase proceeds from this pitch, the downbeat pitches define a succession of descending fifths, culminating with D, and *D'* is subsequently stated as the lowest pitch thus far (bars 143–5). On the basis of register, the bass notes G–F♯–F♮–D may be singled out in bars 131–45 as defining the motion of a descending fourth. The imitative gesture in bars 145–6 introduces D♭, clearly directed towards C, which returns in the bass in bar 147. The D♭ in effect continues the motion descending from G, and we recognize overall in bars 131–47 a fifth progression descending from G to C, with G serving in a conventional sense as dominant in a prolongation of C. The dominant is of course itself prolonged beginning in bar 131. Of particular interest is the voice-leading entailed in the sequential progression of bars 139–42, in which the intervals of the diminished seventh chord on B♮ are unfolded: B♮–D and F–A♭ (by fifth), and B♮–A♭ and F–D (chromatically). This chord is of course derived from V^6_5 of C. Note especially that A♭, the seventh, is expected to resolve downwards to G and – although it is left dangling in bar 142 – ultimately does so in the proper register, with the cadence to C in bar 147. Other elements of the dominant harmony, *b'''* and *D'*, have been stated respectively as the highest and lowest pitches thus far, and do not receive resolutions in the necessary registers at this cadence.

The episode in bars 147–62, based on the accompaniment figuration for the contrasting theme, leads to the restatement of that theme in the key of C. In the transition, the bass descends from tonic to dominant (in C), while the upper voice ascends through the C–F$\sharp$ tritone. The pitches involved in these two spans in fact comprise the characteristic harmony of bars 147–8: C–F$\sharp$–G. Thus the episode, which in a general sense prolongs C, constitutes more specifically the composing out of a harmony of motivic distinction. In the repetition of the contrasting theme, now slightly slower and more expressive than the original presentation, the first six bars contain a literal repetition transposed down three half-steps from the original E$\flat$ major. In bar 169, however, the course of the melody deviates from the original so as to remain in the key of C. In the following bars the bass effects a stepwise descent to the dominant, G, which supports an accented dissonant chord coinciding with the return to Tempo I (bar 179). In the meantime the upper voice has ascended in contrary motion to the bass, arriving at *d''''*, the fifth of this chord and the highest pitch of the piece. In view of the predominance of C major throughout the central portion of the composition, one would expect the chord on G to function as a dominant – in particular, one would expect the sixth and fourth in the chord to resolve as in a conventional cadential $^6_4$. Instead, Bartók allows the stepwise contrary motion of the outer voices to continue a step further to a major seventh chord on F$\natural$, which receives even more emphasis than the chord on G. The deception is enhanced by a violation of the square phrasing which until now has been rigorously upheld. For the chord on F becomes the starting point for a series of four-bar phrases based on the main subject, thereby rendering the preceding bar with the chord on G an odd unit which does not fit neatly into the regular scheme.

While the harmony on F might well function as subdominant of C, subsequent events – especially the failure ever to cadence in C in the remaining bars – indicate that this harmony may serve as a pivot away from C. The bass F links registrally with G$\flat$, which ends the first four-bar phrase. Both *G$\flat$'* and *E$\flat$'* of the next bar (bar 184) link with the lowest pitches thus far, *F'* and *D'* in bars 143–5. Thereafter, the low bass register is abandoned until the final *B$\flat$"*, the lowest pitch of the piece. In the four-bar phrase beginning with E$\flat$ in bar 184, one can trace a chromatic descent of a perfect fourth from E$\flat$ to B$\flat$, also the low and high points of the phrase, and the chromatic ascent from E$\flat$ to E$\natural$, the endpoints of the phrase. The phrase is punctuated at the end by the B$\flat$–E$\natural$ tritone, with B$\flat$ receiving special emphasis, marking its return as a focal point of pitch structure. This tritone is repeated in bar 189 and becomes the basis for the ostinato in bars 191–206. Significantly, the augmented triad which appears in bars 188 and 190 is

identical with the form presented in the first bar of the piece. Here, however, the pitch on the third beat is spelt C$\flat$ (as opposed to B$\natural$ in bar 1), and is treated accordingly as an upper auxiliary to the sforzando B$\flat$. The change in spelling is a significant indicator of a change of direction away from C$^{\cdot}$ and towards B$\flat$. For the remainder of the piece, much tension resides in the opposing tendencies of B$\natural$ and C$\flat$; in fact, the final two phrases of the Scherzo (bars 211–16 and 218–23) hinge on this duality.

As part of the coda (which may well begin with Tempo I in bars 179–80), a variation of the whole-tone theme from bars 97–108 is presented in bars 194–206, but in a much more tranquil mood. Whereas in the earlier version both melody and harmony belonged to the same whole-tone aggregate, in the latter the harmony is based on the diminished seventh chord and is thus in conflict with the whole-tone tune. (Note, however, that the bass notes of the passage, D$\flat$ and G, are members of the whole-tone melodic collection.) This conflict reflects a continued ambiguity in the pitch orientation of the voice-leading. The A–E$\flat$ tritone outlined by the melody connotes a tendency towards B$\flat$, while the bass G, especially in conjunction with the melodic motion about C in bars 205–6, suggests that the tonality of C might still be in force. In fact, the bass G in bars 203–6 is connected registrally with G supporting the dominant chord in bar 179, and it is possible to interpret the progression linking the two Gs as a complex prolongation of the dominant of C. The bass notes F and E$\flat$ (bars 180 and 184) are passing notes connecting G with the next important bass note, D$\flat$ (bars 195–202) – thus unfolding the tritone prolonging the dominant. The validity of this analysis is confirmed by the reciprocal bass motion returning from D$\flat$ directly to G in bar 203.

The ambiguity between the tonal regions of B$\flat$ and C is not resolved in bar 207 with the return of Tempo I. Here the original form (a) of the augmented triad is brought back, but with E$\flat$ as the downbeat note, a continuation of the preceding melodic motion and a reference as well to the preceding whole-tone melody in which E$\flat$ was prominent. In bar 209 this augmented chord is juxtaposed against the diminished seventh chord which was the harmonic underpinning of the preceding bars. The only pitch held in common between the two chords is G – previously significant mainly as the dominant of C. In bar 211 G is taken into the highest register, initiating a precipitous descent in which forms a and b of the augmented triad are alternated. In this passage, reference to C is still strong, the downbeat pitches repeating the cadential motion G–C through several octaves. Nonetheless, in the final phrase focus is shifted abruptly to B$\flat$, presented as the lowest pitch of the piece, with A$\natural$ and C$\flat$ serving as chromatic auxiliaries. The registral connection between the *g'''* (bar 211) and *a'''* (bar 218) may indicate that in the context of the Scherzo *g'''* ultimately serves as a passing note to *a'''*, the leading-note of B$\flat$. Because *a'''* receives no resolution in the highest register, some tension necessarily remains at the close. Significantly, the tension between A♮ and B♭ is central to the voice-leading of the other movements of the *Suite* as well. In the first movement (Allegretto, in B♭) the expectation for $b♭'''$ as the completion of the scalar ascent in the coda was similarly denied. Likewise in the final movement (also in B♭) the final phrases arch only as high as $b♭♭'''$. In the third movement (Allegro molto, in D minor) $b♭'''$ resolves to a''' in the climactic passage of that movement.

Clearly the most important and difficult question posed by Bartók's Scherzo concerns the relation between the predominant key areas of B♭ and C and their respective roles with regard to the coherence of the work (if indeed it is unified). While B♭ is the focal pitch at the beginning and might arguably be prolonged through the first 45 bars, thereafter C governs harmonic structure, at the very least from bar 71 through bar 179 but possibly for the remainder of the piece, with the exception of the final phrase in B♭. After bar 180, B♭ might be heard as more important than C, but it is not clearly the object of prolongation, and the final phrase confirming B♭ comes as something of a surprise. The portions of the piece in which B♭ prevails are not based on a large-scale cadence through its conventional dominant. The only strong F major chord in the work, the climactic chord in bar 180, might be construed as a structural dominant, but its realization as such by a subsequent strong connection to B♭ is not in evidence. In fact, the bass F appears to be superseded by G, the dominant of C, in the same register in bar 203. By contrast, the region of C is conventionally prolonged by means of several large-scale cadences, in which the structural dominant on G is clearly projected. The most extensive prolongation of C spans bars 71 through 147, in which the dominant itself is arpeggiated in bars 131–46. A more straightforward projection of C is accomplished in bars 147–63 through the unfolding in the bass of the descending fourth from tonic to dominant. The bass progression in bars 163–79 constitutes an expansion of the same bass motion. In this instance, of course, the dominant is not followed by tonic. After bar 179, as mentioned, the dominant may in fact be prolonged until the final phrase, although G occurs here only in association with diminished and augmented harmonies.

In view of the extensive and quite conventional prolongations of C major, it would seem that the reappearance of B♭ at the end of the piece does not constitute a tonicization of that pitch, but rather an allusion to its structural importance elsewhere. For that matter, even at the beginning, the role of B♭ as a focal element is illusory: it appears momentarily in the bass as the goal of the first phrase and reappears in bar 41 in the structural bass only as the result of the sequential repetition of a passage heard originally in E♭. Actually, B♭ in the Scherzo is no more than a vestige of the first movement of the *Suite*, in which that pitch functions unequivocally as tonic; as such, B♭ occurs in the second movement essentially as an element of transition. The Scherzo, then, is based in the tonality of C major, with the extraordinary innovation that the exposition of its subject matter takes place in conjunction with the unstable harmonic progressions of a transition. The

failure to close with the tonic, as in the song by Ives, weakens but does not destroy the sense of tonal coherence. Indeed, the references to B♭ that frame the movement help in their own way to create the impression of closure.

The relation of the regions of B♭ and C becomes clear only with an overview of the harmonic scheme of the *Suite* as a whole. As mentioned, the first movement is firmly in B♭ major and the third is equally unproblematic in its projection of D minor. Like the second movement, the fourth and last movement involves conflicting harmonic regions, beginning with D minor and ending with B♭ major – thus presenting in microcosm and in retrograde the harmonic progression spanning the first three movements. Given the signification in the fourth movement of B♭ and D as endpoints of progression, the role of C in the second movement is clarified: it is essentially a passing note connecting B♭ and D, the respective focal elements of the first and third movements. The transitory nature of C is heightened in the second movement by virtue of the lack of closure in its presentation.

4   SUMMARY

The symmetrical balance provided by the harmonic progression of the final movement of Bartók's *Suite* is evidence of his intense concern for structural unity, a concern shared by many of the composers who were attempting to develop new styles and methods at the beginning of the twentieth century. Many found it necessary to avoid the very components by means of which unity had been secured in traditional tonality, for fear that conventional elements – such as a strongly articulated structural dominant – would appear artificial and extraneous and thus disrupt the musical flow. To the extent that they dispensed with conventional relations, however, those striving for coherence were obliged to invent and compose out other relations – often peculiar to individual compositions – thereby obtaining a type of motivic unity. In the first decades of the twentieth century, few composers actually succeeded in (or even aspired towards) abandoning tonality altogether. For the majority of compositions from this era, structure depends on a balance between conventional tonal procedures and non-tonal motivic relations. In approaching this music, therefore, the analyst must first determine the extent to which the laws of conventional tonality are in force – not an easy task given the highly developed state of the art of implicit tonality at the turn of the century. Only then is it possible to evaluate the contribution of special contextual procedures to overall structural coherence.

The four pieces discussed in this chapter were chosen with the aim of providing a broad sample of post-tonal styles. The only other criterion involved in the selection was that each piece should entail problems of conflicting key areas. It is therefore altogether striking that these works, representing four distinct musical traditions, have in common a number of special techniques of voice-leading:

1) All four evince a highly refined use of register, with the function of harmonic definition assumed by the low bass. Registral placement reinforces many non-consecutive pitch relations, especially the most significant long-range connections. The use of register in these works certainly has its origin in tonal voice-leading.

2) These works exhibit symmetry and reciprocal relations at many levels of structure. Although these attributes may be found in the motivic structure of certain tonal music, the intensive and concentrated development of symmetrical relations in these post-tonal works would seem to indicate a much greater dependency on such features for overall structural coherence.

3) All four employ synthetic components – either the augmented triad or the whole-tone scale, or both – apparently chosen for their symmetrical properties and often treated exhaustively so as to complete the chromatic aggregate. These works exhibit a conscious formalism which goes well beyond traditional practice, although some tonal precedents may be found – for instance, the chromatic sequencing of diminished seventh chords in the music of Bach or Liszt.

4) By means of the incomplete span, explicit statements of important harmonies – particularly the tonic – are avoided in these pieces.

It is equally noteworthy that in each of the four compositions a single tonic prevails which is the focus for tonal relations overall. Moreover, in each piece the fundamental tonic is prolonged by means of a conventional cadence from a fundamental dominant. The presentations of these most basic harmonies may be obscure, but in every case their presence and influence may be inferred unequivocally. While these four works do not constitute an adequate basis for drawing general conclusions, they amply demonstrate the adaptability of the traditional tonal system to a variety of twentieth-century styles. The innate strength of tonal relations is such that they may undergo extreme modification and obfuscation without losing completely their cohesive force. It is possible that conventional tonality in the strictest sense underlies a far greater amount of twentieth-century music than we have realized.

NOTES

1 For an account of the controversy, see James M. Baker, 'Schenkerian Analysis and Post-Tonal Music', in *Aspects of Schenkerian Theory*, ed. David W. Beach (New Haven, CT, and London: Yale University Press, 1983), pp. 153–86.

2 The most thorough introduction to techniques of Schenkerian analysis is provided in Allen Forte and Steven E. Gilbert, *Introduction to Schenkerian Analysis* (New York: Norton, 1982).

BIBLIOGRAPHY

Although no comprehensive study of voice-leading in post-tonal music has been produced to date, the literature touching upon the subject is vast. The following listing is offered as a representative sample of this work.

Books

Antokoletz, Elliott, *The Music of Béla Bartók: A Study of Tonality and Progression in Twentieth-Century Music* (Berkeley and Los Angeles: University of California Press, 1984).

Baker, James M., *The Music of Alexander Scriabin* (New Haven, CT, and London: Yale University Press, 1986).

Berry, Wallace, *Structural Functions in Music* (Englewood Cliffs, NJ: Prentice-Hall, 1976).

Forte, Allen, *Contemporary Tone Structures* (New York: Teachers College, Columbia University, 1955).

Hindemith, Paul, *Unterweisung im Tonsatz III: Übungsbuch für den dreistimmigen Satz* (Mainz: B. Schotts Söhne, 1970).

Katz, Adele T., *Challenge to Musical Tradition: A New Concept of Tonality* (1945; repr. New York: Da Capo, 1972).

Lewis, Christopher Orlo, *Tonal Coherence in Mahler's Ninth Symphony*, Studies in Musicology, 79 (Ann Arbor, MI: UMI Research Press, 1984).

Perle, George, *Serial Composition and Atonality* (5th rev. edn, Berkeley and Los Angeles: University of California Press, 1981).

Reti, Rudolf, *Tonality, Atonality, Pantonality: A Study of Some Trends in Twentieth-Century Music* (rev. edn, London: Barrie and Rockliff, 1960).

Salzer, Felix, *Structural Hearing: Tonal Coherence in Music*, 2 vols. (rev. edn, New York: Dover, 1962).

Samson, Jim, *Music in Transition; A Study of Tonal Expansion and Atonality, 1900–1920* (New York: Norton, 1977).

Schoenberg, Arnold, *Theory of Harmony*, trans. Roy E. Carter (Berkeley and Los Angeles: University of California Press, 1978).

Searle, Humphrey, *Twentieth-Century Counterpoint* (London: Benn, 1954).

Stein, Deborah J., *Hugo Wolf's Lieder and Extensions of Tonality*, Studies in Musicology, 82 (Ann Arbor, MI: UMI Research Press, 1985).

van den Toorn, Pieter C., *The Music of Igor Stravinsky* (New Haven, CT, and London: Yale University Press, 1983).

hittall, Arnold, *The Music of Britten and Tippett: Studies in Themes and Techniques* (Cambridge: Cambridge University Press, 1982).

Articles

Babbitt, Milton, 'The String Quartets of Bartók', *Musical Quarterly*, 35 (1949), pp. 377–85.

Baker, James M., 'Schenkerian Analysis and Post-Tonal Music', in *Aspects of Schenkerian Theory*, ed. David W. Beach (New Haven, CT, and London: Yale University Press, 1983), pp. 153–86.

Barkin, Elaine, Benjamin, William E., and Gauldin, Robert, 'Analysis Symposium: Debussy, Etude "Pour les Sixtes" ', *Journal of Music Theory*, 22 (1978), pp. 241–312.

Barkin, Elaine, Forte, Allen, and Travis, Roy, 'Analysis Symposium: Webern, Orchestra Pieces (1913): Movement I ("Bewegt")', *Journal of Music Theory*, 18 (1974), pp. 2–43; 19 (1975), pp. 48–64.

Benjamin, William E., 'Ideas of Order in Motivic Music', *Music Theory Spectrum*, 1 (1979), pp. 23–34.

Bernard, Jonathan W., 'Pitch/Register in the Music of Edgard Varèse', *Music Theory Spectrum*, 3 (1981), pp. 1–25.

Burkhart, Charles, 'Schoenberg's *Farben*', *Perspectives of New Music*, 12 (1973–4), pp. 141–72.

Chrisman, Richard, 'Anton Webern's Six Bagatelles for String Quartet Op. 9: The Unfolding of Intervallic Successions', *Journal of Music Theory*, 23 (1979), pp. 81–122.

Cone, Edward T., 'Stravinsky: The Progress of a Method', in *Perspectives on Schoenberg and Stravinsky*, ed. Benjamin Boretz and Edward T. Cone (Princeton, NJ: Princeton University Press, 1968), pp. 156–64.

DeLone, Peter, 'Claude Debussy, Contrapuntiste malgré lui', *College Music Symposium*, 17, 2 (1977), pp. 48–63.

Fennelly, Brian, 'Structure and Process in Webern's Op. 22', *Journal of Music Theory*, 10 (1966), pp. 300–29.

Forte, Allen, 'Schoenberg's Creative Evolution: The Path to Atonality', *Musical Quarterly*, 64 (1978), pp. 133–76.

Gow, David, 'Tonality and Structure in Bartók's First Two String Quartets', *Music Review*, 34 (1973), pp. 259–71.

Hasty, Christopher, 'Segmentation and Process in Post-Tonal Music', *Music Theory Spectrum*, 3 (1981), pp. 54–73.

Hicken, Kenneth, 'Schoenberg's "Atonality" – Fused Bitonality?', *Tempo*, 109 (1974), pp. 27–36.

Hush, David, 'Modes of Continuity in Schoenberg's *Begleitungsmusik Op. 34*', *Journal of the Arnold Schoenberg Institute*, 8 (1984), supplement.

Jarman, Douglas, 'Doctor Schön's Five-Strophe Aria: Some Notes on Tonality and Pitch Association in Berg's *Lulu*', *Perspectives of New Music*, 8 (1970), pp. 23–48.

Keller, Hans, 'Schoenberg's Return to Tonality', *Journal of the Arnold Schoenberg Institute*, 5 (1981), pp. 2–21.

Lester, Joel, 'Pitch Structure Articulation in the Variations of Schoenberg's *Serenade*', *Perspectives of New Music*, 6, 2 (1968), pp. 22–34.

Lewis, Christopher, 'Tonal Focus in Atonal Music: Berg's Op. 5/3', *Music Theory Spectrum*, 3 (1981), pp. 84–97.

McNamee, Ann K., 'Bitonality, Mode, and Interval in the Music of Karol Szymanowski', *Journal of Music Theory*, 29 (1985), pp. 61–84.

Mark, Christopher, 'Contextually Transformed Tonality in Britten', *Music Analysis*, 4 (1985), pp. 265–87.

Morgan, Robert P., 'Dissonant Prolongations: Theoretical and Compositional Precedents', *Journal of Music Theory*, 20 (1976), pp. 49–91.

Ogdon, Will, 'How Tonality Functions in Schoenberg's Opus 11, No. 1', *Journal of the Arnold Schoenberg Institute*, 5 (1981), pp. 169–81.

Parks, Richard S., 'Harmonic Resources in Bartók's "Fourths" ', *Journal of Music Theory*, 25 (1981), pp. 245–74.

——, 'Tonal Analogues as Atonal Resources and Their Relation to Form in Debussy's Chromatic Etude', *Journal of Music Theory*, 29 (1985), pp. 33–60.

Phipps, Graham H., 'Tonality in Webern's Cantata I', *Music Analysis*, 3 (1984), pp. 125–58.

Rothstein, William, 'Linear Structure in the Twelve-Tone System: An Analysis of Donald Martino's *Pianississimo* (first movement)', *Journal of Music Theory*, 24 (1980), pp. 129–66.

Samson, Jim, 'Schoenberg's "Atonal" Music', *Tempo*, 109 (1974), pp. 16–25.

Schoenberg, Arnold, 'Analysis of the Four Orchestral Songs Opus 22', trans. Claudio Spies, in *Perspectives on Schoenberg and Stravinsky*, ed. Benjamin Boretz and Edward T. Cone (Princeton, NJ: Princeton University Press, 1968), pp. 25–45.

Straus, Joseph, 'A Principle of Voice Leading in the Music of Stravinsky', *Music Theory Spectrum*, 4 (1982), pp. 106–24.

——, 'Stravinsky's Tonal Axis', *Journal of Music Theory*, 26 (1982), pp. 261–90.

Swift, Richard, 'A Tonal Analog: The Tone-Centered Music of George Perle', *Perspectives of New Music*, 21 (1982–3), pp. 257–84.

Travis, Roy, 'Tonal Coherence in the First Movement of Bartók's Fourth String Quartet', *Music Forum*, 2 (1970), pp. 298–371.

——, 'Toward a New Concept of Tonality', *Journal of Music Theory*, 3 (1959), pp. 257–84.

Waldbauer, Ivan, 'Interplay of Tonality and Nontonal Constructs in Three Pieces from the *Mikrokosmos* of Bartók', in *Music and Context: Essays for John M. Ward*, ed. Anne Dhu Shapiro (Cambridge, MA: Harvard University Press, 1985), pp. 418–40.

Whittall, Arnold, 'Tonality and the Whole-Tone Scale in the Music of Debussy', *Music Review*, 36 (1975), pp. 261–71.

Wilson, Paul, 'Concepts of Prolongation and Bartók's Opus 20', *Music Theory Spectrum*, 6 (1984), pp. 79–89.

Zur, Menachem, 'Tonal Ambiguities as a Constructive Force in the Language of Stravinsky', *Musical Quarterly*, 68 (1982), pp. 516–26.

3

Pitch Notations and Tonality: Bartók

MALCOLM GILLIES

I   ORIENTATION

Composers may, as it were, analyse their own music not only in a verbal (or diagrammatic) medium, but also through the notation of a score. The method outlined in this chapter draws its principles from both forms of self-analysis, as found in the output of the Hungarian composer Béla Bartók. In general, the twentieth century has witnessed a growth in the first category of these self-analyses and a dwindling concern for the second. In the early years of the century many composers started to shed the widespread inhibitions of previous eras concerning the sharing of information about compositional practices with the public. For the Schoenberg–Stravinsky–Bartók generation this more open attitude can best be seen in the increasing number of programme notes, score introductions, interviews and short articles by composers (see Somfai, 1978). Most of these self-analyses were addressed to the wider musical public, or even the general public, and were accordingly couched in layman's language. As a result, they rarely afford insight into technical details of the music. Occasionally, however, more revealing commentaries were issued, for the most part addressed to fellow professionals. Of greatest use in this study will be one of Bartók's analyses, that of his Fifth String Quartet (Suchoff, ed., 1976: pp. 414–5), which was undertaken in 1935 to help the critic Alexander Jemnitz construct his own analysis of the work.

But what of the second form of self-analysis, in the score itself? Composers can certainly indicate points of lesser or greater articulation by the deliberate placement of such features as rehearsal cues, thickened or double bar-lines, section timings, slurs and punctuation signs (commas, vertical lines, and so on). They are also able, however, by preferring one pitch spelling over another – G$\sharp$ rather than A$\flat$ – to distinguish the functions of notes within their melodic, harmonic, contrapuntal and, ultimately, tonal contexts. George Perle (1984: p. 101) has neatly summarized this self-analytic potential of a score:

... even though they did not give us analytical surveys of their compositions, the composers of an earlier age were constantly making explicit and detailed analytical assertions, in the very act of writing the notes down. When Beethoven, in the slow movement of the Fifth Symphony, spells ... [a pitch collection] as A$\flat$, C E$\flat$, F$\sharp$ in bar 29 [see example 3.1a] and as A$\flat$, C E$\flat$, G$\flat$ in bar 206 [see example 3.1b], he is engaged in an act of analysis, as well as an act of composition.

Example 3.1a Beethoven: Fifth Symphony, slow movemen bars 28–31

Example 3.1b Beethoven: Fifth Symphony, slow movemer bars 205–9

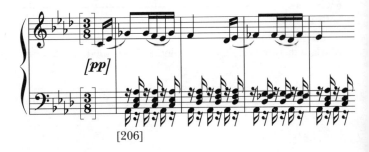

Pitch spellings in music of Beethoven's time reflect, with a fair degree of regularity, harmonic function. In turn, these harmonic spellings reflect tonal function. The presence of G♭ (rather than F♯ or E×) in bar 206 is crucial to an understanding of the pitch collection as a seventh chord. Comparison of the spellings of bar 206 with those of the surrounding bars (example 3.1b): D♭–F–A♭ rather than C♯–E♯–G♯ in bar 207, for instance) suggests that this seventh chord functions as a secondary dominant of the subdominant within the key of A♭ major. An alternative spelling, A♭–C–E♭–F♯, would have reflected a German augmented sixth role entirely out of keeping here, but completely in keeping with the emerging C major environment of bar 29, shown in example 3.1a. So, too, in bar 208, the spelling G–[B♭]–D♭–F♭ (over an A♭ pedal) reflects a function as the diminished seventh chord of A♭ major. An alternative spelling, such as G–[B♭]–D♭–E, would have signified quite a different function, of a secondary diminished seventh, to a submediant chord which is not present here. With the growing chromaticization of music through the nineteenth century the established conventions governing the use of pitch spellings were, of course, increasingly subject to challenge.

Faced with the growing freedom of use of all twelve chromatic notes in twentieth-century music, and the widespread abandonment of triadic harmony, many analysts have assumed the dissolution of those notational conventions of earlier times. They have therefore concluded that distinctions of pitch spelling have little or no significance in twentieth-century music. Indeed, the survival into the twentieth century of five different accidentals (×, ♯, ♮, ♭, ♭♭) and three different spellings for most pitches (E×, F♯, G♭) has been seen by some as a misleading encumbrance which can easily foster false notions because of the suggestions of traditional function inherent in the signs themselves. In the early years of the century Busoni (1910), Bartók (1920), Schoenberg (1924) and Cowell (1927) – to name but a few – called for or proposed new systems of pitch representation. Their cries of dissatisfaction with traditional notational methods were merely in the vanguard of a concerted movement amongst musicians to stress the *aural* nature of music, apparently to redress what was perceived as an excessive concentration on *pictorial* facets of music in earlier times. Alexander L. Ringer (1980: p. 123) has, for instance, written of 'the extent to which musical notation, with all its blessings, has narrowed Western man's understanding of a cultural phenomenon that is always aural in essence and rarely if ever graphic'.

Despite this widespread dissatisfaction with existing methods of visual representation, most composers did continue to employ traditional pitch spellings. Some chose to use the different chromatic inflections randomly in an attempt to cancel out any conventional implications. Others allowed their use of accidentals to be guided by readability alone, preferring, according to the dictates of the moment, a vertical or a horizontal homogeneity in their spellings. A few, notably

Scriabin and Bartók, sought to develop new rules, to allow for consistent representation of their music within the limits of traditional pitch spellings. The prevalence of double sharps and double flats in the music of these composers in itself evidences some special notational purpose. Both experimented with ways of representing more 'progressive' pitch associations such as whole-tone and octatonic structures (see Perle, 1984; Gillies, 1983). As Perle has pointed out (pp. 107–9), in bars 1–4 of his Prelude, op. 74 no. 5 (1914), Scriabin adopted a 'diatonic' principle of successive letter-names (C, D, E etc.) for successive degrees in representing a whole-tone scale: C♭, D♭, E♭, F G A B C♯ D♯ E♯ F×. The octatonic (alternating tone and semitone) basis of bars 13–17 of this piece is notated according to the same principle: A♯ B♯ C♯ D♯ E F♯ G A B♭ C D♭ E♭ F♭ G♭. Scriabin died in the following year, and his experimental notation was not developed into a comprehensive system of pitch representation.

At about the same time as Scriabin, Bartók was confronting similar issues of pitch notation. He managed over many years to develop a sophisticated notational apparatus capable of representing the wide variety of pitch organizations he wished to use in his music. The evolution of this system was not smooth, however. Bartók moved from a Brahmsian chordal practice in his earliest pieces through a more linear phase, influenced by the works of Wagner and Richard Strauss, to a period of greater individuality in which folk-derived pitch structures came to permeate both vertical and horizontal aspects of his music (see Suchoff, ed., 1976: p. 336). In the years 1918 to 1922 Bartók underwent an 'atonal' crisis, during which time he made his much-quoted call for a new system of pitch representation and mentioned the difficulty he experienced in reconciling horizontal and vertical demands in pitch representation (1920: p. 459). Subsequently he moved back to a more decidedly tonal idiom, with a growing emphasis on linear constructions. By 1931 Bartók had established the basic rules for the representation of this style of decidedly horizontal orientation, although he did continue to make minor modifications in his use of pitch spellings until his death in 1945. Many of these modifications were the result of his sustained activity in transcribing folk music during his final decade.

Thus in the pitch notations of his later compositions Bartók left systematic proof of his tonal thinking at the note-by-note level of musical function. His few, more detailed verbal analyses from this period afford the only access to his thinking about broad tonal areas spanning whole sections or even movements of compositions. The hierarchic method proposed below has been based on these two self-analytic foundations. It has been summarized *in toto* in the format of a technical manual since the variety of Bartók's notational usage is not readily encompassed within a few key principles. Following this and a model analysis, suggestions for further study are offered, with a bibliography, to enable the student to consider the applicability of the ideas presented here to a wider repertory.

There is no doubt that Bartók was an especially systematic

Figure 3.1

D	Eb	E	F	F#	G	G#	A	A#	B	C	C#	D	(9:3)
D	Eb	E	F	Gb	G	Ab	A	Bb	B	C	C#	D	(3:9)
B	C	C#	D	D#	E	E#	F#	F×	G#	G×	A#	B	(11:1)
B	C	Db	D	Eb	E	F	F#	G	G#	A	A#	B	(1:11)

composer, and the reader will not need constantly to be reminded that the notational practices studied here, together with the analytical insights they offer, are idiosyncratic. Yet these practices, once discovered, are relatively easily understood and interpreted. They are well worth the study, not only because of Bartók's unquestioned standing as a composer, but also to cultivate the reader's taste for enquiry into the relationship between compositional and analytical processes. This is a taste which can be pursued in many areas of early twentieth-century music, and Bartók's notation is an excellent starting point for such enquiry.

2 METHOD

From 1924 until his death Bartók stated repeatedly that his music was *always* tonal. This is a cardinal assumption of the method presented here. It interprets the composer's pitch notations as a literal expression of that tonality. Pitch notations are used as the fundamental criteria for allocating notes to particular tonal structures (demarcated in the music by the limits of consistency in pitch spellings) and for determining which one or more of the notes of a structure acts as a tonal centre. Sections i–xiii document the various individual tonal structures found in Bartók's later music and their possible notational representations. As the examples show, the application of a particular structure may vary from a few beats in only one of several parts to entire small pieces. In addition, contamination and compromise in Bartók's usage need to be explained (section xiv). As will be clear from sections i–xiii, pitch notations are frequently insufficient for the complete definition of a tonal structure, and so resort must be made to other means of tonal determination (section xv). Finally, the method outlines Bartók's practice in changing from structure to structure (section xvi) and his principles in determining broader aspects of tonal hierarchy (section xvii).

i–xi   Octave tonal structures

i   'Odd numbered' chromatic structures
A majority of Bartók's octave tonal structures are characterized by the presence of two notes of special tonal significance (which we shall call tonal centres) separated by an odd number of semitones. Chromatic structures such as those in example 3.2 – Bartók's own example of bimodality (Suchoff, ed., 1976: p. 367) – are the most frequent of these 'odd numbered'

structures in Bartók's later music, dividing the twelve semitones of the octave in the ratio of 7:5: C Db D Eb E F F# G Ab A Bb B C. Sometimes these structures arise from the chromatic infilling of an originally diatonic structure, but they more commonly result from the union of different modes (which can involve either strict bimodality or the freer mixture of modal elements in modal chromaticism) or from the independent, structural semitonal degrees of Bartók's 'new' chromaticism (see Suchoff, ed., 1976: pp. 366–81). Example 3.2

Example 3.2 Bartók: his own example of bimodality (1943

illustrates that when the notes of the Phrygian and Lydian lines are combined in one scale five letter-names are used twice, and two only once. These two letter-names are chromatically 'encircled' by their semitonal neighbours: B–C–Db, F#–G–Ab. The notation therefore singles out these two tonal centres. The question of the relative significance of the two centres can be determined only on other criteria, such as range, part movement or extremity notes (which are listed in section xv below). In Bartók's example, C is clearly of primary significance, while G acts like a dominant. A 'plagal' version of the chromatic structure is occasionally found, where C is the primary and F the secondary centre: C Db D Eb E F Gb G Ab A Bb B C (5:7). And the relationship of fifths and fourths between the two most important notes in a structure is occasionally abandoned, resulting in structures such as Figure 3.1 above.

ii   'Even numbered' chromatic structures
On those relatively rare occasions when Bartók wished to represent structures with the tonal centres separated by an even number of semitones, the notational principles applying to 'odd numbered' structures could not be implemented fully. As shown in example 3.3 (first movement of the Sonata for Solo Violin, bars 105–7), the encirclement of the two tonal centres C# and G necessitates the encirclement of one other note, E, which nevertheless lacks centric status: C# D D# E

Figure 3.2

B♭	C♭	C	D♭	D	E♭	E	F	G♭	A♭♭	A♭	A	B♭	(8:4)
B♭	C♭	C	C♯	D	E♭	E	F	F♯	G	A♭	A	B♭	(4:8)
F	G♭	G	A♭	A	B♭	B	C	C♯	C×	D♯	E	F	(10:2)
F♯	G	A♭	B♭♭	B♭	C♭	C	D♭	D	E♭	E	E♯	F♯	(2:10)

Figure 3.3

C	D	E	F♯	G	A	B	C	(ascending, Lydian)

C	D♭	E♭	F	G♭	A♭	B♭	C	(descending, Locrian)

C D♭ D E♭ E F F♯↘ G A♭ A B♭ B C (total 5:2:5 structure)
         ↖ G♭

Figure 3.4

E♯↘
C♯ D D♯ E   F♯ G G♯ A A♯ B B♯ C♯ (3:2:7)
         ↖ F

F♯↘
C♯ D D♯ E F G A♭ A B♭ B B♯ C♯ (4:2:6)
         ↖ G♭

Example 3.3 Bartók: Sonata for Solo Violin, bars 105–7

F F♯ G A♭ A A♯ B B♯ C♯ (6:6). As a consequence one further letter-name must be presented in three forms (A♭, A and A♯). Depending on where the single and triple representations occur in the structure several different spellings are possible (compare, for example, C♯ D D♯ E E♯ F♯ G A♭ A B♭ B B♯ C♯). The ranking of centres in 6:6 structures is frequently problematic because of the symmetrical qualities of the structure. Example 3.3 could be considered to involve a change in primary status from C♯ to G over the course of the example. Other 'even numbered' structures are based on the same notational principle (see figure 3.2).

iii Directional chromatic structures

In Bartók's bimodal or modal chromatic writing the pitch spellings of the original modes are generally preserved. While in example 3.2 this creates no conflict, as the scales coincide only at the tonal centres, that is not true of the following cases, where both G♭ and F♯ spellings are presented (see figure 3.3):

This phenomenon originates in the different directions of semitonal leading motions in the two modes, F♯–G in the Lydian, G♭–F in the Locrian, indicating competing secondary centres in the combined structure. Despite these origins, the note-by-note movement of the music need not immediately reflect such directionality. Other 'odd' and 'even numbered' directional structures, such as the following, occur rarely and are not susceptible to simple modal explanation (see figure 3.4):

iv Defective chromatic structures

Frequently Bartók does not present all twelve chromatic notes, thereby creating defective chromatic structures. In example 3.4, written by Bartók in 1943 (see Gillies, 1989: p. 290), probably to demonstrate his modal chromaticism, the lack of D♭ results in only partial encirclement of the primary tonal centre, C: C ( ) D E♭ E F F♯ G A♭ A B♭ B C (11-note). Example 3.4 can be interpreted as an intermingling of C-based Lydian and Aeolian forms, as neither includes the note D♭ (see Oramo, 1980: p. 453). In terms of Bartók's 'new chromaticism' such a structure is simply chromatic, but defective by one degree. A number of increasingly defective chromatic 7:5 structures are shown in figure 3.5.

v Octatonic structures

Bartók sought to represent the independence of the eight scalar degrees (in a pattern of alternating tones and semitones) by employing successive letter-names for successive degrees. This application of diatonic spelling principles results in a rapid flattening of notation in an ascending direction, and a sharpening in a descending one. Because of the uniformity of the letter-name succession, tonal centres often cannot be notationally distinguished from other degrees. In the following

Figure 3.5

C	()	D	E♭	E	F	F♯	G	()	A	B♭	B	C	(10-note)
C	D♭	D	E♭	()	F	()	G	A♭	A	B♭	()	C	(9-note)
C	()	D	()	E	F	F♯	G	()	A	()	B	C	(8-note)
C	D♭	()	()	E	()	()	G	A♭	A	()	B	C	(7-note)
C	D♭	()	()	E	()	()	G	A♭	()	()	B	C	(6-note)

case, however, a centric role can be assigned to F♯ because the regular succession of letter-names can be maintained only from that starting point: F♯ G♯ A B C D E♭ F [F♯]. This example is discussed more extensively in sections 7 and 8 of the model analysis. Notational compromises are sometimes effected, especially to avoid use of double accidentals (see section xiv.a). Defective octatonic structures are found, in which the missing degree corresponds to a missing letter-name.

Example 3.4 Bartók: his own example, probably of modal chromaticism (1943)

vi   Seven-note (diatonic) structures

Because of the diatonic origins of the staff system – with a note on each line or space between the representation of the initial note and its octave – distinctions of pitch spelling are of little help in determining the tonal functions of notes. The variants of letter-names, semitonal encircling motions or flattening/sharpening successions of letter-names which aid the identification of centres in many other structures are seldom relevant to these structures. General factors of tonal determination, such as commencing and concluding pitches or range limits, are frequently decisive in determining the exact nature of a tonal structure, for instance in distinguishing a D-based Dorian mode from an E-based Phrygian structure. Notation may sometimes be relevant in narrowing options, however. A D♯ spelling, in itself, defies any explanation in a G-based traditional mode. An E♭, on the other hand, features in G-based Aeolian, Phrygian and Locrian modes.

vii   Defective seven-note (diatonic) structures

Sometimes one or two degrees of a seven-note structure are omitted, and accordingly there is no representation of the corresponding letter-name (see figure 3.6):

Figure 3.6

D	E	F♯	()	A	B	C♯	D	(6-note major or Lydian)
C	D♭	()	()	G	A♭	B♭	C	(5-note Phrygian)

There is evidence that Bartók considered some pentatonic structures (see section ix) as defective seven-note structures (Suchoff, ed., 1976: p. 363). Defective seven-note octave structures of fewer than five degrees are seldom encountered.

viii   Whole-tone structures

As with octatonic structures, Bartók sought to express the independence of successive scalar degrees by employing successive letter-names. This now results in a sharpening of the notation in an ascending direction, and flattening in a descending direction: C D E F♯ G♯ A♯ B♯(=C). Often, therefore, readability takes precedence over theoretical aspects of representation, particularly when double sharps or flats are involved (as discussed in section xiv.a) or an alternative spelling of a tonal centre would result (B♯, rather than C, above). (See Gillies, 1983: pp. 5–8, and *Mikrokosmos*, no. 136.) Defective whole-tone structures can occur.

ix   Pentatonic structures

As with seven-note structures, the notations *per se* help only to narrow the structural possibilities. Other means of tonal determination (section xv) need to be invoked to determine the exact nature of a structure such as B D E F♯ A B. Even then, difficulties may arise since, as Bartók pointed out, four of the five degrees are approximately equal 'in weight'. Only the degree a fourth above the primary centre behaves like a 'passing tone' (Suchoff, ed., 1976: p. 371).

x   'Triadic' structures

In a small number of situations, such as *Mikrokosmos*, no. 133, bars 25–33 (example 3.5), Bartók's notations indicate a centric status for all three notes of a triad: G A♭ A A♯ B () C♯ D E♭ E F F♯ G (4:3:5). Because of the presence of an even number of semitones in the major third interval found in both major and minor triads, the structure is characterized by a triple representation of one letter-name (A♭, A, A♯, above). 'Triadic

Example 3.5 Bartók: *Mikrokosmos,* no. 133, bars 25–31

Example 3.6 Bartók: Sonata for Solo Violin, fourth movement, bars 80–92

Figure 3.7

<u>A</u>	B♭	B	B♯	<u>C♯</u>	D	D♯	<u>E</u>	F	F♯	F×	<u>G♯</u>	<u>A</u>	(4:3:4:1)
<u>A</u>	B♭	B	<u>C</u>	D♭	D	D♯	<u>E</u>	F	F♯	F×	<u>G♯</u>	<u>A</u>	(3:4:4:1)
<u>A</u>	B♭	B	B♯	<u>C♯</u>	D	D♯	<u>E</u>	F	F♯	<u>G</u>	A♭	<u>A</u>	(4:3:3:2)
<u>A</u>	B♭	B	<u>C</u>	D♭	D	D♯	<u>E</u>	F	F♯	<u>G</u>	A♭	<u>A</u>	(3:4:3:2)

Figure 3.8

| ↑ | | ↑ | | ↑ | | ↑ | | ↑ | | ↑ | | ↑ | |
| B | C | C | C♯ | C♯ | <u>D</u> | D | E♭ | E♭ | E | E | F | F | F♯ |

inversions' can also be found, although the primary tonal centre is not necessarily best assigned to the traditional root.

xi 'Seventh' structures

On rare occasions, as in the Divertimento for Strings, second movement, bars 50–1, Bartók encircles four notes, all of which could be considered tonal centres: G× <u>A♯</u> B B♯ <u>C♯</u> D D♯ <u>E</u> F F♯ <u>G</u> A♭ A <u>B♭</u> (3:3:3:3). These centres always appear to form some kind of seventh chord, as shown in figure 3.7. The primary tonal centre is not necessarily best assigned to the traditional root of the seventh chord. Notational compromises are sometimes needed if a pattern is to be duplicated with the same spellings in another octave (see the A♭ notations in figure 3.7).

xii – xiii Non-octave structures

xii Sub-octave structures

Chromatic, diatonic, pentatonic and quartertone structures can all be found from time to time in a 'narrow range', where only a segment of the potential octave structure is presented. When a chromatic structure contains only three or four adjacent chromatic degrees Bartók frequently stressed their independence by writing a successive letter-name for each successive degree: F× G♯ <u>A</u> B♭. Because of the regular succession of letter-names notation is of little help in identifying the tonal centre, although notes with double sharp or double flat spellings can automatically be excluded. When more than four or five chromatic degrees were involved this principle became too cumbersome and Bartók

Figure 3.9

<u>A</u>	B♭	B	C	C♯	D	<u>D♯</u>	E	F	F♯	G	G♯	<u>A</u>	(actual notation)
<u>A</u>	B♭	B	C	C♯	C𝄪	<u>D♯</u>	E	F	F♯	G	G♯	<u>A</u>	(theoretical notation)

<u>C♯</u>	E♭	F	G	A	(actual notation)
<u>C♯</u>	D♯	E♯	F𝄪	G𝄪	(theoretical notation)

Figure 3.10

Structure 1:   F   G♭   G   <u>A♭</u>   B♮   B♭   C♭   C   D♭   (Piano 1) (bars 12–13)
Structure 2:   B   C   C♯   <u>D</u>   E♭   E   F   F♯   G   (Piano 2)

Structure 1a: F   F♯   G   <u>A♭</u>   A   A♯   B   C   C♯   (Piano 1) (bars 13–14)
Structure 1b: F   F♯   G   <u>A♭</u>   A   B♭   B   C   C♯   (Piano 2)
Structure 2:   B   C   C♯   <u>D</u>   E♭   E   F   F♯   G   (both pianos)

introduced variant accidentals for letter-names: <u>A</u> B♭ B C C♯. As the number of degrees increases the possibility of secondary or tertiary tonal centres needs to be admitted: <u>A</u> B♭ B C C♯ <u>D</u> E♭. Diatonic and pentatonic sub-octave structures behave, in their spelling, as simple segments of their respective octave structures.

In several of his later works Bartók introduced short passages of quartertone writing. His use of quartertone elevating and lowering arrows was consistent within individual works, although he adopted slightly different principles in each work. Tonal centres in the extensive quartertone sections of the Sonata for Solo Violin (1944) are indicated by the lack of variant accidentals for a letter-name. Example 3.6 shows bars 80–92 of the fourth movement (as in Nordwall, 1965: pp. 2–3), where D is the tonal centre:

Comparison of the semitone and quartertone versions of example 3.6 makes it clear that Bartók's quartertone structures generally result from compressions of octave chromatic structures.

xiii   Super-octave structures

Structures with successive centres separated by the interval of a fourth, or of a fifth, are encountered in Bartók's later music. The distance between these centres may be filled out by diatonic, chromatic or even pentatonic steps. The occasional different spelling of the same pitch-class, as with D♯ and E♭ below, reflects the different functions of notes within different octaves – D♯ is the lower semitonal neighbour of the E centre, while E♭ is the upper neighbour to D: D♯ <u>E</u> F F♯ G G♯ <u>A</u> B♭ B C C♯ <u>D</u> E♭ E F F♯ <u>G</u> A♭. The notation of a structure of fourths very gradually flattens itself in an ascending direction, while a structure of fifths gradually sharpens itself. Defective structures are frequently found.

Occasionally Bartók wished to fill, in a tonally indefinite way, the space between tonal centres separated on the surface of the music by a considerable distance. This purpose is shown in the maintenance of dual accidentalizations of each letter-

name until the required tonal centre is reached: <u>D♭</u> E♮ E♭ F♭ F G♭ G A♭ A B♭ B C C♯ D D♯ <u>E</u>.

xiv   Compromises and contaminations

Had Bartók employed his pitch notations consistently as described above, analysts would soon have 'decoded' his tonal structures. However, in numerous situations he was influenced by other factors relevant to the effective presentation of his work. Although his late music is decidedly linear in conception, issues relating to vertical pitch homogeneities and more general concerns of score readability could not be ignored entirely. By the 1930s none the less, so consistent had Bartók's notational practice become that most of these situations of notational anomaly can also be categorized. They are elaborated more fully in Gillies (1989: pp. 69–91).

xiv.a   Over-sharpening and over-flattening

When the application of notational principles would result in the introduction of awkward passages in double sharps or double flats, Bartók frequently inserts a more readable spelling. Examples are the first movement of the Sonata for Solo Violin, bars 101–3 (see figure 3.9, first example), and *Mikrokosmos*, no. 136, bars 21–7, left hand (see figure 3.9, second example).

xiv.b   Legibility of simultaneous structures

Where individual performers are called upon to play simultaneously a number of parts, in allegiance to a number of different tonal structures, the spellings of one structure may contaminate another or a compromise notation may be effected. Vertical considerations of the total readability of the player's part may outweigh considerations of notational purity in individual parts. Bartók usually admits such contamination only when the theoretically appropriate accidentals in the various parts would be widely varied. In the first movement of the Sonata for Two Pianos and Percussion, two structures

Figure 3.11

G	A♭	A	B♭	B	C	D♭	D	E♭	E	F	F♯	G	(tonal integrity)
C	D♭	D	E♭	E	F	F♯	G	A♭	A	B♭	B	C	
G	A♭	A	B♭	B	C	C♯	D	E♭	E	F	F♯	G	(intervallic integrity)
C	D♭	D	E♭	E	F	F♯	G	A♭	A	B♭	B	C	

are presented on different pianos (bars 12–13), and then both played on both instruments (bars 13–14) (see figure 3.10).

The variant a and b spellings of Structure 1 (bars 13–14) reflect Bartók's desire to accommodate its originally flat spellings to the more accidentally 'balanced' spellings of Structure 2.

xiv.c Intervallic, motivic and thematic integrity

It is not possible to notate a full series of any given interval within a chromatic system without interfering in some way with the representation of the tonal structure. For instance, when seeking to maintain the interval of a perfect fifth within a full 7:5 chromatic structure, the composer is forced to decide in favour of tonal integrity (in which case one 'fifth' will be represented as a diminished sixth, F♯–D♭) or intervallic integrity (in which case the C♯ spelling will undermine the semitonal encirclement of the primary tonal centre, C) (see figure 3.11).

Bartók's responses in situations of intervallic maintenance were not entirely consistent, although the evidence of his *Mikrokosmos* pieces based on set intervals suggests that he strove to uphold tonal integrity as far as was practicable.

A motif or theme can also briefly distort the representation of a tonal structure if the composer seeks to maintain the interval patterns or actual letter-names of the original motif or theme in different tonal settings. Such distortion can be discerned in a comparison of Music for Strings, first movement 1–5, with bars 199–204 and 224–8 of the second movement.

xiv.d Instrumental idiosyncrasies

Technical limitations or capacities of instruments significantly influenced Bartók's pitch spellings. As the companion pieces in his Forty-four Duos and *Petite Suite* illustrate, his writing for piano was inclined to be influenced by issues of vertical spelling homogeneity more than his writing for strings, where concern for open string or finger positions is evident. Bartók's spellings of transposing woodwind and brass parts in orchestral scores, however, do not always reflect the niceties of his original tonal structures, which are best seen in his piano or short scores.

xiv.e Pre-compositional, compositional and publishing compromises

The published score is merely the final statement of Bartók's tonal thinking. Many of his notational compromises were effected, however, before he put pen to paper, or at the stages of sketch, fair copy or proof (see Vinton, 1964: plate 1; Suchoff, 1967–8: pp. 4, 6). From time to time Bartók was also prompted by his publishers to make changes in his pitch notations (see Dille, ed., 1968, pp. 241–2). As a result of the preparation for publication of his 'American' works by several friends, further inauthentic changes in pitch spellings have been introduced. The various Viola Concerto scores, prepared by Tibor Serly, are particularly unreliable in this regard.

xiv.f 'Default' notation

Exceedingly rarely, the complexities of the notational representation of his ideas lured Bartók into complete abandonment of a tonally based pitch representation. In these circumstances his notation 'defaulted' to that of the dominating structure of the movement. Such 'default' occurs in the first movement of the Fifth String Quartet (1934), bars 146–51, where Bartók's notation accords with the B♭-based structure that begins and ends the movement, although his own analysis of the passage considers it to be in A♭ (Suchoff, ed., 1976: p. 414).

xv Other criteria of tonal determination

Excepting this last situation, (xiv.f), Bartók's tonal structures always accord in some way with his pitch notations. This does not mean, however, that those notations are necessarily sufficient for precise identification of a structure. As a general rule, the less chromatic a section, the less its notation will indicate definitely its tonal structure. Other general criteria of tonal determination therefore need to be invoked to narrow further the possibilities admitted by the notation. These criteria include range limits, commencing and concluding pitches, symmetries, pitch reiterations and retentions, metrical and accentual features, as well as voice-leading and functional harmonic procedures.

xvi Tonal change (modulation)

xvi.a Tonal change by juxtaposition

A change in the spelling of a pitch-class in most cases indicates some change in tonal structure. Such changes can occur both through time between sections of the music (modulation) and

Example 3.7 Bartók: Viola Concerto, first movement, bars 204–7

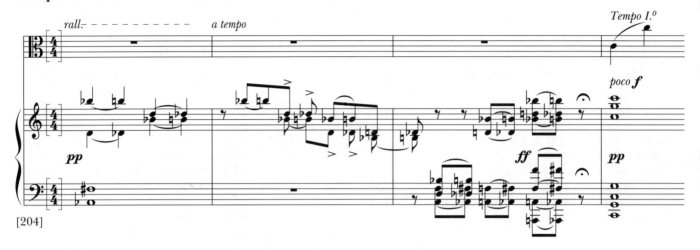

[204]

Figure 3.13

<u>B</u>   ()   C♯   ()   D♯   E   E♯   <u>F♯</u>   ()   G♯   ()   A♯   <u>B</u>   (bars 51–60)

<u>F♯</u>   ()   G♯   A   ()   B   ()   <u>C♯</u>   D   ()   E   ()   <u>F♯</u>   (bars 61–6)

Figure 3.14

<u>F♯</u>   ()   G♯   A   ()   B   ()   <u>C♯</u>   D   ()   E   ()   <u>F♯</u>   (bars 61–6)

<u>D♭</u>   ()   E♭   ()   F   G♭   ()   <u>A♭</u>   ()   B♭   C♭   C   <u>D♭</u>   (bars 67–75)

simultaneously between parts (as in polytonal textures). In much of Bartók's music, particularly his more highly sectionalized pieces, tonal structures are simply juxtaposed. The change is abrupt, and is often associated with a point of formal articulation. Figure 3.12 from *Mikrokosmos*, no. 141, shows Bartók changing at a major formal division from a fifths structure centred on B♭ to a fourths structure with a centre of B.

Figure 3.12

<u>E♭</u>   F   G♭   A♭   <u>B♭</u>   C   D   E♭   <u>F</u>   (bars 1–14)

<u>F♯</u>   G   A   <u>B</u>   C♯   D♯   <u>E</u>   (bars 15–22)

xvi.b   Transitional strategies

Several techniques of transition can be observed, though all occur fairly rarely. The second movement of the Sonata for Solo Violin, bars 94–9, provides an example of Bartók's use of intervallic integrity to create tonal ambiguity at the end of a section before emerging into tonal clarity at the beginning of the following section. A second technique is the 'breaking' of a notational scheme just before a natural point of articulation. This transitional technique can be used either to create a very small, incompletely defined tonal structure – a kind of 'buffer' – as at bars 12–14 of the first movement of the Fifth String Quartet, or to prepare a 'notational link' between the

end of one passage of the music and the beginning of the next, as at bar 21 of the same music. A variant of this technique is seen in Bartók's notational preparation for the arrival of important tonal centres. This is demonstrated in example 3.7, from the first movement of the Viola Concerto: [<u>C</u>] D♭ D () () F F♯ [<u>G</u>] A♭ A B♭ B [<u>C</u>]. The primary C and secondary G centres are semitonally encircled but not actually played during bars 204–6. They enter only with the soloist, at bar 207.

xvi.c   Partial tonal relationships

Because of the presence of two or more tonal centres in much of Bartók's music, it is possible for some centres to change while others are unaltered. In 'Párnás táncdal', from Twenty-seven Choruses, F♯ is a common centre to both structures, fulfilling a secondary role in the first and a primary role in the second (see figure 3.13).

xvi.d   Enharmonic tonal relationships

An enharmonic relationship exists between two structures when their centre or centres are spelt different but assert the same pitch-class or classes. These spelling distinctions may result from broader considerations of tonal hierarchy. A further case in 'Párnás táncdal' shows a hybrid, partial enharmonic relationship between two structures (figure 3.14):

Example 3.8 Bartók: Second Violin Concerto, second movement, bar 106

Example 3.9 Bartók: Sketch for violin solo part, first movement, bars 15–6

xvi.e Ornamental notations

In Bartók's scores, as in his ethnomusicological treatises, an ornamental notation is sometimes employed. Ornamental notes are written with small note-heads to show clearly their ancillary function. In example 3.8, a solo part in the second movement of the Second Violin Concerto, the ornamental B naturals occurring in the heptatuplet pattern do not override the later structural C♭ notations: B♭ C♭ C () D () E () F♯ G A♭ A B♭ (9:3).

Caution is needed, however, as in several passages of Bartók's later music the pattern of the pitch spellings indicates the presence of an ornamental level even where small note-heads have not been employed (for example, bars 21–6 of the fourth movement of the Sonata for Solo Violin).

xvi.f Microtonicization

Bartók's music provides occasional evidence of momentary tonicizing activity quite distinct from ornamental figurations. This microtonicization is indicated by a short-term deviation from the structural pitch spellings, reflecting the passing attraction of a note or chord within the structure. The B♯ spelling in example 3.9, Bartók's sketch for a violin solo part for the Second Violin Concerto, shows the momentary centric role of C♯ within an overall defective E–B chromatic structure (see Somfai, 1981: p. 105). The 'correcting' C♮ which follows clarifies that this is only a microtonicization: E () () G () () () B C C♯ D D♯ E (7:5).

xvii Tonal hierarchy

While notationally based analysis can provide a comprehensive inventory of tonal structures, notational factors are of minimal assistance in determining the relative significance of these structures in a movement or entire composition. The only substantial guide to the establishment of such a hierarchy among Bartók's tonal structures is found in the composer's verbal self-analyses. In his analysis of the first movement of the Fifth String Quartet (Suchoff, ed., 1976: pp. 414–15) Bartók identified the following symmetrical scheme:

Figure 3.15

Exposition			Development	Recapitulation		Coda
B♭	C	D	E	F♯	A♭	B♭ [B♭]

His analysis of the fifth movement likewise expressed a formal-tonal correlation:

$$A \; + \; B \; + \; C \; + \; B_{var.} \; + \; A_{var.} \; + \; Coda$$
$$B♭ \quad C♯ \quad E \quad G \quad B♭ \quad [B♭]$$

At a higher level still Bartók emphasized the importance of the B♭–E–B♭ progression which spans both movements. Comparison with a notationally based analysis of the first movement reveals that each of Bartók's tonal areas consists of a number of individual tonal structures (Gillies, 1989: pp. 210–62). Although not all of these individual structures maintain the tonal centre of the prevailing area (as analysed by Bartók), his area centres are nonetheless an accurate summary of the centres which predominate within the individual tonal structures. From Bartók's own practice, it seems that the most relevant criteria in establishing higher levels of tonal function are those which concern, firstly, commencing and concluding centres (especially of principal formal sections), and, secondly, duration, reiteration and repetition of centres.

Figure 3.16

Allegro

bars	section														
1–12	[1]	**D**	E♭	E	F	F♯	G	G♯	**A**	B♭	B	C	C♯	**D**	
13–23	[2]	**A**	B♭	()	C	C♯	()	D♯	E	F	F♯	G	G♯	**A**	(A♯ **B**, bars 22–3)
24–33	[3]	**A**	B♭	()	C	C♯	()	()	E	F	()	G	G♯	**A**	
34–41	[4]	**E**	F	F♯	()	G♯	**A**	B♭	B	C	C♯	()	D♯	**E**	
41–51	[5]	**A**	B♭	()	()	C♯	[**D**]	E♭	E	F	()	()	G♯	**A**	

Molto più calmo, lugubre

bars	section														
52–7	[6]	**C**	D♭	D	E♭	()	F	G♭	G	A♭	B♭♭	()	B	**C**	
57–62/4	[7]	**F♯**	G	G♯	A	()	**B**	C	()	**D**	E♭	()	E♯/F	**F♯**	
62–4	[8]	**A**	()	B	C	()	D	D♯	()	()	F♯	()	G♯	**A**	

Tempo I

bars	section														
65–74	[9]	**D**	E♭	E	F	F♯	()	G♯	**A**	B♭	B	C	C♯	()	D♯	**E**
74–82	[10]	**D**	E♭	E	F	F♯	G	G♯	**A**	B♭	B	C	C♯	**D**	

3   MODEL

'Free Variations', *Mikrokosmos*, no. 140 (1933), is a fine example of Bartók's varied use of tonal structures and modulatory techniques. The piece also provides several instances of compromised, contaminated and insufficiently prescriptive notations. Central to Bartók's variation strategy is the mirroring of tonal structures around A. This is best seen in his careful use of $D♯$ and $E♭$ spellings. Figure 3.16 is a summary of the structures of the piece, with the primary tonal centres highlighted.

Section 1, of twelve bars, unfolds a fully chromatic structure in which the right-hand part is devoted primarily to the chromatic infilling of A to D (bars 7–12) while the left fills in D to A (bars 1–12). Overall, therefore, the tonal centres of A and D are defined by semitonal encirclement, although neither part fully encircles both centres. A is clearly the primary centre, although factors other than pitch notation weigh heavily in this assertion: it is established first and maintained throughout this section in the left hand. The importance of the secondary centre of D grows through the section, however. It acts as the goal of the left-hand motion of bars 1–7, and from bar 7 onwards is maintained consistently in the right hand. As the left hand moves towards this D, it traces an octatonic segment, A–G♯–F♯–F–E♭–D. This formation is significant only within the framework of the prevailing D–A chromatic structure, as the notation reveals through its denial of letter-name integrity to the octatonic scalar degrees. Bartók's comma at the conclusion of bar 12 neatly signals the end of section 1 and a partial modulation, by juxtaposition, to the following section.

In section 2, bars 13–23, the primary tonal centre of A is maintained. Because of the inversion of material and exchange of hand roles the secondary centre is now E. This is shown by the regular appearance of $D♯$ spellings, instead of the $E♭$s found in section 1. The octatonic segment is now found in the right hand working towards the goal of E, along the path A–B♭–C–C♯–D♯–E. Through its notation, involving two representations of letter-name C, the segment's continuing subservience to the prevailing chromatic structure is indicated. This octatonic quality of the upper line is more clearly delineated here than in section 1 because of the lack of chromatic infilling in the A–E fifth portion of the structure. As well as A, the notes C and C♯ are reiterated in the left hand, reflecting an interest of Bartók in major-minor constructions which will be brought to the fore in section 3. Just before that section is reached, however, Bartók introduces a microtonicization of the note B, signified by the $A♯$ notation in bar 23. The result is a momentary impression of a structure of fifths, as E–B is added to the prevailing A–E. The centric significance of B is fleeting, nonetheless, as the cancelling $B♭$ spelling of bar 24 recognizes. Microtonicization creates a smooth modulation into the following section. The crescendo in bar 23, leading to the sforzando chord of bar 24, shows further Bartók's desire to merge rather than juxtapose sections 2 and 3. Indeed, he does not in the end change the primary centre: A remains as the chief tonal focus, although the scalar base is reduced from ten to eight notes. The exact demarcation of these sections is not indicated by the notation or a definitive point of articulation such as the comma at the end of section 1. Clearly the change must occur between the $A♯$ of bar 23 and the $B♭$ of bar 24. I have placed the change at the bar-line which separates bars 23 and 24 because of the playing of the $C♯$–C chord (which so characterizes section 3) on the downbeat of bar 24 and the change to a regular 2/4 metre at that same point.

In section 3, bars 24–33, A is semitonally encircled (G♯–A–B♭). It is not possible to identify a secondary centre conclusively, as the scale of only eight notes is insufficient for such identification. Section 3 acts as a bridge connecting the first variation (section 2) with the second, freer variation (section 4).

With the move to section 4 at bar 34 wider pitch activity is restored. A ten-note A–E structure is activated, the primary centre of A being maintained by the thumbs of both hands. The octatonic nature of the theme is compromised, however, through the admission of a B♮ in the right-hand part (bars 36 and 40), and the reduction in range from the expected perfect fifth (D–A) to a diminished fifth (D♯–A) in the left hand. This causes a chromatic 'squashing' of the intervening notes. The notational integrity of the left hand's thematic statement is also undermined. Its D♯ (rather than E♭) spellings are signs of contamination by the right hand's inverted A–E structure and, consequently, of a partial denial of the part's origins in the opening D–A structure of bars 1–12. From Bartók's sketch, it appears that he initially wrote out this left-hand passage with a D–A range (Vinton, 1966: p. 62). Given his eventual adoption of a juxtaposition of D–A (ordinary) and A–E (inverted) structures for the first section of his formal recapitulation (bars 65–74), it is probable that he rejected his initial idea for section 4 because of its potential to pre-empt that point of recapitulation. The notational consistency of section 4 is broken unexpectedly at bar 41 by the introduction of the E♭ in place of D♯ in the lower part. Bartók hesitated over which notation to use at this point, changing several times in his sketch between a prospective E♭ or a retrospective D♯ notation. With E♭, he introduces the fifth tonal section of the piece.

Section 5, from the end of bar 41 to bar 51, is still based on the primary centre of A. Despite the limited scale content, A is fully and repeatedly encircled by A–B♭ (right hand) and G♯–A (left hand figurations). C♯ and E♭ spellings also indicate the secondary tonal centre of D (D is not actually played). The modulation from section 5 to section 6 is by juxtaposition. The G♭ notation which starts bar 52 indicates that a quite different tonal structure has been adopted. Bartók does prepare melodically for section 6, although his notation bears no prospective signs. F and C♯ at the extremities of each part at the conclusion of bar 51 lead by contrary semitonal motion to the initiating notes, G♭ and C, of section 6.

The change in tonal structure between sections 5 and 6 (bars 51–2) is accompanied by changes in tempo, metre and playing mode. In this contrasting legato music Bartók unfolds a ten-note structure. The right-hand melody is a 'free variation' of the piece's opening in which the octatonic character of section 1 is developed to embrace seven of the octatonic degrees. These pitches are now spelt according to the principle of a new letter-name for each scalar degree and exhibit a rapid flattening (in an ascending direction): C D E♭ F G♭ A♭ B♭♭. As with sections 1 and 2, however, the octatonic melody is subsumed into the overall prevailing tonal structure defined by the totality of notes presented in both hands. This is the 'triadic' structure C–F–A♭. (Given the lack of a lower

encirclement to F, the alternative interpretation, of a C–E♭–A♭ structure, is possible. The repeated, strong upper semitonal G♭–F motions, however, lead me to favour C–F–A♭.) One telling sign of this 'triadic' structure is the presence of B♭♭ and B♮ notations. Notationally based argument is not sufficient for the determination of the hierarchy of the three tonal centres presented in section 6. C would appear to be the primary centre, by virtue of its position as the goal of the right-hand melodic motion from bar 52 to bar 56 as well as its foundational position at the bottom of the left hand (bars 52–5). F, as the dominating note of the right-hand melodic movement in bars 52–5, is best accorded secondary status, while A♭ is clearly the least significant of the three centres. Modulation to section 7 is by juxtaposition, to a similar 'second inversion' triadic structure a tritone distant.

Section 7, commencing with the upbeat to bar 58, shows the octatonic melody in the left hand, with the accompanying motif in the right. Bartók's seven-note octatonic segment is again spelt with one letter-name per degree: F♯ G♯ A B C D E♭. The octatonic characteristics are, nonetheless, subsumed into a 'triadic' structure when the right-hand part and also the G left-hand upbeat are taken into account. By analogy with section 6, an F♯–B–D interpretation is best, although the lack of conclusive encirclement of both B and D means that other interpretations are possible. One sign of this triadic structure is the presence of both E♭ and E♮ notations. But Bartók was inconsistent here. In his sketch, he wrote E♮ notations in the right-hand part throughout bars 58–62, only to change the final two E♮ notes, in bars 61 and 62, to F naturals in his fair copy (Vinton, 1966: pp. 62–3). This is best explained as a case of contamination of the right hand's notation by the left hand's octatonic spellings. F is the correct notation for the last note needed to complete the F♯-based octatonic scale: F♯ G♯ A B C D E♭ F. Perhaps the additional length and lower position of the left-hand E♭ at bars 60–1, in comparison with the corresponding right-hand B♭♭ at bar 54, also induced Bartók to make these changes.

Towards the end of section 7 the hands assume somewhat different functions for two bars, creating a sense of tonal ambivalence. While the left hand still pursues its section 7 goal of F♯ octatonically, the right hand moves at bars 63–4 (section 8) into a notation which looks forward to the return of the movement's opening material, with its A-based structures. The right-hand D♯ notation introduced in bar 63 is the sign of the start of this brief section 8. But the left-hand notation at bars 62–4 allows for both A–E chromatic and F♯-based octatonic interpretations.

For the return at bar 65 of his opening material, introducing section 9, Bartók overlays section 1's left-hand and section 2's right-hand part. This creates the mirroring of parts and consequent tonal structure that Bartók had originally investigated in his sketch for section 4. Both hands now pursue their octatonic paths unimpeded and achieve their goals of D (left hand) and E (right hand) in bar 72. A remains the primary

Example 3.10 Bartók: The ternary form of *Mikrokosmos*, no. 140, 'Free Variations'

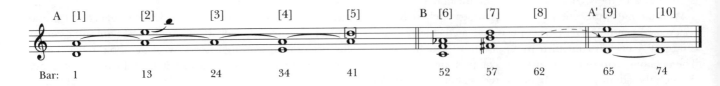

tonal centre of both the lower D–A structure and its mirrored right-hand A–E structure. It is the axis of symmetry and is played constantly in both hands, and in combination the parts evidence a symmetrical three-element structure of fifths. The notational signs of the competing upper E and lower D secondary centres are the D♯ (right-hand) and E♭ (left-hand) spellings of bars 68, 72 and 73, which act as chromatic leading-notes to the appropriate secondary centres.

The point of change from section 9 to section 10 is ill-defined. Indeed, the transition between these two sections is more a large-scale example of contamination by one part of another than a strict modulation. Bartók withdraws from his D–A–E mirror tonal structure to the D–A structure with which the composition began. That involves the right-hand notation falling into line with the spellings of the D–A structure already prevailing throughout section 9 in the left hand. The point of this change can be located only approximately, between the right hand D♯ at the start of bar 73 and E♭ midway through bar 74. Until the end of bar 73, also, both hands reiterate A, while from bar 74 C♯, D and A reiterations are found. Section 10 might, therefore, begin at the start of the left-hand part in bar 74. As in section 1 (but no other portion of the piece), this concluding section employs all twelve chromatic notes. It has rejected the octatonic melodic movements which characterized most intervening sections and adopted a consistently chromatic part-writing. The final supremacy of A as tonal centre is asserted by its constant repetition in both hand parts from bar 77, and the final chromatic convergence on this pitch-class.

The larger-scale tonal planning of 'Free Variations' is an important contributory factor to the clear ternary form of this piece. As example 3.10 shows, the first main group of sections (bars 1–51) is unified by the presence of primary tonal centre A and symmetrically disposed secondary centres. Bars 52–64 present tonal contrast by introducing triadic structures with primary centres of C and F♯ (sections 6 and 7). But here, too, the centres are disposed symmetrically around A, to which the notation gravitates in bars 62–4. In the varied reprise (bars 65–82) the original secondary centres are presented simultaneously (section 9) before the piece concludes in allegiance to its opening structure (section 10). Example 3.10 suggests that, at a higher tonal level, 'Free Variations' is best interpreted as a symmetrical movement around the centre of A by minor third intervals:

Figure 3.17

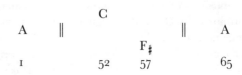

Such simple symmetrical patterns are frequently found between the broader tonal areas of Bartók's later compositions. Indeed, the same progression of centres as shown here is found between the movements of his Music for Strings.

4   GUIDED READING AND ANALYSIS

i   Reading

For the reasons listed in the Orientation section of this chapter, only a few music analysts have paid sustained attention to the connection between pitch notations and tonality in early twentieth-century composition. See Oramo, Perle and Gillies entries in the bibliography. Perle's article concerns Scriabin's practice while the others refer to Bartók's usage. Because of the highly idiosyncratic nature of Bartók's pitch notations, most analysts of his music have felt compelled to make some statement about their significance or lack of significance. See Stevens (1953: p. 117), Lendvai (1971: p. 60) and Antokoletz (1984: pp. xiv–xv). For other analyses of, or statements about *Mikrokosmos*, no. 140, see Suchoff (1971: pp. 122–3), Frank (1977: pp. 187–90) and Waldbauer (1985).

ii   Analysis

The analytical method is best applied to Bartók's output from 1931 onwards, as the evidence on which it is based has been drawn from that period. As an introduction to the method, analysis might be undertaken of various of the more chromatic themes found in Bartók's works of this period. Bartók himself listed many of these in his Harvard Lectures of 1943 (Suchoff, ed., 1976: p. 380). Following this, Bartók's educational works of the 1930s provide simple, more extended examples for analysis: Forty-four Duos, Twenty-seven Choruses, *Mikrokosmos* (earlier volumes). The more difficult *Mikrokosmos* pieces present a great variety of notational issues, especially concerning contamination and compromise procedures. See, in particular, nos. 109, 122, 131–6. Analysis of the major compositions of the period might now be attempted, although the complexities can at times be bewildering. It is therefore advisable to begin with the chamber works for strings, as these present fewer problems of notational orientation: Divertimento, Music for Strings, Fifth String Quartet, Sixth String Quartet. Where available, Bartók's sketches, drafts and verbal self-analyses should be consulted; see Vinton (1966: pp. 41–69), Suchoff, ed. (1976: pp. 414–31), Antokoletz (1984: pp. 77–8). Many of the principles of the method can be applied more widely, to Bartók's earlier works, and to the output of some other composers (Scriabin, Rakhmaninov, Kodály). An increasing number of difficulties will be encountered, however, unless an attempt is made to adapt the method to the particular usage of the composer and period.

BIBLIOGRAPHY

Antokoletz, Elliott, *The Music of Béla Bartók* (Berkeley: University of California Press, 1984).

Bartók, Béla, 'The Problem of the New Music' (1920), in *Béla Bartók Essays*, ed. Benjamin Suchoff (London: Faber and Faber, 1976), pp. 455–9.

Busoni, Ferruccio, *Versuch einer organischen Klavier-Noten-Schrift* (Leipzig: Breitkopf & Härtel, 1910).

Cowell, Henry, 'Our Inadequate Notation', *Modern Music*, 4, 3 (1927), pp. 29–33.

Dille, Denijs, ed. [Letters to Bartók], *Documenta Bartókiana*, 3 (1968), pp. 241–2.

Frank, Oszkár, *Bevezető Bartók Mikrokozmoszának világába* [Introduction to the World of Bartók's *Mikrokosmos*] (Budapest: Zeneműkiadó, 1977).

Gillies, Malcolm, 'Bartók's Last Works: A Theory of Tonality and Modality', *Musicology*, 7 (1982), pp. 120–30.

——, 'Bartók's Notation: Tonality and Modality', *Tempo*, 145 (1983), pp. 4–9.

——, *Notation and Tonal Structure in Bartók's Later Works* (New York: Garland, 1989).

Lendvai, Ernő, *Béla Bartók: An Analysis of his Music* (London: Kahn & Averill, 1971).

Nordwall, Ove, 'The Original Version of Bartók's Sonata for Solo Violin', *Tempo*, 74 (1965), pp. 2–4.

Oramo, Ilkka, *Modaalinen Symmetria* (Helsinki: Suomen Musiikkitieleellinen Seura, 1977).

——, 'Modale Symmetrie bei Bartók', *Musikforschung*, 33 (1980), pp. 450–64.

Perle, George, 'Scriabin's Self-analyses', *Music Analysis*, 3 (1984), pp. 101–22.

Ringer, Alexander L., 'Melody', *New Grove Dictionary of Music and Musicians* (London: Macmillan, 1980), Vol. 12, pp. 118–27.

Schoenberg, Arnold 'A New Twelve-Tone Notation' (1924), in *Style and Idea*, ed. Leonard Stein (London: Faber and Faber, 1975), pp. 354–62.

Somfai, László, 'Self-analysis by Twentieth-century Composers', in *Modern Musical Scholarship*, ed. Edward Olleson (London: Oriel, 1978), pp. 167–79.

——, *Tizennyolc Bartók-tanulmány* [Eighteen Bartók Essays] (Budapest: Zeneműkiadó, 1981).

Stevens, Halsey, *The Life and Music of Béla Bartók* (New York: Oxford University Press, 1953).

Suchoff, Benjamin, 'Structure and Concept in Bartók's Sixth Quartet', *Tempo*, 83 (1967–8), pp. 2–11.

——, *Guide to Bartók's Mikrokosmos* (rev. edn, London: Boosey & Hawkes, 1971).

Suchoff, Benjamin, ed., *Béla Bartók Essays* (London: Faber and Faber, 1976).

Vinton, John, 'New Light on Bartók's Sixth Quartet', *Music Review*, 25 (1964), pp. 224–38.

——, 'Toward a Chronology of the Mikrokosmos', *Studia musicologica*, 8 (1966), pp. 41–69.

Waldbauer, Ivan, 'Interplay of Tonality and Nontonal Constructs in Three Pieces from the *Mikrokosmos* of Bartók', in *Music and Context: Essays for John M. Ward*, ed. Anne Dhu Shapiro (Cambridge, MA: Harvard University Press, 1985), pp. 418–40.

4

Dodecaphony: Schoenberg

MARTHA HYDE

I ORIENTATION

Schoenberg developed the twelve-tone method and wrote music using it immediately following World War I in the midst of the intense turmoil and trauma of Austrian defeat. In Austria, more than in any country except perhaps Russia, the war brought a drastic break with nineteenth-century social, political and cultural institutions, a break which the long rule of the Habsburgs and the stable ascendancy of the bourgeoisie only intensified. By the turn of the century, the bourgeoisie had come to dominate Austrian social and cultural institutions, especially in Vienna, and had created a society that cultivated stability above any other values. Bourgeois life tended to affirm disciplined conformity, good taste guided by tradition, reason and belief in orderly social progress. In the decade preceding the war, to be sure, eloquent voices of dissent might occasionally be heard, and some Austrians were not without premonitions of unknown social horrors. Writers such as Karl Kraus and Stephen Zweig, the poets of the *Jung Wein* and the artists known as the Expressionists all attacked the constraints of bourgeois life and art. But few were prepared for the upheavals, hardships and discontinuities of defeated Austria.

Defeat produced despair and cynicism in some, but others recognized in broken cultural continuity an opportunity for the humanist renaissance that inspired at least two major works of cultural history: Allan Janik and Stephen Toulmin's *Wittgenstein's Vienna* and Carl I. Schorske's *Fin-de-siècle Vienna*.[1] 'Hell lay behind us', Zweig wrote in his memoirs, 'What was there to frighten us after that! Another world was about to begin'.[2] The peace treaty of Versailles effectively dismantled the Habsburg Empire. Postwar Austria therefore faced the task of rebuilding its polity. A constitution had to be framed, a parliament established and an effective system of social democracy put in place. The times seemed to demand fresh thinking, bold innovation, new institutions freed from the dead weight of the past. This spirit of construction, self-determination and independence extended to the arts as well. By the turn of the century bourgeoisie had largely replaced

aristocrats as patrons of the arts, but the arts themselves continued as before. It took war and its aftermath to produce a radical break with earlier styles and conventions and inaugurate in all the arts a period of intense innovation. Poetry, literature, film, painting, architecture and music all showed concentrated technical experimentation. Artists shed many of the preoccupations and doubts that characterized the prewar years, and a progressive attitude prevailed, as well as a general sympathy towards artistic diversity. With so much to be accomplished, so little taken for granted or exempt from challenge, artists felt encouraged to strike out and validate their own experimental paths.[3]

In this particular cultural milieu, Schoenberg decided to formalize and adopt a new method of composition – radically new even though he claimed to have struggled with its conceptual ingredients since before World War I:

> After many unsuccessful attempts during a period of approximately twelve years, I laid the foundations for a new procedure in musical construction which seemed fitted to replace those structural differentiations provided formerly by tonal harmonies. I called this procedure *Method of Composing with Twelve Tones which are Related Only with One Another*. This method consists primarily of the constant and exclusive use of a set of twelve different tones.[4]

This matter-of-fact account of an autonomous decision to proceed with the twelve-tone method perhaps reflects an objectivity attained only after the fact. For the nature of Schoenberg's artistic decision – its rejection of the expressive forms and technical means that mark his earlier, also revolutionary atonal style – resonates so strongly with postwar developments in other artistic fields that it must reflect Schoenberg's own engagement with, his own constructive response to, the tumultuous social and cultural upheavals of the time.

Schoenberg's later writings contain barely a hint that he ever questioned his decision to adopt the twelve-tone method, and from 1923 until his death in 1950 he composed almost exclusively with it, resurrecting his earlier chromatic and atonal styles only infrequently. Schoenberg asserted, in his 1934 lecture 'Composition with Twelve Tones', that the twelve-tone method resolved problems of brevity that he had not managed to overcome in atonal forms.[5] In other words, he identified generating extended forms as the twelve-tone method's decisive capacity. Perhaps it was this as-yet unproven potential that prompted in 1921 the famous remark to Josef Rufer that he had 'made a discovery which will ensure the supremacy of German music for the next hundred years'.[6] Towards the end of his life, his claims for the twelve-tone method became no weaker or less confident: 'Forty years have since proved that the psychological basis of all these changes was correct. Music without a constant reference to a tonic was comprehensible ...'[7] Schoenberg never wavered in the conviction that the twelve-tone method was born of artistic necessity, that it represented the inevitable culmination of the highly chromatic and atonal styles that had flourished before World War I.

This assessment of the method (and of Schoenberg's music that embodies it) has never been universal or even general among musicians, critics and composers, either during his lifetime or after. In fact, throughout his career he suffered criticism the unanimity and virulence of which is probably unmatched among twentieth-century composers (fist-fights after concerts, for example, or reviews printed in the crime columns of the Vienna press). Some of this virulence subsided after Schoenberg went to the United States in 1933. In Europe he had been branded as 'The Twelve-Tone Constructor', 'The Atonalist'. In the United States his works were no longer attacked because they were not performed, but he himself enjoyed – or rather suffered – public attention as a theoretician rather than as a composer. Only at the end of his life did the twelve-tone method and Schoenberg's achievement in it enjoy an enthusiastic re-evaluation and development by other composers.

While works using the twelve-tone method were rarely performed until after World War II and therefore unfamiliar to the general public, composers had begun to appreciate the flexibility of the method through the highly varied twelve-tone styles of such proponents as Webern, Berg, Krenek, Casella and Dallapiccola. But the fresh interest accorded twelve-tone and more general serial techniques after World War II resulted directly from the International Summer Course for New Music established at Darmstadt, Germany, in 1946 in order to expose German composers to modern achievements that had been denied or denigrated by the Nazis. Postwar interest by distinguished composers such as Boulez, Stockhausen, Nono and Berio steadily extended serial techniques to musical domains other than pitch (for example, rhythm, articulation, dynamics and register). These same composers had become disenchanted with their serial experiments by 1956, but curiously, and perhaps significantly, it was Webern's music, and not Schoenberg's, that had served as their model. Even those who advocated serial procedures after the war often found Schoenberg's serial rigour uncongenial.

The general nature of the postwar criticism of Schoenberg deserves attention, for it both highlights the compositional issues that made Schoenberg's music difficult to penetrate and explains why even now composers and critics disagree on his place in the history of twentieth-century music. I hope the analysis I shall develop of Schoenberg's *Klavierstück*, op. 33b, will show that what many have regarded as unresolved problems in his method are in fact its most sophisticated resources.

Schoenberg's postwar critics have identified two apparent problems in his twelve-tone method or two discrepancies between his music and the claims he made for it. The first of these might be called 'the harmonic problem', and the second 'the form problem'. In 'Composition with Twelve Tones', Schoenberg made one claim for his serial method that many composers and critics have thought unjustified: not only that the melodies of his music were derived from the basic set, but also that 'something different and more important is derived from it with a regularity comparable to the regularity and logic of [tonal] harmony'.[8] And he goes on to claim, 'The association of tones into harmonies and their successions is regulated (as will be shown later) by the order of [the pitches of the basic set]'.[9] The problem is that Schoenberg never really showed later how a twelve-tone basic set regulates harmonies and their successions, a failure that critics have taken to signal either irresolution in Schoenberg's use of his method, or a failure in the method itself. The tonal system, critics have argued, orders and integrates both horizontal and vertical dimensions of a piece of music, but the twelve-tone system can order only a single dimension and consequently, in itself, cannot produce an integrated musical texture. In this view, Schoenberg's twelve-tone pieces contain many harmonic events unrelated to the basic set. They therefore fail to justify his claim that the twelve-tone row regulates both harmonies and their successions, and they suggest that the method itself is not really comparable with tonal harmony, not a rigorous and radical new practice, but a curious oddity of twentieth-century modernism.[10]

The second apparent problem, 'the form problem', has been most forcefully diagnosed by Pierre Boulez. In an essay called 'Schoenberg is Dead', published in 1952, one year after Schoenberg's death, and in several later writings, Boulez attacks what he views as major shortcomings in Schoenberg's application of his own method.[11] These criticisms reveal, in turn, why Webern's serial music, rather than Schoenberg's, served as a model for those at Darmstadt who sought to extend serial techniques. Boulez concentrates on the potential of the serial method to sustain extended forms comparable with those of tonal compositions. Against the earlier view that Schoenberg went too far in trusting to a method that lacks structural principles comparable with those of tonal harmony, Boulez argued that Schoenberg did not go far enough. Schoenberg failed to explore the potential of the twelve-tone method to generate its own forms, but rather imposed on his new method inappropriate, ready-made tonal forms, such as sonata form in his quartets or the Baroque dance forms of op. 25.

> The pre-classical and classical forms ruling most of his compositions were in no way historically connected with the twelve-tone discovery; the result is that a contradiction arises between the forms dictated by tonality and a language [the twelve-tone method] of which the laws of organization are still only dimly perceived. It is not only that this language finds no sanction in the forms used by Schoenberg, but something more negative: namely, that these forms rule out every possibility of organization implicit in the new material.[12]

Boulez complains further of Schoenberg's use of 'clichés typical of a romanticism at once ostentatious and outmoded': particularly accompanied melody, counterpoint based on principal and subsidiary voices (*Hauptstimme* and *Nebenstimme*), rhythmic structure based on strong and weak beats, false appoggiaturas, broken chords and repetitions. These complaints lead to the conclusion that Schoenberg's twelve-tone music did not make a clear break with tonal principles, as Schoenberg always claimed it did, because it maintained melody, harmony and counterpoint as separate functions. The irony in Boulez's attack – that even 'though Schoenberg's work is essentially experimental, it lacks ambition'[13] – is that throughout the 1920s and 1930s Schoenberg issued statements (some quoted above) showing him to be ambitious precisely where Boulez would find him timid: in developing the twelve-tone method's potential for extended forms.

Many would agree in identifying Schoenberg as the most influential composer of the twentieth century (rivalled only by Stravinsky), but persistent and largely unanswered complaints about twelve-tone harmony and form have resulted in radically different assessments of the historical legacy of the twelve-tone method and of Schoenberg himself. Two representative accounts will illustrate this predicament, and I hope will explain why any analysis of Schoenberg's twelve-tone music – no matter how elementary – must address forthrightly the issues of twelve-tone harmony and form.

The first account comes from an exemplary book on twentieth-century music by Bryan Simms, who reaffirms much of Boulez's earlier indictment. Simms argues that the upheavals of World War I marked the *end* of musical progressivism for Schoenberg, who afterwards only consolidated and systematized the compositional advances of the preceding decades. Schoenberg's return to conventional, tonal forms after 1921 represents retrenchment for Simms, who argues that, after more than 60 years,

> it is now clear that musical style has not unfolded with the predictability that [Schoenberg] anticipated. The [twelve-tone] method unquestionably produced masterpieces by European composers between the world wars, and ... by several Americans before and after World War II.... But the evolution of style has since led composers on new paths, pushing 12-tone composition, at least for the time, into the background.[14]

The events of the same period call forth the opposite judgement from the eminent composer Charles Wuorinen, who with Stravinsky and Milton Babbitt, has been one of the principal proponents of serialism in America. For Wuorinen, 'there are in fact only two principal systems in Western music: the tonal and the 12-tone systems'.[15] In his view, the tonal system was 'replaced ... by the 12-tone system, first initiated by Schoenberg, and subsequently developed into a world of chromaticism extending far beyond the domains originally envisioned for its use'.[16] The expansion of serial procedures after World War II is not a failed experiment, but a successful generalization of the concept of the twelve-tone set: 'sets become more global in their organizing power, more abstracted and general, and broader in the domain of their compositional influence'.[17] Where Simms sees recent trends towards highly chromatic music as an implied rejection of serial techniques, Wuorinen believes that it could not have been conceived except for the twelve-tone method which produced a more generalized principle of ordered interval succession. And this achievement holds promise for the future:

> If the principle of ordered interval succession becomes a sufficiently generalized generator of form, then (as is already the case in some 12-tone music) the principles of pitch organization derived from interval content [that is, principles derived from the tonal system] ... can be reintroduced into what is basically order-determined music. This appears to be the direction of highly chromatic music of the present day.[18]

These radically opposed, yet representative evaluations reach back as far as the innovations of 1920 and extend to the most recent developments in twentieth-century composition. Perhaps the irreconcilability of these received opinions has helped in the last decade to prompt an intense re-evaluation of Schoenberg's music, a re-evaluation that stresses his techniques for structuring twelve-tone harmony and form. The following analysis of the *Klavierstück*, op. 33b, aims to suggest some of the fruits of this re-evaluation and begins with the conviction that harmony and form represent the crucial issues for understanding Schoenberg's twelve-tone music.

2 METHOD

To bring these issues into sharper focus, we must return to 'Composition with Twelve Tones' to reconsider how Schoenberg himself conceived of the twelve-tone method and its basic elements. He begins quite simply by defining the basic set and describing its function:

> This method consists primarily of the constant and exclusive use of an ordered set of twelve different tones. This means, of course, that no tone is repeated within the series and that it uses all twelve tones of the chromatic scale, though in a different order.... Such a basic set (BS) consists of various intervals.... The association of tones into harmonies and their successions is regulated ... by the order of these tones. The basic set functions in the manner of a motive. This explains why such a basic set has to be invented anew for every piece. It has to be the first creative thought.[19]

Example 4.1   Basic set with three transformations

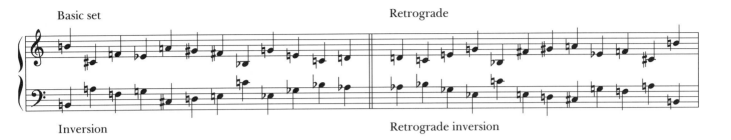

Basic set

Retrograde

Inversion

Retrograde inversion

An example of a basic set follows with an explanation of how to derive from it three additional transformations (which he terms the retrograde set, the inversion and the retrograde inversion).

Example 4.1 gives the basic set (P) for op. 33b with its three transformations, using Schoenberg's notation as in 'Composition with Twelve Tones'. The example shows that one obtains the retrograde of a basic set (RP) by reversing the order of its pitches – that is, beginning with its twelfth pitch and proceeding in reverse order to the first. The inversion (I) of the basic set is derived by inverting each of its successive intervals about some fixed pitch; in example 4.1, the fixed pitch is the first, B♮. Unlike the retrograde, the inversion associates new pitches, but the exact succession of intervals in their inverted form remains constant. The retrograde inversion (RI) simply reverses the order of the inversion – that is, by reading the inversion from right to left.

Transposition, Schoenberg continues, yields a total of twelve forms (eleven plus the original) of each of the four transformations of the basic set. One can derive by transposition twelve 'prograde' forms of the basic set, by beginning on the twelve available pitches of the chromatic scale. Similarly, there are twelve retrograde forms, twelve inversions and twelve retrograde inversions, giving a total of 48 available forms of a single basic set.

In its simplest formulation, these set-forms represent the essential elements of the twelve-tone method as Schoenberg presents it in his lecture-manifesto. And, in most of Schoenberg's twelve-tone compositions, a single basic set and its various transformations can in fact account for all pitches. But such an account achieves only the most rudimentary kind of analysis, analogous perhaps merely to identifying the keys and melodies of a tonal piece. To proceed further, we need a more precise definition of the basic set itself and a clearer conception of what Schoenberg meant by twelve-tone harmony. As will become clear, the ambiguity inherent in 'Composition with Twelve Tones' explains much of the later confusion that has surrounded the problems of twelve-tone harmony and form.

Schoenberg consistently describes a basic set as a succession of intervals rather than as a series of individual pitches. He stresses that each tone does not function independently, since each 'appears always in the neighbourhood of two other tones' – that is, each functions only in relation to its adjacent pitches.[20] He makes clear that he has included all twelve pitches in the basic set so that no single pitch is repeated more frequently than any other and all pitches are equally emphasized. In naming his new technique 'Method of Composing with Twelve Tones which are Related Only with One Another' he indicates that the twelve tones are mutually dependent and, most important, that they are perceived primarily in terms of each other. It is thus misleading to conceive of the basic set as a series of twelve ordered pitches. Rather, it is primarily a series of intervals set forth by twelve ordered pitch-classes.[21]

According to Schoenberg, the intervals of the basic set delineate all the twelve-tone harmonies for a given piece. But he asserts that listeners will recognize a twelve-tone harmony regardless of the internal ordering of its pitches. Because musical ideas are recognizable in inverted and retrograde forms, the identity of a musical idea or harmony is determined by the absolute relation of its elements – that is, by its total intervallic content and not merely by a single ordering of its pitches.[22] Schoenberg also states that, while the pitches of the basic set usually occur in their original order, a similar restriction need not apply among its partitioned segments. Thus several examples in 'Composition with Twelve Tones' use a basic set that is partitioned into three tetrachords, and the tetrachords themselves need not occur in order, but rather function as if they were independent small sets. In other words, the harmonies of the basic set do not have to occur in a fixed order, but can function independently. (The importance of this last feature will become evident in example 4.2.) To summarize: first, the basic set is best considered as a group of harmonies defined by an ordered series of intervals; second, these harmonies are identified primarily by their *total* intervallic content, not merely by a single series of pitches; and third, when partitioned, their segments can function as independent small sets.

A final property of the basic set, as Schoenberg conceived it, is that its harmonies need not be restricted to a fixed pitch-class content. 'Composition with Twelve Tones' does not state this property explicitly, but strongly implies it in its

Figure 4.1 Combinatorial property of basic set

(a) Vertical aggregates:

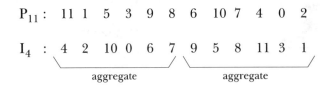

P_{11} : 11 1   5   3   9   8   6   10 7   4   0   2

I_4 : 4   2   10 0   6   7   9   5   8   11 3   1

‿‿‿‿‿‿‿‿‿ ‿‿‿‿‿‿‿‿‿
     aggregate   aggregate

(b) Horizontal aggregate:

P_{11} RI_4

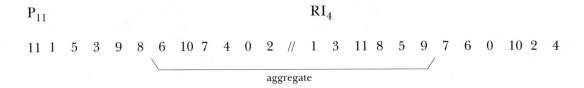

11 1   5   3   9   8   6   10 7   4   0   2 // 1   3   11 8   5   9   7   6   0   10 2   4

‿‿‿‿‿‿‿‿‿‿‿‿‿‿‿‿‿‿
              aggregate

discussion of how twelve-tone harmony works, as well as in the musical examples it provides. For instance, an early version of 'Composition with Twelve Tones' ambiguously redefines what constitutes a harmony under the new method:

> ... the concept whereby the vertical and horizontal, harmonic and melodic, the simultaneous and the successive were all in reality comprised within one unified space. It follows from this that whatever occurs at one point in that space, occurs not only there but in every dimensional aspect of the spatial continuum, so that any particular melodic motion ... will not only have its effect upon the harmony, but on *everything* subsequently that is comprised within that spatial continuum.[23]

Schoenberg evidently does not conceive of harmony as merely a vertical event − pitches sounding simultaneously − but asserts that melodic events − pitches sounding successively − also have harmonic implications. A legitimate harmony comprises all pitches, both simultaneously and successively, that are temporally associated or, as he describes it, 'comprised within the same spatial continuum'. But what defines this spatial continuum? What sets its bounds? A brief example from op. 33b will clarify this obscure invocation of what Schoenberg later called 'multi-dimensional musical space', and will show precisely its importance both for harmonic structure and for form. But the example requires that first I review one further property of hexachords that Schoenberg discusses in 'Composition with Twelve Tones', one that is now usually termed 'combinatoriality'.[24]

In some basic sets, when an operation (transposition, retrograde transposition, inversion or retrograde inversion) is performed on the first hexachord, the result is a new hexachord which includes none of the pitches of the original. Together the two hexachords produce an 'aggregate' whose combined pitch-class content is the same as the universal set of twelve pitch-classes. This property of 'combinatoriality' depends on segmental or hexachordal pitch-class content, but not at all on the ordering of elements within those segments. It provides a further means of ensuring the constant recycling of the twelve pitch-classes, in addition to that already provided by the repetition of the basic set itself.

Figure 4.1 illustrates hexachordal combinatoriality in op. 33b's basic set. I represent the basic set in numeric rather than musical notation, as in example 4.1, because we must now treat the row as a series of *pitch-classes* rather than as a series of specific pitches. Row forms are conventionally labelled by the operations P, RP, I and RI, followed by an integer that represents the first pitch-class of the designated row form, whether prograde or inverted. Pitch-class integers remain fixed; they do not shift. (The twelve pitch-classes are designated by the integers 0 through 11. Pitch-class 0 refers to all notated pitches C, B♯ and D♭♭; pitch-class 1 refers to all notated pitches C♯, D♭ and B×, and so on.) Figure 4.1, then, presents the initial form of op. 33b's basic set; it begins on B♮ and is therefore labelled P_{11}. Below it appears the inversion of the prograde form that begins on E♮ − that is, I_4. Notice that when the first hexachord of P_{11} is inverted around pitch-class 11 and then transposed up five semitones (that is, by interval-class 5), a new hexachord results which excludes the pitch content of the first. This new hexachord is, of course, the first hexachord of I_4, and since the two hexachords do not overlap in pitch content (the initial hexachords of P_{11} and I_4) they produce an aggregate which contains all twelve pitch-classes. (The same is true for the second hexachords of P_{11} and I_4.) Aggregates can unfold either vertically, as in figure 4.1a, or horizontally, as in figure 4.1b (the formation of the aggregate here requires one row form to unfold in retrograde); the former configuration generates two aggregates vertically, where the latter allows only one horizontally.[25] As we shall see, Schoenberg uses both horizontal and vertical aggregates throughout op. 33b to create additional dimensions of harmonic structure.

One example from op. 33b will clarify Schoenberg's concept of 'multi-dimensional musical space' and his typical method of structuring twelve-tone harmony, as well as illustrate why harmonies of the basic set should be defined principally by their *total* intervallic content rather than by a single ordering of intervals or pitch-classes. Example 4.2 shows the third phrase (bars 11–16) of op. 33b, which unfolds the successive row forms P_{11} and RI_4. (Order numbers 1–12 mark the first occurrence of successive pitches in each row form, but not later occurrences.) As everyone immediately hears, this phrase represents a kind of varied repetition of op. 33b's opening, differing only in the inverted contour of its cantabile melody and in the pitch repetition and registral expansion of its accompaniment. As in the opening, these row forms unfold what Schoenberg regards as an ordered presentation of the basic set. The partitioned dyads in the upper voice seem to enter too late with respect to those in the bass (for example, in bar 12 the pitch marked by order-number 5 in the left hand enters before that marked by order-number 4 in the right hand), but this kind of configuration is typical of Schoenberg's style and exemplifies the feature mentioned above, namely his use of partitioned segments as 'independent small sets'. Analysis of the harmonic structure of this phrase, however, will reveal criteria governing *how* these partitioned segments are used independently, criteria that Schoenberg only hinted at in his vague invocation of 'multi-dimensional musical space'.

The phrase occurs in two connected dimensions of harmonic structure, as indicated by brackets in figure 4.2. (Order numbers indicate the relative position or register of the pitches that make up the two principal voices – melody and accompaniment – marked by separate stemming in the score.) What we can call the 'primary dimension' includes the entire phrase and simply reproduces the ordered, successive pitches of P_{11} and RI_4. The primary harmonic dimension, in other words, contains contiguous elements of the basic set and is bounded within each of its ordered statements. The 'secondary dimension' spans each individual row form and represents the tetrachordal harmony of the melody (marked pitch-class set 4–2) and the complementary eight-note harmony of its accompaniment (marked pitch-class set 8–2).[26] Notice that the tetrachordal harmony of the melody contains pitches non-adjacent in the basic set (order-numbers 3, 4, 9, 10), but this

harmony is nonetheless equivalent to a linear segment of the basic set (order-numbers 6, 7, 8, 9). (Linear segments are marked on the basic set that appears at the bottom of figure 4.2, and 'equivalent' here means that they are not identical in pitch content, but are related by transposition or inversion, or both.) In other words, the melody of bars 12–13 unfolds a tetrachord containing pitches with the non-successive order numbers 3, 4, 9 and 10, but this harmony is equivalent to (being a transposition of) the tetrachord with the successive order numbers 6, 7, 8 and 9. Hereafter, 'secondary harmonic sets' refer to pitch-class sets such as these which structure secondary harmonic dimensions. Secondary harmonic sets can be derived from one or more forms of the basic set and always have non-successive order numbers, but are nonetheless equivalent to linear segments of the basic set. In bars 12–13, the secondary harmonic tetrachord (the melody, pitch-class set 4–2) contains pitches in the same order as the equivalent tetrachord in the basic set, but such identical ordering is rare. It does not occur, for example, in the secondary harmonic dimension that structures the accompaniment in bars 12–13.

There are a number of reasons why the harmonies of a basic set must include not only all of its linear segments but also the complements of these segments – in this example, why both the linear segment 4–2 and its complement pitch-class set 8–2 should be regarded as harmonies of the basic set. Pitch-class set 8–2 has order numbers 1, 2, 3, 4, 5, 10, 11, 12 and therefore represents a linear segment only if the basic set is taken as a kind of loop, so that order-numbers 12 and 1 are successive order numbers. The most important reason for accepting these round-the-corner segments as harmonies of the basic set can be inferred from 'Composition with Twelve Tones'. Here Schoenberg refers to the 'separate selection of the tones for their respective formal function, melody or accompaniment', thereby suggesting that pitches of the basic set function within one of two principal harmonic dimensions, as part of the melody or as part of the accompaniment.[27] Since any linear segment of the row can form the principal voice, the accompaniment always contains the complementary set, a set frequently composed of non-adjacent linear segments from both ends of the row. Thus, because complementary sets usually delineate the two principal harmonic dimensions of Schoenberg's music, we must regard as harmonies of the basic set the complements of all its linear segments. This conclusion is valid, of course, only if we accept his claim that a single basic set regulates all harmonies and their successions and can thereby produce an integrated musical texture.[28]

We can see now that, no less than the melody, the accompaniment in example 4.2 comprises a secondary harmonic dimension. But the internal structure of this secondary dimension serves to illustrate further a crucially important feature – that harmonies defined as equivalent to those of the basic set need not maintain the same internal ordering of their pitches. Notice that the accompaniment in each row form unfolds two tetrachords (pitch-class sets 4–11 and 4–24), each

Example 4.2 Op. 33b, bars 11–16

Row forms and order numbers marked

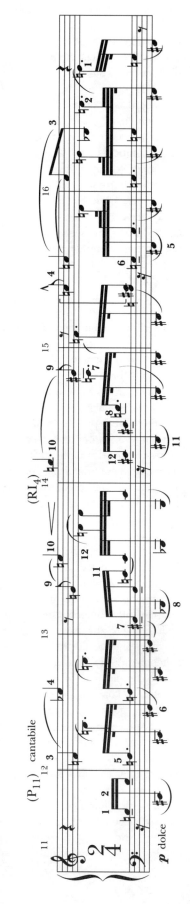

Figure 4.2 Order-number transcription with secondary harmonic sets

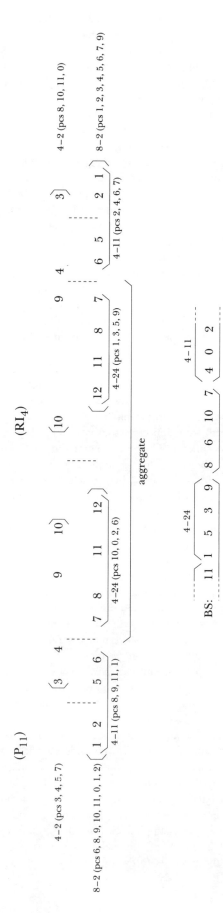

containing non-adjacent pitches in the basic set (order numbers 1, 2, 5, 6 and 7, 8, 11, 12). Both of these tetrachords are equivalent to linear segments of the basic set and thus represent secondary harmonic sets, but these sets, unlike the melody, do not duplicate the ordering of the basic set. The example demonstrates, then, that secondary harmonic sets, though equivalent to linear segments of the basic set, need not include the same succession of intervals. Example 4.2 also illustrates Schoenberg's use of an aggregate to provide an additional dimension of harmonic structure; here the aggregate links together the final hexachord of P_{11} with the initial hexachord of RI_4 (marked in figure 4.2). The aggregate, along with the complementary sets 4–2/8–2, thus comprises two secondary dimensions of harmonic structure derived from the basic set that serve to connect non-adjacent elements within and between successive row forms.

This example shows how Schoenberg could legitimately assert that a single twelve-tone row can integrate all harmonic and melodic dimensions of a composition, and also shows the rudimentary techniques implied by that assertion. Many composers and scholars have misunderstood, however, and complained that because pitches adjacent in the melody are not adjacent in the row Schoenberg imposed an extrinsic harmonic structure on his theme. The row itself must therefore be insufficient to generate a complete musical texture. Boulez never mentions this specific example, but it is easy to infer from his general argument what he would say. He would complain that Schoenberg's attempt to combine twelve-tone serialism with a typically tonal texture of theme and accompaniment led to arbitrary and contradictory restrictions. Boulez might argue, for instance, that the predominantly crochet pulse of the melody serves to separate it rhythmically from the faster accompaniment, but also thwarts a rhythmic and harmonic structure that is uniquely serial. Our analysis shows, however, how Schoenberg's multiple dimensions of harmonic structure delineate a four-bar phrase subdivided into two two-bar segments of equal length. The form and structure of this phrase thus is not an arbitrarily imposed tonal texture, but rather emerges from twelve-tone techniques alone.

Example 4.2 and figure 4.2 conveniently illustrate, then, three principles of twelve-tone harmonic structure that are worth reiterating. First, twelve-tone harmonies need not be simultaneous: they do not occur only in the vertical dimension. In 'two-or-more-dimensional space' no categorical distinction exists between the vertical and the horizontal, and harmonies are defined as pitches occupying the same 'spatial continuum'. In this example this concept allows Schoenberg to regard a tetrachord unfolded by the melody as a harmonic entity, even though its elements unfold successively.

Second, a single harmonic event necessarily affects *more* than one dimension. In this phrase, for instance, each pitch functions simultaneously in at least two different harmonic dimensions. This principle is confirmed by statements in 'Composition with Twelve Tones'.

Any particular melodic motion – for instance, a chromatic step – will not only have its effect upon the harmony, but on everything subsequent that is comprised within that spatial continuum.... This circumstance ... enables the composer to assign one part of his thinking to ... the vertical, and another in the horizontal.[29]

Because, in Schoenberg's view, musical ideas necessarily affect both vertical and horizontal dimensions, a composer must structure both simultaneously, and not merely attend to the unfolding of the row.

Third, and most important, the order of the twelve pitch-classes defines the harmonies of the basic set, but it defines them primarily by total intervallic content rather than by pitch-class content. Moreover, these harmonies need not be presented by the same succession of intervals as in the basic set, that is, the internal ordering of their pitches need not be the same. But because they are related by transposition or inversion or both, their total intervallic content will always be the same. These three principles of harmonic structure provide the foundation for analysing Schoenberg's twelve-tone music. Analysis of a specific piece needs, of course, to consider other essential features, such as motivic structure, rhythm, development and form; but, as I hope the following analysis demonstrates, these features derive from Schoenberg's method of structuring twelve-tone harmony.

3 MODEL

Analysis of a piece of twelve-tone music must begin with the basic set in itself and not in any of its particular occurrences in the piece. Schoenberg asserted that a basic set 'functions in the manner of a motive', and that therefore each piece requires a unique basic set, but these assertions can confuse inexperienced twelve-tone analysts because crucial differences distinguish a basic set from a motif. Most importantly, the basic set determines only those features that pertain both to pitch and to pitch-class relations. That is, the basic set governs how the twelve pitch-classes are used, but, unlike a motif, does not govern features related only to pitch, such as register or motivic contour. The local context in the piece governs these features, but not features that pertain to pitch-class relations which are predetermined and thereby assume greater structural importance. We should try to hear a twelve-tone piece, then, not only in itself, but also in reference to its basic set and to the operations of the twelve-tone system (transposition, inversion and retrogression).

The basic set determines both those features pertaining to pitch and pitch-class relations and the constituent harmonies of the piece. I have already set forth a definition of Schoenberg's twelve-tone harmony and his principle of harmonic structure, but I must emphasize that, while the basic set restricts the harmonies that can structure a piece, it does not determine which of these the composer actually uses. Schoenberg himself usually limits his structural harmonies to as few as ten or twelve in an entire piece or movement.

Schoenberg's criteria for choosing some structural harmonies from those determined by the basic set can sometimes be guessed from its overall succession of interval classes or from differences among the segments of its principal partitionings (that is, hexachordal, tetrachordal and trichordal). Such guesses may prove erroneous, but often they do reveal general features that convey the temporal unfolding of the basic set or create the piece's form. Op. 33b's basic set provides one such example, for on first hearing several features stand out that later prove crucial to analysis. First, because many of its three-, four- and five-note segments represent whole-tone sets, a whole-tone sound dominates its overall interval-class succession. This feature, however, pertains only to some of the segments derived from the three principal partitionings. Partitioning the set into two hexachords produces two versions of pitch-class set 6–34 – [11, 1, 5, 3, 9, 8] and [6, 10, 7, 4, 0, 2] – the 'almost' whole-tone hexachord that uses five of the six possible tones of a whole-tone scale. Partitioning into three tetrachords also produces predominantly whole-tone sets, since each tetrachord contains at least one three-note whole-tone segment: [11, 1, 5, 3], [9, 8, 6, 10] and [7, 4, 0, 2]. But trichordal partitioning produces a different result: of the four trichords, only the first and last represent whole-tone sets: [11, 1, 5], [3, 9, 8], [6, 10, 7] and [4, 0, 2]. Through this whole-tone feature, then, trichordal partitioning provides for temporal differentiation of the middle of the row from its beginning and end.

What means, if any, has Schoenberg used to differentiate the hexachords and tetrachords with their uniformly predominant whole tones? First, the basic set's two hexachords unfold the interval-class successions [2, 4, 2, 6, 1] and [4, 3, 3, 4, 2] which each contain unique interval classes, that is, ones absent from the other partition. Interval-classes 1 and 6 mark the one hexachord and two occurrences of interval-class 3 mark the other. Unique interval classes similarly differentiate the interval-class succession of the three tetrachords; the first, [2, 4, 2], progresses only by whole tones or their composite intervals, the second, [1, 2, 4], contains the single instance of interval-class 1 and the third, [3, 4, 2], the single instance of interval-class 3. (A listener may perceive this feature initially by hearing the strongest contrast between the first tetrachord, with its emerging tritone between order-numbers 1 and 3, and the last tetrachord, with its major/minor triad spanning order-numbers 9 to 11.) This kind of intervallic differentiation among the basic set's partitions is crucially important for hearing – as well as analysing – op. 33b, for it enables a listener to perceive the temporal progress of the basic set as it unfolds in any of its three principal partitions, even if he or she cannot at any given moment identify its exact transformation (that is, R, I or T).

This kind of general observation about the basic set often suggests related issues fruitful for analysis. Here, having observed how Schoenberg uses unique interval classes to differentiate partitions, we might well ask why he simultaneously maintains their uniformity through recurring whole-tone segments, and the question will reveal the use of a secondary harmonic structure such as those discussed in example 4.2. This one relies upon the association of non-adjacent dyads to form harmonies equivalent to linear segments of the basic set itself, and op. 33b's basic set proves to have remarkable properties of this type, which in turn rely upon the whole-tone segments recurring in the row. As figure 4.3 shows, if one partitions the basic set into six dyads, and then associates all pairs of non-adjacent dyads, more than half such associations (six out of ten) produce a tetrachord equivalent to a transposed or inverted linear segment of the row – that is, a secondary harmonic set. This illustrates, then, how analysis of the basic set's interval-class succession and principal partitions can suggest criteria that influence the composer's choice of structural harmonies. Analysis of the music itself would no doubt eventually reveal these criteria, but they may be concealed or emerge only late in the piece. But the issue is not just efficiency: getting the best results for the least analytical labour. The analyst needs to remember that the composer has created the basic set as well as the piece, and in that order.

Figure 4.3 Dyadic partitioning and derivation of secondary harmonies

P_{11}: 11 1 5 3 9 8 6 10 7 4 0 2

Dyads: 1   2   3   4   5   6

$Dyads$	$=$	$Tetrachord$	
1 + 3	=	4–11	(pcs 8, 9, 11, 1)
1 + 5	=	4–27	(pcs 1, 4, 7, 11)
1 + 6	=	4–1	(pcs 11, 0, 1, 2)
2 + 5	=	4–2	(pcs 3, 4, 5, 7)
3 + 6	=	4–Z15	(pcs 8, 9, 0, 2)
4 + 6	=	4–24	(pcs 10, 0, 2, 6)

P_{11}: 11 1 5 3 9 8 6 10 7 4 0 2

4–24   4–2   4–11
4–2   4–1
4–Z15   4–27

Example 4.3 Principal theme, op. 33b, bars 1–5

Rhythmic analysis

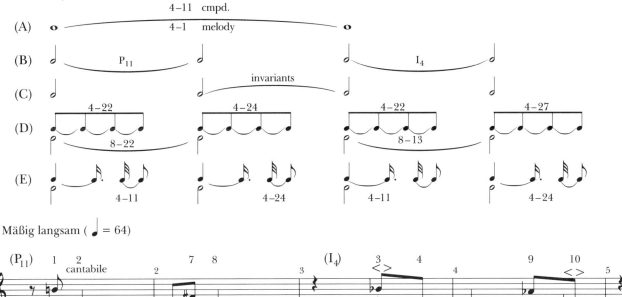

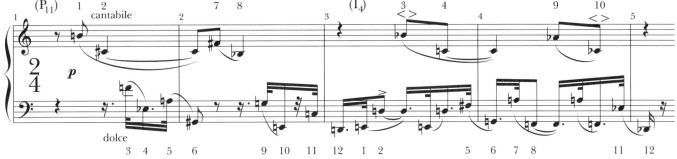

After studying the basic set, a twelve-tone analysis can proceed to the piece's important motifs or themes. In Schoenberg's music these usually appear at the beginning of the piece, or at the beginning of its principal sections. Let us for a moment consider beginnings in general, since they pose problems for composers that are often overlooked by analysts. Risking the obvious, one can advance several generalizations about what an effective beginning does. First, and most obvious, its beginning distinguishes a piece of music from other pieces; it presents features that make a piece itself. Second, a beginning usually implies criteria for inclusion and exclusion. That is, it specifies a compositional method – which techniques are admissible, and which are not – and thereby creates expectations in the listener that have been thought almost to constitute a contract between composer and listener. More specifically, a beginning usually implies rules for prolonging and developing motifs – that is, explicit or implicit modes of continuation. One mark of an effective beginning is the ability to generate continuations particular to the work it introduces.[30]

If we return from the safety of abstraction, Schoenberg's beginnings can be seen to illustrate well these generalizations. First, Schoenberg's beginnings usually set forth the regular ordering of the basic set, and since his method requires that

all a piece's melodies and harmonies derive from this set, his beginnings do introduce the basis of its identity. Similarly, only rarely do Schoenberg's beginnings lack secondary harmonic dimensions that will serve in turn to generate the overall form of the piece. Clear use of secondary harmonic dimensions at the beginning creates expectations about the kind of harmonic structures that will organize and continue the piece. Schoenberg's principal technique for building extended forms – what he terms 'developing variation' – in fact ensures that continuations fulfil the expectations promised by the beginning. In my view, the challenge to the twelve-tone analyst is to arrive at an understanding of how the music works in time on actual listeners. It may help to know how the piece was composed, but that is not the real goal. For these reasons, I want to begin by examining op. 33b's opening section and show how it leads to later continuations, thereby generating form. I will begin with harmonic structure and then move on to rhythmic and motivic structure. The result may seem a lengthy discussion of the piece's opening, but that discussion will be more helpful than any superficial survey. The first nine bars present the basic material that, varied and developed through the piece, creates op. 33b's form.

The form of op. 33b divides into two parts (bars 1–31 and

Figure 4.4

(a) Harmonic analysis (ONs)

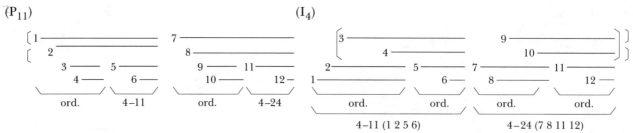

(b) Harmonic analysis (ONs) ♪'s

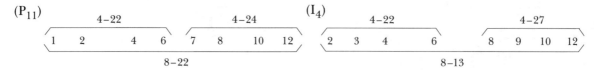

(c) Basic set (PCs)

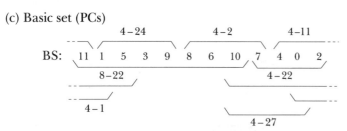

bars 32–56), followed by an extended coda-like passage (bars 57–68); only the first part divides clearly into sections (bars 1–18 and bars 19–31). Both parts employ two contrasting themes, the first derived from dyadic partitioning of the basic set and the second from trichordal partitioning. But their contrast extends beyond partitioning, for each uses a unique harmonic structure that Schoenberg varies and develops along with their distinctive rhythms and motifs.

The piece begins with the first theme (example 4.3), whose harmonic structure derives from the kind of properties shown in figure 4.4, and the texture highlights these properties. That is, by placing specific dyads in the right hand against those in the left, Schoenberg associates temporally dyads that are not connected in the row. Notice that, in this phrase, the left and right hands together unfold two ordered forms of the basic set, P_{11} and I_4. (These two row forms are combinatorially related (see figure 4.1) and are the only two used (along with their retrograde forms) in the entire piece.) Thus in the horizontal or primary dimension of the theme, the row is perfectly ordered; but in the vertical or secondary dimension, a kind of temporal re-ordering occurs. The first two pitches of the right hand, for example, are sustained to overlap with the fifth and sixth pitches in the left hand, thus creating the row segment 4–11. As figure 4.4a shows, each of the dyads extracted from the row and put into the melody creates this same kind

of secondary dimension. (In figure 4.4a, b and c and those following I mark only secondary harmonic dimensions; those harmonies that contain only successive order numbers are marked 'ordered'.) One can hardly imagine a texture that would exhibit this dyadic property of the basic set more strongly than this opening phrase.

The principal theme's rhythmic structure depends directly on this secondary or vertical harmonic dimension. To explain this, I need first to analyse its various rhythmic strata and then show how the interaction of these strata creates metre.[31] A general theory of musical rhythm in Schoenberg's music deals with the regular recurrence of related events. Rhythm is not abstract; one must speak of the rhythm of definite events, and those events must be related by similar features or analogous functions. Recurrence establishes a logical class of events in which an occurrence and all recurrences are members, and some criterion must specify this logical class. Criteria can include such features as quality of attack, dynamic level, timbre, and pitch or harmonic function. If events that belong to the same class recur at equal intervals of time, then they define a *rhythmic stratum*; they have a simple periodicity in which each recurrence begins a cycle that ends with the next recurrence. A rhythmic stratum thus contains more than one event; all its events recur at equal intervals of time, and all are characterized by the same criterion. In this example, I want to deal only with the rhythmic strata created by pitch or harmonic function.

First, the two ordered row forms, P_{11} and I_4, each spanning two bars, comprise the primary harmonic dimension and form a stratum (marked B in example 4.3) in which the recurrence interval is four beats. A second stratum (marked C) derives from the combinatorial property; each of the four successive hexachords spans two beats, or one half-bar, but the pitches contained in the second and third hexachords are identical, thus forming not an aggregate, but a type of pitch or hexachordal palindrome. These held or invariant pitches create a kind of syncopation, shown in stratum C, by the tie that slurs together the second and third minims. Of greater significance are the strata derived from the phrase's secondary harmonic dimensions. Consider, for example, how the secondary harmonic tetrachords discussed above help delineate the stratum marked E. They in fact are essential to this stratum, for the alternation of ordered tetrachords with secondary harmonic tetrachords creates a recurring pattern of durations that recurs every two beats. Moreover, in the second part of the phrase, these secondary harmonic tetrachords make explicit the pattern's two-beat interval of recurrence. Without these tetrachords and the secondary harmonic dimension they create, stratum E would not exist. And without stratum E (as well as stratum D, discussed below), the phrase would lose its duple metre. Any implied duple metre would be quite trivial, for it would derive merely from the hexachordal partitions and their periodic unfolding.

Several other secondary harmonic dimensions, ones that Schoenberg will develop later in the piece, reinforce the duple metre of this passage. Probably the most important emerges from the four melodic dyads in the right hand, creating the effect of a compound melody. The initial pitches of the four dyads, always higher in register, create the tetrachord marked 4–11, a linear segment of the row as well as the segment formed by the association of its first and third dyads (see figure 4.3). Likewise, the four second pitches, always lower in register, create tetrachord 4–1, again a linear segment of the row and the set formed by joining its first and last dyads. This secondary harmonic dimension is crucial to form, since it spans the entire phrase and joins its parts into a whole; its completion, then, creates a twelve-tone analogue to a tonal cadence.

A last harmonic dimension (figure 4.4b) again uses secondary harmonies displayed in figure 4.3. Although covert here, its secondary harmonies become increasingly important later in the piece. At the beginning they form a stratum (D) that reinforces the duple metre of strata B, C and E. Stratum D is formed by each pitch that occurs on the notated quaver pulse; in other words, stratum D contains all pitches except those that fall on the recurring demisemiquaver pick-ups. The secondary harmonic sets structuring this stratum are shown in figure 4.4b. Its successive secondary tetrachords (4–22, 4–24, 4–22, 4–27) form a stratum whose recurrence interval is minims. At the same time, successive tetrachords pair together to form two eight-note secondary harmonies, 8–22 and 8–13, and thereby create a stratum whose recurrence interval is four beats. The secondary dimensions of this stratum thus reinforce the duple metre established by those of strata C and D.

The secondary harmonic sets of this opening phrase and the duple metre they set forth introduce the principal harmonic and rhythmic features that Schoenberg employs through much of the piece. A third essential feature, motivic contour, can conclude our analysis of the principal theme. No less important than harmony and rhythm, motivic contour is more difficult to analyse. Unlike pitch-class and rhythmic relations, motivic contour does not lend itself to quantification. In Schoenberg's music, the associative and formal power of purely motivic features often seems to increase as they become more elusive, harder to define, as if their richness resides in flexibility or ambiguity. While I argue above that essential differences distinguish a basic set from a motif and that the pitch-class relations determined by the basic set have greater structural importance, I must emphasize that our perception of pitch-class relations, as well as the harmonic structures that derive from them, depends subtly on motivic contour. Op. 33b illustrates how Schoenberg uses motivic contour, first, to contrast the two principal themes, and then, as the piece progresses, to vary and develop their distinctive features – not just separately, but simultaneously. The motivic contours that at the beginning keep the principal themes separate serve at the end to bring them together and emphasize their common structures.

Only recently have analysts begun to investigate how motivic contour functions in twentieth-century music. I cannot offer a thorough discussion of this topic, but can present two tools for analysing motivic contour that prove especially useful in the analysis of twelve-tone music: Contour Adjacency Series and Contour Class.[32] Both are somewhat rudimentary, but do allow one to describe how, and to what degree, distinct contours relate to one another.

A Contour Adjacency Series (CAS) merely describes the ordered series of directional moves up and down ($+$, $-$) in a motif or theme. For example, the CAS for the first hexachord of P_{11}, bar 1, is $< -, +, -, +, - >$ and the CAS for the right hand, bars 1–2, is $< -, +, - >$ (see example 4.4). A CAS disregards immediately repeated pitches, and because it does not indicate the contour relation between non-consecutive pitches, does not indicate non-consecutive repeated pitches. That is, the CAS $< +, - >$ does not reveal whether the third pitch is identical to, or higher or lower than, the first. Thus CAS gives only a blunt description of a series of moves between temporally adjacent pitches.

Nonetheless, CAS can effectively describe a general kind of contour equivalence, one that can even include relations integral to the twelve-tone method itself (such as inversion and retrogression). For instance, if we compare the CASs for the four hexachords of the principal theme (right hand + left hand), we see that none are identical, but that two can

Example 4.4 Principal theme: CAS and CC analysis

be derived from one another: the retrograde of the second hexachord's CAS, $<-, -, -, +, ->$, produces that of the fourth hexachord, $<-, +, -, -, ->$. Thus CAS can reveal contour equivalencies among components, as well as provide a means of describing the contour structure they may comprise; in this contour structure, only the second and fourth among the theme's four components are related. Such a structure can be represented as: a–b–c–Rb. But a very different structure emerges if we compare these same four components using the CASs of the right- and left-hand motifs separately. The CAS for the right-hand motif in bars 1–2, $<-, +, ->$, is identical to that of bars 3–4; and this same CAS also marks all but one

(the third) of the four left-hand motifs. In contrast to the overall CAS, this CAS by hands reveals a highly repetitive structure in which only the third component stands out: a–a–b–a. CAS thus reveals two distinct yet simultaneous motivic structures in op. 33b's principal theme. A complete analysis of the piece will show that Schoenberg most often connects new motifs with earlier ones in ways discernible by analysing CAS. Either the CAS of the earlier motif or a contour structure derived from earlier motifs will recur.

Contour Class (CC) is a more precise tool for comparing motifs because it describes contour relations among all the pitches of a motif, not merely adjacent pitches, and also indicates repeated pitches. In a CC, o is the lowest pitch, and n–1 (n = the number of *different* pitches in a motif) is the highest pitch. Using integers to indicate overall registral position, a CC shows the relative registral position of a motif's consecutive pitches. For example, the CC of the right hand in bars 1–2 is <3–1–2–0>, whereas the CC of the theme's first hexachord (right hand + left hand) in bar 1 is <5–3–4–1–2–0> (see example 4.4). (If this motif included a repeated pitch, then its CC would show one integer occurring twice.)

Analysis of the principal theme in terms of Contour Class reveals several structures that coincide with some, but not all those revealed by Contour Adjacency Series. For example, the CC of the right hand in bars 1–2, <3–1–2–0>, recurs as the first, second and fourth CC of the left hand's four figures; only the CC of the third figure stands out. The resulting motivic structure, a–a–b–a, is the same as that arrived at through the CAS. CC reveals a second structure in the final four-note segment of each complete hexachord. If we reduce this segment as a four-element CC, a kind of rhyming pattern emerges that associates the endings of the first two hexachords and those of the last two, thus forming a contour structure that divides into two equal parts, a–a–b–b:

<5–3–4–1–2–0>   <5–4–3–1–2–0>
    <3–1–2–0>   <3–1–2–0>
      a   a

<0–2–5–4–3–1>   <3–1–5–4–2–0>
    <3–2–1–0>   <3–2–1–0>
      b   b

Like a–a–b–a, this contour structure also appears among those revealed by the CAS for these same hexachords. The CC and CAS of this theme agree in pointing towards the same contour structures and suggest the kind of reinforcement that makes them highly audible. The CAS structure, a–b–c–Rb, which has no CC equivalent, is less perceptible, at least to my ear. CCs and CASs can diverge or coincide. Taken together, the two tools can indicate not only various kinds of contour equivalence, but also the relative importance of the contour structures that result.

This brief discussion will suggest how CC and CAS can reveal several types of contour equivalence, as well as how these types can be related. In analysing Schoenberg's music, the two tools are particularly useful in understanding how the new motifs that often emerge towards the end of a piece are related to earlier motifs. In fact, motivic structures seem often to be subtly planted and left dormant, only to emerge late in the piece as Schoenberg seeks new sources for motivic development. In op. 33b, CC and CAS are particularly helpful because, as I will discuss later, they reveal features common to its two contrasting themes that never become obvious, although they serve later to develop both themes simul-

taneously. Before I take up this topic, however, let me conclude my discussion of the principal theme by explaining how its harmonic, rhythmic and motivic structure serves to develop and delimit the piece's first section (bars 1–18).

Immediately following the principal theme (bars 1–5), Schoenberg presents a second, contrasting theme (bars 5–10), which is followed by a brief transition (bars 10–11) leading into the varied repetition of the principal theme discussed in example 4.2. The harmonic structure of the principal theme and its varied repetition both derive from the association of non-adjacent dyads to form linear tetrachords of the row, those tetrachords shown in figure 4.3. On the surface, Schoenberg varies the principal theme in bars 10–16 by changing the contour and pitch-class content of its melody; inverting the contour of the original melody, bars 10–16 twice join dyads 2 and 5, whereas the original joined them only once. More importantly, the varied repetition, now using the retrograde of I_4, creates an aggregate to join its two forms. The changes in melodic contour are especially interesting here, but I must leave it to the reader to analyse how Schoenberg varies the contour structures revealed by the respective CASs and CCs. I do want to point out one method of variation here, because Schoenberg uses it repeatedly in his music. In the analysis of the opening theme I mentioned that the pitch-class invariants between the final hexachord of P_{11} and the first hexachord of I_4 (bars 2–4) create a pitch-class palindromic that spans the entire phrase. In the variation shown in example 4.2, Schoenberg blocks this palindrome and creates instead a horizontal aggregate joining the two row forms. Notice, however, that the changes in contour in the right hand re-create or transpose the palindrome to the melodic line and that, as in the beginning, the palindrome spans the entire phrase. (Both the CC and the CAS of the melody reveal this palindrome structure.) What sounds in the variation like a short, two-bar change in melodic contour, then, actually re-creates an earlier structure, presented by different means and spanning the entire five-bar theme. This example illustrates one aspect of Schoenberg's technique of developing variation: he seldom varies surface features without also developing structures previously set forth.

Figure 4.5 Melodic palindrome (ONs):

(RP_{11}) (I_4)

12   11   6   5   5   6   11   12
  4–Z15   4–Z15
                   4–1

The two-bar phrase that concludes the first section (bars 17–18) can illustrate this same generalization. Initially we might

Example 4.5 Final phrase of first section, bars 17–18

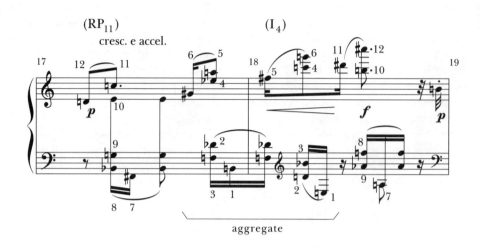

not hear this phrase as a variation of the principal theme since its overall texture and rhythm hardly recall the opening, but important features make it a fitting conclusion to the opening section. If we compare the secondary harmonic tetrachords that structure both the theme and its variation (examples 4.2 and 4.3) with those listed in figure 4.3, we will discover that only pitch-class set, 4–Z15 (formed by joining dyads 3 and 6), does not recur. Precisely these dyads and the resulting tetrachord 4–Z15 are what Schoenberg uses to structure the melody of the concluding phrase (see example 4.5). Only the contour of this melody recalls the principal theme and suggests a connection to the principal theme. Perhaps even more important, this final phrase uses both a pitch-class palindrome and an aggregate, features that separately structured the theme and its first variation. (The aggregate is self-evident; the pitch-class palindrome arises from the melody's overlapping secondary tetrachords, 4–Z15/4–1/4–Z15, figure 4.5, both of which appear as secondary tetrachords in figure 4.3.) Op. 33b's first section ends, then, just when the dyadic properties that Schoenberg exploits to create the theme's harmonic structure (those shown in figure 4.3) have been fully explored. What determines this major part of the whole form is not just sufficient variation of some idea, but sufficient development of that idea through variation.

Schoenberg builds the form of op. 33b first by presenting two highly contrasting themes, and then by developing their features independently. As shown above, the piece's first section focuses largely on the principal theme; similarly, its second section (bars 19–31) – which rounds out the form's first part – develops the second theme. Analysis of the second section will show that it develops exactly those features of the second theme that contrast most strongly with the first. Two of these features are most important: first, a harmonic structure derived from trichordal rather than dyadic partitioning of the row,

and second, a metre that uses a triple, rather than duple, division of the metrical pulse. (This change, occurring in bar 21, coincides with the notated change from 2/4 to 6/8 metre.) Finally, the second section presents both row forms simultaneously, rather than successively, again according with the second theme and contrasting with the first.

The melody of the second theme (right hand, bars 5–9) unambiguously sets forth a trichordal partitioning of the basic set (see example 4.6). In contrast to the uniform contour of the principal theme (right hand), the contour of the second theme is highly differentiated. Analysis using CAS and CC shows that, in the second theme, Schoenberg varies contour to create a palindrome motivic structure that spans the complete phrase, like those in bars 12–16 and 17–18. Unlike the first theme, the second theme lacks clear secondary harmonic dimensions that would create a distinctive harmonic structure. Its rhythms may seem to continue the duple metre established in the principal theme, but this impression is illusory, since no secondary harmonic dimensions work here to reinforce the duple metre. (The two aggregates that structure the second theme merely divide it approximately in half.) One clue does foreshadow the metre that the second theme will eventually adopt, however. Its palindromic motivic structure creates a rhythmic stratum containing three durations of approximately equal length (see top line of example 4.6), thus anticipating the forthcoming triple metre.

Except for the two vertical aggregates, the harmonic structure of the second theme lacks definition, largely because the repetitive texture of the accompaniment blocks the formation of unambiguous secondary dimensions. But, as in its metrical foreshadowing, the second theme does allude to the distinctive harmonic structure it will eventually assume. Figure 4.6a uses order numbers to show how the successive pitches in the theme's two row forms unfold horizontally. Notice that each

Example 4.6 Second theme, op. 33b, bars 5–10

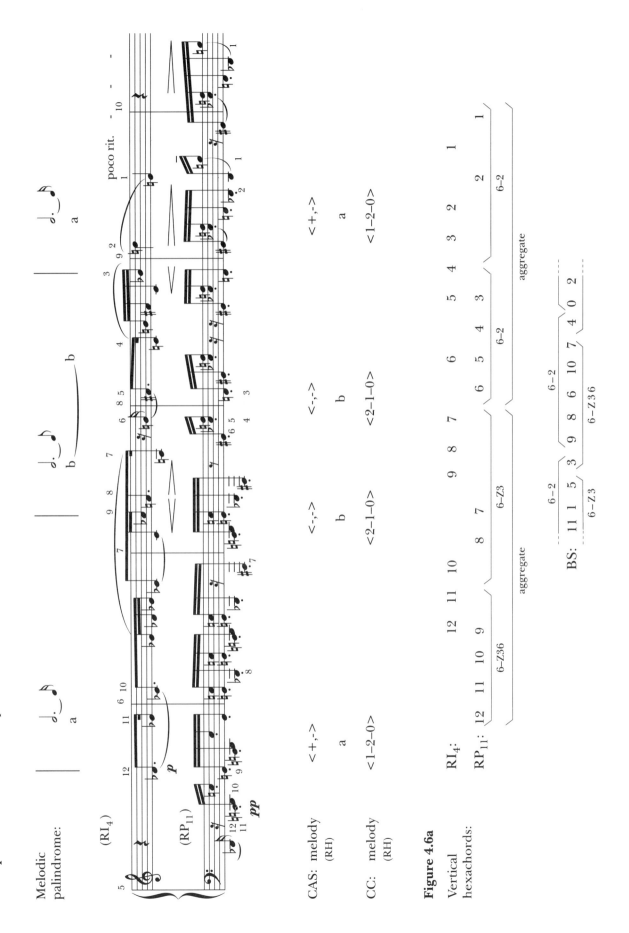

Melodic
palindrome:

CAS: melody
(RH)

CC: melody
(RH)

Figure 4.6a

Vertical
hexachords:

Example 4.7 Op. 33b, bars 10–11

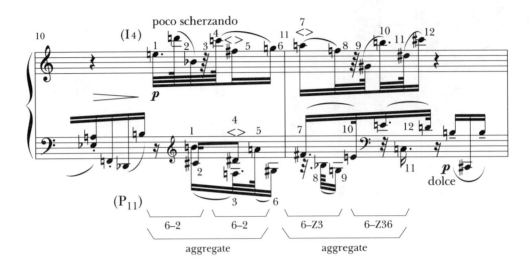

of the four vertical hexachords always contain, not three pitches from each row as one might expect, but two pitches from one and four from the other:

Figure 4.6b

(RI$_4$)	12	11				10	9	8	7		6	5			4	3	2	1
								:			:			:				
(RP$_{11}$)	12	11	10	9		8	7				6	5	4	3		2	1	

This design does create a secondary harmonic dimension comprised of the hexachords 6–Z36, 6–Z3, 6–2 and 6–2. As the piece progresses, precisely this secondary harmonic dimension will serve to differentiate the harmonic structure of the second theme's two vertical aggregates. In the two-bar phrase that immediately follows the second theme (bars 10–11), this distinctive harmonic structure becomes somewhat more explicit. As shown in example 4.7, this phrase reverses the order of the four secondary hexachords alluded to in the second theme (that is, 6–2, 6–2, 6–Z3, 6–Z36), thereby suggesting a long-range palindromic structure with the second theme that sets up the return of the principal theme in bar 11.

To conclude the analysis of the second theme, I want to suggest briefly that, despite the contrast between the piece's two themes and the resulting impression that they lack connection, the second theme nevertheless draws its distinctive motivic shape from components of the principal theme, in fact those that create the retrograde motivic structure discussed above (a–b–c–Rb). If the reader will work out the CAS and CC of the second and fourth hexachords of the principal theme, but partition each into two trichordal components, he or she will uncover the exact motivic structure that generates the melodic palindrome of the second theme. Schoenberg's desire to make this connection audible may, in fact, account

for the abrupt juxtaposition of the two themes, unusual in his twelve-tone works.

To explain how Schoenberg develops his second theme, I need to pause for a moment to qualify some previous assertions, and to introduce one further compositional technique. This added complexity is, I believe, essential to understanding how Schoenberg builds twelve-tone forms beyond their openings. The model analysis I have presented so far cannot reveal how form develops in Schoenberg's works, nor what brings them to a satisfactory conclusion.

I hope the reader has grasped the derivation of structural harmonies from linear segments of the basic set, but Schoenberg also uses a second technique to derive harmonies, not from the internal structure of the basic set, but from invariant segments occurring between specific inversions and transpositions of the basic set. The first technique develops the intervallic structure of the basic set; the second develops a group of specific transformations of that same basic set and elegantly solves the compositional problem of relating the form of a piece to its generative row forms.[33]

These new structural harmonies, termed 'invariant harmonies', almost always emerge in the latter half of long sections or towards the ends of movements. They seem to provide a source for the motivic and harmonic variety needed to generate large-scale form. To put it another way, they keep forms from becoming too repetitive. Schoenberg's technique of deriving invariant harmonies is simple and elegant; he merely joins invariant segments that occur between two row forms in order to create larger harmonies which then serve, like secondary harmonies, to structure secondary harmonic dimensions. Also like secondary harmonies, invariant harmonies are not restricted to a single ordering or a specific pitch-class content. Let me give a simple example of invariant harmonies, and then proceed to a more complex example in op. 33b. Consider the two forms of a basic set given in figure 4.7, in which some, but not all, of their invariant segments are underlined:

Figure 4.7

P₄: 4 3 1 7 <u>2 5</u> 0 6 9 <u>8 11</u> 10

P₁₀: 10 9 7 1 <u>8 11</u> 6 0 3 <u>2 5</u> 4

                4–28   4–28

Joining these two invariant segments (pitch-classes 2, 5 and 8, 11) produces the 'diminished seventh' tetrachord, pitch-class set 4–28, which is not a linear segment of the basic set. This new tetrachord is an 'invariant harmony' and can be used, like a secondary harmony, as an unordered pitch-class set to structure secondary harmonic dimensions.

Invariant harmonies, as well as secondary harmonies, serve in op. 33b to develop the second theme beginning in the second section of Part I. But because op. 33b uses only two row forms which do not have any invariant segments (except their combinatorial hexachords), Schoenberg devises an artificial source of invariant segments. These artificial invariants then produce two invariant harmonies, pitch-class set 6–1 [0, 1, 2, 3, 4, 5] and pitch-class set 6–8 [0, 2, 3, 4, 5, 7], which in turn structure many secondary harmonic dimensions.

The invariant harmony represented by pitch-class set 6–1 emerges beginning in bar 21 as follows.[34] The first hexachord of one row form occurs in two separately stemmed voices, each containing three non-consecutive pitches in the row; the three non-consecutive pitches in both voices duplicate trichordal segments of the second hexachord of the other row form. Together, these two invariant trichords create two occurrences of pitch-class set 6–1. Figure 4.8 illustrates this technique:

Figure 4.8

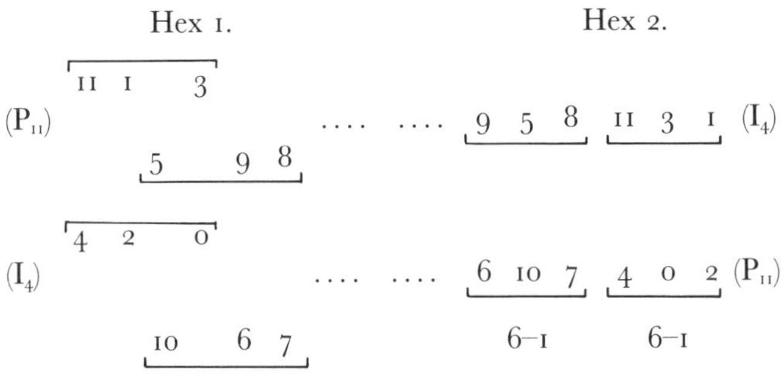

The same technique applied to the second hexachord of each row form produces the second invariant harmony, pitch-class set 6–8, as illustrated by figure 4.9.

Figure 4.9

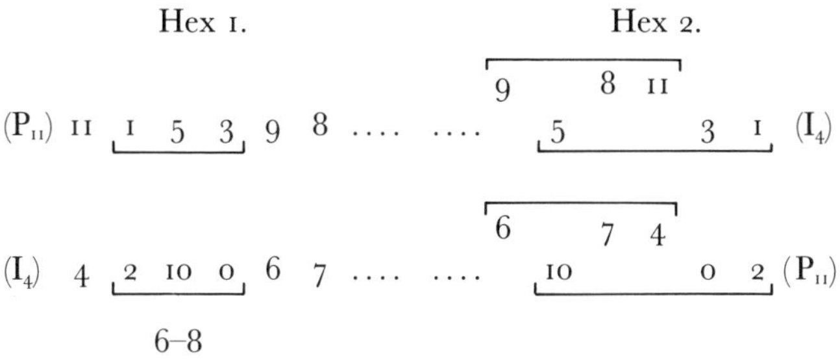

Having derived these two invariant harmonies, Schoenberg then devises three segmentations of the row, each again presented in voices that join three non-consecutive pitches, to produce these two invariant harmonies simultaneously in multiple secondary dimensions (see figure 4.10). (As one might expect, these three segmentations include both of the hexachords noted in the above diagrams.) Among the twelve trichords formed by the separate voices of these three segmentations, all but two represent secondary trichords, that is, trichords equivalent to linear segments of the row. Because these invariant harmonies derive from secondary harmonies, in using them Schoenberg ensures at least two simultaneous secondary harmonic dimensions. We are now equipped to discover exactly how these invariant harmonies and multiple dimensions work in op. 33b.

I shall skip for the moment the short two-bar transition that begins the second section and discuss instead the following two phrases (bars 21–4), in which Schoenberg first develops his second theme by means of invariant harmonies derived from the three segmentations given in figure 4.10. The phrases appear in example 4.8 and an order-number transcription in figure 4.11. The transcription marks with horizontal brackets the trichords of the separately stemmed voices and also shows how the trichords join to form multiple occurrences of the invariant harmonies 6–1 and 6–8. In addition to these two invariant harmonies, one secondary harmony, hexachord 6–2, helps develop the second theme. Schoenberg produces the numerous occurrences of hexachord 6–2 by joining separately stemmed trichords from different row forms. This hexachord is important, since it makes explicit the connection between these two phrases and the second theme. As discussed above, the secondary harmony 6–2 differentiates the harmonic structure of the second theme's final aggregate (see examples 4.6 and 4.7).

Figure 4.11 shows how the development of the second theme employs what we might call a twelve-tone analogue of invertible counterpoint. The separately stemmed trichords move freely through the voices (S, A, T, B), always pairing to form the invariant hexachords 6–1 and 6–8, and the secondary hexachord 6–2. One important exception needs to be explained, for it reveals Schoenberg's overriding interest in devising

Figure 4.10 Three row segmentations for invariant harmonies

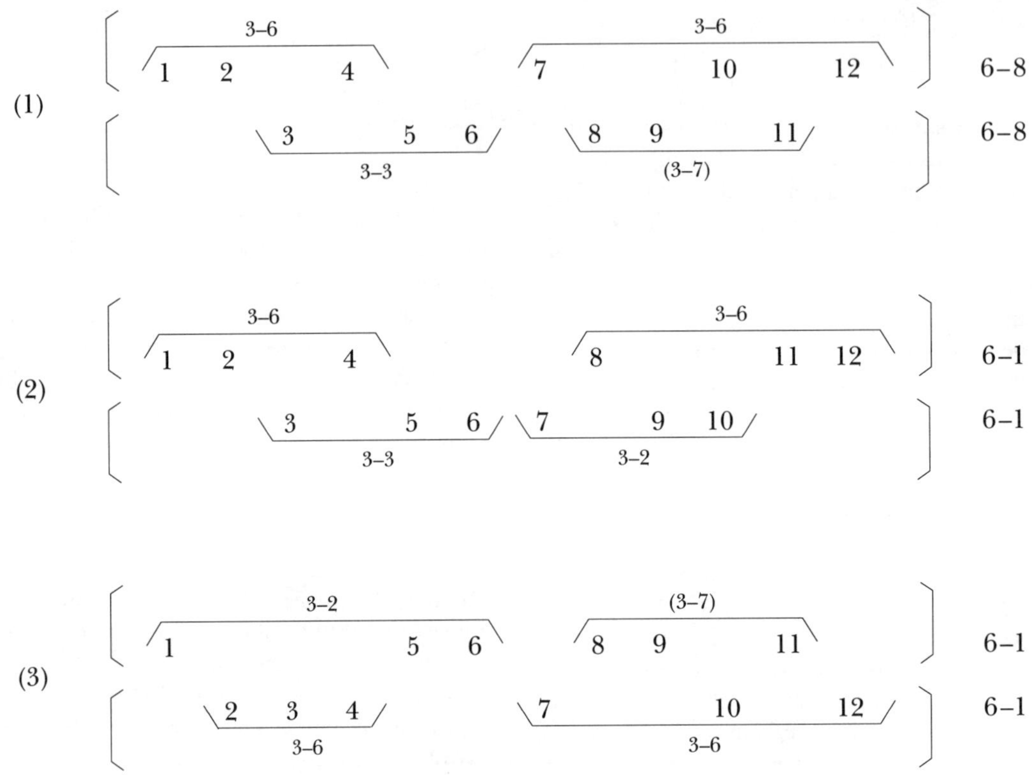

long-range secondary dimensions that can join successive row forms into a single phrase. As figure 4.11 shows, the soprano and alto in bar 22 do not project forms of the invariant harmony 6–1, but rather pitch-class set 6–33, a hexachord that is neither secondary nor invariant and receives little emphasis in the piece. We can explain this inconsistency if we analyse the melodic line that spans bars 21–2. In fact, this specific line recalls most strongly the second theme, since both consist of four partitioned trichords unfolded successively. In the second theme these trichords represented an ordered presentation of the row, but here they are all secondary harmonic sets. Nonetheless, all four secondary trichords join to form the secondary harmony 8–22, identical to the first eight-note segment of the row. If bar 22 followed the pattern of bar 21 (forming the invariant harmony 6–1 by switching the trichords in the soprano and alto at the end of bar 22), the melodic line that spans bars 21–2 would not represent a secondary or invariant harmony, and thus no secondary dimension would unify the bars into a single phrase. The melody that spans the following two-bar phrase (bars 22–3) strongly suggests that Schoenberg intentionally structured the melody in this way.

Again using four secondary harmonic trichords, it too unfolds a large secondary harmony, this time pitch-class set 8–1. As in bars 21–2, only this secondary dimension makes these two bars a single phrase.

I now shall return to the two-bar transition that begins the second section in order to explain how it prepares for the development of the second theme, as well as foreshadows the developmental technique employed in Part II. This short transition combines unique features of both themes, but does not yet make use of invariant harmonies. The dyadic partitioning of its four successive row forms recalls the first time, but the trichordal partitioning of its melody, as well as its motivic contour, strongly suggest the second (see example 4.9). Superficially, then, the phrase seems to allude to both themes, but its secondary harmonic dimensions move the phrase away from the first theme and closer to the second, achieving an effect not unlike a tonal modulation between keys. The harmonic structure of the first theme relies principally on secondary harmonic tetrachords, we found, and that of the second on secondary harmonic hexachords. But in this phrase, the dyadic partitions that allude to the first theme do not uniformly

Example 4.8 Part I, section two, invariant harmonies

(a)

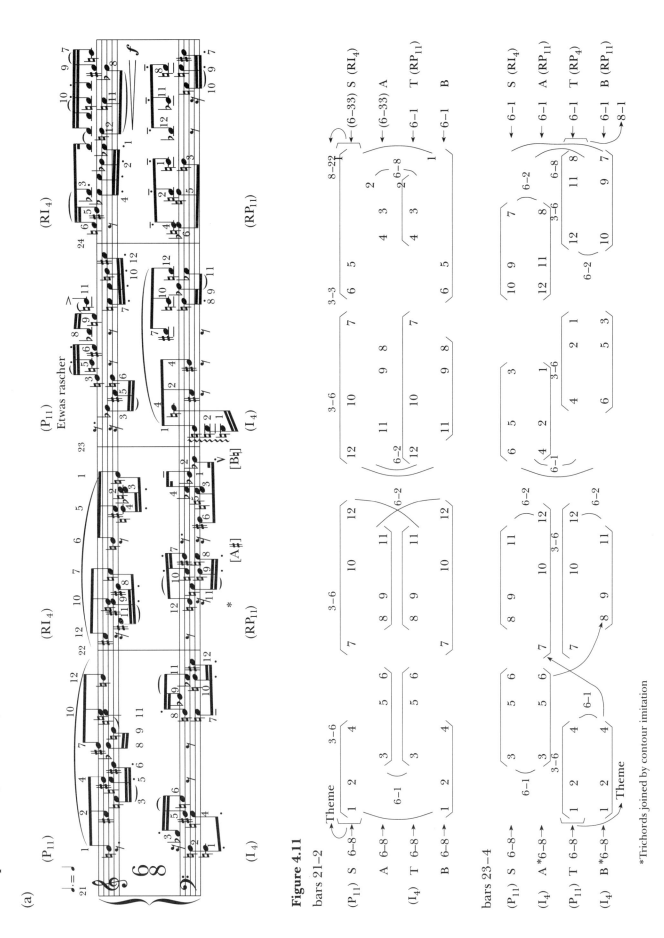

Figure 4.11

bars 21–2

bars 23–4

*Trichords joined by contour imitation

Example 4.9 Part I, section two, transition (bars 19–20)

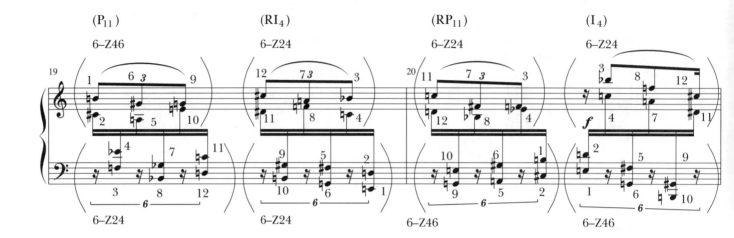

form secondary tetrachords, but rather secondary hexachords (6–Z24, 6–Z46), so that the secondary harmonic structure suggests the second theme. Together with the secondary trichords that structure its melodic line (3–3, 3–3, 3–5, 3–11), this phrase more deeply resembles the second theme and prepares the listener for the intense development of the second theme that follows. At least as important, the simultaneous allusion to both themes points towards op. 33b's second part, where Schoenberg uses a new technique for developing and relating his themes. This technique is crucial to the form of the piece because, by distinguishing the two parts from one another, it makes the second part not just a variation on the first, but a continuation or development; thus op. 33b does not consist of two related parts, but one whole.

Part II introduces no new structural harmonies. As in Part I, the six secondary tetrachords of the first theme (see figure 4.3) and the five secondary or invariant hexachords of the second theme (6–Z3, 6–Z36, 6–2, 6–2) continue to structure multiple secondary harmonic dimensions. But unlike the phrases of Part I, which developed the two themes separately, those of Part II almost without exception develop features of both simultaneously. I only have space to give one example, which I hope will serve the reader as a model for analysing phrase structure throughout Part II.

Part II opens with a five-bar phrase that begins sounding like a varied reprise of the principal theme. After the first three bars, however, the texture slowly transforms, until by the last bar the rhythm and contour of the upper voice clearly recall the second theme. This melodic reference to both themes would remain superficial – merely a clever manipulation of motivic contour and rhythm – were it not for the secondary harmonic dimensions that structure the accompaniment. As example 4.10 shows, the new and rather

dense texture of the accompaniment joins with the melody to form a series of vertical secondary harmonies, all of which strongly recall either of the two principal themes. The phrase begins with two occurrences of pitch-class set 8–12, followed by pitch-class set 8–21, and ends with pitch-class set 8–Z15 – all complements of tetrachordal row segments that have been featured prominently in the principal theme and its variations. (For instance, in example 4.5 notice how pitch-class set 8–Z15 prominently structures the accompaniment against the melodic dyads forming pitch-class set 4–Z15.) The middle of the phrase contains three occurrences of the secondary hexachord 6–2, whose association with the second theme has already been discussed. One last secondary harmony, hexachord 6–34, is the principal hexachord of the basic set. The allusion to both themes in this phrase, then, is more than superficial: it runs also in the deepest levels of harmonic structure.

This double allusion to the two themes becomes a synthesis in the Coda, which I would particularly encourage readers to analyse for themselves. The texture Schoenberg devises for its initial phrase (bars 57–60) brilliantly integrates all of the two themes' principal harmonies: not only the second theme's hexachords 6–Z3 and 6–Z36 along with the large eight-note complements occurring at the beginning of Part II, but also secondary tetrachords set forth by a new melodic imitation between bass and soprano. Regardless how we join the motifs of this complex and elusive texture, we will hear one of the limited number of harmonies that structure the entire piece.

Especially to beginners, serial music can easily seem to have the least unified of all forms – just an arbitrary and unordered set of variations on the series. One way to grasp the aesthetic wholeness of op. 33b, as well as the meaning of Schoenberg's term 'developing variation', is to imagine hearing or playing

Example 4.10 Part two, first phrase, bars 32–6

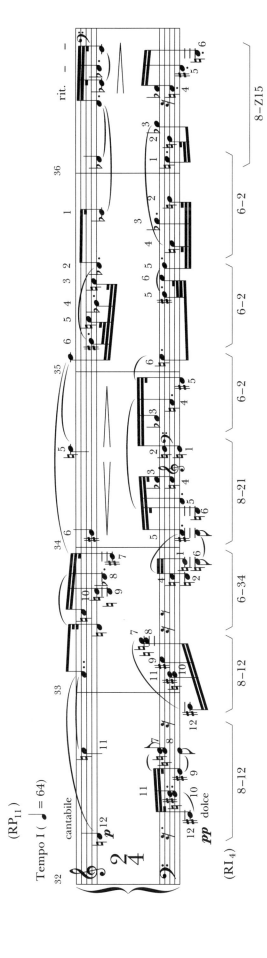

the two parts in reverse order. Part II would be an incomprehensible jumble. No phrase in Part II (possibly excepting bars 52–4) presents either theme in clear association with 'its' harmonies, as in Part I. No one, I should think, could recognize the form of the piece if confronted with the synthesis before the thesis and antithesis. I have not had space or inclination to present a 'complete' analysis of op. 33b, and to my mind a complete analysis is not one that plods through every bar, but one that grasps the piece's completeness. I have left much for my reader to do in following out and testing this analysis, but I hope I have provided the essential tools.

4 CODA

Some pages ago I suggested that musical analysis aims at understanding how music works on actual listeners, and I should like to conclude by following out an obvious implication of that suggestion. If analysis invokes, not ideal, but actual listeners, then they must listen to actual, not ideal, performers. What can the analyst of op. 33b learn from actual performances? What, in turn, can an analysis like this one teach performers?

Let us focus these questions on the opening phrase of op. 33b and approach them through two well-known recordings that offer an instructive contrast in use of the pedal and articulation of melody and accompaniment, performance issues crucial to how, or if, we hear harmonic structure or metre. The recordings are by Maurizio Pollini and Eduard Steuermann.[35] If you have access to them, listen particularly for differences in pedalling and in projection – or relative balance in tone – between the opening theme and accompaniment. Otherwise, you will have to rely on my description.

However we react to these two performances, some general comparisons seem clear. Pollini produces a much smoother, more beautiful tone. He keeps rhythms fairly regular and clearly separates melody from accompaniment. The melody, in the right hand, sounds decidedly louder than the softer – or 'dolce' – accompaniment. Moreover, the melody is projected by a highly legato touch, reminiscent perhaps of Chopin. Pollini often uses the pedal, probably to ensure an even left-hand legato. The variation of the opening phrase in bar 11 uses much wider and faster leaps in the left hand – and just here the pedalling becomes pronounced and extended, probably to match the left-hand legato of the opening.

By contrast, Steuermann's recording sounds quirkier, even eccentric. Rhythms are jagged and irregular, articulations more varied, and the accompaniment often seems as loud as the melody. There is almost no pedalling. Whatever composer Steuermann's playing might recall, it is certainly not Chopin.

In light of our analysis of this theme, which performance best accords with its harmonic and metrical structure? The answer must be Steuermann's, which our analysis makes more

comprehensible if not clearly superior. By equalizing the tone of the left and right hands, Steuermann makes it easier to hear the vertical tetrachordal harmonies that structure the phrase's secondary harmonic dimensions and are essential to its duple metre. Schoenberg's dynamic markings may themselves suggest this balance: the 'piano' appearing between the systems seems to refer to both parts, and the 'dolce' in the left hand could be achieved other than by a softer dynamic – for example, with contrasting articulations.

The question of pedalling seems even clearer. Any extended use of the pedal emphasizes one harmonic dimension over another, especially when they overlap or intersect, as in this example. Pedalling according to the right hand will obscure or obliterate many of the harmonic dimensions marked in figure 4.4a. Pollini's light pedalling in the first phrase forces him to use more in its variation, where the pedal works against and, to my ear, obscures these secondary harmonic structures.

Eduard Steuermann studied composition with Schoenberg and became a disciple, friend and musical confidant. He gave the first performances of most of Schoenberg's piano pieces (and chamber pieces with piano). Steuermann's rendition of op. 33b is therefore more than just one early performance. It is one the composer is known to have approved; it has something like the status of a document: a sketch, a letter, a performance score.[36] To question whether Steuermann's performance might corroborate our analysis is therefore in a small way to undo some of the breaches that, at least in America, divide our discipline, to play for a moment all three parts in the trio of those whose profession is interpreting music.

NOTES

1 Allan Janik and Stephen Toulmin, *Wittgenstein's Vienna* (New York: Simon and Schuster, 1973); Carl E. Schorske, *Fin-de-Siècle Vienna: Politics and Culture* (New York: Alfred A. Knopf, 1961).
2 Stefan Zweig, *The World of Yesterday: An Autobiography*, (New York: Viking Press, 1943), p. 280.
3 Janik and Toulmin, *Wittgenstein's Vienna*, pp. 239–55.
4 Arnold Schoenberg, 'Composition with Twelve Tones (1)', in *Style and Idea*, ed. Leonard Stein, trans. Leo Black (New York: St Martins Press, 1975), p. 218.
5 Schoenberg, 'Composition with Twelve Tones', pp. 217–18.
6 H. H. Stuckenschmidt, *Arnold Schoenberg: His Life, World and Work*, trans. Humphrey Searle (New York: Macmillan, 1978), p. 277.
7 Schoenberg, 'My Evolution', in *Style and Idea*, p. 88.
8 Schoenberg, 'Composition with Twelve Tones', p. 219.
9 Ibid., p. 219.
10 Scepticism about the harmonic structure of Schoenberg's twelve-tone compositions began during Schoenberg's life and has continued until the present. The following items can be said to represent it fairly: Ernst Krenek, 'New Developments of the Twelve-Tone Technique', *Music Review*, 4 (1943), pp. 81–97; Peter Stadlen, 'Serialism Reconsidered', *The Score*, 22 (1958), pp. 12–27; Seymour Shifrin, 'A Note from the Underground', *Perspectives of New Music*, 1 (1962), pp. 152–3; George Perle, *Twelve-tone Tonality* (Berkeley and Los Angeles: University of California Press, 1977), pp. 23–4.

11 Pierre Boulez, 'Schoenberg is Dead', *The Score*, 6 (1952), pp. 18–22. See also Boulez, *Notes of an Apprenticeship* (New York: Alfred A. Knopf, 1968) and *Conversations with Célestin Deliège* (London: Eulenburg, 1976).

12 Boulez, 'Schoenberg is Dead', p. 20.

13 Ibid., p. 21. See also 'Trajectories: Ravel, Stravinsky, Schoenberg' in *Notes of an Apprenticeship*, pp. 256–8.

14 Bryan R. Simms, *Music of the Twentieth Century: Style and Structure* (New York: Schirmer, 1986), p. 172.

15 Charles Wuorinen, *Simple Composition* (New York and London: Longman, 1979), p. 15.

16 Ibid., p. 3.

17 Ibid., p. 6.

18 Ibid., pp. 8–9.

19 Schoenberg, 'Composition', pp. 218–19.

20 Schoenberg, 'Composition with Twelve Tones (2)' in *Style and Idea*, pp. 246–7. This short essay is undated, but evidence suggests that it was written after 1946 and perhaps as late as 1948.

21 My technical terms and definitions largely follow those of Allen Forte, *The Structure of Atonal Music* (New Haven, CT, and London: Yale University Press, 1973) and Bo Alphonce, 'The Invariance Matrix' (dissertation, Yale University, 1974). *Pitch-class* denotes all pitches of the same relative position in all octave transpositions of a twelve-tone scale. The twelve pitch-classes are designated by the integers 0 through 11.

22 *Total intervallic content* refers to the collection of interval-class representatives formed by taking the absolute value differences of all pairs of elements of a pitch-class set. The twelve intervals reduce to six *interval classes*, designated by the integers 1 to 6 (the interval 11 is designated by interval-class 1, interval 10 by interval-class 2, and so forth). Total intervallic content requires the calculation of intervals between all unordered pairs of pitch-class integers in a given pitch-class set and the conversion of the resulting numbers to interval-class integers, where required. For example, to derive the total intervallic content of a given tetrachord, one must calculate a total of six intervals expressed as interval classes. The total intervallic content can be shown as an ordered array of numerals enclosed in square brackets which is termed the *interval vector*. The first numeral gives the number of intervals of interval-class 1, the second gives the number of intervals of interval-class 2, and so forth. For example, the interval vector [121110] designates a tetrachord that has one interval of interval-class 1, two of interval class 2, and so forth.

23 Schoenberg, 'Vortrag / 12 T K / Princeton', ed. Claudia Spies, *Perspectives of New Music*, 12 (1974), p. 83.

24 In 'Composition with Twelve Tones' Schoenberg only discusses hexachordal combinatoriality, even though this property can pertain to trichords and tetrachords.

25 This horizontal aggregate is conventionally termed a 'secondary set', but because this term overlaps with what I call a 'secondary harmonic set' I use 'aggregate' to refer to both types (that is, horizontal and vertical).

26 See chapter 6.

27 Schoenberg, 'Composition with Twelve Tones', p. 234.

28 For a more complete discussion of the reasons why we must regard as harmonies of the basic set the complements of all its linear segments, see my *Schoenberg's Twelve-Tone Harmony: The Suite Op. 29 and the Compositional Sketches*, Studies in Musicology, ed. George Buelow (Ann Arbor, MI: UMI Research Press, 1982), pp. 9–11.

29 Schoenberg, 'Vortrag / 12 T K / Princeton', p. 88.

30 For a more extensive discussion of how beginnings work in Schoenberg's twelve-tone music, see my 'A Theory of Twelve-Tone Meter', *Music Theory Spectrum*, 6 (1984), pp. 14–51.

31 I have presented here only a rudimentary description of metre in Schoenberg's twelve-tone music; for a more thorough discussion, see my 'A Theory of Twelve-Tone Meter'. The reader should not assume that metre structures the twelve-tone music of composers such as Webern and Berg. Rather, it seems that each devises unique methods for structuring rhythm. This apparent lack of consensus, however, should not discourage the reader from trying to answer how rhythm works in twelve-tone compositions.

32 For a fuller discussion of these analytical tools, as well as an original and important discussion of contour in Schoenberg's twelve-tone music, see Michael L. Friedman, 'A Methodology for the Discussion of Contour: Its Application to Schoenberg's Music', *Journal of Music Theory*, 29 (1985), pp. 223–48.

33 For a more extensive discussion of Schoenberg's use of invariant harmonies and their relation to form, see my 'Musical Form and the Development of Schoenberg's Twelve-Tone Method', *Journal of Music Theory*, 29 (1985), pp. 85–143.

34 I am indebted to Wayne Petty for having first noticed how Schoenberg creates artificial invariants in op. 33b.

35 Edward Steuermann, 'Schoenberg: Complete Piano Music', Columbia Masterworks, ML 5216, *c.* 1945; Maurizio Pollini, 'The Piano Works of Arnold Schoenberg', Hamburg: Deutsche Grammophon, 423 249–2, *c.* 1988.

36 Schoenberg worked extensively with Steuermann in preparation for the performance of his piano works and enthusiastically endorsed his pianistic abilities. In light of this relationship, we might give due weight to Steuermann's comments published with this recording, which are particularly revealing about this passage from op. 33b:

> The novelty and originality of Schoenberg's piano style is often overlooked.... The pianist is confronted with new problems. It is mainly the extremely scarce use of pedal which often deprives the sound of the romantic vibration for which the piano is known, and the polyphony requires the most exact differentiation by the use of all kinds of touch.

BIBLIOGRAPHY

Alphonce, Bo, 'The Invariance Matrix' (dissertation, Yale University, 1974).

Boulez, Pierre, 'Schoenberg is Dead', *The Score*, 6 (1952), pp. 18–22.

——, *Notes of an Apprenticeship* (New York: Alfred A. Knopf, 1968).

——, *Conversations with Célestin Deliège* (London: Eulenburg, 1976).

Forte, Allen, *The Structure of Atonal Music* (New Haven, CT, and London: Yale University Press, 1973).

Friedman, Michael L., 'A Methodology for the Discussion of Contour: Its Application to Schoenberg's Music', *Journal of Music Theory*, 29 (1985), pp. 223–48.

Hyde, Martha, *Schoenberg's Twelve-Tone Harmony: The Suite Op. 29 and the Compositional Sketches*, Studies in Musicology, ed. George Buelow (Ann Arbor, MI: UMI Research Press, 1982).

——, 'A Theory of Twelve-Tone Meter', *Music Theory Spectrum*, 6 (1984), pp. 14–51.

——, 'Musical Form and the Development of Schoenberg's Twelve-Tone Method', *Journal of Music Theory*, 29 (1985), pp. 85–143.

Janik, Allan, and Toulmin, Stephen, *Wittgenstein's Vienna* (New York: Simon and Schuster, 1973).

Krenek, Ernst, 'New Developments of the Twelve-Tone Technique', *Music Review*, 4 (1943), pp. 81–97.

Perle, George, *Twelve-tone Tonality* (Berkeley and Los Angeles: University of California Press, 1977).

Schoenberg, Arnold, 'Vortrag / 12 T K / Princeton', ed. Claudia Spies, *Perspectives of New Music*, 12 (1974), pp. 00–00.

——, 'Composition with Twelve Tones (1)', in *Style and Idea*, ed. Leonard Stein, trans. Leo Black (New York: St Martins Press, 1975), pp. 214–45.

——, 'Composition with Twelve Tones (2)', in *Style and Idea*, pp. 245–9.

——, 'My Evolution', in *Style and Idea*, pp. 79–92.

Schorske, Carl E., *Fin-de-Siècle Vienna: Politics and Culture* (New York: Alfred A. Knopf, 1961).

Shifrin, Seymour, 'A Note from the Underground', *Perspectives of New Music*, 1 (1962), pp. 152–3.

Simms, Bryan R., *Music of the Twentieth Century: Style and Structure* (New York: Schirmer, 1986).

Stadlen, Peter, 'Serialism Reconsidered', *The Score*, 22 (1958), pp. 12–27.

Stuckenschmidt, H. H., *Arnold Schoenberg: His Life, World and Work*, trans. Humphrey Searle (New York: Macmillan, 1978).

Wuorinen, Charles, *Simple Composition* (New York and London: Longman, 1979).

Zweig, Stefan, *The World of Yesterday: An Autobiography* (New York: Viking, 1943).

5

Tonality and the Series: Berg

CRAIG AYREY

I   ORIENTATION

From the standpoint of the historical evolution of style the topic 'Tonality and the Series' implies an antithesis. Schoenberg's final formulation in 1925 of the rules of twelve-tone composition, using a series of all twelve pitch-classes 'related only to one another', was a solution to the problems and limitations (as he saw them) of free atonality; this in turn was both a natural outgrowth of the chromatic tonality of the late nineteenth-century (in Wagner, Wolf, Mahler, Richard Strauss and early Schoenberg) and an attempt to renew what seemed to have become a decadent and therefore impoverished musical language. Historically, then, twelve-tone composition appeared as the furthest point in a progression away from the hegemony of functional tonality in Western music.

However, once the twelve-tone system had been established in theory, both Schoenberg and Alban Berg (1885–1935), his pupil until 1910, explored the possibilities of constructing or manipulating a series to incorporate triadic features or to provide a serial work with a triadic, if not tonally prepared,

goal. In Schoenberg's *Ode to Napoleon* (1942), for example, the series is constructed in a way that limits the 48 serial permutations usually available (under the operations of transposition, inversion and retrograde) to only four non-equivalent forms. Example 5.1 shows the series divided into two equivalent hexachords, each of which can be segmented to produce four interlocking triads, a property increasingly exploited as the piece progresses. This leads to a logical, serially prepared and therefore non-arbitrary arrival at the final cadence on an E♭ major triad.

The series of many of Berg's twelve-tone works contain triadic configurations, yet 'tonality' in these works is just as elusive as in Schoenberg. In general, the structure of Berg's series produces sweetly triadic passages or sections within a work which nevertheless seem to lack the goal direction essential to functional or extended tonality. Berg's Violin Concerto (1935) is well-known for the explicit triadic features of its series (shown in example 5.2a) constructed as a progression of overlapping statements of dominant-related triads (G minor, D major, A minor and E major) followed by a four-

Example 5.1 Schoenberg, *Ode to Napoleon*, series

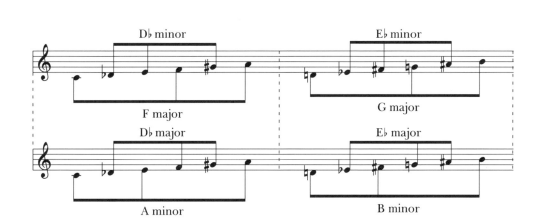

Example 5.2a Berg, Violin concerto, series

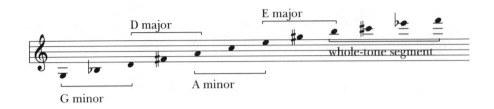

Example 5.2b Berg, Violin concerto: part 1 (Andante), bars 11-15

note segment of the whole-tone scale. In the opening section of the work these triads are used simply as in example 5.2b, so that in each bar consecutive notes of the series are present. Later, the series is transformed and manipulated to allow the introduction of a (tonal) Carinthian folksong (Part I, Allegretto, bars 213–28) and the Bach chorale 'Es ist genug' (Part II, Adagio, bar 136ff), which begins with an ascent from B♭ to the tritone E♮ thus using the whole-tone segment of the series; thereafter, the triadic content of the remainder of the series is freely exploited.

Such compositional procedures and their implications for analysis have rarely received full-scale consideration by music analysts and scholars of the music of the Second Viennese School, although analysts have often focused on the implicit tonality of free atonal music (discussed elsewhere in this book). Similar approaches to twelve-tone music have been relatively few.

In the case of Schoenberg, debate has centred on the issue of the presence of a tonal 'background' in this repertory. Oliver Neighbour's view that Schoenberg's twelve-tone harmony is 'an extension of post-Wagnerian chromatic writing' (Neighbour, 1952: p. 16) leaps over the transitional period of free atonality and is regarded by George Perle as 'highly doubtful' (Perle, 1981: p. 89). The consistent employment of a tonal interval does not justify, for Perle, an interpretation of any serial piece in the terms of tonal harmonic relations since harmonic relations in twelve-tone music 'cannot in general

[…] depend upon a borrowed harmonic language, based on premises that have no general meaning in the twelve-tone system' (1981: p. 90). Hans Keller nevertheless continued to argue that tonal 'backgrounds' can control the serial 'foreground' in Schoenberg (see Keller, 1977: p. 189); yet, as Arnold Whittall objected, there is no analytical evidence for such an interpretation, challenging Keller to demonstrate the existence of a tonal background by means of Schenkerian or Salzerian voice-leading techniques (Whittall, 1980: p. 29). The terms of this debate are determined by differing modes of perceiving this music. Nineteenth-century rhythmic techniques and texture characteristic of much of Schoenberg's serial music tend to emphasize, melodically, certain pitch-classes of the series and invite a tonal interpretation of the accompanying harmony; but an opposed way of hearing accepts Schoenberg's melodic and rhythmic structures as a foreground patterning of an essentially atonal, serial control of pitch, and therefore privileges dodecaphonic factors over fleeting tonal configurations.

In Berg scholarship, though, the perspective is somewhat different. Berg's structuring of a series, derivation of tonally implicative subsets (or 'tropes') and combination of row forms to produce triadic collections all point to a concern with tonality that goes beyond the short-lived role that (with the exception of the *Ode to Napoleon*, the Piano Concerto (1942) and other works composed in the early 1940s) tonal intervals normally play in Schoenberg. The prominence of tonal features in Berg has led most writers to detail effectively the ways in

Example 5.3 Berg, 'Schliesse mir', series

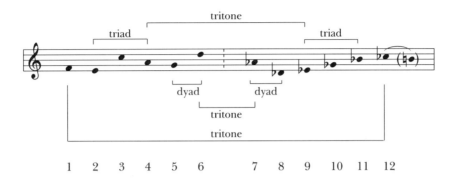

which tonal considerations can determine Berg's twelve-tone procedures. Perle makes a distinction between, on the one hand, works such as *Der Wein* (1929) and the Violin Concerto, in which the structure of the row itself invites a tonal interpretation, and, on the other, *Lulu* (1935) and the *Lyric Suite* (1926), in which explicit tonal configurations are not present in the series but whose 'harmonic texture includes diatonic, chromatic and dodecaphonic elements integrated into "some kind of tonality"' (Perle, 1981: pp. 88–9).

Douglas Jarman (Jarman, 1979) has made the most sustained attempt to describe and classify the varieties of tonal procedure in Berg. Principally, he identifies collections of notes acquiring a particular significance at a fixed pitch level, which, although not always, frequently may be tonal. Such collections are the basis for 'tonal areas' grounded on what he calls 'primary tonal centres'. In many works such passages are extensive and seem to operate according to traditional tonal criteria, but Jarman admits that 'traditional music theory has no word or phrase that adequately describes the way in which these "tonal areas" function in Berg's music' (1979: p. 93). He notes that tonal areas in Berg do not exist in conjunction with a 'completely ordered hierarchy' of secondary areas which can govern all vertical and linear formations. Nor do the areas exert any sense of tonal attraction; thus, they do not have any type of large-scale function as does a tonic in tonal music. Jarman's concept of tonality in Berg is limited to the creation of 'some kind of hierarchy of relationships among the notes of the set and frequently amongst the different set forms and transpositional levels as well' (1979: p. 93).

The analytical attitudes summarized here are essentially concerned with a single issue: the relationship of a triadically implicative series to the finished composition. Although triadic construction of the series does not guarantee 'tonality' in a work, it may sustain a web of recurrent references to tonal

music. Structuring a series is an initial, 'precompositional' stage of writing which can open up a range of possibilities and lay the ground for a relatively circumscribed field of compositional choices. On the other hand, although the various series of Berg's *Lulu* are not triadically constructed, they can easily be transformed by the derivation of triadic tropes which maintain serial control of the resultant triadic configurations. But a central problem for the study of tonality in serial music remains almost virgin territory: the degree to which triadic configurations and 'tonal areas' in Berg can be heard independently of their serial origin and associated with one another. This issue will be the primary focus of this chapter and will determine my analytical approach to Berg's song 'Schliesse mir die Augen beide' (1925).

This song (annotated in example 5.6a below), a second setting of the poem 'Schliesse mir die Augen beide' ('Close my eyes') by Theodor Storm first set by Berg in 1900 in a late nineteenth-century tonal idiom, was the composer's first twelve-tone composition. The series of this work is the same as that of the first movement of his next work, the *Lyric Suite* for string quartet, for which it has recently been established that 'Schliesse mir' is a study (see Perle, 1985: p. 10). Much of Berg's twelve-tone music (except the concert aria *Der Wein*) has important extra-musical references to his relationship with Hanna Fuchs-Robettin (the sister of the eminent Viennese writer Franz Werfel). In 'Schliesse mir' and the *Lyric Suite* the personal 'programme' extends to the structure of the series itself (example 5.3). The first and last notes of the series, F and B (F and H in German notation) are Hanna Fuchs's initials reversed. Once the series is repeated, as it is in the piece, the B of the first statement becomes immediately adjacent to the F of the second statement and establishes the correct order; and since the penultimate note of the series is B♭ (B in German notation), Berg's own second initial is always closely associated

Example 5.4

with F and B. In the song, however, Berg does not exploit the potential of combining the initials as explicitly as in the *Lyric Suite*, in which the basic motivic cell is B–F–A–B♭ (H–F–A–B in German notation).

From the technical point of view, the tritone span of the series (F–B) represents its atonal aspect; this is confirmed by the pitch-class relationships within it. Like the series of Schoenberg's *Ode to Napoleon*, the series is divided into hexachords with, in this case, all the 'white' notes (except C♭/B♮) in the first hexachord and all the 'black' notes in the second. This division, at notes 6 and 7, forms a central tritone D–A♭. But, since the other intervals between adjacent notes are mostly diatonic in aggregate, the remaining notes can be collected into tonally implicative triads and dyads which are palindromically placed within each hexachord. Notes 2, 3 and 4 form the A minor triad and reflect the E♭ minor triad formed by notes 9, 10 and 11. The two dyads are formed by notes 5 and 6 (G, D) and 7 and 8 (A♭, D♭). These collections represent the tonal aspect of the series (see also Perle, 1981: pp. 89–90). Yet, as Berg explained to Schoenberg in a letter of 13 July 1926 (quoted in Rauchhaupt, 1971: pp. 90–2), if the dyads and triads are stated in root position they too are tritone related: A minor–E♭ minor, G/D–D♭/A♭. Thus the potential for tonal or atonal (serial) deployment of the series is inherent in every aspect of its construction.

It seems likely, too, that the triads have a special, programmatic role to play in the piece (see example 5.4), partially determined by the text. At two points the A minor and E♭ minor triads are unfolded simultaneously: in bar 9 (piano) and bar 18 (voice and piano left hand). Each occurrence is accompanied by images of peace and love: 'all becomes peaceful beneath your hand' ('*unter deiner Hand zur Ruh*'), bar 9; 'you fill all my heart' ('*füllest Du mein ganzes Herz*'), bar 18. The significance of this is that each triad contains one of Berg's initials, A. B. (A, B♭ in English notation), and that in each case the series is arranged so that Hanna Fuchs's notes are also present: in bar 9¹, B(H)–F (piano left hand), and bar 18¹⁻³, F–B(H) (piano). Conversely, at the two points where the E♭ minor triads are unfolded simultaneously (bars 7–8 and 11–12), the text speaks of 'anguish' ('*was ich leide*') and 'pain' ('*Und wie leise sich den Schmerz*') and Hanna's notes are absent, implying the absence of Hanna herself. In this way Berg personalizes the text; and since the poem hinges on the polarity of love and pain these correspondences (also dependent on the polarity of tritone-related triads and the F–B tritone itself) function as symbolic, extra-musical references.

Such a symbolic role for the triads suggests that they may exist 'outside' the real structure of the work, on the supposition that they have only an extra-musical meaning. But to accept this would be to ignore the problem of the organic nature of the pitch structure of the song which contains both tonal and serial formations. A method of analysing the song as a potentially integrated structure is therefore required; this is described in section 2 and applied in section 3.

2 METHOD

A variety of methods has been formulated to demonstrate the existence of tonality in non-functional tonal and atonal music. Beginning with the 'extended tonality' of late nineteenth-century and early twentieth-century music, analysts and theorists have used or adapted Schenkerian techniques to reveal an implicit or explicit tonal centre (see, for example, Ayrey, 1982). A further development of this approach takes as axiomatic the concept of a 'dissonant tonic sonority' (see Travis, 1959), so that even insignificantly triadic music can be analysed by replacing the Schenkerian hierarchy of diatonic prolongations with categories of dissonant prolongations (see Morgan, 1976). Such analogies with the Schenkerian model allow a form of tonality to be revealed in atonal and even serial compositions.

Other theorists have emphasized harmonic or vertical considerations over the predominantly linear interpretations of extended voice-leading techniques. Schoenberg himself in the *Theory of Harmony* of 1911 (Schoenberg, 1978) established a theoretical basis for compositions exploring extended tonality and 'fluctuating [*schwebend*] tonality' in which the tonic is referential but absent. (An application of Schoenbergian theory to his song 'Traumleben', op. 6 no. 1 (1905) can be found in Wintle, 1980.) Extensions of this approach have also been diverse, ranging from Hindemith's classification of non-diatonic chords in *The Craft of Musical Composition* (1945), to theories of 'fused bitonality' in Schoenberg (Hicken, 1974) and George Perle's *Twelve-Tone Tonality* (1977) predicated on a theory of interval cycles and pitch arrays.

None of these approaches seems wholly appropriate to the issues raised by Berg's tonally implicative serial music. Those which seem to have the greatest explanatory potential are the theories of extended tonality and Schoenberg's theory of chromatic harmony, since they preserve the role of the triad in complex tonal structures and incorporate concepts of chromatic or scalic alteration. The other methods, by contrast, rely on a redefinition of the notion of tonality itself (usually centred on a 'referential sonority') and are therefore more appropriately applied to non-triadic music.

Perhaps the most successful though inconclusive attempt to formulate a method for Berg's serial music that respects its triadic content is a study by Anthony Pople (Pople, 1983), a consideration of the interaction of serial and tonal aspects of pitch structure in Act III of Berg's *Lulu*. In his discussion of the problems inherent in a Schenkerian approach to the work, he discounts the relevance in Berg analysis of theories of non-triadic harmony and gives a concise summary of the theoretical issues involved:

> The most coherent theory of tonality we have is Schenker's, but this cannot easily be applied to such music as *Lulu*.... The most successful applications of Schenkerian concepts to music from the period 1900–20 have been concerned with what might be called 'non-triadic tonality'. In such analysis the central

concept of a hierarchy of functional layers – which may still be characterised by Schenkerian terms such as 'background', 'middleground' and 'foreground' – is maintained. But here, unlike classical tonality, the layers ultimately articulate not a triad, but some other collection of pitches. As in Schenker's work, though, each layer also articulates its neighbours in the hierarchy – the middleground elaborates the background, for example – and this articulation has generally been expressed in terms reminiscent of Schenker's and which, like his, derive from the concepts and distinctions of counterpoint. Even though in non-triadic tonality this cannot be the strict counterpoint that Schenker uses, the result of such analysis is still a reading which interprets the piece under consideration as a unified structure, unified that is to say, in its basically self referential articulation of a kernel sonority by contrapuntal means. This unity is compromised only in that the principles of counterpoint are not immanent to the kernel sonority, whether or not it is triadic. The resultant tension is more apparent in non-triadic tonality, where the use of counterpoint may be regarded as a stylistic reference to tonality of the earlier kind. (pp. 46–7)

Pople's immediate topic is the potential for an interpretation of Act III, bars 83–230, the 'Marquis's chorale variations', based in diatonic tonality; but, as the above statements imply, he is careful to avoid suggesting that the full complement of Schenkerian levels is applicable to the extract. In fact, he regards the 'fully fledged' referential function of C major in the piece as a cause of 'disunity in the musical discourse' (p. 47), describing the variations as 'successions of small structures' articulating a series of 'images' of C major which can be classified as various types of 'tonality' in the piece. He identifies a 'clear' C major ('Lied des Mädchenhändlers', bar 103 ff); pitches diatonic to C but without functional support ('English waltz', bar 158 ff); chord sequences susceptible to tonal interpretation; a free contrapuntal section (Variations 7 and 8, bars 192–207) with an emphasis on certain pitches which can be integrated into an overall tonal reading of the piece; and textures saturated with the diminished seventh, which can be interpreted as a succession of dominant sevenths and ninths (Variations 9–11, bar 208 ff). These events are then connected in an analytical reduction that resembles a Schenkerian middleground graph (see example 5.5). However, because few of the structures are the product of a larger contrapuntal structure, the further levels in the hierarchy are not available. The middleground graph (example 5.5) therefore 'stands between a non-unified foreground and a non-unified background' that is, between a musical surface which is not diatonically coherent, and an ideal assumed level that could show the diatonic origin of the chord sequences. He decides, then, that the 'connections' of example 5.5 are established by more or less literal identities of pitch or by the redistribution of the notes of a vertical collection. The tonal interpretation of the piece is regarded by Pople as a 'referential aspect of interpretation rather than a functional aspect of structure' (p. 48).

Speaking of *Lulu* as a whole, Pople concludes:

Tonal allusions abound in this work: Jarman [1979] has identified several key areas associated with individual characters, though he has understandably not pursued any detailed investigation of the ways in which they operate. In fact, it must be doubted whether we yet have analytical techniques which can represent (as opposed to misrepresent) the status of each of these local and global tonalities, and the relationship between them, in the detail which is expected of serious analysis. (p. 49)

Of course, the task of analysing a work the length of *Lulu*, or even the 147 bars of the chorale variations, is bound to be more problematic than uncovering the implicit tonality of the twenty bars of 'Schliesse mir'. But, for the analysis of Berg's song, Pople's demonstration of a method is a fruitful beginning. Its most suggestive feature is the double reading it invites, since it exhibits both a progression of chords that, with little difficulty, could be given traditional harmonic descriptions, and a bass arpeggiation (following Schenker) of the C major triad. Since this analytical approach is largely experimental, it will be sufficient at this stage to assume that a bass-line graph will ground the 'tonal' analysis of 'Schliesse mir' and that a similarly 'tonal' progression of chords might also be present. It is also to be expected that the bass-line graph, while being tonally coherent, will exhibit some of the characteristics of extended tonality and that the chord progression will be predominantly chromatic.

These assumptions imply a dual method of analysis, in which successions of chords will interact with a bass-line graph showing the prolongation of the tonic through a series of scale steps and arpeggiations. We may begin by taking Pople's method as a starting point, although it must be modified and extended in the full analysis of 'Schliesse mir'. In particular, 'fully fledged' tonal areas will be privileged in the analysis and, unlike Pople's, will be regarded as causes of unity (not 'disunity') in the piece. Once this method is applied, a more precise formulation of a method for the song will be possible.

First, then, in an attempt to replicate Pople's results, the piece can be scanned for unequivocal triadic collections in order to ascertain the potential for long-range connections of the type he finds in *Lulu*, Act III. Example 5.6a shows a segmentation of the song identifying 19 vertical triadic collections (numbered 1–19). Because the texture is predominantly contrapuntal, few of these are simultaneities, but prolongations of one chord over another have been accounted for (that is, they are not included) and some notes foreign to the chords are excluded (indicated by parentheses).

The 19 chords fall into two classes: firstly those formed by notes in both the piano and the voice (nos. 1, 7, 8, 9, 10, 12, 14–19); and secondly, those formed by the piano (right and left hand) alone (nos. 2–6, 11, 13). The exceptions are chords 17–19 (class i), since the voice is silent at the end of the piece. Example 5.6b summarizes the chords in order, with chords of class ii enclosed in square brackets. Following Carner's observation that the song 'finally comes to rest on the bass F, the implied tonality of the setting' (Carner, 1983: p. 108), the

Example 5.5 [from Anthony Pople, 'Serial and tonal aspects of pitch structure in Act III of Berg's *Lulu*', *Soundings* No. 10 (1983)]. Example reproduced by permission of the author.

C major middleground of chorale variations (Act III, bars 83-230)

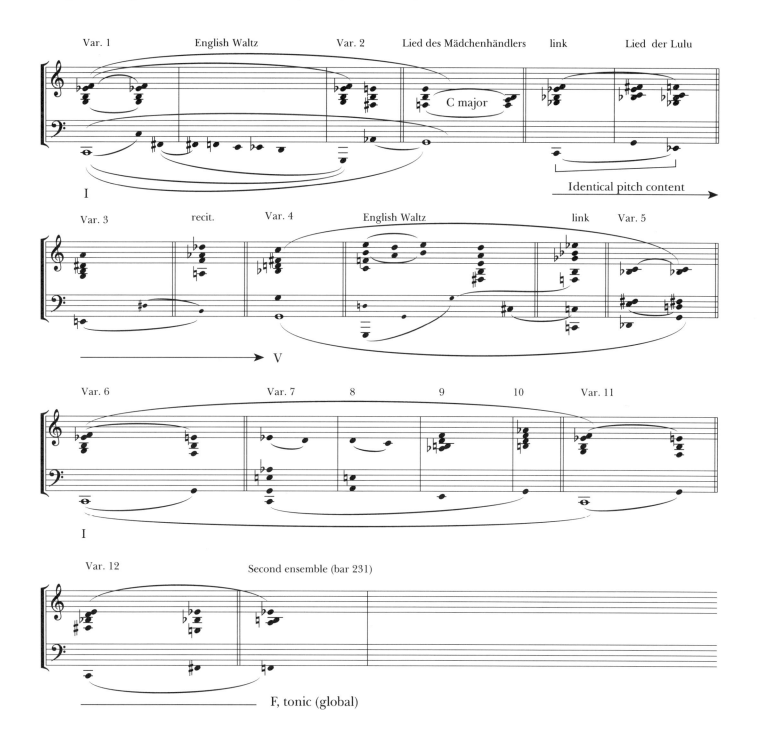

final F is provisionally assigned as tonic, and on this assumption class i chords are given a roman-numeral description in example 5.6c. (Class ii chords represent only part of the texture and pose the problem of integrating the vocal line with the piano: they are therefore reserved for a later stage of the analysis.)

The most obvious feature of this listing is the clear cadential progression of chords 17–19 (II_5^6, V^7, I). Such an interpretation is suggested by Berg's beaming of the notes within the collection aggregated in bars 19–20, particularly the first four notes of Form 1 of the series (F E C A) which, when combined with the notes of the simultaneities they form, reveal an intention to establish a serially clouded perfect cadence progression (see example 5.6a). As far as the other chords are concerned, there is a certain lack of harmonic direction, although the initial ♭VI could be connected to the final cadential progression, giving ♭VI–II_5^6–V^7–I, without loss of harmonic logic. But this does not address the problem of the intervening chords which seem to be connected more by the linear progression of the bass notes than by functional harmonic connections. Example 5.6c above makes the linear progression explicit and resembles Pople's bass-line graph, except that there is no complete arpeggiation of the tonic F, only a directed motion towards it.

There are of course two issues here determined by the differing approaches to harmonic structure. First, the status of the chords is unclear, since most appear haphazardly spaced in the piece. The problem, as Pople identified, lies in connecting the chords both with one another and with the intervening material. (Although this could be achieved by uncovering linear connections between the chords, this would not necessarily solve the problem of their non-functional relationship.) However, it is obvious that the class i chords are not only non-functional but are also relatively complex: that is to say, they are variously chromatic, added-note chords, or in harmonically 'weak' inversions. Here we must make a distinction between triadic content and tonal function, since example 5.6 accounts for the triads but gives only an inadequate model of tonality. A method is therefore required that will restore the functional connection of the chords, and, because these connections often remain implicit rather than explicit in the song, the best method will be to adopt an explanatory hypothesis in the form of a diatonic model from which all 19 chords and the intervening material of the piece could be derived.

In accordance with traditional principles of transformation and substitution, the diatonic model will undergo several stages of development, leading from a simple diatonicism to a harmonically complex version expanded in length; this last stage can then be mapped on to the piece to reveal the implicit tonality of the serially controlled surface. In effect, this method is a simple version of a process by which a complex result is 'generated' from a less complex, normative model by means of a series of transformational levels. In this respect the method resembles the procedures of Schenkerian analysis, which,

although it begins (analytically) with a process of reduction (that is, going from surface to model), is also intended to be understood in the opposite way as a process of diminution, or elaboration, of the simpler, more fundamental levels. The method proposed here differs from Schenker's, though, in that it is based on transformations of chords or chord progressions, while Schenker's concern is with contrapuntal elaboration and therefore exemplifies a predominantly linear conception of musical structure.

Nevertheless, this vertical approach to harmonic structure is not wholly incompatible with concepts of linearity. In the *Theory of Harmony* Schoenberg frequently stresses the importance of part-writing, or 'voice-leading', in the control and production of complex chromatic chords. He notes, in the discussion of 'non-harmonic tones' which often produce unclassifiable chords, that the historical evolution of harmony 'sometimes arrives at chords by way of part-writing; at other times it makes the part evolve over the chords' (Schoenberg, 1975: p. 314); later he suggests that 'there are no traditional experiences on which to base the use of these chords: instead, in the rules of voice-leading, we have tested and approved methods for controlling them' (p. 331). Since the serial technique of 'Schliesse mir' is mostly linear, a triadic interpretation of complex simultaneities will be controlled and produced as much by linear movement as by vertical construction, and will thus effect a structural link with the linear organization of the bass.

Further, as Pople has shown, the potential in Berg's serial music for a linear organization of the bass does not rely absolutely on local functional connections between chords. This is already suggested by example 5.6c, and it is here that an application of aspects of Schenkerian theory is appropriate. The result of the final stage of chord generation will be to clarify the structural and subordinate chords of the model and, by extension, of the song itself; this will allow a more sophisticated bass-line graph than that of example 5.6c to be constructed in order to reveal the large-scale motion towards the tonic more clearly than does the chord progression alone. In this example the motion of the bass resembles Schenker's normative bass arpeggiation of the tonic triad only insofar as it is directed towards the tonic and assigns structural weight to the dominant and tonic scale degrees. A complete 'arpeggiation' will therefore be absent, as will the top-voice Fundamental Line which, in conjunction with the bass, according to Schenker, would normally complete the linear, contrapuntal projection of the tonic triad through a composition.

These theoretical provisos are important because they suggest forcibly that the tonal structure of 'Schliesse mir' will not emerge as a late, complex example of 'classical tonality' for which Schenker's theory was formulated. What will emerge is an extended tonal structure exhibiting some features of functional tonality that can be captured in the process of analysis: this will form the 'background' to the pitch structure of the piece, a background that, through a process of serial manipulation, is radically transformed in the song itself.

Example 5.6a Berg, 'Schliesse mir': Triadic collections

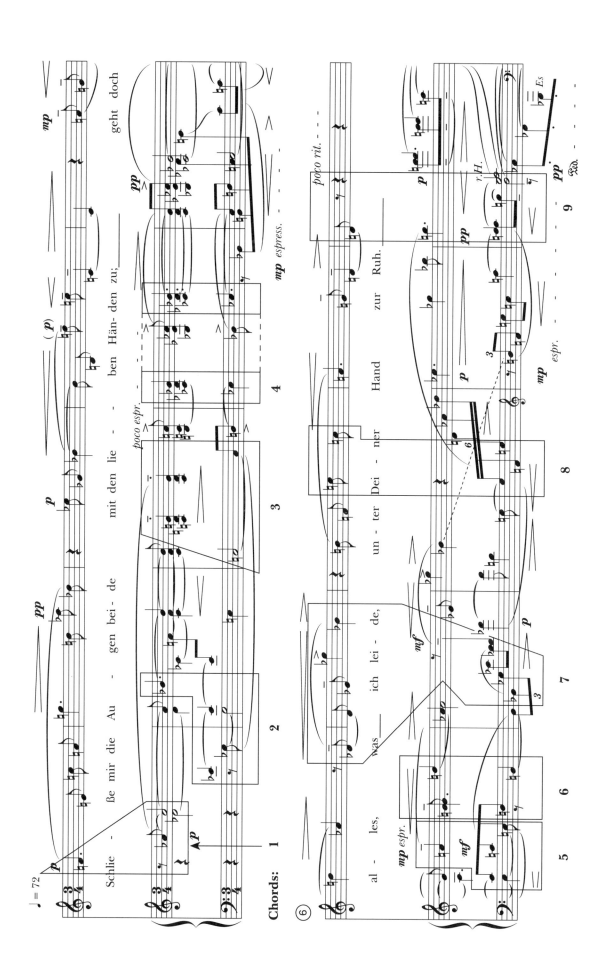

Example 5.6a contd

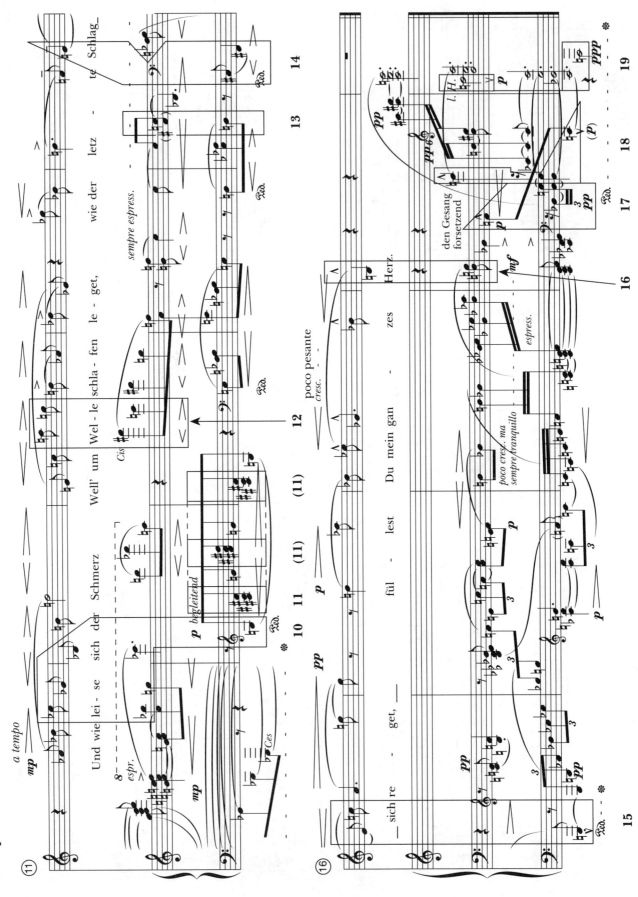

Example 5.6 b/c

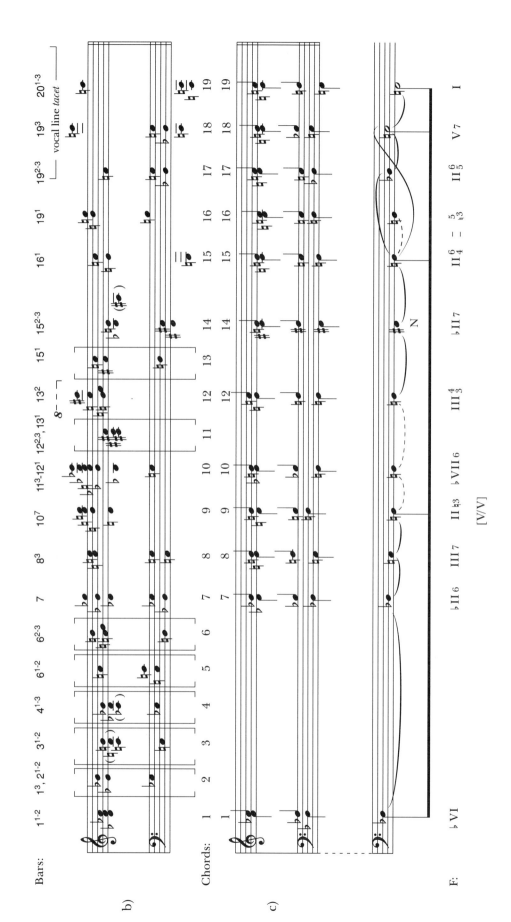

Example 5.7

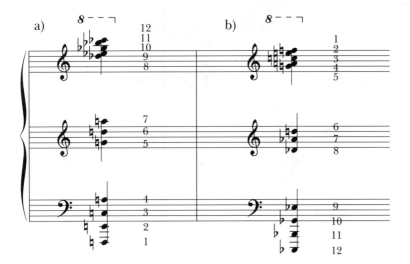

3   MODEL

The full analysis of 'Schliesse mir' will comprise five stages:

i) an examination of the twelve-tone structure of 'Schliesse mir';
ii) the construction of a diatonic model and transformations of the song, leading to a highly chromatic, 'extended' tonal version;
iii) the construction of a bass-line graph on the basis of the results of ii), in order to redefine the progression given in example 5.6c;
iv) the connection of the final, most complex version of the diatonic model with the harmonic structure of the piece by mapping the tonal chord progression onto the predominantly atonal surface of the song;
v) explanation of connections between the tonal model and Berg's serial procedures.

i   Examination of the twelve-tone structure of 'Schliesse mir'

The series of the song (see example 5.3 above) has the property of being an 'all interval' series, a type discovered by Berg's pupil Fritz Heinrich Klein in 1924 (see Klein, 1925). Following Klein, Berg terms the series *Mutterakkord* ('mother chord'), since it can be arranged vertically to contain all the intervals, not only inversional equivalents (for example, the semitone and major seventh). Example 5.7a reproduces Klein's diagrammatic description of the chord, here transposed to the pitch level of Berg's series as it appears in the precompositional sketches for the work (see Smith, 1978, for a reproduction of Berg's original: some minor errors have been corrected in example 5.7a/b). In example 5.7b the pitches of the chord are arranged in descending order without change to the vertical succession of intervals of example 5.7a. Example 5.7c shows the progression of intervals linearly as they appear in the series (Berg's notation).

In this basic form, the construction of the series has important consequences for the creation of a tonal dimension in the song, since the major and minor scales also contain all the intervals, although not between consecutive pitches (see example 5.8). This, in addition to the triadic content of the series (see example 5.3), maximizes the potential for the exploitation of both linear and vertical tonal forms in the piece.

The all-interval series therefore suggests a further connection with the tonal system. Jarman (1979: p. 131) notes that while

Example 5.8

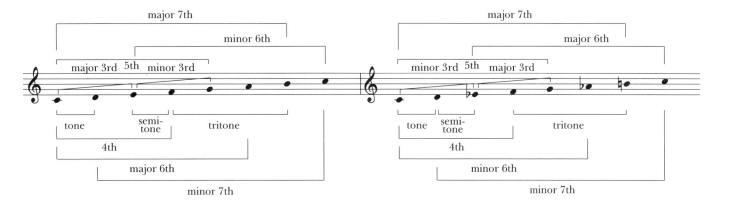

Example 5.9

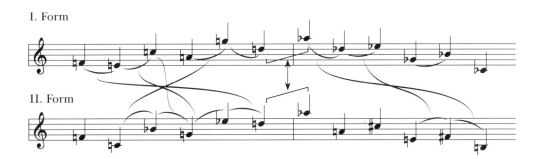

there is no difficulty in reconciling scalic and triadic formations in tonal music – because they represent different formations of the same 'exclusive' collection of notes (that is, the scale of the key) – in twelve-tone music the relation of vertical and horizontal formations is one of the more problematic areas of analysis. The problem is especially acute when the twelve-tone technique is simply applied; when, for example, chords are created by the simultaneous statement of consecutive notes of the series. As the chords proceed they produce new linear intervals in each strand of the texture, intervals which are not present in the series itself. But in the case of an all-interval series this is not the case: all intervals created by non-consecutive notes of the series will also be included in it. In this respect the series can be regarded as a serial analogy to the major and minor scales.

In preparation for an examination of these tonal forms, a description of Berg's treatment of the series itself is necessary. When the song was first published in the February 1930 issue of the periodical *Die Musik* (Vol. 22, No. 5), Berg provided a preface in which he spoke of 'the enormous distance covered as music has gone from tonal composition to the "method of composing with twelve Tones which [are] related only to one another", from the C-major triad to the "Mutterakkord"'

(quoted in Redlich, 1960: p. 7). And in a letter to Anton Webern (1883–1945) written on 19 August 1925, Berg mentions 'a (love) song ... my first attempt at strict twelve-note serial composition. However, in that art I am unfortunately not as far advanced as you are' (quoted in Redlich, 1960: p. 8). The first of these statements reveals Berg's conception of progress in composition from tonal to serial music, and the second his diffidence in publishing the second setting of 'Schliesse mir' which he feared would demonstrate a less sophisticated technique than Webern's (and of course Schoenberg's). It is only later, in 1926, writing to Schoenberg about the composition of the *Lyric Suite*, that he shows confidence in his command of twelve-tone technique and reveals the continuing concern with tonality which was absent in his *Die Musik* preface (see Harris, 1981: p. 13).

These comments have led some writers to take Berg at face value and to assume that his treatment of the series in the song is 'primitive' (see Redlich, 1960: p. 10; Barilier, 1978: p. 145; Perle, 1985: pp. 9–10). Certainly the series is used in a simpler and less sophisticated manner than in the *Lyric Suite*, but the comparison draws attention from the considerable complexity of the serial construction of the piece. Two of the three extensive commentaries on the song (Smith, 1978; Perle,

Example 5.10

Form 1 = Form 1a

Example 5.11

Form 1a (Po)

Form 2 (I9 of Form 1a)

1985) note the derivation in Berg's precompositional sketches of a second all-interval series from the first. Example 5.9 reproduces the content of the sketch and reveals Berg's method: within each hexachord the order of intervals is reversed while retaining the tritone (F–B) span of the series and the tritone D–A♭ between the hexachords. Schematically, the process can be set out as in figure 5.1, with the intervals expressed in terms of the number of semitones they contain:

Figure 5.1

Semitones:

1 8 3 10 5 6 7 2 9 4 11

5 10 3 8 1 6 11 4 9 2 7

The hexachords of Form 1 are, like the triads and dyads of the series, palindromically related by inversion (semi-tone –

major seventh, minor sixth – major third, etc.), and this property is preserved in Form 2 (fourth – fifth, minor seventh – tone, etc.). Berg produces the second form by treating the series as an interval series rather than a pitch series. This suggests a continuity between Berg's conception of tonal and serial structure, since the diatonic scale is not only a pitch series but a collection of pitches that form tonal relations only when arranged in a series (or simultaneity) of tonal intervals.

Further, on the evidence of the song itself, it is clear that Berg is also using a third form of the original series (Form 1a), from which the second form can be derived by the normal means of serial permutation. In the opening bars of the song the piano begins with the second hexachord of the series and continues with the first (see example 5.10). A serial inversion of the series beginning with the hexachords reversed (Form 1a) produces a new form transposed by nine semitones, as in example 5.11. The reversed hexachord version is designated Form 1a, further designated Po because it is stated at the original pitch in original, or 'prime', form. The inverted and transposed version, identical with example 5.9, is therefore designated I9.

The three forms of the series (1, 1a and 2) are deployed in the song (see example 5.12) to reflect the formal structure of the text which falls into two four-line stanzas. In this way the binary form of the piece is created. Form 1 is stated in the voice at the beginning of the song and is repeated four times in sequence, a procedure that recalls Schoenberg's in his first completely serial piece, the *Sonnett* movement of the Serenade, op. 24 (1924). Simultaneously with the first statement of Form 1, Form 1a is stated in the piano (bars 1–5) after which it proceeds with Form 1. A complementary procedure is adopted in Section B (bars 11–20), where the voice begins with the second hexachord of the series. This connects with the first hexachord which ended Section A (see bars 8–10) to complete the third full statement of Form 1. But it also gives the illusion of a statement of Form 1a in bars 11–13, and since the piano right hand simultaneously has Form 2 (i.e., Form 1a at I9) the second half of the song is distinguished from the first by utilizing two forms (P0 and I9) of Form 1a. (The simultaneous statement of the two hexachords of Form 1 in bars 1–2 also gives the illusion of a complete statement of Form 1 only, but the completion of Form 1a at bar 5 (piano) followed by Form 1 marks Form 1a as the distinct form of the series here.) The formal function of Forms 1 and 2 is confirmed by the 'cadential' sonorities at the end of each section. Section A builds up a complete statement of Form 1 in bars 9–10, while the final chord (*Mutterakkord*) of Section B (bar 20) is a vertical statement of Form 2. Thus, Redlich's view that 'we are confronted in the case of Lied II with a comparatively primitive application of twelve-note technique which in this special case totally refrains from utilising any variant in the order of the basic set' (Redlich, 1960: p. 10) already appears to be highly inaccurate.

Pursuing the serial analysis further we find four additional classes of serial permutation in example 5.12.

i) retrograde (R0) of Form 1 in:
  a) piano left hand, bars 6^3–8^3, which pivots on note 4 to connect with a segment of Form 1 (P0) to produce a palindromic succession of intervals and pitches;
  b) bars 16^2–19^2: two overlapped statements in the piano right hand and left hand, the first also overlapping with P0 (bar 18^2), the second pivoting on notes 5 and 6 (bar 19^1) to connect with a four-note segment of P0, thus forming a subsidiary hexachord;
ii) a) bars 12–14^2, piano left hand: a P5 segment of Form 1;
  b) bars 14–16^1, piano right hand and left hand: a statement of segments of I9 (notes 1–4 and 5–11) with the order of the notes not strictly observed. Note 4 of the first (right hand) segment is a pivot to P0, note 5, in left hand bar, 16^1.
iii) Repetitions of segments of the row in the piano, bars 3–5, 12–15^1, 18, 20 (final bass F). Such repetition is usually avoided in twelve-tone composition because it tends to

create a hierarchy among the pitches, but it is of course Berg's intention here to prolong tonally implicative segments (see example 5.14 below).
iv) The free ordering of Form I in bar 19 to establish an obscured tonal cadence (compare example 5.6a and example 5.12) and the vertical statement of Form 2 described above.

These procedures and departures from the 'rules' of twelve-tone composition are at least as advanced as the technique of Schoenberg's earliest serial works (for example, the Suite for Piano, op. 25 (1925)) and surpass the very strict application of the method in Webern's first serial compositions. In these works Schoenberg and Webern used series that were far less rigorously structured and determinant of the pitch relationships in the finished composition than in Berg's song. They were, therefore, quick to explore various complex methods of combining serial forms to exert stricter control over simultaneities. This is a less urgent concern in Berg. As we have seen, the forms of the original series can be stated simultaneously to produce recurrent 'tonal' sonorities with extra-musical meaning; and as will become evident, the 'law' governing simultaneity in the song (i.e., vertical collections and heterophonic lines) is grounded in tonality itself.

What gives 'Schliesse mir' the appearance of demonstrating a 'comparatively primitive treatment' of the series is Berg's attempt from the outset of his serial period to maintain the character and style of his atonal compositions, in which, uniquely among the composers of the Second Viennese School, the tradition of tonality was also consistently explored. Although Berg does not experiment at this stage with complex serial permutations, this is rendered unnecessary by the careful construction of a series incorporating both 'tonal' and atonal pitch and interval relations. 'Schliesse mir' can be seen as a study in the maintenance of a continuity of style, and in this attitude Berg is close to Schoenberg's view of twelve-tone technique as more a compositional device than a new 'language'. Schoenberg's comment on his own approach to serial composition is equally true of Berg: 'One has to follow the basic set; but, nevertheless, one composes as freely as before' (Schoenberg, 1975: p. 224).

ii   The diatonic model and its transformations

As described in section 2 (Method), the progressions of chords in example 5.6b are drawn directly from the song. They are therefore fixed in the structure and must eventually be incorporated in the harmonic analysis as they stand. But because they lack firm harmonic or functional connections they give only a partial and, for the present, complicated picture of tonal motion towards the final tonic F. Furthermore, the class ii chords of example 5.6b are not integrated into a normative harmonic progression. The construction of a dia-

Example 5.12 Berg, 'Schliesse mir': Serial structure

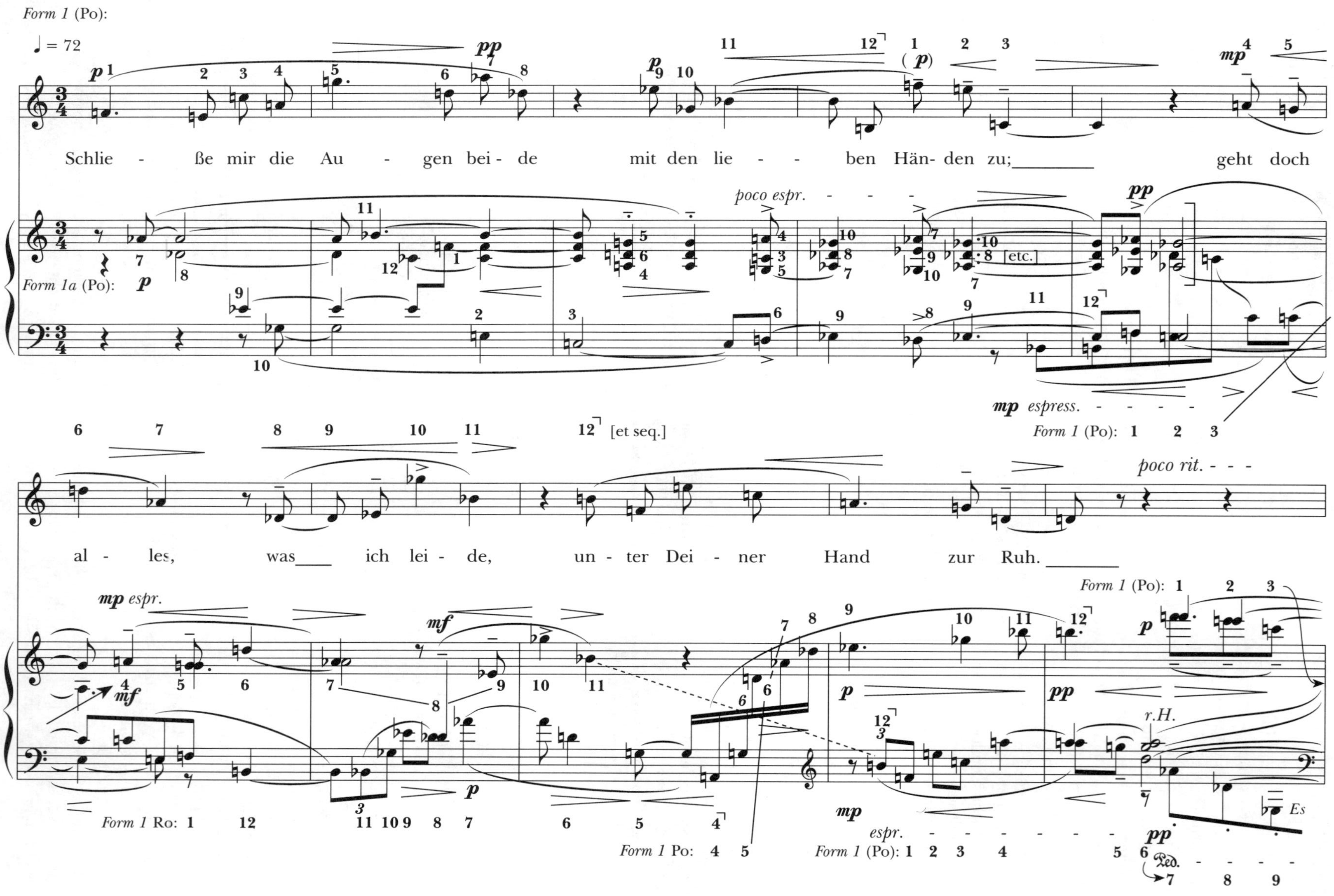

Example 5.12 contd

tonic model must therefore integrate class i and ii chords and provide a clear and complete tonal model. For this to be achieved, a provisional reinterpretation of the 19 chords is necessary, since many of the chords and the progressions they imply are already transformations of simpler diatonic forms. Example 5.13a (aligned here with example 5.6b/c) shows such a reinterpretation.

The chords are numbered corresponding to those of the original sequence; those which do not reproduce the originals are marked with an asterisk. At this level all asterisked chords are diatonic or inversional equivalents of the originals. These operations allow a normative progression to emerge which exemplifies the norms of good progression, essentially moving by strong scale degrees and applied dominants. Inversions appear in order to ensure the smooth progression of the bass. Two further operations have been applied to complete the model: firstly, insertion of chords (indicated by square brackets), and secondly, omission of chords in the initial sequence which remain outside the diatonic progression; the latter will be incorporated in subsequent transformations of the model.

Even at this degree of abstraction from the original, some features of the song itself are already apparent. Most noticeably, the progression does not immediately imply its final F major cadence. Up to chord 9, the local tonic is clearly G major, after which C major is weakly implied by the IV^6_4–I progression of chords 15–16 which is quickly succeeded by the cadential progression in F. Although the whole progression appears to begin in one key and to cadence in another, distantly related key, it would be equally true to observe that it shows the potential, if not yet the realization, of the harmonic outline of a piece exploring 'fluctuating tonality', as Schoenberg explained it:

> [A] piece can also be intelligible to us when the relationship to the fundamental is not treated as basic; it can be intelligible when the tonality is kept, so to speak, flexible, fluctuating (*schwebend*). Many examples give evidence that nothing is lost from the impression of completeness if the tonality is merely hinted at, yes, even if it is erased. (1978: p. 128)

However, in example 5.13a the tonic is finally present: it is the dominant, C, which is 'hinted at' (in chords 15–16) and is entirely absent between chords 1–9. But since the latter progression firmly establishes G major, C is not completely 'erased' but is represented by its dominant. Here, as in the song itself, the tonality must be understood in retrospect, that is, in relation to the final F major cadence, so that the apparently distantly related G major can be designated as V of V.

In example 5.13b the strength of G major begins to weaken with the introduction of stepwise chromatic movement in the bass. (Asterisked chords here indicate transformations of those of example 5.13a; insertions in the previous example are numbered 2a, 5a, etc.) This produces firstly, a prolongation of A minor from chords 2a–5a, realizing the implications of the VI^{6-5}_{4-3} progression in example 5.13a (chords 5 and 5a); and secondly, a weakened progression to the G major chord 15 by

means of the transformation of chord 10 back to its original E♭ major, the introduction at this level of chord 11 (G♭/F♯ major) and the chords inserted between chords 12 and 13. The A minor prolongation implies C, its relative major, while the chromatic progression between chords 10 and 15 begins to reduce the clarity of G major here, making this key dependent on the relation of chords 9 and 13 (in G: I–V). This connection and chromatic expansion (which never achieves a full close in G) smooths over the two-part division of the diatonic progression in example 5.13a and therefore strengthens the drive towards the final F by increasing the suggestion that the C major of chord 15, though in second inversion, is the absent fundamental of the preceding progression.

Example 5.13c increases the chromaticization of the bass but also introduces sevenths, ninths and substitutions. Chords 1 and 2, transposed down a semitone, are substitutions of those in example 5.13b, but they reproduce (enharmonically) the first two chords of the original sequence (see example 5.6b). This reveals a clearer connection to the following progression in A minor, than did the enharmonic notation (D♭–G♭) of the original sequence. A comparison of example 5.13c with the diatonic progression of example 5.13b shows how the opening progression in C♯ (chords 1–2) uses chord 2a as a pivot to the A minor progression of chords 2a–5a, which itself contains transformations. In particular, chord 4 becomes an augmented sixth, not functioning in the traditional manner, but controlled by the chromatic movement of the four voices. Chord 7, an augmented sixth in example 5.13b, becomes a G♭ major chord in first inversion, while chords 8–8a are transformed from a functional II–V progression to a prolongation of the seventh chord of chord 8 leading weakly to the G major of chord 9. Here the bass connecting chords 6 to 9 is linear and strong functional progressions are completely absent. G major as a local tonality is therefore compromised and the progression becomes only a linear chromatic connection of the two G major chords (6 and 9). Thus, C emerges more clearly as the implied local tonic because it follows the progression in A minor, to which it is more closely related than is G (as example 5.13b shows). Following this, G as tonic is represented only by the move to V at chord 13, via a complex chromatic elaboration of the II–V–I progression (chords 12–13). Chords 14–16 further weaken the tonicity of G: chord 14 becomes an F major chord after which the C major of chord 15 leads to a G major seventh at chord 16, suggesting that the larger progression between chords 9 and 16 is, again, best understood as a complex chromatic elaboration of a move to V in C major (at chord 16) – this allows the final F major cadence to begin from an implicit C major progression, that is to say, from its dominant.

It is in example 5.13d that the progression begins to resemble the harmonic content of the song itself. All 19 chords of the original sequence are reinstated, but they are integrated in a highly chromatic progression involving functional relationships that are connected predominantly by chromatic 'inessential'

Example 5.13 a/b/c

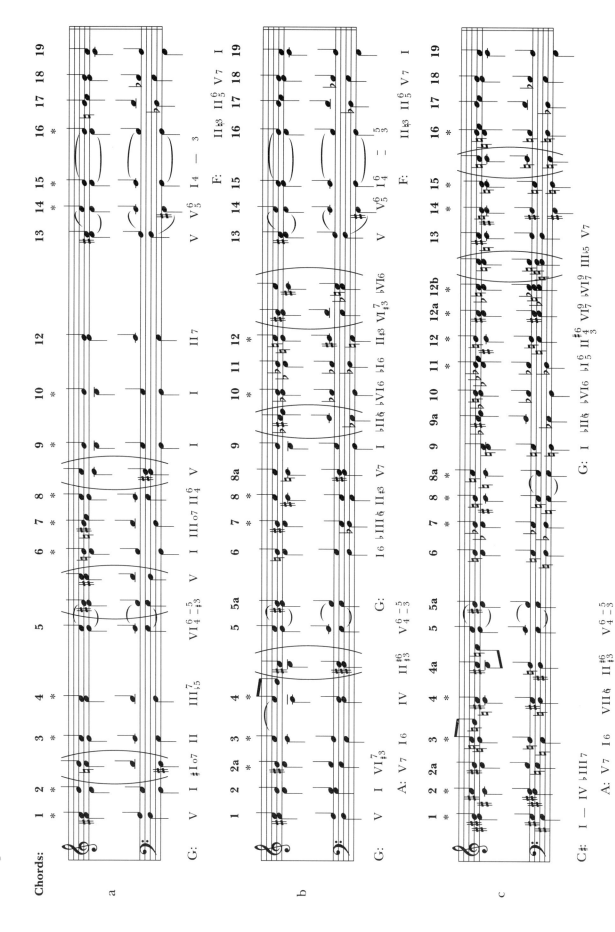

Example 5.6 b/c (bis)

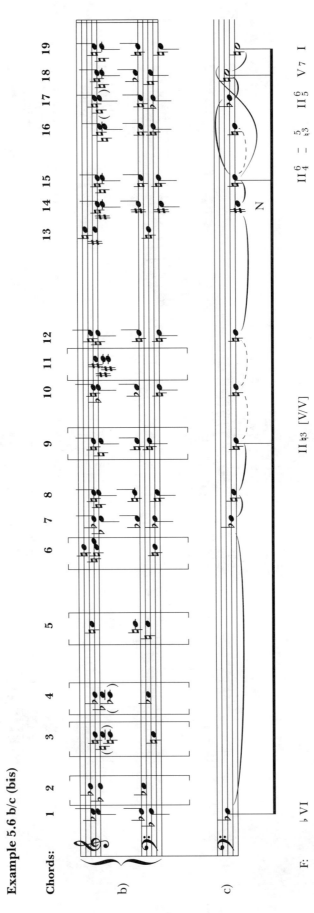

notes and chords. Transformations here are determined by the reinstatement of the form of the chords in the original sequence; inserted chords and passing notes appear in order to encompass forms in the song which cannot otherwise be mapped onto the harmonic progression of example 5.13d. (These additions are numerous and are not bracketed in example 5.13d, but their function is made clear in example 5.14.) Although the progression is much expanded in surface content, harmonic coherence is preserved in the progression of functionally related chords represented on a 'middleground' level by roman-numeral classifications. At this stage in the transformational procedure it is possible to read the progression from chords 1 to 16 as an extended tonal progression in C, beginning with $\flat$II (chord 1)–I (chord 3). The transformation of chord 3 from A minor to C major (and appoggiatura) reduces the influence of the A minor local tonic of example 5.13b and c, and allows the progression to appear as a chromatic approach to the dominant (chord 6); the bass progression C–(D$\sharp$)E–B (I–III–V^6) arpeggiates a tonic third C–E, while the vertical harmonies maintain a chromatic, potentially atonal context. Thus there is a certain tension between the diatonic form of the bass and the harmonies it supports: this will emerge in example 5.14 as characteristic of the analysis and as a distinctive feature of the song itself. The subsequent prolongation of V (chords 6–9) by means of a non-functional linear bass can be read as a neighbouring-note progression of scale steps V (chord 6)–VI (chords 8, 8a)–V (chord 9), a progression typical of, and basic to, extended tonality.

The motion from chords 9 to 13 is similar to the earlier progression from chords 3 to 6. The G (V) of chord 9 is prolonged chromatically, then moves in the bass to the minor third of the triad; it eventually attains its dominant (in C: II$^{\sharp7}$, chord 13) via the prolonged E of chords 12 and 12b. Thus the minor triad is outlined in the bass, yet, as before, the harmonies are chromatic and do not confirm the diatonic implications of the bass. However, the dominant of C is confirmed by the long chromatic prolongation of V^7 between chords 15 and 16, at which point the final cadence in F begins with a chromatic pivot (V$^6_5$ of C [chord 16] leading to II$^6_5$ of F [chord 17]).

iii Construction of a bass-line graph

Example 5.13e summarizes the linear motion of the bass, annotated with scale degrees in F, the implied tonic of the progression. This further clarifies the bass motion of example 5.13d and reveals a large-scale progression $\flat$VI–V–V/V–II$^6_5$–V^7–I prolonged by full or partial arpeggiations of the scale degrees. At this level of abstraction, all subordinate degrees comprising the arpeggiations are triadic and define the implicit tonality of the song. That these subordinate degrees are not always functionally related indicates why we need to move from a vertical to a linear study of the tonality, as the diatonic model becomes chromatically more elaborate. Since it is impossible to classify harmonically all the vertical collections in the piece, the (linear) bass-line graph gives the best representation of tonality, while the chords and passing motions of the upper parts represent the tendency towards the atonality of example 5.13d, which is fully realized in the song itself. Note, though, that example 5.13e is a more coherent tonal structure than example 5.6c; the latter lacks a dominant prolongation and offers no functional explanation for the connection of the first $\flat$VI (chord 1) to the chords preceding the final V^7 (chord 18). The result of the transformation of the diatonic progressions is therefore the specification of a functional bass, elaborated diatonically and supporting complex harmonies which can account for the non-diatonic pitch content of the song.

iv Mapping of the final transformation of the diatonic model (Ex. 13d) onto the surface of 'Schliesse mir'

In mapping the progression in example 5.13d onto the song itself the objectives are to account for each note of the piece and to show how the piano and vocal lines, though harmonically distinct and largely independent, can be derived from the harmonically integrated linear model (as shown in example 5.14a). Since the harmonic structure of the song is not overtly tonal, except in the case of the class i chords and where one triadic segment is overlaid with another to form a momentary 'bitonal' area, the mapping involves a freer demonstration of the relation of the model (example 5.13d) to variant (the song itself) than in the transformations of the diatonic model. However, some constraints have been applied and will be explained in conjunction with the mapping procedure.

As far as possible, notes forming linear or vertical triads are related to chords in the model, while notes which appear to have a subordinate 'tonal' function are related to subordinate notes in the model. This principle is relatively unproblematic in the model-to-piano-texture mapping since the simultaneities usually define structural and subordinate tones. The model-to-vocal-line mapping is more difficult since, except for the class i chords, there appear to be fewer points of integration of the row form with tonally implicative simultaneities. This means that the metrical position of a vocal note, which would usually indicate its structural or subordinate status, must often be ignored so that an apparently 'structural' vocal pitch will often be defined in the mapping as subordinate (see, for example, the first beat of bar 2, where the first vocal pitch, G, appears as a chromatic passing note in the bass of the model).

The chords of the model are mapped directly onto the linear or triadic segments of the piece in order to avoid an 'oblique' (anticipated or delayed) appearance of the chords in the song itself. At several points, though, this principle has been liberally observed. In bars 5–8 there is a brief canon

Example 5.13 d/e

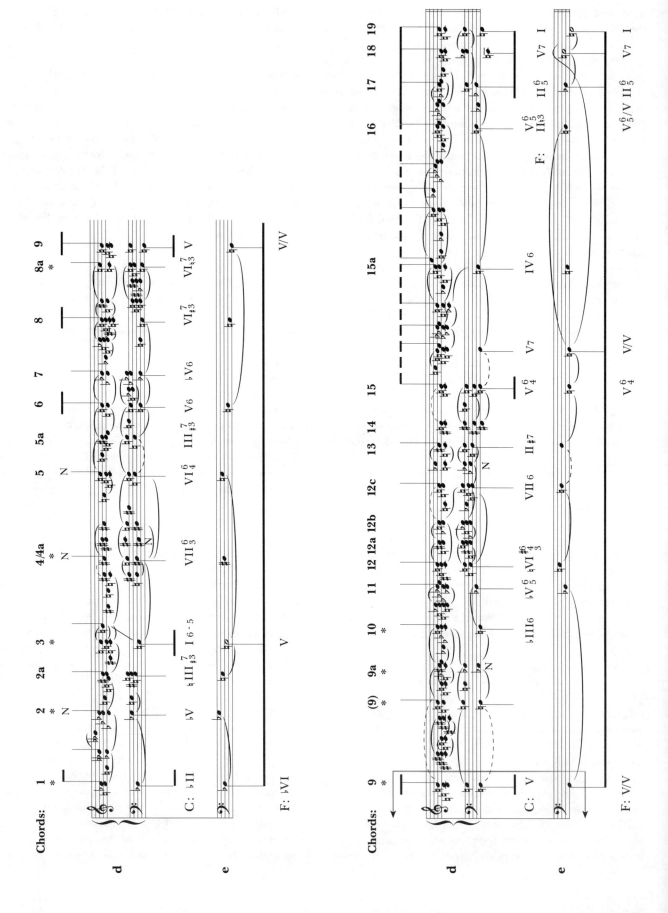

Example 5.14a Berg, 'Schliesse mir', mapping of diatonic model

Example 5.14a contd

Example 5.14a contd

Example 5.14a contd

Example 5.14b

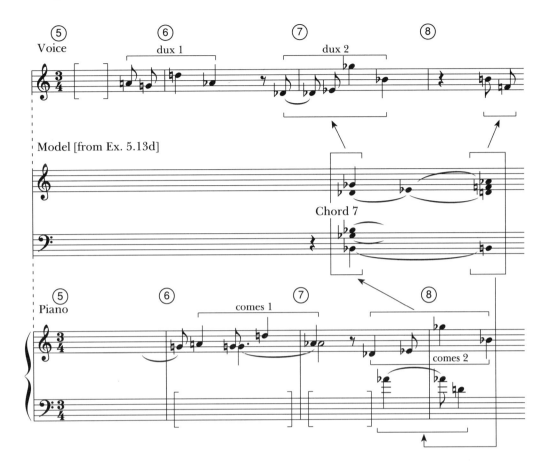

(voice, piano right hand) which necessitates the mapping of chord 7 (G♭ major) formed by notes 8–11 of the series (in the voice bars 6–7) onto the same notes of the piano imitation (bars 6–7). This reveals a harmonic superimposition in the piano: the left-hand notes A♭ and D♮ belong to the following chord in the model, which is completed by the first two notes (B, F) of the voice in bar 8 (see example 5.14b).

As explained in section I (Orientation), the phenomenon of superimposed triadic segments is deliberately and symbolically exploited by Berg using the E♭ minor and A minor triads; but these do not pose a problem of integration if enharmonic spellings are applied (see bar 9 and bar 18 illustrated in example 5.14c).

A more problematic and pervasive feature is the prolongation of one triadic segment, over another, resulting in an overlapping progression of chords, as in the piano, bars 1–2. In such cases no attempt is made to modify the model to take account of the simultaneities on each beat. This type of overlapping is accepted as a clouding of the tonal structure which preserves the effect of atonality in the song; it frequently

concerns the relation of the vocal line to the piano part, so that where enharmonic spellings do not enable integration with the piano an overlapped or 'oblique' relation is maintained (as in bar 3^3, illustrated in example 5.14d). Other examples occur in bars 8^3–9^2 and 15^{1-2}.

Because this feature is clearly related to the serial clouding of the final tonal cadence in bars 19–20 (discussed in section 2) it can be identified as a strategy of the work, a definitive feature of Berg's serial style. To attempt to describe the complex 'tonal' formations this strategy produces would be to assert a false interpretation of Berg's compositional technique: that is to say, the triadic formations are undoubtedly heard, but their potential tonal function is 'liquidated' almost as soon as the triads are perceived. The function of the mapping is therefore to specify incipient, rather than the actual, tonality. Although there is no functional tonality in the song, the best explanation of the relationship of clear tonal forms (represented by class i chords) to the material that connects them is a tonally coherent model, given that the techniques of its radical transformation in the piece are specified.

Example 5.14c (part 1)

Example 5.14 c (part 2)

Example 5.14d

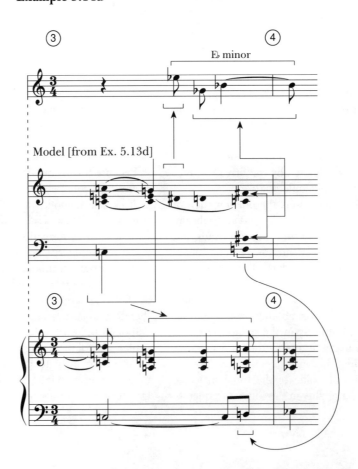

v Explanation of connections between the tonal model and Berg's serial procedures

The essential ambiguity of the pitch structure of 'Schliesse mir' has become evident. The work is both serial and tonal, and the relative weightings of the two systems of pitch relationship fluctuate throughout. Yet Berg's serial technique also suggests that some procedures are determined by the intention to create the conditions for an extended tonal 'background'. Example 5.15a shows example 5.13e annotated to reveal correspondences between the row forms of the song and the bass-line graph of the model. No attempt is made to construct a voice-leading graph directly from the musical surface.

Example 5.13d remains the nearest approach to a background structure for the song's foreground. Such voice-leading connections as there are in the top line of example 5.13d (predominantly the overall motion from the opening A♭ to the long prolongation of G leading finally to F) are features of the model only, not of the song itself (see example 5.15b). The progressions connecting chords 15 and 16 (indicated by a broken beam) show the only clear example of directed motion in the piece that can be revealed without falling into those false applications of Schenkerian concepts which were discussed in section 2. That these progressions prolong the top voice G confirms the prolongation of G in the model and shows how tonal features come to the surface in the last four bars. This alone justifies the retrospective tonal interpretation of the rest of the piece given in the transformations of the diatonic model, but it does not imply that conventional voice-leading techniques could be unproblematically applied.

However, it is possible to reveal a correspondence between the fully realized serial structure of the piece itself and the fully realized tonal structure of the model. The 'tonal' function of the row transformations detailed above is made explicit in example 5.15a: every structural note or arpeggiation in the bass is defined by a change of row form. In the first part of the song the opening D♭–G♭ progression of the model is defined by Form 1a (Po), while the subsequent arpeggiation of C introduces Form 1 (Po). This form is present up to the progression B–A–G which confirms the V/V cadence in bar 10. Each bass note is distinguished by a different transformation of Form 1: Ro(B)–Po(A)–Po(G). The attainment with Po is further emphasized by the unusual central position of G in the sequence: where Po normally has G as note 5, in bars 9–10 the sequence begins with note 12, giving the six notes 12, 1, 2, 3, 4, 5 up to the cadence (see example 5.15c). The row is then continued in bar 9^{2-3} as the transition to Section B. Berg establishes a relation between the two-part form of the song and the 'tonal' cadence at this point by deploying the row symmetrically around G, thus creating a sense of serial and formal half-closure.

The row forms of Section B are similarly definitive of structural notes (see example 5.15a). The move to B♭ in the bass (bar 12), arpeggiating the G *minor* triad, is introduced by a P5 segment signalling the move away from the major

triad and weakening the tonicity of G: subsequently the bass progression E–D–G is accompanied by the sequence P5, Form 2 (Form 1a: I9), Form 1: Po, so that the reattainment of G in bar 16 brings also a return to Form 1: Po of bar 9. The 'resolution' of V_4^6 to V_5^6/V reintroduces Ro, which also accompanies the ascent to A only to be replaced by Po on the following B, the pivot chord V_5^6 (G *major*), after which the perfect cadence in F maintains Po segmented (1, 2, 3, 4), (11, 5, 9, 6), (7, 8, 10, 12), to create the linear and vertical cadential forms discussed in section 2 above, illustrated in example 5.15d.

Reviewing the complete bass progression and attendant row forms, a larger structural principle emerges. All the fundamental scale degrees (as they appear in the piece: V, V/V, II, V, I) are invariably accompanied by Form 1 or its transformations: V by Po, V/V by either Ro or Po, II (the diatonic form of V/V) and I by Po. These correspondences isolate the opening progression and the subsidiary 'prolongational' degrees. In retrospect it can be seen that the C chord (V_4^6) at bar 16 is not ultimately subordinate to the following V_5^6/V, its local resolution, since as a C major triad it is associated by row form with the other appearances of V in bars 3 and 19. However, since V/V shares both Po and Ro, V_4^6 is also weakly associated with the resolution, so that the fluctuation of tonality at this point is reflected in the ambiguity it introduces into the otherwise direct pairing of row forms and scale degrees.

vi Conclusion

Although the analysis has revealed a number of structural principles which unite the serial and tonal features of the song – primarily the notion of a tonal background transfigured in the foreground by serial procedures, and the correspondence of structural scale degrees in the bass with the different row forms – there remains a discontinuity between example 5.13d as 'background' and the actual music. The connections of tonal to atonal forms are not absolutely explicit and do not show enough regularity to draw a set of general principles from the mapping procedure. Thus, while the increasingly chromatic versions of the diatonic model (example 5.13) are easily generated from the simpler forms, no such procedure is available to connect example 5.13d to the fabric of the song. In this respect the analysis is inconclusive in the same way as Pople's analysis discussed in section 2. Pople explains that in *Lulu* the chorale chord sequence (which forms the basis of the chorale variations) is only tangentially related to a serial ordering, and that

> the final appended chord ... cannot be said to result from any serial statement. Its presence at the end of the sequence may perhaps be explained as a reference to quite a different kind of musical coherence: both this chord and the initial sonority of the sequence would, in a supportive context, be recognisable as cadential – that is, tonality-defining – harmonies in C major. (1983: p. 45)

Example 5.15a

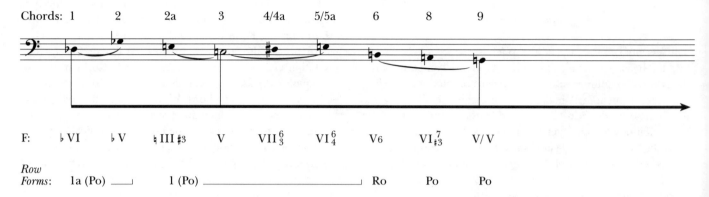

Example 5.15b Summary of Ex. 5.13 d/e

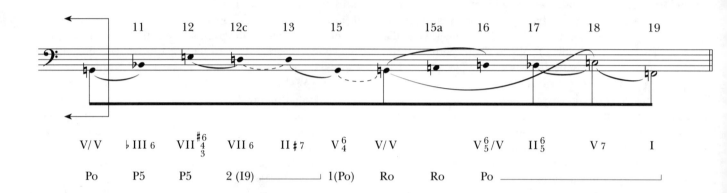

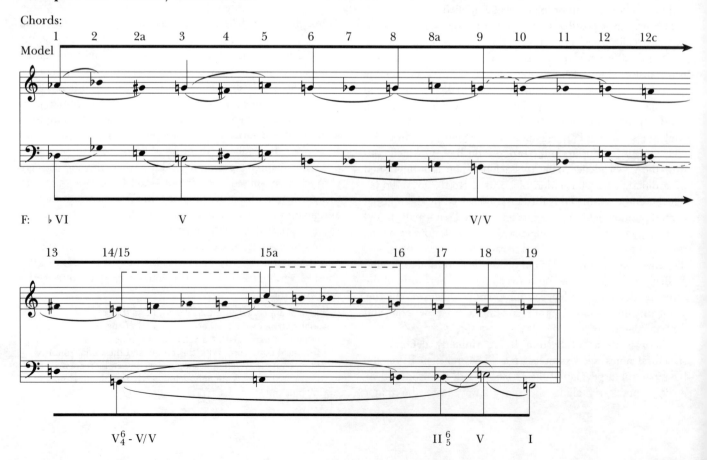

Example 5.15c

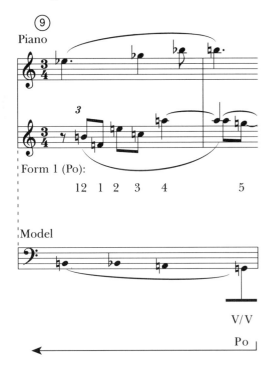

Example 5.15d

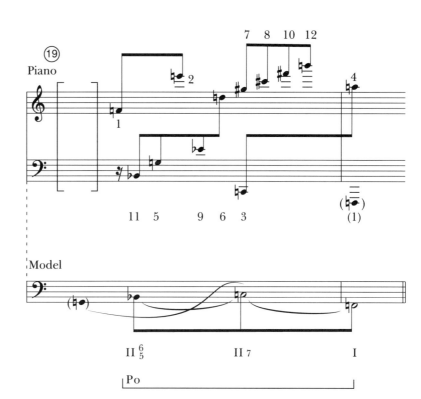

Since the intervening chords are not functionally related and are not the result of linear prolongations, it is not possible to connect all the chords of the chorale sequence in a tonal model: Pople suggests that, as 'the crisis points for serial coherence occur at the beginning and end of an ordered unit' (p. 45), tonal references may be regarded either as Berg's particular solution to a problem of (serial) composition or as a listener's solution to the problem of understanding the complex processes of serial pitch structure.

This is not the case in 'Schliesse mir'. Unlike parts of *Lulu*, all the tonal formations of the song are produced by relatively straightforward serial manipulation, so that the analyst is continually confronted with the possibility of a dual system of organization. The piece therefore stands as a more ambiguous, more closely integrated tonal-serial structure than the chorale variations of *Lulu*. Thus, the attempt to integrate the triadic forms with the serial organization of 'Schliesse mir' can be pursued only to the point reached in example 5.14a, by mapping one system of pitch organization onto another. Example 5.14a can therefore be read not only as an attempt to synthesize these systems, but also as a representation of the pitch ambiguity of the song by extrapolating the implied tonal system from it in

order to reveal the types of reference to that system produced by serial procedures normally employed to eliminate any such reference. 'Schliesse mir' is indeed a 'complicated' structure, since it essentially opposes serial and triadic (rather than tonal) forms: *Lulu*, on the other hand, is a 'complex' structure in which references to the tonal system itself – references that are not easily assimilable in the predominantly serial organization of the work – are basic. This at least suggests the possibility of a model that could eventually show how one system may influence another in a global sense; with 'Schliesse mir' however, this is a more remote possibility if the pitch ambiguity of the song is to be respected.

4   GUIDED READING AND REPERTORY

i   Reading

The most extensive discussions of 'Schliesse mir die Augen beide, II' are found in Hans Redlich, 'Afterword' (1960, and in George Perle, *The Operas of Alban Berg*, Vol. 2 (1985: pp. 7–10).

Joan Allen Smith, in 'Some Sources for Berg's "Schliesse mir die Augen beide" II' (1978), gives a valuable account of the sketch material and of the source for Berg's choice of series, Fritz Heinrich Klein's 'Die Grenze der Halbtonwelt' (1925).

The serial structure of the song and its relationship to *Lulu* is considered in detail in Wolfgang Budday, *Alban Bergs Lyrische Suite* (1979: pp. 20–4), and in Douglas Jarman's *The Music of Alban Berg* (1979: pp. 129–31).

A more superficial coverage of this topic appears in Etienne Barilier, *Alban Berg* (1978: pp. 145–6), and in Mosco Carner, *Alban Berg* (1983: p. 108).

A comprehensive treatment of tonality in Berg's serial music appears in Jarman (1979): pp. 93–4, 101–3, 131–40, 143–6). See also Anthony Pople, 'Serial and Tonal Aspects of Pitch Structure' (1983), for the first attempt to pursue this topic analytically, and his chapter on 'Harmony, Tonality and the Series', in *Berg: Violin Concerto* (1991: pp. 65–90).

Tonal configurations in Berg's atonal and serial music are approached in Adorno's *Alban Berg* (1991: especially pp. 1–8), and are mentioned in passing in many of the essays collected in Douglas Jarman (ed.), *The Berg Companion* (1989) and in David Gable and Robert P. Morgan (eds), *Alban Berg* (1991).

George Perle's *Serial Composition and Atonality* (1981: pp. 87–90), contains a general discussion of tonality and serialism in the music of the Second Viennese School. This issue is also considered more briefly in Hans Keller, *1975 (1984 minus 9)* (1977), and in Arnold Whittall, 'Schoenberg and the English' (1980).

ii Repertory

Tonal formations in the twelve-note music of the early twentieth century are almost exclusively found in the later works of Berg and Schoenberg. In particular see Berg's *Lyric Suite for String Quartet* (1926), the concert aria *Der Wein*, Part I (1929), *Lulu* (1935) and the Violin Concerto, Part II, Adagio (1935). For Schoenberg, see the Fourth String Quartet, third movement (1936), the *Ode to Napoleon* (1942), and the Piano Concerto, first movement (1942).

BIBLIOGRAPHY

Adorno, Theodor W., *Alban Berg: Master of the Smallest Link*, trans. Juliane Brand and Christopher Hailey (Cambridge: Cambridge University Press, 1991).

Ayrey, Craig, 'Berg's "Scheideweg": Analytical Issues in Op. 2/ii', *Music Analysis*, 1, 2 (1982), pp. 189–202.

Barilier, Etienne, *Alban Berg: Essai d'interprétation* (Lausanne: Editions l'Age d'Homme, 1978).

Budday, Wolfgang, *Alban Bergs Lyrische Suite: satztechnische Analyse ihrer zwölftönigen Partien* (Neuhausen-Stuttgart: Häussler, 1979).

Carner, Mosco, 1983: *Alban Berg: Life and Work* (2nd edn, London: Duckworth, 1983).

Gable, David, and Morgan, Robert P., eds, *Alban Berg: Historical and Analytical Perspectives* (Oxford: Clarendon Press, 1991).

Harris, Donald, 'The Berg–Schoenberg Correspondence: a Preliminary Report', *International Alban Berg Society Newsletter*, (1981), pp. 11–14.

Hindemith, Paul, *The Craft of Musical Composition*, trans. Arthur Mendel (rev. edn, New York: Associated Music Publishers, 1945).

Hicken, Kenneth L., 'Schoenberg's "Atonality" – Fused Bitonality?', *Tempo*, 109 (1974), pp. 27–36.

Jarman, Douglas, 1979: *The Music of Alban Berg* (London: Faber and Faber, 1979).

——, *The Berg Companion* (London: Macmillan, 1989).

Keller, Hans, *1975 (1984 minus 9)* (London: Robson, 1977).

Klein, Fritz Heinrich, 'Die Grenze der Halbtonwelt', *Die Musik*, 17, 4 (1925), pp. 281–6.

Morgan, Robert P., 'Dissonant Prolongations: Theoretical and Compositional Precedents', *Journal of Music Theory*, 20, 1 (1976), pp. 49–92.

Neighbour, Oliver, 'In Defence of Schoenberg', *Music and Letters*, 33 (1952), pp. 10–27.

Perle, George, *Twelve-Tone Tonality* (Berkeley: University of California Press, 1977).

——, *Serial Composition and Atonality* (5th edn, Berkeley: University of California Press, 1981).

——, *The Operas of Alban Berg*: Vol 2, *Lulu* (Berkeley: University of California Press, 1985).

Pople, Anthony, 'Serial and Tonal Aspects of Pitch Structure in Act III of Berg's *Lulu*', *Soundings*, 10 (1983) pp. 36–57.

——, *Berg: Violin Concerto* (Cambridge: Cambridge University Press, 1991).

Rauchhaupt, Ursula von, ed., *Schoenberg, Berg, Webern. The String Quartets: A Documentary Study*, trans. Eugene Hartzell (Hamburg: Deutsche Grammophon Gesellschaft, 1971).

Redlich, Hans, 'Afterword', in *Alban Berg: Zwei Lieder (Theodor Storm)* (Vienna: Universal Edition, 1960), pp. 7–11.

Schoenberg, Arnold, *Style and Idea*, trans. Erwin Stein (London: Faber and Faber, 1975).

——, *Theory of Harmony*, trans. Roy E. Carter (London, Faber and Faber, 1978).

Smith, Joan Allen, 'Some Sources for Berg's "Schliesse mir die Augen beide" II', *International Alban Berg Society Newsletter*, 6 (1978), pp. 9–13.

Travis, Roy, 'Towards a New Concept of Tonality', *Journal of Music Theory*, 3 (1959), pp. 275–84.

Whittall, Arnold, 'Schoenberg and the English: Notes Towards a Documentary, *Journal of the Arnold Schoenberg Institute*, 4, 1 (1980), pp. 24–33.

Wintle, Christopher, 'Schoenberg's Harmony: Theory and Practice', *Journal of the Arnold Schoenberg Institute*, 4, 1 (1980), pp. 50–68.

6

The Theory of Pitch-Class Sets

BRYAN R. SIMMS

I INTRODUCTION

The *set* is a fundamental concept in all branches of modern mathematics. It has proved a flexible and productive tool in technological research – especially in relation to the computer – and since the 1940s it has been applied to music as a way of understanding the relations which can exist among musical elements. A set is a clearly defined collection of entities. These may be objects of any sort, such as numbers, or musical materials, such as pitches. After sets have been defined, their relationships and transformations can be precisely and thoroughly investigated.

A set is normally symbolized by an upper-case letter; its constituent elements are usually enclosed in braces. In order to simplify typography in the discussion that follows, braces are replaced by brackets. For example, a set A consisting of all odd numbers 1 to 9 will be represented: A = [1, 3, 5, 7, 9]. Since the constituents of this set can be entirely specified, A is a *finite set*. Finite sets are the ones that have the greatest relevance to traditional music. The number of elements in a finite set is its *cardinal number* or *cardinality*. Set A shown above has the cardinal number 5.

Sets are generally *unordered* collections. If A = [1, 5, 8] and B = [5, 8, 1], for example, the two are functionally identical, and we can say that A = B. Such unordered sets are useful to represent pitch structures in 'freely' atonal music, in which composers often do not systematically preserve the order in which pitches occur. Relations of order can also be defined in a set, under certain conditions. Simply stated, a total order in a set stipulates that its elements exist in a relation of precedence to one another. If *a* and *b* are elements of a totally ordered set, *a* will either precede *b* or *b* will precede *a*, according to a predefined rule. Ordered sets are especially useful in depicting the notes of a tone row, since the order of occurrence of such notes is a fundamental compositional factor.

A basic relationship between two sets of different cardinalities is *inclusion*. If, for example, set A = [1, 2, 3, 4, 5] and B = [1, 2, 3], then B is included in A, or is a *subset* of A. In general, B is a subset of A (symbolized B ⊂ A) if and only if all elements of B are also found in A and if B is not identical to A (that is, B ≠ A). If B is a subset of A, then A will be called a *superset* of B.

Two sets of the same or different cardinalities may interact in a few basic ways, among which *union* (or addition), *intersection* and *complementation* have important musical analogies. The union of sets A and B (symbolized A ∪ B or A + B) produces a new set whose elements include all constituents of both A and B. If A = [1, 2, 4, 5] and B = [1, 2, 3], then A ∪ B = [1, 2, 3, 4, 5]. The intersection of sets A and B (symbolized A ∩ B or AB) produces a new set made of all elements found in common in both A and B. Thus, A ∩ B (see above) is the set [1, 2]. The complement of a set A (symbolized A' or Ā) is understood in terms of a larger or 'universal' set of which A is a subset. The complement of A is the set consisting of all elements of the universal set not found in A. If the universal set, for example, is [0, 1, 2, 3, 4, 5, 6, 7, 8, 9] and A = [1, 2, 4, 5], then A' = [0, 3, 6, 7, 8, 9].

Sets may be transformed by *functions* or *mappings*. A function is a rule which assigns to every element of the set one and only one entity. If A = [1, 2, 4, 5] and the rule of the function commands that every element of A be doubled, then the function transforms the elements of A, shown in the left column below, into the numbers shown in the right column:

Figure 6.1

$$1 \rightarrow 2$$
$$2 \rightarrow 4$$
$$4 \rightarrow 8$$
$$5 \rightarrow 10$$

The set A = [1, 2, 4, 5] is said to be the *domain* of the function and the new set into which it is transformed, [2, 4, 8, 10], is called the *range*. Certain musical transformations such as transposition and symmetrical inversion can be performed speedily and accurately by applying simple functions to sets of pitches which are represented by numbers.

2   ORIENTATION

If we represent musical elements as sets of numbers, we have begun to create a *model* of musical structure. Models are relatively simple interpretations of more complicated phenomena or processes. In the sciences, models are often constructed to provide analogies of phenomena that cannot be directly observed; these facilitate the prediction and discovery of still unknown facts. In music, the function of a model is primarily explanatory. Musical models (in the sense specific to this chapter) depict in a formal way the elements and relations inherent in sophisticated musical systems and literature and show their logical connections. Models of musical structure do not necessarily refer to compositional techniques or methods. Indeed, it is not significant whether a model was or was not consciously used by the composer as a working guide.

A model of musical structure provides the analyst with a theoretical apparatus to account for the organization of specific musical works. For a model to be successful, it must accommodate all musical phenomena pertinent to it. If the model deals with pitch, for example, there must be no structures of pitch that cannot be represented by it.

An analytic model must provide a formal language capable of its own logic and development, but it must also reflect the style and artistic content of the musical works which it represents. Thus, our investigation of the set-theoretical model will of necessity have two orientations: first, towards a general artistic and stylistic assessment of the music under consideration and, second, towards the mathematical apparatus. For the model to be meaningful as an analytical tool, the analyst must develop its abstract logic, but must also be guided in this development by musical understanding, sensitivity and insight.

Although many styles or systems of music are susceptible to analysis by set theory, post-tonal music of the twentieth century has proved especially amenable to such an interpretation. The first significant application of sets to music was made by the American composer and theorist Milton Babbitt.[1] Babbitt relied on his training as a mathematician to investigate precisely the formal properties inherent in the twelve-tone method of composition, a method which had been devised by Arnold Schoenberg and first put into practice in the early 1920s.

In the theory of ordered sets, Babbitt found a model by which a twelve-tone row and its manipulations could be represented concisely. This model then served to represent other aspects of music, such as rhythmic durations, and the same functions which generated transformations of sets of pitches (including transposition, inversion and retrograde motion) were applied to all non-pitch components of a musical work. Set theory guided Babbitt in his composing of 'totally serialized' music, in which all elements of a piece were integrated by their derivation from a single mathematically conceived source.

Babbitt recognized that ordered sets of pitches were not always primary factors in twelve-tone music, especially in Schoenberg's later dodecaphonic compositions. In some pieces, Schoenberg creates twelve-tone structures whose order of notes is unrelated to the order of the basic series. He does so by freely juxtaposing halves (or 'hexachords') of forms of the basic series, so that new presentations of all twelve notes will arise.

Example 6.1 Schoenberg: Fourth String Quartet, bar 27

An illustration of this technique is found in bar 27 – the beginning of a transitional passage in a free sonata form – of the first movement of Schoenberg's Fourth String Quartet (example 6.1). As shown by the boxes in this example, the violins state the basic series:

D C♯ A B♭ F D♯ E C A♭ G F♯ B
beat 1   2   3   4

The lower two instruments state the inversion of this row a fifth below:

G A♭ C B E F♯ F A C♯ D E♭ B♭
beat 1   2   3   4

Since the first hexachord of the inversion has no notes in common with the first hexachord of the basic series, their presentation in tandem in beats 1 and 2 creates a statement of all twelve notes. This statement is independent of the order of the basic series.

Babbitt used the term 'combinatoriality' to describe the general property of a tone row which allows for the formation of new chromatic aggregates. The phenomenon of combinatoriality is dependent not upon the order of notes within the hexachords of a row, but only upon their total content of pitches. So the model of the ordered set of pitches is not entirely appropriate to represent or to explain this important aspect of the twelve-tone system.

Schoenberg's manipulation of hexachords to create freely ordered chromatic aggregates pointed the way towards a new application of set theory to music based on *unordered* collections of notes. The first theorists after Babbitt to investigate the properties of such sets as they occur in twelve-tone music were David Lewin (1959, 1960, 1962) and Donald Martino (1961). Lewin suggested that unordered collections of pitches could be defined and differentiated from one another by their total *intervallic content*, that is, by the total numbers of different intervals that each note within such sets could form with every other note. Lewin also investigated 'segmental' associations in selected dodecaphonic works by Schoenberg, using the model of unordered sets. A segment in Lewin's usage is a contiguous subgroup of notes occurring in a form of a basic series. The identity of a segment is not determined by the order of its notes, but, instead, by the unordered content of its pitches and by its intervallic inventory. Martino devised a way to represent the total intervallic content of a segment and investigated how these collections could be combined into twelve-tone aggregates.

The American theorist Allen Forte (1964, 1973b) reinterpreted Babbitt's mathematical model for serialized music and put the studies of intervallic properties of unordered sets by Lewin and Martino to a new use. Forte developed the concept of the unordered set of pitches as a tool for harmonic analysis of freely atonal music. This repertory, which will henceforth be referred to simply as atonal music, includes works composed from about 1908 by such diverse figures as Schoenberg, Berg, Webern, Scriabin, Stravinsky and Bartók. Atonal music bypasses traditional tonality as a means of organization, and it also avoids the constraints of order imposed by serial methods of composition. Its harmonic vocabulary consists primarily of dissonant chords, and it may use traditional textures and traditional principles of motivic exposition and development. It is a body of music that is especially susceptible to the model of unordered sets, since the pitch materials of such works exhibit no abstract or pre-compositional order.

Perhaps reflecting a general decrease of attention to serial composition in the last fifteen years, theoretical writings in English during this time have come to identify the set-theoretic model with the way that it is used by Forte, that is, as a tool for the analysis of atonal music. Forte's application of the model, which has become the best known of several related systems, will be the basis for the following explanation, with references made, as appropriate, to other authors. The assumptions about the nature of atonal harmony which underlie Forte's mathematical model have a history extending well before Babbitt's research into twelve-tone music. The evolution in the theoretical literature of these assumptions and discoveries is sketched as this discussion progresses.

3   METHOD

Musical set theory is a model for harmonic analysis of atonal music. It provides a summary and explanation of the relations among structures of pitch and interval in this repertory. The mathematics of the theory are simple and rudimentary; much more important are the musical generalities and assumptions which inform the model. Its main elements are derived from two considerations: simplicity and flexibility in the mathematical apparatus and conformity to the general style of atonal music. We shall first survey those general stylistic features of the atonal repertory which are incorporated into the model and then summarize refinements in its mathematical dimension, which makes the theory simple, consistent and workable.

The most basic element of set theory derived from musical phenomena is the *octave equivalence* of notes. According to this observation, notes separated by one or more octaves are structurally equivalent. This assumption is also an element of traditional tonal theory, and it is supported by acoustical fact and by context in numerous atonal works. Let us compare, for example, two chords appearing in analogous positions in Anton Webern's song 'So ich traurig bin', op. 4 no. 4 (example 6.2). (This song will be the object of a more complete harmonic analysis later in this chapter.) The work is in a small ternary form (ABA'), in which the middle sections (bars 9–13) is made distinct from the outer sections by its more angular vocal line and by its contrasting texture in the piano part. The chords shown in Examples 2a and 2b begin the A and the A' sections, respectively. These chords contain the same notes – E F G G♯ B C – but five of the six occur in bar 13 in different registers compared with their position in bar 1. Clearly, it is misleading to interpret the chords as structurally distinct. Their parallel musical context and their similarity in sound show them to be equivalent.

Example 6.2a Webern: 'So ich traurig bin'

Bar 1

Example 6.2b Webern: 'So ich traurig bin'

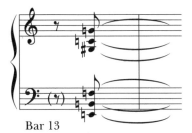

Bar 13

The concept of *pitch-class* is derived from the phenomenon of octave equivalence. A pitch-class is a representation of all notes separated by one or more octaves. All Cs, B♯s and D♭♭s in all registers, for example, are members of a single pitch-class. There are twelve pitch-classes in atonal music, and the basic elements of set theory are collections of these entities.

The pitch structures or 'harmonies' of set theory are not only vertical chords, but also lines or intersections of lines and chords. In general, atonal harmonies are constellations of *adjacent* pitches, although, occasionally, non-contiguous notes can be analysed as constituents of a pitch-class set if they are strongly associated by some musical context.

This integration of the vertical and horizontal in atonal harmony has precedents in tonal music, for example, in the linearized harmonies of an arpeggiated accompaniment. The presentation of harmonic units as lines or motifs is more often encountered in the atonal repertory. Schoenberg several times spoke of the identity of vertical and linear presentations of an atonal pitch structure. 'Tones of the accompaniment', he wrote in *Structural Functions of Harmony*, 'often come to my mind like broken chords, successively rather than simultaneously, in the manner of a melody'. In his essay 'My Evolution', Schoenberg was more explicit: 'A melodic line, a voice apart, or even a melody derives from horizontal projections of tonal relations. A chord results similarly from projections in the vertical direction'.[2]

Schoenberg's Piano Piece, op. 23 no 4, contains an illustration of the integration of horizontal and vertical presentations of harmonic structures. The principal motif of this work and a chord from the first bar of the coda are shown in example 6.3. Both statements contain the same six pitch-classes: G B♭ B D D♯ E. At the beginning, the set takes a linear, motivic shape; in bar 29, the presentation is essentially vertical. The work is unified by recurrences of both the motivic element, characterized by its rhythm, metre and contour, and the harmonic entity which the motif embodies, whose recurrences lend the piece intervallic unity.

The nature and constitution of chords in atonal music is a controversial matter requiring a brief survey of theoretical writings on atonal harmony. The basic harmonic units of

atonal music may consist of any combinations of the twelve pitch-classes. No single type of chord, such as symmetrical or tertian structures, has priority in this musical idiom. Atonal music is much more diverse in its harmonic vocabulary than tonal music, in which chords made from consonant intervals (i.e., triads) and other tertian structures such as seventh and ninth chords have a decided structural priority. To be sure, all the major composers of atonal music have exhibited their own distinctive harmonic vocabularies, but, in the atonal literature in general, no category of chords takes precedence a priori over any other.

Example 6.3a Schoenberg: op.23, no. 4, bar 1

Example 6.3b Schoenberg: op.23, no. 4, bar 29

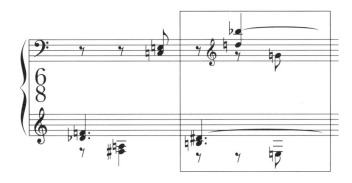

This assertion about the nature of atonal harmonies may appear unorthodox. Indeed, to the present day, writers on modern harmony assert that atonal music is built primarily upon tertian structures, which are usually distorted in sound and pitch content by melodic or voice-leading processes, by harmonic alteration, or by conflation into 'polytonal' formations.[3] Other writers have maintained that fourth chords or symmetrical harmonies are central.[4]

It should be recognized, however, that these theories of chords do not conform to the way that the music sounds; an appraisal at face value of the chords of atonal music supports the conclusion that all combinations of notes have been used as basic harmonies. This expanded view of atonal chords first began to appear in the 1920s in the writings of several German and Austrian theorists. Bruno Weigl's *Harmonielehre* (written in 1922, published in 1925) contains illustrations of 2,019 'chromatic chords' of between three and twelve pitch-classes. These resources, Weigl remarked, 'open a huge new field of countless harmonic combinations – at present still largely unused – whose

Figure 6.2

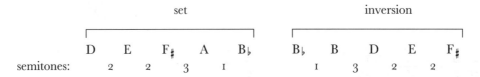

effect demands an entirely new and transformed framework for our musical perception, in a word, a completely new orientation of our sense of hearing'.[5] Weigl's chords are formed by ordered successions of intervals read vertically among notes limited to an octave in total span.

Fritz Heinrich Klein (1925) used mathematical processes to 'show the outer limits of our tonal universe'. He computed the total number of 'source chords' (*Urklänge*) which were available to the modern composer. 'I call source chords', he wrote, 'any groups of notes (without repetitions) to which absolutely any musical chord of one or more tones can be reduced'.[6] Klein's enumeration was accurate and exhaustive. He found a total of 4,095 source chords, in which figure he included all distinct unordered combinations of one to twelve pitch-classes.

Alois Hába pursued a similar goal in his *Neue Harmonielehre* (1927). 'The chords of new music', he stated, 'are vertical combinations of two to twelve notes of the chromatic scale placed in different interval relations – not exclusively consisting of thirds or fourths.'[7] In an attempt to illustrate 'the most comprehensive collection of harmonic constructs', Hába enumerated 620 chords of between three and eleven pitch-classes, in which he included unordered collections of notes which cannot be made identical by transposition. Although his tables are highly inaccurate, his theory, like Klein's and Weigl's, is evidence of a growing sensitivity to the comprehensive harmonic resources of modern music.[8]

The necessity for simplicity in the set-theoretical model prevents us from adopting Klein's 4,095 source chords as basic pitch sets. To do so would be unwieldy and would ignore relationships which are exhibited in atonal harmony. Systematic and musically justified principles of equivalence are needed to reduce the number of distinct set types.

According to Weigl's standard of equivalence, two chords are of the same type if they exhibit the same vertical order of intervals among pitch-classes. A chord spelt C D F, reading from bottom to top, for example, is equivalent to one spelt D E G or to any three-note collection that contains a major second and a perfect fourth above its bass note. We will see the limitations of this theory by applying it to the chords shown in example 6.2. These harmonies would, in Weigl's system, be judged non-equivalent, since they have different vertical intervallic structures. But this interpretation is untenable in light of their audible and contextual kinship.

Hába's principle of equivalence by transposition among unordered collections of pitch-classes more accurately reflects musical context. Let us compare the two accompanimental

chords which conclude the A and A' sections, respectively, of Webern's song (example 6.4). Their analogous context suggests that they are akin, despite their sharing only two pitch-classes in common and despite their different vertical order of intervals. Their relationship is through transposition and reordering, which can be observed if we place the contents of the two in a close, scalewise arrangement.

Example 6.4 Webern: 'So ich traurig bin'

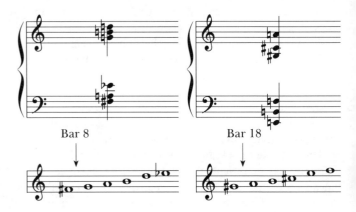

Hába's erroneous enumeration of non-equivalent collections of pitch-classes was corrected by the Czech composer and theorist Karel Janeček (1903–74) in his *Základy moderní harmonie* (written 1942–9, published in 1965). Janeček shows that there are 351 possible combinations of between one and twelve pitch-classes, if transposed collections are eliminated and if the order of presentation of the elements of a chord is not taken in account. Equivalence by transposition and reordering, likewise, is an assumption of set theory.

An additional principle by which collections of notes can be defined as equivalent is *inversion*. This term is used in set theory differently from its meaning in tonal theory. In the former, inversion is a symmetrical rotation of a set of pitches about one invariable note. We can invert the set D E F♯ A B♭, for example, by allowing its last note, B♭, to remain unchanged and then rotating the intervals formed by its other notes symmetrically around this pivot note. Therefore, A, a half-step below B♭, becomes B, a half-step above B♭; F♯, four semitones below B♭, becomes D; E remains E; and D becomes F♯. The symmetrical aspect of inversion is seen in figure 6.2 above.

The pivot tone B♭ is arbitrarily chosen: if any other pitch within the original set were chosen, the resulting inversion

Example 6.5 Berg: 'Nacht', bars 31–2

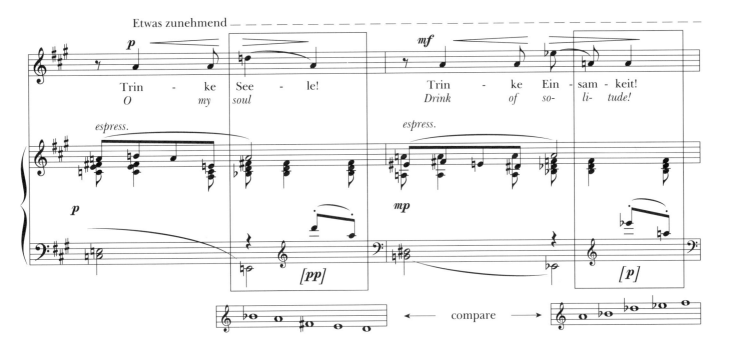

would be a transposition of or the same as the one shown above. We shall see shortly that the general conception and computation of inversions are much clearer using a mathematical model.

As with reordered and transposed sets, those varied by inversion often occur in 'equivalent' or analogous locations. An example of such a usage is found in 'Nacht' (*c.* 1908), from Alban Berg's *Seven Early Songs*. Bars 31 and 32 (example 6.5) contain passages with textual parallels ('Trinke Seele!/Trinke Einsamkeit!') and similar music. The second of these bars is but a slight motivic variant of the first. The last chord in bar 31 (boxed in the example) contains the pitches B♭, A F♯ E D (placed below the example, for purposes of comparison, in a close, scalewise order); the parallel chord in bar 32 has the pitch-class content A B♭, D♭, E♭, F. The relationship between the two chords is through inversion (followed by transposition). In set theory, such chords will be considered equivalent.

Equivalence by inversion has no important analogy in classical tonal harmony. The symmetrical inversion of a dominant seventh chord, for example, yields a half-diminished seventh – two chords which have entirely different functions in normative tonal progressions. A theoretical recognition of equivalence by inversion in modern harmony was first made by the German-American theoretician Bernhard Ziehn (1845–1912). His interest in the technique was stimulated by its appearance in strict canonic practices. Ziehn found that variants of tonal harmonic progressions in a chromatic, late romantic style could be obtained

simply by performing symmetrical inversion upon chords and lines.

The role of inversion in post-tonal music of the twentieth century was clarified by studies of the twelve-tone method of composition. In Schoenberg's classic formulation of this technique, basic pitch structures (i.e., tone rows) maintain their identity subsequent to inversion, transposition, or both. This perception was brought to the analysis of atonal music by Howard Hanson (1960). Hanson used the term 'involution' to denote symmetrical inversion, about which he writes, 'every sonority in music has a counterpart obtained by taking the *inverse ratio* of the original sonority. The projection *down* from the lowest tone of a given chord, using the same intervals in the order of their occurrence in the given chord, we may call the *involution* of the given chord' (p. 17). According to Hanson's theory, chords are equivalent despite reordering, transposition, involution, or a combination of the three. He enumerates a total of 216 'forms' or 'types' of non-equivalent chords of between three and twelve notes, and he also delves with great originality into the intervallic properties and interrelationships of these chordal types.

Hanson's theory of chords and intervallic structures is similar to Forte's, although the latter uses the language of set theory to expand upon harmonic relationships, while Hanson avoids mathematical models. Certain contemporary theorists who have used or commented upon set theory – including Howe (1965), Regener (1974) and Browne (1974) – reject as excessively general the principle of equivalence by inversion. There are, however, three arguments in its favour: the frequent occurrence

Example 6.6 Hauer: Piano Étude, op. 2, no. 1

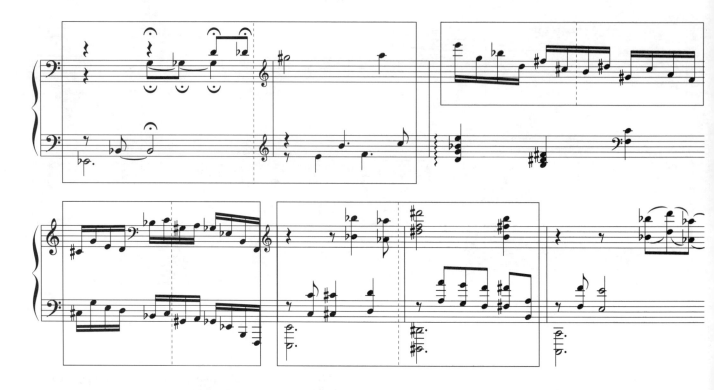

Example 6.7 Berg: *Wozzeck,* act 3, scene 4

Bar 219   220

of inversionally related sets in analogous musical contexts, the simplification in total numbers of set types, and the relationship of pitch-class inversion to total intervallic content. This last consideration will be explained later in this chapter.

Reordering, transposition and inversion establish relations among pitch-class sets which are sufficiently strong to be deemed equivalence. Relations of a different sort are created by complementation, similarity and inclusion. Two sets are *complementary* if they contain no elements in common and if their union produces the universal set of all twelve pitch-classes. The compositional juxtaposition of complementary sets is especially prominent in atonal music by composers such as Josef Matthias Hauer, Jefim Golyscheff, Herbert Eimart and

Nicolai Roslavetz, for whom the formation of complete chromatic aggregates was a paramount objective. Complementary sets are also commonly found in close proximity in the atonal music of Schoenberg composed just before his embarking on the twelve-tone method.

Example 6.6 is drawn from the beginning of Hauer's Piano Etude, op. 22 no. 1 (1922–3). It illustrates the constant juxtaposition of complementary hexachords (shown in the example by boxes and broken lines) which typifies this composer's music after 1919. Perpetual chromatic recirculation of tones was part of what Hauer termed the 'law' of atonal melody: 'within a particular succession of notes, no tones may be repeated and none omitted'.[9] From 1922, Hauer referred

Example 6.8 Berg: *Wozzeck*

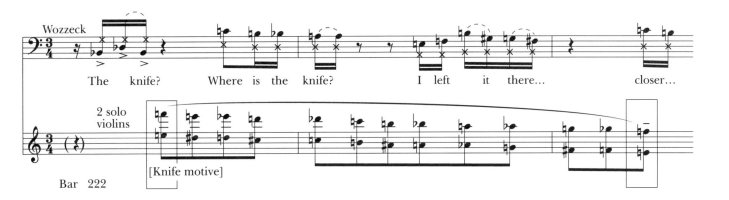

Example 6.9a Webern: 'So ich traurig bin'

Bar 13

Example 6.9b Webern: 'So ich traurig bin'

Bar 18

to such pairs of freely reorderable complementary hexachords as 'tropes'.

The association of complementary sets in other atonal works need not create complete twelve-tone aggregates if one of the sets is varied by inversion or transposition. The beginning of Act III, Scene IV, of Berg's *Wozzeck* (example 6.7) contains an example of this more abstract use of the principle of complementation. The chord in the trumpets and trombones in bar 219 is answered by another chord in the woodwinds and horn in bar 220. The harmony in the woodwinds forms the complement – varied by inversion and transposition – of the chord in the brass. This relationship may be illustrated by these steps:

set of pitches in bar 219: A B C D E F;

complement of this set: F♯ G G♯ A♯ C♯ D♯;

inversion of this complement about D♯: D♯ F G♯ A♯ B C;

transposition of this inversion up five semitones = the set of pitches in bar 220: G♯ B♭ C♯ E♭ E F.

The chords in bars 219 and 220 are not literally complementary,

since they share the pitch-classes E and F. Such notes which are maintained despite a transformation of a set are called *invariants*. They often receive special musical emphasis. In the immediately ensuing passage of *Wozzeck*, they form the boundary points of the Knife Motif, which is stated in the solo violins while Wozzeck frantically searches for the murder weapon (example 6.8).

Similarity is a measure of likeness between two non-equivalent sets of the same cardinality. It can apply either to pitch or to intervallic content. Let us compare the opening and closing hexachords which frame the reprise of Webern's song 'So ich traurig bin' (example 6.9). Since these hexachords share a common four-note subset (E F G♯ B), which occurs as the four lowest tones of both chords, we can conclude that the two are moderately similar as regards pitch.[10]

The *inclusion* relation is the most basic mode of interaction between two sets of different cardinalities. In Webern's song, the recurrence of major or minor triads (inversional forms of a single atonal set type) as subsets of larger chords lends the song a relatively familiar sonority. An E major triad, for example, is a subset of the accompanimental chords both at the beginning and end of the song (example 6.10).

Example 6.10a

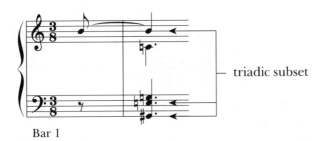

Bar 1

triadic subset

Example 6.10b

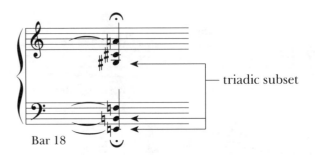

Bar 18

triadic subset

Example 6.11

Bar 1

Inclusion and complementation often occur simultaneously in Webern's song, as they commonly do in works by all the Viennese atonalists. This phenomenon, which Forte calls *embedded complementation*, is seen in the first bar of 'So ich traurig bin' (example 6.11). The five-note set that arises on the third beat of this bar, [E, G, G♯, A, C] (circled in the example), is evidently a subset of the seven-note collection made up of all notes of bar 1. The circled pentad is also a transposition of the complement of the larger set. This multiple relationship can be summarized by these steps:

set of all pitches of bar 1: E F G G♯ A B C;

complement of this set: B♭ C♯ D E♭ F♯;

transposition of this complement up six semitones = subset pentad: E G G♯ A C.

In fact, any set can be transformed by transposition, inversion, or both, so that it will be a subset or superset of its complement, with the sole exception of the pentad A B♭ C D E♭. This collection cannot occur in any form within its complement – a unique and remarkable property that led Hanson (1960) to dub it the 'maverick' sonority.

We now turn to the mathematical part of the theory,

by which musical phenomena that we have observed are represented in set-theoretical language. In atonal set theory, pitch-classes are represented by numbers such that C = 0, C♯ = 1, up chromatically to B = 11. The principle of octave equivalence requires that any operation or function on these numbers be carried out in 'modular' arithmetic, specifically, modulo (or 'mod.') 12. Stated simply, when we reach 12 in any operation, we return to 0.

To represent pitch-classes by integers facilitates operations within the model, and integers also provide a good analogy with the musical entities that they depict. Both are equally spaced, both are abstract entities, and numbers avoid the antiquated aspect of our tonal nomenclature, which suggests naturalness or priority in the diatonic collection A, B, C, D, E, F and G at the expense of 'accidentals'. Diatonic collections exhibit no general priority in atonal music. We shall also use the numbers 0 to 11 to represent the *interval* between two pitch classes; these numbers correspond to the number of semitones from one pitch class 'upward' to the second note. Operations on interval numbers must also be computed mod. 12.

The final chord of Webern's song 'So ich traurig bin' (see example 6.9b) contains the pitch classes E, B, F, G♯, C♯ and A; this chord is represented by the set [4, 11, 5, 8, 1, 9]. Even though the order of its elements does not affect the identity of the set, it will be useful for purposes of comparison to establish a standard referential sequence in which elements of a set will always be displayed. This will be termed *normal order*.[11] The normal order of a set meets three criteria: first, its elements are arranged in ascending numerical order (mod. 12); second, the interval between the first and last elements is as small as possible; and third, if two arrangements have the same minimal boundary interval, normal order is the one with the smaller intervals at the beginning.

To find the normal order of the set occurring at the end of Webern's song, we first put its elements into numerical order, thus [1, 4, 5, 8, 9, 11]. Next, we compute the intervals between each element as well as the interval between the last pitch-class and the first. This set of intervals is (3, 1, 3, 1, 2, 2), using parentheses to distinguish it from the notation of pitch-class sets. We then rotate this intervallic set (i.e., progressively place the first element at the end) until we find the rotation in which the largest interval is at the end. Since 3 is the largest interval and it occurs twice in the intervallic set, there are two such rotations: (1, 3, 1, 2, 2, 3) and (1, 2, 2, 3, 1, 3). The latter of these has the smaller intervals towards the beginning, so it represents normal order. Finally, we place the pitch-class numbers in a sequence which conforms to the intervallic set (1, 2, 2, 3, 1, 3), which gives [8, 9, 11, 1, 4, 5] as the normal order of this collection.

Transpositions and inversions of a set can be easily obtained by simple functions. A transposition is computed by adding (mod. 12) to each element a number from 1 to 11, corresponding to the number of semitones upward that the set is to be transposed. A transposition of our sample set up three semitones yields the new set [11, 0, 2, 4, 7, 8]. To compute the inversion we simply subtract every number in the original set from 12, allowing 0 to remain as 0. The inversion of the sample set is [4, 3, 1, 11, 8, 7], whose normal order is [7, 8, 11, 1, 3, 4].

Since we have postulated that all transpositions, inversion, and transpositions of the inversion of any set are equivalent, a pitch-class set will be a member of a collection of equivalent sets. We will call such collections *set classes*. Each class contains a maximum of 24 sets, but fewer if its sets are symmetrical or if its cardinal number is very high or very low.

It will be useful to establish as referential one set within a set class, just as we usually think of the root position of a triad or seventh chord in tonal music as the referential form by which this chord and all its inversions are known. This referential set which identifies its entire class is called *prime form*. It can be found as follows. Compare the normal order of a set and its inversion after these have been transposed so that their first elements equal 0. Since the sample set is [8, 9, 11, 1, 4, 5] and its inversion is [7, 8, 11, 1, 3, 4], we shall compare their transpositions down eight and seven semitones, respectively, which render the sets [0, 1, 3, 5, 8, 9] and [0, 1, 4, 6, 8, 9]. Prime form will be the one of these two with the smaller intervals towards the beginning, thus, [0, 1, 3, 5, 8, 9].

Forte (1973b, pp. 179–81) has arranged these prime forms into lists according to their cardinality and intervallic properties and assigned labels to them and to the set classes which they represent. His nomenclature for a set class consists of a number telling its cardinality, then a hyphen, then a number telling its position in his list. The set class represented by the prime form [0, 1, 3, 5, 8, 9] is labelled '6–31', that is, its prime form occurs as the thirty-first among set classes of six elements. Forte's lists are constructed so that complementary set classes occupy the same relative positions among sets of their own cardinal numbers. For example, the complement of any set within class 7–21 will be a member of class 5–21.

A basic characteristic of a set is its total *intervallic content*, which is an inventory of all intervals that each of its elements can form with every other. Since the elements of sets are pitch-classes rather than pitches in specific registers, the intervallic

distance between any two such entities is properly an *interval class* rather than an interval. An interval class is a collective representation of any interval, its inversion (i.e., octave complement) and octave compounds. Thus, the major third, minor sixth and major tenth all belong to a single interval class. There are six interval classes in atonal music. These will be represented by numbers from 1 to 6, such that the minor second belongs to interval class 1; the major second to interval class 2; and so forth, up to the tritone, which is a member of interval class 6.

To find the intervallic potential of the sample set [8, 9, 11, 1, 4, 5], we pair off its elements and record the interval class which separates them (see figure 6.3). The array of six numbers at the bottom depicts the total intervallic content of the set: Forte calls it the interval *vector*. It will be apparent that this total is not altered when a set is transposed or inverted, so the vector is the same for all sets within a class (in this case, the set class 6–31).

Figure 6.3

interval class:

	1	2	3	4	5	6
8–9	×					
8–11			×			
8–1					×	
8–4				×		
8–5			×			
9–11		×				
9–1				×		
9–4					×	
9–5				×		
11–1		×				
11–4					×	
11–5						×
1–4			×			
1–5				×		
4–5	×					

| Total: | 2 | 2 | 3 | 4 | 3 | 1 |

Even though all sets within a class share the same vector, it does not follow that all sets with the same vector are in the same class. In other words, not all sets with the same total intervallic content are inversionally or transpositionally equivalent. Consider, for example, the two tetrachords [0, 1, 4, 6] and [0, 1, 3, 7]. These have the same vector, [111111], but they cannot be made identical in pitch content by any combination of transposition or inversion.

Attention was first called in the theoretical literature to these 'twins' by Hanson (1960) and Lewin (1960). Forte refers to them as *Z-related* set classes, and he prefixes their set-class label with the letter Z. The tetrachords just cited are members of classes 4–Z15 and 4–Z29, respectively, which are the only Z-

Example 6.12 Berg: 'Warm die Lüfte'

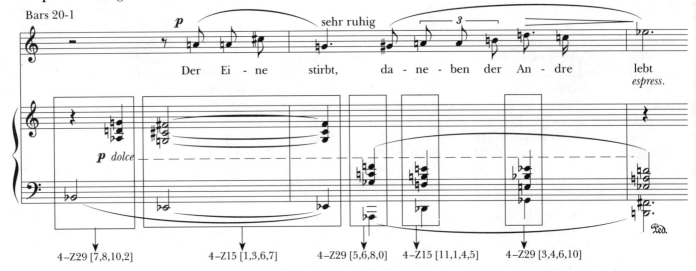

related set classes of cardinal number 4. There are a total of 23 such Z-related pairs of set classes, all of which have a cardinality of four to eight.

Z-related sets are often closely associated in the atonal repertory. An illustration is found in bars 20–1 of Berg's song 'Warm die Lüfte', op. 2 no. 4 (*c*. 1908–10) (example 6.12). The piano part in this passage is constructed of an alternation of forms of these two Z-related tetrachords. Claude Debussy later borrowed (perhaps unconsciously) this striking progression note-for-note in his fourth *Épigraphe antique*.[12]

Multiplicative operations are functions which generate sets related in novel ways. According to these functions, elements of a set are multiplied (mod. 12) by some factor. Multiplication by 11 (abbreviated 'M11') produces an inversion of a set. Multiplication by 5 transforms each semitone separating pitch-classes into a perfect fourth, and multiplication by 7 transforms each semitone into a perfect fifth. The result of the M5 transformation of any set will be the inversion of the result of the M7 operation.

The theorist and composer Herbert Eimert (1950) first called attention to the M5 and M7 operations as ways of transforming twelve-tone rows into new forms which were not among the classic 48 forms produced by transposition, inversion or retrograde arrangement. Eimert discovered that the M5 and M7 operations invariably transformed a twelve-tone row into a new row in which there could be no repetitions of pitch-classes. Whether these functions have applicability to atonal analysis is still undemonstrated. The M5 and M7 operations can transform some sets into their Z-related twins, but the operations do not consistently have this property.[13]

An analysis of most atonal works will reveal the presence of relatively large numbers of pitch-class sets of the same and of different cardinalities. Most of the relations between sets which have been defined so far – equivalence, similarity and Z-relatedness – pertain only to those of the same cardinality, and these are sufficiently restrictive to leave the relation between many sets uninterpreted. It is desirable to have a principle which can establish the relatedness of such sets as they occur over broad spans of music – a principle, that is, comparable with that of the tonic–dominant axis in tonal music, which organizes harmonic motion throughout entire movements.

A logical basis for such connections among sets is *inclusion*: the phenomenon in which one set is a subset of another. Inclusion of a literal sort is normally an isolated occurrence in atonal music. Of greater importance to the establishment of long-range connections among atonal harmonies is the abstract concept of inclusion among set classes.

To illustrate this principle, let us return to example 6.10 and compare the opening chord of the piano part in Webern's song with the closing chord. The first is the pentad [4, 7, 8, 11, 0], which is a form of class 5–21; the second chord is [8, 9, 11, 1, 4, 5], which is contained in class 6–31. One aspect of the relationship between these two harmonies, which was noted earlier, is the similarity of their pitches, since both sets contain an E major triad. The two chords are also related in a more abstract way. If the opening pentad were transposed up nine semitones, the resulting set, [1, 4, 5, 8, 9], would be literally contained in the final chord. Since there is at least one form of class 5–21 which is a subset of a form of 6–31, we shall say that 5–21 is a *subclass* of 6–31.

Forte uses the term *set-complex* to designate an entire collection of subclasses and superclasses of a given class. There are two types of set-complexes, which Forte labels K and Kh. The former is the more inclusive, since it consists of the central set class (which is called the *nexus*), its complement class, and all sub- and superclasses of either one. The more restrictive complex Kh consists of the nexus class, its complement class, and all sub- and superclasses of both. Set class 5–21 is clearly

Figure 6.4a Bars 1–5

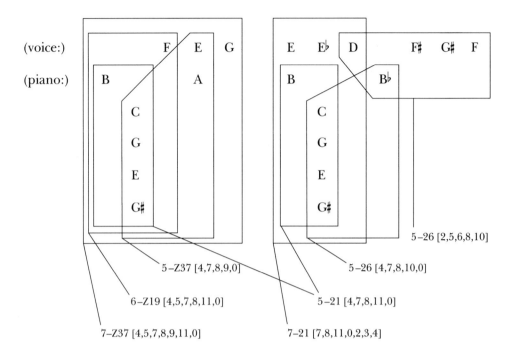

Figure 6.4b Bars 5–9

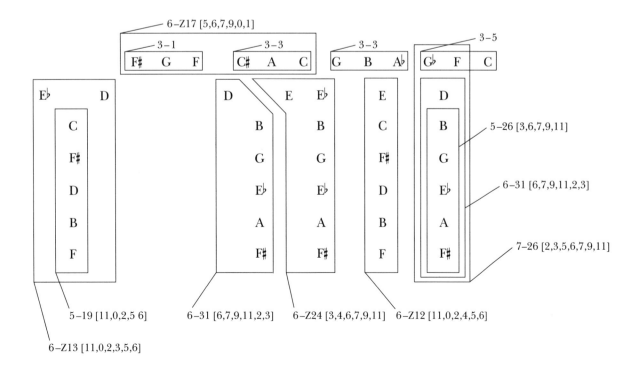

Figure 6.4c Bars 9–13

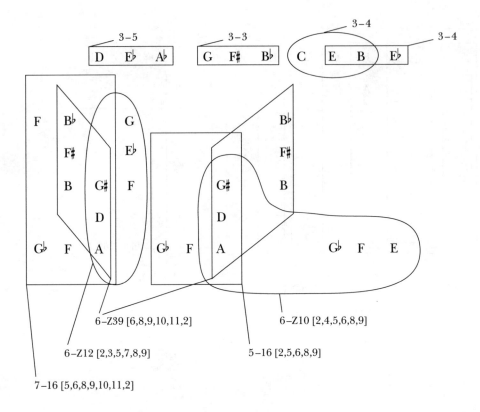

Figure 6.4d Bars 13–18

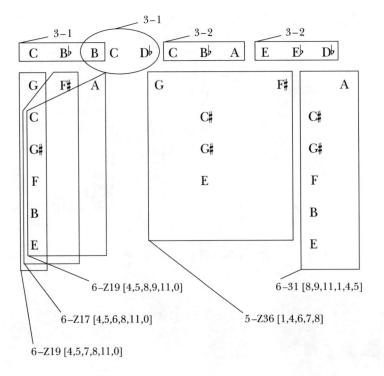

in the complex K of the nexus 6–31, since it is a subclass of 6–31. To be in the complex Kh of 6–31, 5–21 would also have to be contained in the complement class of 6–31. But 6–31 does not have a distinct complement class, since the complement of any of its sets remains in 6–31. For this reason, its K and Kh complexes are identical.

The set classes of atonal music are sometimes highly connected into K or Kh collections about one or a few nexus sets. Other works, such as the Webern song, are relatively unconnected by this abstract extension of the principle of inclusion.

4   MODEL

'So ich traurig bin' will now be the object of a brief harmonic analysis using the techniques and assumptions of set theory.[15] This piece was among Webern's first atonal compositions. It was written in either 1908 or 1909 as one of a group of fourteen settings of poetry by Stefan George. After experimenting with various combinations and orderings of these songs, Webern selected five to be published in 1919 as op. 3 (revised in 1921) and five more to be published in 1923 as op. 4. The remaining four were published posthumously as *Four Stefan George Songs* (1970).

The elegance of language and refinement of tone that characterizes the poetry of George were an inspiration to all the Viennese atonalists, especially to Schoenberg, who set George's verse in his opp. 10, 14 and 15. 'So ich traurig bin' is a poem in prose (using the authentic capitalizations) drawn from George's *Das Buch der Sagen und Sänge*:

So ich traurig bin	I am sad
Weiss ich nur ein ding:	And know but one thing:
Ich denke mich bei dir	I dream of being with you
Und singe dir ein lied.	And singing you a song.
Fast vernehm ich dann	Then I can almost hear
Deiner stimme klang,	The sound of your voice;
Ferne singt sie nach	From afar it sings back to me,
Und minder wird mein gram.	And my sorrow is lessened.

Webern's musical setting of these words is cast into a small ternary form (ABA'). Typically of his music in general, each of the three sections is articulated by a slowing of the tempo at its end and a return to a stable tempo at the beginning of the next section. The texture of the work is relatively simple. The piano accompaniment is chordal except for a linear figure in the top part. The vocal line is predominantly stepwise and chromatic in pitch content, and it contains no overt motivic recurrences.

The first step in a set-theoretical harmonic analysis is one of the most difficult and most crucial. This is the correct division or 'segmentation' of pitches into discrete collections. The analyst must be guided by divisions created by rhythm and metre, presentation of notes as chords, placement of rests,

groupings of notes under a slur or phrase mark, motivic elements and disjunctions in register or colour; he or she must also seek more covert units that are not immediately suggested by the musical context. The segmentation should be musically objective, but it must also aim towards discovering equivalent or closely related sets. In general, contiguous or adjacent notes are those which create significant harmonies.[16]

A segmentation of the entire song is given in figure 6.4a, b, c and d. Pitch-classes are shown by letter notation, without rhythm, metre or other details. This synoptic presentation of pitches should be compared with the complete musical text. The segmentation emphasizes sets of cardinal numbers 5, 6 and 7. Smaller sets are also operative, especially the tetrachord types 4–18 and 4–19. The vocal line is organized primarily by a succession of trichords, but these units are occasionally subsumed into larger sets.

Figure 6.4a shows pitches of the first half of the A section. Pitch-class numbers are put into normal order within brackets, and set classes are labelled according to Forte's terminology. Especially notable is the appearance of set class 6–Z19 at the beginning; the same set will recur to mark the reprise in bar 13. Also noteworthy are the embedded complements: 5–Z37 in 7–Z37 and 5–21 in 7–21. This integrated presentation of subsets and complements is a basic aspect of the harmonic language of the song.

The conclusion of the A section is depicted in figure 6.4b. Here the trichords of the vocal line are shown as segments, since they are only partially contained in important larger sets. The set class of the final harmony, 6–31, recurs to mark the conclusion of the song, so, like 6–Z19, it must be recognized as a basic element in the harmonic superstructure. The embedding of a complement is seen again at the end of this passage in the pair of classes 5–26/7–26.

The harmonies of the middle section of the song, represented in figure 6.4c, are generally different from those of the A sections. The association of Z-related set classes 6–Z10/Z39 is a new feature.

The reprise (figure 6.4d) recapitulates sets from the opening passage, including the articulative classes 6–Z19 and 6–31. The vocal line returns to its chain of fully or nearly chromatic trichords (3–1 and 3–2).

5   SUMMARY

This brief harmonic analysis accomplishes two objectives. First, it serves to point out specific relationships which might otherwise not be noted. Primary among these is the recurrence of set 6–Z19 in bars 1 and 13 and of set class 6–31 in bars 8 and 18, both of which contribute to a clarification of the ternary form of the piece. Second and more generally, the analysis presents a concise harmonic *summary* of the work, showing operative harmonic collections and depicting their relatedness or distinctness. A more detailed analysis could identify larger and smaller sets and assess the extent to which set classes are connected into set complexes. Other issues, such as voice-leading, harmonic progression and pitch centricity, can then be investigated in a meaningful context.

NOTES

1 An unpublished essay entitled 'The Function of Set Structure in the Twelve-Tone System' (1946) was Babbitt's first major writing of its type. It was followed by several published articles in which his theory is developed. See Babbitt, 1955, 1960, 1961 and 1973–4.

2 Schoenberg, *Structural Functions of Harmony*, ed. Leonard Stein (Rev. edn, New York: Norton, 1969), p. 194; Schoenberg, 'My Evolution', in *Style and Idea*, ed. Leonard Stein (Berkeley and Los Angeles: University of California Press, 1975), p. 87.

3 Edwin von der Nüll, in his *Moderne Harmonik* (Leipzig: F. Distner and C. F. W. Siegel, 1932), asserts that the bases of atonal harmony are diatonic collections of notes, which are diversified by mixing modes, simultaneous or successive bitonality, alteration and unresolved embellishing notes. Darius Milhaud ('Polytonalité et atonalité', *Revue musicale*, 4 [1923], p. 41) remarks, 'atonal music has its origins in chromaticism; ... chromaticism is based on the chord of the dominant seventh'. Other authors analysing atonal works in diatonic, triadic and tonally functional terms include Hugo Leichtentritt (*Musical Form*, 1951), Reinhold Brinkmann (*Arnold Schönberg: Drei Klavierstücke*, 1969) and Will Ogden ('How Tonality Functions in Schoenberg's Opus 11, Number 1', *Journal of the Arnold Schoenberg Institute*, 5 [1981]).

4 The view that atonal harmonies stem from fourth chords received support from a speculative chapter in Schoenberg's *Harmonielehre* (1911). See the translation by Roy E. Carter, *Theory of Harmony* (Berkeley and Los Angeles: University of California Press, 1978), chapter 21. Schoenberg's initiatives were developed in Hermann Erpf, *Studien zur Harmonie- und Klangtechnik der neueren Musik* (Leipzig: Breitkopf & Härtel, 1927), in which the author asserts that atonal or 'non-functional' harmony consists of symmetric chords such as those built of fourths, 'mixtures' (by which he refers to chords moving in parallel), or chords having several intervals of the semitone. Elmar Budde (*Anton Weberns Lieder Op. 3*, Wiesbaden: Franz Steiner, 1971) analyses the harmonies of Webern's early atonal songs by recourse to 'altered' fourth chords or chords which extend symmetrically from a central axis.

5 'Sie eröffnet ein neues, ungeheuer weites Feld zahlloser, derzeit zumeist noch unverbrauchter Klangkombinationen, deren Wirkung eine von Grund auf neue und veränderte Einstellung unserer musikalischen Aufnahmefähigkeiten, mit einem Worte eine vollkommene Neuorientierung unseres Gehörsinns.' Weigl, *Harmonielehre* (Mainz: B. Schott's Söhne, 1925), p. 372.

6 'Urklänge nenne ich jene Tongruppen (ohne Tonverdoppelung), auf die schlechterdings alle Akkorde (Ein- oder Mehrklänge) der Musik zurückzuführen sind.' Klein, 'Die Grenze der Halbtonwelt', *Die Musik*, 17 (1925), p. 281.

7 'Die Zusammenklänge in der neuen Musik sind vertikale Kombinationen von zwei zum zwölf Tönen der chromatischen Leiter in verschiedenen Intervallabständen, also nicht ausschliesslich in den Terzen oder Quarten.' Hába, *Neue Harmonielehre* (1927); repr., Vienna: Universal Edition, 1978), p. 111.

8 Hába's list of chords is highly redundant. See George Perle, 'The Possible Chords in Twelve-Tone Music', *The Score*, 9 (1954), pp. 54–8.

9 'Ihr "Gesetz" ... besteht darin, dass innerhalb einer gewissen Tonreihe sich kein Ton wiederholen und keiner ausgelassen werden darf.' Hauer, *Vom Wesen des Musikalischen* (Leipzig and Vienna: Waldheim-Eberle, 1920), p. 53.

10 Forte has defined precise measurements of pitch and intervallic similarity, which he labels Rp, R0, R1 and R2. See Forte, 1973b, pp. 46–60; see also Lord, 1981.

11 The related concept of *normal form* was put forward by Babbitt (see Babbitt, 1961, p. 77, and Howe, 1965, p. 49): Forte's definition of 'normal order' differs in minor details from Babbitt's. The method described here for obtaining normal order is taken from Regener, 1974.

12 H. H. Stuckenschmidt, 'Debussy or Berg? The Mystery of a Chord Progression', *Musical Quarterly*, 51 (1965), pp. 453–9.

13 Other aspects of these operations are discussed in Wuorinen, 1979, and Rahn, 1980.

14 See Forte 1973b, pp. 200–8, for an inventory of all Kh complexes about set classes of cardinalities 4 to 8. There is no published enumeration of K complexes.

15 For further practical information regarding set-theoretic analysis, see Forte, 1973b; Forte, 1978 (Introduction); Beach, 1979; and Schmalfeldt, 1983 (chapter 1).

16 See Forte 1973b, pp. 83–92, for further information on segmentation.

BIBLIOGRAPHY

i General

Babbitt, Milton, 'Some Aspects of Twelve-Tone Composition', *Score*, 12 (1955), pp. 53–61.

——, 'Twelve-Tone Invariants as Compositional Determinants', *Musical Quarterly*, 46 (1960), pp. 246–59.

——, 'Set Structure as a Compositional Determinant', *Journal of Music Theory*, 5 (1961), pp. 72–94.

——, 'Since Schoenberg', *Perspectives of New Music*, 12 (1973–4), pp. 3–28.

Baker, James M., 'Coherence in Webern's Six Pieces for Orchestra, Op. 6', *Musical Theory Spectrum*, 4 (1982), pp. 1–27.

——, *The Music of Alexander Scriabin* (New Haven, CT, and London: Yale University Press, 1986).

Beach, David W., 'Pitch Structure and the Analytic Process in Atonal Music: An Interpretation of the Theory of Sets', *Music Theory Spectrum*, 1 (1979), pp. 7–22.

Benjamin, William E., 'Review' of *The Structure of Atonal Music* by Allen Forte, *Perspectives of New Music*, 13 (1974), pp. 170–90.

——, 'Towards a Typology for Pitch Equivalence', *In Theory Only*, 1, 6 (1975), pp. 3–7.

Brinkmann, Reinhold, 'Die George-Lieder 1908/09 und 1919/23: Ein Kapitel Webern-Philologie', *Beiträge der österreichischen Gesellschaft für Musik* (1972–3), pp. 40–50.

Browne, Richmond, 'Review' of *The Structure of Atonal Music* by Allen Forte, *Journal of Music Theory*, 18 (1974), pp. 390–415.

Budde, Elmar, *Anton Weberns Lieder Op. 3: Untersuchung zur frühen Atonalität bei Webern*, Archiv für Musikwissenschaft, vol. 9 (Wiesbaden: Franz Steiner, 1971).

Chapman, Alan, 'Some Intervallic Aspects of Pitch-Class Relations', *Journal of Music Theory*, 25 (1981), pp. 275–90.

Chrisman, Richard, 'Identification and Correlation of Pitch-Sets', *Journal of Music Theory*, 15 (1971), pp. 58–83.

——, 'Describing Structural Aspects of Pitch-Sets Using Successive-Interval Arrays', *Journal of Music Theory*, 21 (1977), pp. 1–28.

——, 'Anton Webern's "Six Bagatelles for String Quartet", Op. 9: The Unfolding of Intervallic Successions', *Journal of Music Theory*, 23 (1979), pp. 81–122.

Clough, John, 'Pitch-Set Equivalence and Inclusion (A Comment on Forte's Theory of Set-Complexes)', *Journal of Music Theory*, 9 (1965), pp. 163–71.

——, 'Aspects of Diatonic Sets', *Journal of Music Theory*, 23 (1979), pp. 45–62.

——, 'Use of the Exclusion Relation to Profile Pitch-Class Sets', *Journal of Music Theory*, 27 (1983), pp. 181–202.

Crotty, John E., 'A Preliminary Analysis of Webern's Opus 6, No. 3', *In Theory Only*, 5, 2 (1979), pp. 23–32.

Daniel, Keith W., 'A Preliminary Investigation of Pitch-Class Set Analysis in the Atonal and Polytonal Works of Milhaud and Poulenc', *In Theory Only*, 6, 6 (1982), pp. 22–48.

Dean, Jerry, 'Schoenberg's Vertical-Linear Relationships in 1908', *Perspectives of New Music*, 12 (1973–4), pp. 173–9.

Dobay, Thomas R. de, 'The Evolution of Harmonic Style in the Lorca Works of Crumb', *Journal of Music Theory*, 27 (1984), pp. 89–112.

Eimert, Herbert, *Lehrbuch der Zwölftontechnik* (Wiesbaden: Breitkopf & Härtel, 1950).

Enderton, Herbert B., *Elements of Set Theory* (New York: Academic Press, 1977).

Eriksson, Tore, 'The IC Max Point Structure, MM Vectors and Regions', *Journal of Music Theory*, 30 (1986), pp. 95–111.

Erpf, Hermann, *Studien zur Harmonie- und Klangtechnik der neueren Musik* (Leipzig: Breitkopf & Härtel, 1927).

Falck, Robert, 'Schoenberg's (and Rilke's) "Alle, welche dich suchen"', *Perspectives of New Music*, 12 (1973–4), pp. 87–98.

Forte, Allen, 'Context and Continuity in an Atonal Work: A Set-Theoretical Approach', *Perspectives of New Music*, 1 (1963), pp. 72–82.

——, 'A Theory of Set-Complexes for Music', *Journal of Music Theory*, 8 (1964), pp. 136–83.

——, 'The Domain and Relations of Set-Complex Theory', *Journal of Music Theory*, 9 (1965), pp. 173–80.

——, 'Sets and Nonsets in Schoenberg's Atonal Music', *Perspectives of New Music*, 11 (1972–3), pp. 43–64.

——, 'The Basic Intervallic Patterns', *Journal of Music Theory*, 17 (1973a), pp. 234–73.

——, *The Structure of Atonal Music* (New Haven, CT, and London: Yale University Press, 1973b).

——, 'Analysis Symposium. Webern: Orchestral Pieces (1913), Movement 1 ("Bewegt")', *Journal of Music Theory*, 18 (1974), pp. 13–43.

——, *The Harmonic Organization of the Rite of Spring* (New Haven, CT, and London: Yale University Press, 1978a).

——, 'Schoenberg's Creative Evolution: The Path to Atonality', *Musical Quarterly*, 64 (1978b), pp. 133–76.

——, 'The Magical Kaleidoscope: Schoenberg's First Atonal Masterwork, Opus 11, No. 1', *Journal of the Arnold Schoenberg Institute*, 5 (1981), pp. 127–68.

——, 'Pitch-Class Set Analysis Today', *Musical Analysis*, 4 (1985a), pp. 29–58.

——, 'Tonality, Symbol and Structural Levels in Berg's *Wozzeck*', *Musical Quarterly*, 71 (1985b), pp. 474–99.

Gilbert, Steven E., 'The "Twelve-Tone System" of Carl Ruggles: A Study of the Evocations for Piano', *Journal of Music Theory*, 14 (1970), pp. 68–91.

——, 'An Introduction to Trichordal Analysis', *Journal of Music Theory*, 18 (1974), pp. 338–63.

Hába, Alois, *Neue Harmonielehre* (1927. Reprint, Vienna: Universal Edition, 1978).

Hanson, Howard, *Harmonic Materials of Modern Music: Resources of the Tempered Scale* (New York: Appleton-Century-Crofts, 1960).

Hasty, Christopher, 'Segmentation and Process in Post-Tonal Music', *Music Theory Spectrum*, 3 (1981), pp. 54–73.

Hauer, Josef Matthias, *Vom Wesen des Musikalischen* (Leipzig and Vienna: Waldheim-Eberle, 1920).

——, 'Sphärenmusik', *Melos*, 3 (1922), pp. 132–3.

——, 'Die Tropen', *Anbruch*, 6 (1924), pp. 18–21.

——, *Vom Melos zur Pauke: Eine Einführung in die Zwölftonmusik* (Vienna and New York: Universal Edition, 1925a).

——, 'Die Tropen und ihre Spannungen zum Dreiklang', *Die Musik*, 17 (1925b), pp. 257–8.

Hoover, Mark, 'Set Constellations', *Perspectives of New Music*, 23 (1984–5), pp. 164–79.

Howe, Hubert S., Jr, 'Some Combinational Properties of Pitch Structures', *Perspectives of New Music*, 4 (1965), pp. 45–61.

Hrbacek, Karel, *Introduction to Set Theory* (2nd rev. edn, New York: M. Dekker, 1984).

Hyde, Martha MacLean, 'The Roots of Form in Schoenberg's Sketches', *Journal of Music Theory*, 24 (1980a), pp. 1–36.

——, 'The Telltale Sketches: Harmonic Structure in Schoenberg's Twelve-Tone Method', *Musical Quarterly*, 66 (1980b), pp. 560–80.

——, 'Musical Form and the Development of Schoenberg's Twelve-Tone Method', *Journal of Music Theory*, 29 (1985), pp. 85–143.

Janeček, Karel, *Základy moderní harmonie* (Prague, 1965).

Johnson, Peter, 'Symmetrical Sets in Webern's Op. 10, No. 4', *Perspectives of New Music*, 17 (1978), pp. 219–29.

Joseph, Charles M., 'Structural Coherence in Stravinsky's *Piano-Rag-Music*', *Music Theory Spectrum*, 4 (1982), pp. 76–91.

Kielian-Gilbert, Marianne, 'Relationships of Symmetrical Pitch-Class Sets and Stravinsky's Metaphor of Polarity', *Perspectives of New Music*, 21 (1982–3), pp. 209–40.

Klein, Fritz Heinrich, 'Die Grenze der Halbtonwelt', *Die Musik*, 17 (1925), pp. 281–86.

Kolneder, Walter, *Anton Webern: An Introduction to His Work*, trans. Humphrey Searle (Berkeley and Los Angeles: University of California Press, 1968).

Lansky, Paul, 'Pitch-Class Consciousness', *Perspectives of New Music*, 13 (1974–5), pp. 30–56.

Lewin, David, 'Intervallic Relations Between Two Collections of Notes', *Journal of Music Theory*, 3 (1959), pp. 298–301.

——, 'The Intervallic Content of a Collection of Notes, Intervallic Relations Between a Collection of Notes and its Complement: An Application to Schoenberg's Hexachordal Pieces', *Journal of Music Theory*, 4 (1960), pp. 98–101.

——, 'A Theory of Segmental Association in Twelve-Tone Music', *Perspectives of New Music*, 1 (1962), pp. 89–116.

——, 'Forte's Interval Vector, My Interval Function, and Regener's Common-Note Function', *Journal of Music Theory*, 21 (1977a), pp. 194–237.

——, 'Some Notes on Schoenberg's Opus 11', *In Theory Only*, 3, 1 (1977b), pp. 3–7.

——, 'Some New Constructs Involving Abstract PC Sets, and Probabilistic Applications', *Perspectives of New Music*, 18 (1979–80), pp. 433–44.

——, 'On Generalized Intervals and Transformations', *Journal of Music Theory*, 24 (1980), pp. 243–52.

——, 'Transformational Techniques in Atonal and Other Music Theories', *Perspectives of New Music*, 21 (1982–3), pp. 312–71.

Lewis, Christopher, 'Tonal Focus in Atonal Music: Berg's op. 5/3', *Music Theory Spectrum*, 3 (1981), pp. 84–97.

Lissa, Zofia, 'Geschichtliche Vorform der Zwölftontechnik', *Acta musicologica*, 7 (1935), pp. 15–21.

Lord, Charles, 'Intervallic Similarity Relations in Atonal Set Analysis', *Journal of Music Theory*, 25 (1981), pp. 91–114.

Maegaard, Jan, 'The Nomenclature of Pitch-Class Sets and the Teaching of Atonal Theory', *Journal of Music Theory*, 29 (1985), pp. 299–314.

Marra, James, 'Interrelations Between Pitch and Rhythmic Structure in Webern's Opus 11, No. 1', *In Theory Only*, 7, 2 (1983), pp. 3–33.

Martino, Donald, 'The Source Set and its Aggregate Formations', *Journal of Music Theory*, 5 (1961), pp. 224–73.

Marvin, Elizabeth West, 'The Structural Role of Complementation in Webern's *Orchestral Pieces (1913)*', *Music Theory Spectrum*, 5 (1983), pp. 76–88.

Mead, Andrew, 'Pitch Structure in Elliott Carter's String Quartet No. 3', *Perspectives of New Music*, 22 (1983–4), pp. 31–60.

Moldenhauer, Hans, and Moldenhauer, Rosaleen, *Anton von Webern: A Chronicle of His Life and Work* (New York: Alfred A. Knopf, 1979).

Morris, Robert, 'A Similarity Index for Pitch-Class Sets', *Perspectives of New Music*, 18 (1979–80), pp. 445–60.

——, 'Set Groups, Complementation, and Mappings Among Pitch-Class Sets', *Journal of Music Theory*, 26 (1982), pp. 101–44.

——, 'Set-Type Saturation Among Twelve-Tone Rows', *Perspectives of New Music*, 22 (1983–4), pp. 187–217.

Neumeyer, David, *The Music of Paul Hindemith* (New Haven, CT, and London: Yale University Press, 1986).

Parks, Richard S., 'Pitch Organization in Debussy: Unordered Sets in "Brouillards"', *Music Theory Spectrum*, 2 (1980), pp. 119–34.

——, 'Harmonic Resources in Bartók's "Fourths"', *Journal of Music Theory*, 25 (1981), pp. 245–74.

——, 'Tonal Analogues as Atonal Resources and their Relation to Form in Debussy's Chromatic Etude', *Journal of Music Theory*, 29 (1985), pp. 33–60.

Perle, George, 'The Possible Chords in Twelve-Tone Music', *The Score*, 9 (1954), pp. 54–8.

——, *Serial Composition and Atonality* (4th edn, Berkeley and Los Angeles: University of California Press, 1977).

Pinter, Charles C., *Set Theory* (Reading, MA: Addison-Wesley, 1971).

Rahn, John, 'Relating Sets', *Perspectives of New Music*, 18 (1979–80), pp. 483–98.

——, *Basic Atonal Theory* (New York and London: Longman, 1980).

Regener, Eric, 'On Allen Forte's Theory of Chords', *Perspectives of New Music*, 13 (1974), pp. 191–212.

Rothgeb, John, 'Some Uses of Mathematical Concepts in Theories of Music', *Journal of Music Theory*, 10 (1966), pp. 200–15.

Rouse, Steve, 'Hexachords and their Trichordal Generators: An Introduction', *In Theory Only*, 8, 8 (1984), pp. 19–33.

Sargeant, Winthrop, 'Bernhard Ziehn: Precursor', *Musical Quarterly*, 19 (1933), pp. 169–77.

Schiff, David, *The Music of Elliott Carter* (London: Eulenburg, 1983).

Schmalfeldt, Janet, *Berg's Wozzeck: Harmonic Language and Dramatic Design* (New Haven, CT, and London: Yale University Press, 1983).

Simms, Bryan R., 'Line and Harmony in the Sketches of Schoenberg's "Serophita", op. 22, no. 1', *Journal of Music Theory*, 26 (1982), pp. 291–312.

Starr, Daniel, 'Sets, Invariance and Partitions', *Journal of Music Theory*, 22 (1978), pp. 1–42.

Starr, Daniel, and Morris, Robert, 'A General Theory of Combinatoriality and the Aggregate', *Perspectives of New Music*, 16 (1977–8), pp. 3–35, 50–84.

Teitelbaum, Richard, 'Intervallic Relations in Atonal Music', *Journal of Music Theory*, 9 (1965), pp. 72–127.

van den Toorn, Pieter, *The Music of Igor Stravinsky* (New Haven, CT, and London: Yale University Press, 1983).

Weigl, Bruno, *Die Lehre von der Harmonik der diatonischen, der ganztönigen und der chromatischen Tonreihe* (Mainz: B. Schott's Söhne, 1925).

Williams, Edgar Warren, Jr, 'On Mod 12 Complementary Interval Sets', *In Theory Only*, 7, 2 (1983), pp. 34–43.

Wittlich, Gary, 'Interval Set Structure in Schoenberg's Op. 11, No. 1', *Perspectives of New Music*, 13 (1974–5), pp. 41–55.

Wood, Jeffrey, 'Tetrachordal and Inversional Structuring in Arnold Schoenberg's Herzgewächse, Op. 20', *In Theory Only*, 7, 3 (1983), pp. 23–4.

Wuorinen, Charles, *Simple Composition* (New York and London: Longman.

Ziehn, Bernhard, *Canonical Studies* (Milwaukee: Kaun, 1912).

ii   Analyses

The following works are analysed by set-theoretic means in the publications indicated.

Bartók, Béla, *Mikrokosmos*, vol. 5: 'Fourths': Parks, 1981.

Berg, Alban, Orchestral Songs, op. 4 no. 3 ('Über die Grenzen'): Forte, 1973.

——, Four Pieces for Clarinet and Piano, op. 5 no. 3: Lewis, 1981.

——, *Wozzeck*, Act I, scene I, and passim: Schmalfeldt, 1983.

——, *Wozzeck*, Act III, scene I, variation 5: Forte, 1985.

Debussy, Claude, *Préludes*, book 2: 'Brouillards': Parks, 1980.

——, *Etudes*, book 2: 'Pour les degrés chromatiques': Parks, 1985.

Hindemith, Paul, Sonata for Solo Cello, op. 25 no. 3: Neumeyer, 1986.

Ruggles, Carl, Evocations for Piano, nos. 1–4: Gilbert, 1970.

——, *Evocation* for Piano, no. 2: Chapman, 1981.

Schoenberg, Arnold, Three Piano Pieces, op. 11 no. 1: Forte, 1981.

——, Three Piano Pieces, op. 11: Lewin, 1977b.

——, Fifteen Verses from *The Book of the Hanging Gardens*, op. 15 nos. 2, 6 and 11: Dean, 1973–4.

——, Five Orchestral Pieces, op. 16 no. 2: Lansky, 1974–5.

——, Five Orchestral Pieces, op. 16 no. 3: Forte, 1973.

——, Five Orchestral Pieces, op. 16 no. 3: Rahn, 1980.

——, Six Little Piano Pieces, op. 19: Forte, 1963.

——, *Herzgewächse*, op. 20: Wood, 1983.

——, Four Songs, op. 22 no. 1 ('Seraphita'): Simms, 1982.

——, Four Songs, op. 22 no. 2 ('Alle, welche dich suchen'): Falck, 1973–4.

Scriabin, Alexander, Piano Sonata no. 4, op. 30: Baker, 1986.

——, Piano Sonata no. 5, op. 53: Baker, 1986.

——, *Poem of Ecstasy*, op. 54: Baker, 1986.

——, *Feuillet d'album*, op. 58: Baker, 1986.

——, Prelude, op. 59 no. 2: Baker, 1986.

——, *Poem of Fire*, op. 60: Baker, 1986.

——, Piano Sonata no. 10, op. 70: Baker, 1986.

Stravinsky, Igor, Four Studies for Orchestra, no. 2: Forte, 1973.

——, *Piano-Rag-Music*: Joseph, 1982.

——, *Rite of Spring*: Forte, 1978.

Webern, Anton, Five Movements for String Quartet, op. 5 nos. 1 and 5: Teitelbaum, 1965.

——, Five Movements for String Quartet, op. 5 no. 4: Beach, 1979.

——, Five Movements for String Quartet, op. 5 no. 4: Forte, 1964.

——, Six Pieces for Large Orchestra, op. 6: Baker, 1982.

——, Six Pieces for Large Orchestra, op. 6 no. 3: Crotty, 1979.

——, Four Pieces for Violin and Piano, op. 7 no. 3: Forte, 1973.

——, Six Bagatelles for String Quartet, op. 9: Chrisman, 1979.

——, Five Pieces for Orchestra, op. 10 no. 3: Beach, 1979.

——, Five Pieces for Orchestra, op. 10 no. 4: Johnson, 1978.

——, Three Little Pieces for Violoncello and Piano, op. 11 no. 1: Marra, 1983.

——, Orchestral Pieces (1913), no. 1: Forte, 1974.

——, Orchestral Pieces (1913): Marvin, 1983.

7

Foreground Rhythm in Early Twentieth-Century Music

ALLEN FORTE

I ORIENTATION

The term 'foreground rhythm' refers to rhythmic patterns of smaller scale, usually those formed by adjacent components (pitches or rests). It is intended to describe the more immediate rhythmic surface of the music, as distinct from rhythmic patterns of large scale. Yet, although this chapter concentrates on foreground rhythm it does touch upon rhythms of larger scale here and there, those patterns that engage non-contiguous elements.

In order to limit the scope of the chapter to elementary considerations, I define rhythmic pattern as a set of successive durations with a first component (onset) and a last component (terminal). For the purpose of this chapter we may regard a rhythmic pattern either as a durational succession formed in a single horizontal strand of music or, going one step further, as determined in one strand by the interaction of one pattern with another. Both types of elementary pattern are illustrated in the analysis that follows.

As suggested above, in the ensuing discussion I shall concentrate on the durational aspect of rhythm, and assume that the duration of a particular event is its essential rhythmic characteristic. Other rhythmic attributes such as accent, contour and registral placement, while important, are complementary and subsidiary.[1]

For the purpose of the present discussion I will avoid questions of metre, since analysis of foreground rhythm in non-tonal music more often than not places regular accentual pattern in the background. Indeed, it is likely that such constructs may be more appropriate to the analysis of tonal music, with its highly determinate syntax.

The annotated bibliography contains references to the relevant literature, which is not extensive, for this is a relatively new field of enquiry – excluding from consideration, of course, an older literature that consists almost exclusively of recitations of rhythmic schemes divorced from other aspects of structure, notably pitch. An exhaustive discussion of various current approaches and issues will not be undertaken here, although I will make some comments in connection with the bibliography that will guide the reader towards further study in this vital and interesting area.

I shall not attempt to deal with every aspect of the work that serves as model for this chapter, but will direct the reader's attention mainly to pitch organization as it relates to rhythm (or vice versa), for this is perhaps the major analytical issue in recent music theory, both for tonal and non-tonal music. In the past there has been a strong tendency to separate the analysis of pitch structure from the analysis of rhythm – for example, to deal with rhythmic features such as isorhythms and canons and to specify harmonic content and relations, but to disregard the question of correspondences between the domains of rhythm and pitch. I will try to avoid that artificial separation in this essay.

Bartók's piano composition the eighth of the *Fourteen Bagatelles*, op. 6, stands at the very threshold of early twentieth-century music, along with the avant-garde music of Schoenberg, Webern and Ives. Written in 1908, it is among the earliest of Bartók's iconoclastic compositions, works which retained an element of folk music, here most obviously in the declamatory nature of the melodic phrases and the improvisational feeling of the whole, while reaching forth into new domains of pitch and rhythmic organization.

Although it is an early work, much can be learned from the *Bagatelle* that applies to the study of Bartók's later music, in which the coordination of pitch and rhythmic structures is developed in more systematic and perhaps more obvious ways. It may also be said that some of the musical procedures revealed in this work – in particular, the often intricate association of rhythm and pitch in which rhythm plays a differential as well as a unifying role – are exhibited in the music of other early twentieth-century composers. It is hoped therefore that the present brief study may have applicability beyond the confines of this short model.

Example 7.1 First subject

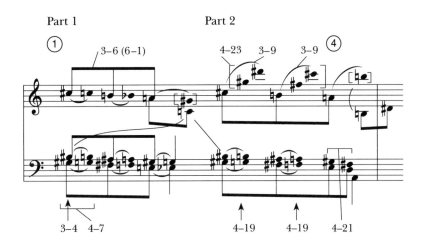

2   METHOD

The theory of pitch-class sets (see chapter 6) and this author's research in rhythm of non-tonal music underlie the analytical method, which also incorporates aspects of linear analysis, since Bartók's music appears to lend itself in a convincing and natural way to adaptations of linear techniques. The term 'linear techniques' refers to that part of the analytical method that employs elementary reductive procedures to uncover underlying essential horizontal motions. An introductory example is given below.

In the absence of a fully fledged theory of linear structural levels for non-tonal music, we proceed on a piece-by-piece, localized basis – a 'contextual' approach. However, since we will consistently refer to a specific theoretical framework (pitch-class set theory), this approach is not to be equated with the *ad hoc* methods that are frequently devised in an effort to explain the musical content of the atonal work.

After a brief look at the succession of parts in the *Bagatelle*, its 'form', I shall begin to carry out the most elementary of analytical operations, the identification of pitch-class sets. This basic, but most important step in the analytical procedure necessarily entails making decisions about 'segmentation', determining the musical units that are to be the object of analytical consideration. Here we will begin in the simplest manner possible, taking the surface configurations at face value. Subsequently, however, on the basis of information obtained about pitch and rhythmic structures over the span of the entire composition, we may modify and refine our reading of pitch-class components to reveal slightly concealed connections. As an uncomplicated example of this, we take the upper-voice melody of bar 1 to consist of $c\sharp'$–b'–a' filled in by passing notes to create the complete chromatic motion descending from $c\sharp'$ to a'. This is justified because the composer himself supplies a reduction in his variant of the upper-voice motion in bars 3–4, where the chromatic passing notes are omitted. This is the uncomplicated example of the reductive linear technique mentioned above.

3   MODEL

i   Form

The overall design of this piece resembles that of a miniature sonata.[2] The exposition encompasses bars 1–11 and consists of two parts: a first subject of four bars and a second, contrasting subject six bars in length. There follows a transitional passage of four bars (bars 12–15) that leads into the development section, marked Sostenuto. Following the rhapsodic single-line passage in bars 20–3 a variant on the first subject of the exposition returns (bars 24–6) together with a variant on part of the second subject (bar 27). A coda five bars in length (bars 28–32) follows. The subsequent discussion is organized according to these sections of the large-scale form.

ii   Exposition

Example 7.1 displays salient features of the pitch-class set organization of the first subject in the exposition. Perhaps the most general observation to be made in connection with this opening music is that the pitch materials represents whole-tone, diatonic and chromatic collections, a considerable diversity. The diatonic element is not as immediately evident as the

Example 7.2a Correspondences of ic4 and ic5

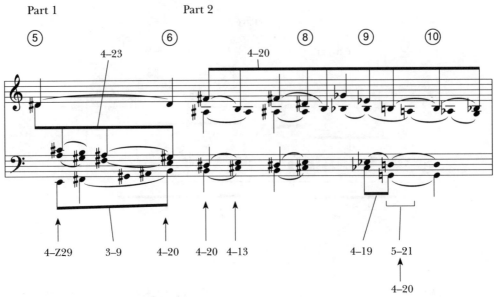

Example 7.2b Fibonacci numbers as durations

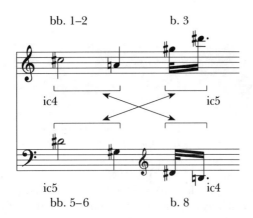

others, consisting of the boundary pitches of the bass motion of the first phrase, $g_\sharp$–$e_\flat$, combined with the boundary pitches of the soprano, $c_\sharp'$–$g_\sharp'$. The latter note is only implied, as indicated by the brackets, on the analytical assumption that the final and unexpected melodic descent to c' refers back to the tenor c' ($b_\sharp$) at the beginning of the passage, where it was associated with $g_\sharp$.

However, the diatonic component becomes more evident in the second phrase, where fifths replace the chromatic passing motion in the soprano of the first phrase to form tetrachord 4–23, the archetypical diatonic tetrachord because it contains more fifths (3) than any other tetrachord (example 7.1). Not only does this variation create a new harmonic structure in the upper part, but it also introduces a new tetrachord when it combines with the passing chromatic notes in the lower part. Example 7.1 shows that this new tetrachord is 4–19, a

favourite of Bartók's. Whereas the rhythmic figure carried by these upper-voice fifths seems at first to be new, it derives from the rhythm of the left-hand part of the first phrase – a feature to which I will return below.

The rhythm of the second phrase clarifies the segmentation of the first phrase in the following way. Instead of an undifferentiated succession of single quavers, the soprano now groups the lower parts into quaver duplets, since each soprano sub-pattern, consisting of quaver–demisemiquaver–dotted semiquaver, corresponds to a quaver duplet.

This rhythmically determined segmentation of the lower parts yields adjacent forms of tetrachord 4–7, the first of which is $g_\sharp$–$b_\sharp$, g–b. We will see that this tetrachord occurs at significant junctures later in the composition. At the end of the second phrase of the subject (example 7.1) 4–21 replaces 4–7, one of the whole-tone tetrachords. Here the two symmetrical tetrachords 4–7 and 4–21 associate harmonically on the basis of the major thirds (two intervals of class 4)[3] they share; they associate rhythmically as well on the basis of what begins as an equivalent pattern, the last component of which, however, is extended by the duration of a crotchet.

Example 7.2a shows the second subject in its entirety. From the standpoint of pitch, perhaps the most obvious feature of this section is its diatonic organization: the first part (bars 5–8) could be described as 'in B major'. Here the rhythm of the first subject, the succession of quavers grouped into crotchets, is associated with a descending diatonic motion from $d_\sharp'$ to $g_\sharp$, a motion spanning a fifth which the soprano motion $f_\sharp'$–b (bars 6–7) then imitates. In this way, since they have the same pattern of durations, the motion spanning a descending major third in the first subject is associated with the motion spanning a descending fifth in the second subject, a correspondence to which we will return in a moment (example 7.2b).

The subsequent motion $f_\sharp$'–b in the soprano of part 2 of the second subject has the contour and rhythm of the soprano of bar 2 of the first subject, the cadential succession of two crotchets, with the second crotchet expressed here as quaver–quaver rest. Moreover, when this gesture occurs the second time (bars 7–8) it incorporates the demisemiquaver–dotted semiquaver rhythmic motif of bar 3. That motif, originally associated with the interval of the fifth (ic5) is now associated with the interval of a major third (ic4).

The complete set of correspondences between rhythmic pattern and interval class is displayed in example 7.2b. The relation between interval class 4 and interval class 5, as well as interval class 1, is given in the very first moment of the piece, in the vertical trichord 3–4: $g_\sharp$–$b_\sharp$–$c_\sharp$. Odd interval classes 1 and 5 as well as even classes 2 and 4 pervade the harmonic texture in this portion of the music, as expressed in the special tetrachord 4–20, which is the only tetrachord that contains two intervals of class 4 and two of class 5.

In the second part of this second subject the alto voice expresses interval class 1 as b–$a_\sharp$ (bar 7). The melodic potential of this dyad, in terms of the thematic motifs already established, is realized only at the end of the phrase, where $a_\sharp$ becomes $b_\flat$ and descends chromatically to g, accompanying the cadential melodic motion b'–$b_\flat$ in the soprano. It should also be noted that the soprano and alto over the first quaver of bar 8 form a trichord that replicates the trichord on the downbeat of bar 1, a reference that is assisted by the distinct rhythmic configuration of those voices at that moment in the music.

Because the second subject differs so markedly at the surface level from the first subject with respect to harmonic content, it is clear that rhythmic pattern provides the basic connective tissue here, unifying the two sections and clarifying the fundamental intervallic associations that their constituents form.

In this regard, the climax of the second subject on the downbeat of bar 9 appears as a significant harmonic as well as rhythmic-accentual event in the work: from the rhythmic standpoint it features the demisemiquaver–dotted semiquaver figure first heard explicitly in bar 3, although implied in the very opening music, while from the harmonic standpoint set 5–21 comes into play (see example 7.2a), a special pentad whose tetrachordal subsets are 4–7, 4–17, 4–19 and 4–20 – all tetrachords that play major roles in this piece, as will become apparent.

Example 7.2c displays these tetrachords as they occur in 5–21 in bar 9. If we were to grant special status to the upper trichord, 3–4, consisting of $e_\flat$'–$b_\flat$–b, by virtue of rhythmic emphasis and contiguity, then we could say that 4–7 and the two forms of 4–19 are most prominent in the foreground here, since they incorporate that trichord, whereas the other tetrachords do not. However, 4–17 is the tetrachord that sounds after the initial demisemiquaver $e_\flat$' and 4–20 is the tetrachord formed on the downbeat of bar 9. Thus, all tetrachordal subsets deserve analytical status, although most auditors would probably confer priority upon the two simultaneities 4–17 and 4–20.[4]

Example 7.2c Tetrachordal subsets of 5-21 in bar 9

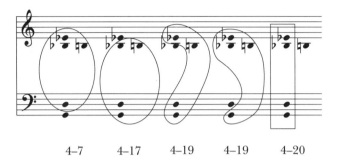

4–7   4–17   4–19   4–19   4–20

An additional rhythmic feature in the second subject now requires attention: in the bass of bar 5 the new figure, dotted quaver followed by two demisemiquavers, segments the bass as shown in example 7.2a into a motion of a second, e–$f_\sharp$, followed by the fourth from $f_\sharp$ to b, since the short note values are understood to have a connective function, filling in the fourth from $F_\sharp$ to B. Thus the overall bass motion from E to B incorporates yet another interval of class 5 ($F_\sharp$–B), with the remarkable result that trichord 3–9 now emerges as E–$F_\sharp$–B, a replica of the trichord type that was first heard in the upper parts of bar 3 (example 7.1) and a further instance of the fundamental role played by interval class 5 in this piece.

Here a new rhythmic figure has created an association with a previously heard pitch configuration, and that configuration, in turn, affects the rhythmic segmentation by providing a further basis for it in the contextual pitch domain of this work. The connection between this first part of the second subject and the beginning of the second part of the first subject (bar 3) is further strengthened by the formation of tetrachord 4–23 in both: $g_\sharp$''–$d_\sharp$'''–f'–$c_\sharp$''' in the uppermost stratum of bar 3 and $d_\sharp$'–$c_\sharp$'–$a_\sharp$'–$g_\sharp$' between the two upper parts of bar 5 (see example 7.2a). The second, of course, is an unordered transposition of the first (t = 7), which is significant because of the prominent role played by interval class 5 in this piece, here represented by the interval of transposition. From the standpoint of the correspondence of pitch-class and rhythmic patterns, $g_\sharp$''–$d_\sharp$''' of bar 3 with rhythmic shape demisemiquaver–dotted semiquaver finds its counterpart in the durational succession minim–crotchet of bars 5–6: a ratio of 1 to 3. This, of course, is a more remote correspondence, since those durational events are disjoint in the work. A more immediate proportional relation is discussed below in connection with the upper voice of bars 5–10, spanning the entire second subject.

There is a strict correspondence between horizontal and vertical dimensions in both parts of the second subject (example 7.2a). In the first part (bars 5–6) the descending soprano motion from $d_\sharp$' to $g_\sharp$ combines with the ascending bass motion from E to B to form tetrachord 4–20, precisely the vertical on the

Example 7.2d Second subject

first crotchet in bar 6. In the second part of the subject the process is reversed: the vertical 4–20 on the second crotchet in bar 6 is gradually unfolded horizontally in the soprano over the remainder of this section, ending on $b_\sharp$ in bar 10 within a G minor triad.[5]

Example 7.2d shows the main upper-voice melodic components of the second subject, with part 1 reduced to the motion $d_\sharp{}^1$–$g_\sharp$, comprising 'soprano' and 'alto' endpoints, since it is the fifth $d_\sharp$–$g_\sharp$ which they delineate that is then reiterated as $f_\sharp$–b in part 2 of the second subject, as shown. Below the stave in example 7.2d are given (in crotchets) the durations of each melodic gesture, forming the numerical succession 3 2 2 5. The duration 5 further divides into 2 + 3, as shown, and duration 3 within 5 divides into 2 + 1. Now, it happens that these numbers comprise the first five numbers of the Fibonacci sequence, a numerical construct of considerable interest to mathematicians because of its relation to number theory and geometry (of which the golden section is an ancient instance) and a sequence that has attracted attention from a number of students of Bartók's music – notably Ernő Lendvai.[6] Whether this series has extensive explanatory power with respect to rhythm in Bartók's music has yet to be demonstrated convincingly. Here the proportions are attractive because the final grouping (5) can be understood as the sum of the durational parts of the previous gestures (2 + 3). Suffice it to say that such proportions based upon numbers of the Fibonacci series seem to be not atypical in Bartók's music.

iii   Transitional section

The four-bar transition that connects exposition with development, bars 12–15, is shown in example 7.3a. Clearly based upon the first subject, it differs from it in significant ways. The lower parts now begin with motion in whole steps, creating the whole-tone tetrachord 4–21 over each group of two quavers, as shown. The last two components, however, depart from the pattern to form 4–7 as in the first subject (example 7.2a). Here the two contrasting tetrachords 4–21 and 4–7 are associated not only on the basis of their intervallic constituents – both contain two intervals of class 4 – but also on the basis of foreground rhythmic pattern. Moreover, over the span of the entire progression, 4–7 is formed again, as indicated by the

Example 7.3a Transition

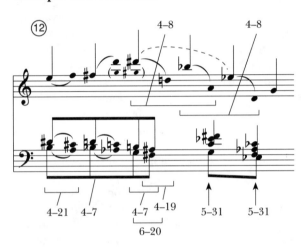

Example 7.3b Transition: rhythmic links

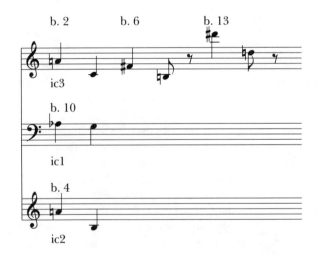

beams in example 7.2a. The bass thus traverses the descending fourth from B to $F_\sharp$ and also expresses the motivic tetrachord 4–7 as B–$B_\flat$–G–$F_\sharp$.

Like 4–7 in the lower parts, 4–8 in the upper (example 7.3a) is also symmetrical. Here there are two interlocking forms of 4–8: $D_\sharp$–D–$B_\flat$–A and $B_\flat$–A–$E_\flat$–D. This configuration prepares the way for yet another symmetrical tetrachord to which 4–8 is closely akin, 4–9, a sonority that dominates the scene at the end of the composition (bars 28–32).

Again, in this transitional passage (bars 12–15) rhythm performs a linking function, summarized in example 7.3b. The last statement of the cadential rhythmic motif crotchet–crotchet (bar 2, soprano) occurred in the alto of bar 10 with pitches *a*♭–*g*. The motif then enters in the soprano at the end of the first phrase of the transition as *d*♯‴–*d*″; the descending second has become a descending ninth – the interval has been inverted and expanded by octave displacement. It is the pitches associated with this rhythmic motif that form the interlocking tetrachords of class 4–8 described above.

At first it seems that rhythm-to-pitch analysis does not illuminate the soprano voice of the transition (example 7.3a) to any great extent. This voice begins as a literal inversion of the soprano of bar 1 as *e*″–*f*″–*f*♯″, then breaks out of the pattern, leaping upwards to *d*‴, which then continues by half-step to the accented *d*♯‴, a pitch-specific reference to that note in part 2 of the first subject (bar 3). This then becomes the head note of the rhythmic and contour motif first heard at the end of the first phrase in the soprano of bar 2, as indicated above, the first of three occurrences. Thus, the second part of the transition coincides rhythmically with the second part of the second subject (bars 6–9), with its three statements of that rhythmic motif, while the first part of the transition derives from the first subject.

Example 7.3c summarizes the derivation of the actual soprano of the transition from the 'theoretical' soprano that would have resulted had the inversion been continued: in place of the expected *g*″–*g*♯″, the soprano has *d*‴–*d*♯‴, a transposition by fifth, one of the basic structural intervals in the piece. Following upon this is another transposition downwards by fifth (t = 7), bringing into play *a*–*b*♭. Finally, and coinciding with the third of the successive rhythmic motifs, the dyad is transposed up a fifth (t = 5), the inverse transposition, so that the passage ends with *e*♭″–*d*′, replicating the first form of the motif in the soprano of bar 13 with respect to pitch-class.

Example 7.3c Transition: theoretical derivation of soprano line

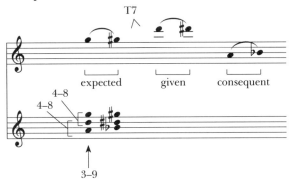

In bars 14–15, the second part of the transition, the tail note of the soprano melodic motif receives an accent from the chord notated on the lower stave. The harmonic analysis of this chord in example 7.3d reveals that a marked change in intervallic content coincides with the rhythmic stresses; the principal harmonic component here is 5–31, a sct in which interval-class 3 (the minor third) is predominant, whereas the previous sonorities have featured other intervals. The preceding sonority in bar 13, in particular, is 6–20, a hexachord in which interval-class 4 is predominant. As shown in example 7.3d, the accented *g*′ that enters unexpectedly on the last quaver in bar 15 fits into the final harmonies of the transition as it forms yet another image of 5–31 with the previously sounding lower parts. Rhythmically it associates with the anticipation that precedes bar 1, an unmeasured duration that we have assumed to approximate a demisemiquaver. (Cf. bars 28–30, where the semiquaver becomes the notated value of an analogous passage.)

Example 7.3d Harmonic analysis of bars 14-15

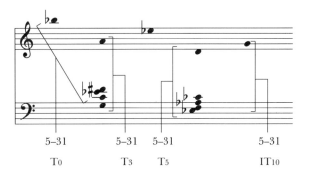

iv Development

The beginning of the development section in bar 16 provides an occasion for a general comment – one that is perhaps gratuitous – on rhythm as it relates to tempo in a contrapuntal context: although there is a slowing of the tempo here (Sostenuto), any rhythmic correspondences between this and the previous music will remain intact because of the proportional relations between horizontal strands. Thus, when a new figure, quaver–two semiquavers–quaver, occurs, this is understood as a subdivision of the crotchet motion of the opening music, even though the duration of the crotchet is now greater than it was. Observe that the crotchet has only been subdivided twice in the previous music, by the demisemiquaver–dotted demiquaver figure in bars 8–9.

The development section (bars 16–23) divides naturally into two parts; each begins with material that recalls the first subject and each ends with a rhapsodic, cadenza-like single line that bears no immediately obvious relation to any of the previous material. The latter will be of particular interest to our analysis.

Example 7.4a Development, part 1

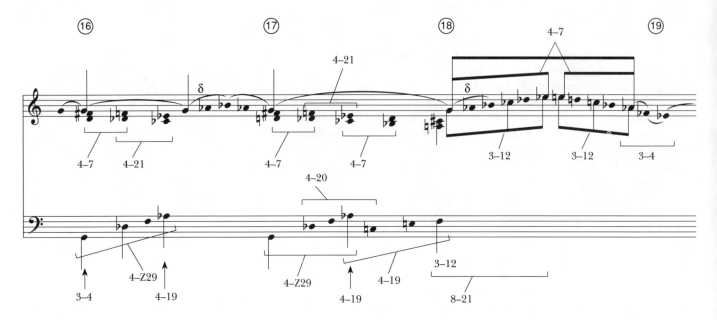

Example 7.4a shows the pitch organization of the first section of the development. Against the quaver pattern in the voices below the soprano the bass introduces a new rhythmic figure, the quaver–two semiquavers–quaver pattern mentioned above. This new rhythmic figure, in turn, appears to introduce a new set in the composition, tetrachord 4-Z29, one of the two 'all-interval' tetrachords. However, this set has occurred before in a corresponding location: as the vertical on the second quaver in bar 5, just at the beginning of the second subject (see example 7.2a). The harmonic reference here thus effects a further and very precise connection between the opening of the development and the previous thematic materials.

The effect of the double semiquaver figure in the left-hand part of bar 16 is twofold: to emphasize the major third component of the figure ($d\flat–f$), which doubles the third above it at the octave, and to provide rhythmic impetus towards $a\flat$, the terminal note. The pitch-motivic reference here is hardly obscure: the ninth from G to $a\flat$ is the inversion of the descending ninth figure that began in the soprano of bar 13, which, in turn, relates by contour and rhythm to the characteristic component of the first subject that first occurred in bar 2, as noted above. Hence, this bass motion in the development is a direct descendant of that original sixth, $a'–c'$, to which it relates by inverse contour and equivalent underlying rhythm.

As a refinement of simple linear succession, rhythmic pattern plays an important selective role here in this 'new' gesture in the bass of bar 16 under discussion, selective in the sense that certain pitches are brought forth by the pattern, with the result that there is a corresponding selection of intervals out of the total interval content of the tetrachord. This is shown in example 7.4a where three of the four pitches of the figure are supplied with stems, based upon rhythmic segmentation. In

terms of the entire piece, this is the first strong linear appearance of 3-5, a trichord featured within tetrachord 4-9 in the coda, to be discussed below.

Continuing with our examination of the rhythmic features of the development, we note that the three semiquaver figure in the soprano of bar 16, $a\flat'–b\flat'–a\flat'$, prepares the beginning of the cadenza-like gesture of bar 18, which is based upon the semiquaver and the accelerated semiquaver within the quintuplet.

More interesting and of greater general interest with respect to the analysis of foreground rhythm is the new syncopated bass figure at the end of bar 17: semiquaver–quaver–semiquaver, expressing $a\flat–c–e$, the augmented triad, trichord 3-12. This symmetrical figure also distinguishes 4-Z29, which ends on $a\flat$, from 4-19, which begins on that note. The latter function is also greatly assisted by contour, of course: $a\flat$ is the peak of the ascending and descending motions. In this regard it should also be observed that the completion on $a\flat$ of the linear form of 4-Z29 in the left-hand part coincides exactly with the vertical occurrence of a form of 4-19 (as $a\flat$, $c\flat'$, $e\flat'$ g') the tetrachord that then unfolds in the bass line as $a\flat–c–e–f$ (see example 7.4a). In this situation $a\flat$ is axis pitch between the two transpositionally related (t = 3) forms of 4-19, a role that is quite in accord with the special accent it receives.

Example 7.4b provides an additional perspective on the rhythm of the bass figure in bar 17. Two more sets emerge in this analysis, formations that may be regarded as secondary: first, the grouping of four semiquavers (bracketed) articulates tetrachord 4-20, the principal sonority of part 2 of the second subject (example 7.2a) and prepares for the continuous successions of semiquavers that begin in the next bar. Also shown in example 7.4b is the slightly concealed form of 3-9 (soprano,

Example 7.4b Trichord 3-9 in bass figure

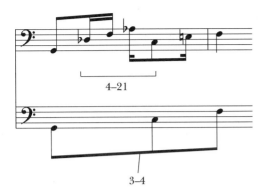

4–21

3–4

Example 7.4c Development, bar 18: effect of syncopation

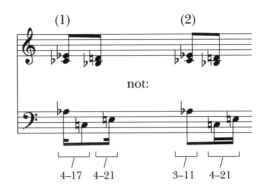

(1)　　　　　　　(2)

not:

4–17　4–21　　　3–11　4–21

bar 3) carried by the first note of the pattern, the quaver *G*, the quaver *c*, and the tail note of the figure, the crotchet *f*. Thus, the rhythmic pattern of the bass in bar 17 carries three of the characteristic tetrachords of the work: 4–Z29, 4–19 and 4–20, with the last-named set corresponding exactly to the group of four semiquavers. In addition, the pitch-motivic trichord of the second part of the first subject is also expressed by non-contiguous elements of the pattern. All these distinctions depend upon differences in durational values in the pattern; in bar 18 and in bar 21, where we encounter long strings of equal durations, we shall take another analytical approach to ascertain pitch-rhythm correspondences.

These are important rhythmic aspects of the bass line of bar 17 considered alone. If we consider the upper parts as well as the bass, a more elegant and idiomatic effect of the syncopation is revealed (example 7.4c). Without the syncopation and following the preceding quaver–two semiquavers pattern, the trichord 3–11 and the whole-tone tetrachord are brought into play, as shown at (2). But with the syncopation, as shown at (1), 4–17 is created within the same timespan. Although tetrachord 4–17 has not been prominent previously (example 7.3d), its occurrence in this complex of tetrachords together with 4–21 is quite natural, since both belong to a group of tetrachords that feature two intervals of class 4. Perhaps the most prominent of these is 4–7, the first tetrachord formed in the lower parts at the beginning of the piece (example 7.1). And, to refer to a more general idea in connection with the effect of the syncopation in bar 17, we have here an instance of rhythmic structure apparently being influenced by pitch structure; the pitches that form major thirds, a characteristic and prominent interval from the first subject, are given maximum exposure here in the foreground detail.

From the standpoint of rhythmic pattern alone, the figure that begins in the left-hand part on the second crotchet of bar 17 may be understood as a completion of the left-hand figure of the previous bar. In this sense it has a complementary function, one that suggests a rhythmic process more determinative with respect to pitch structure than indicated in the

preceding discussion. The bass figure in bar 17 also contributes in very direct and lucid fashion to the uninterrupted succession of semiquavers that comprises the rhythmic aspect of bar 18 (to be discussed in some detail below). The related figures in the left-hand part of bars 16 and 17 are repeated in bars 19 and 20, with extensions that develop the three-note syncopated unit. Only in bar 22, with the approach to the climax of the development, does this syncopated figure emerge exposed, without contrapuntal 'interference'. And then in bar 23 it becomes the rhythmic essence of the climax itself, at which point its association with the demisemiquaver–dotted semiquaver motif is unmistakable. In this way the development section is arrested, literally, by a reference to the opening music, music that is about to return with the beginning of the reprise in bar 24. I return now to a more detailed consideration of the interaction of pitch and rhythm in the main body of the development.

With bar 18 begins the improvisation-like portion of the development, which, although it projects a definite feeling of independence from the preceding music, relates to it through very specific and artistic musical means, among which rhythm is primary. I have analysed the cadenza-like gesture in bar 18 as shown by beams and set names on example 7.4a. Here rhythmic pattern as a determinant of segmentation is conditioned by contour and dynamics, the latter clearly indicated by the composer as a crescendo towards the peak note *e''*, with a dropping off in dynamic level thereafter. The resulting segmentation is extremely interesting from several standpoints, not least of which is the development of procedures of diminution in Bartók's early avant-garde music.

As shown in example 7.4a, the ascending motion from *g'* to *e♭''* combined with the descending motion from *e''* to *a♭'* – both traversing minor sixths – produces tetrachord 4–7, by now a familiar harmony in this composition. Notice that the stepwise motion breaks at the end of the quintuplet with the skip from *a♭'* to *f♭'*, thus confirming the underlying arpeggiated augmented triad (3–12) which also occurs within the immediately preceding ascending sixth.

Example 7.5a Development, part 2

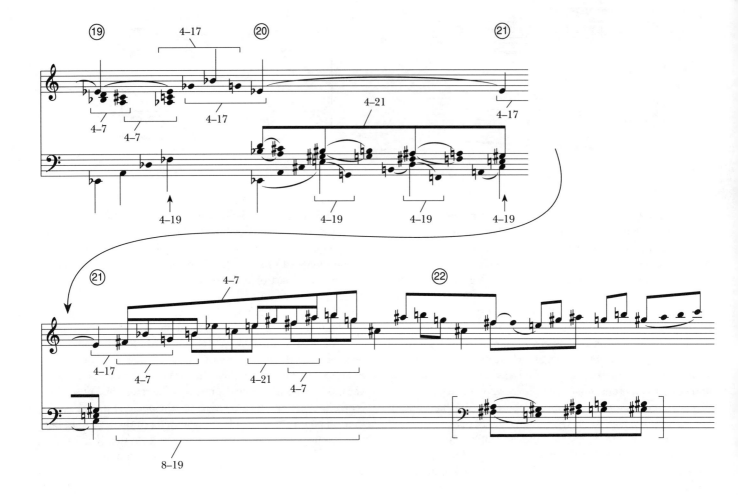

Although a detail, it is worthwhile to observe that Bartók does not compose a complete descending whole-tone scale from e″, but breaks off at a♭′, thus articulating the descending sixth e″–a♭′ that matches the ascending sixth g′–e♭′. To preserve the pattern of even-note values he expresses this motion within the quintuplet – another instance, albeit a minuscule one, of pitch-determined rhythm.

A pitch analysis of the second and last section of the development is represented in example 7.5a. That this begins with a transposition at the interval of a major third of the trichord 3–4 at the beginning of the first section of the development (bar 16) should be no surprise, since interval-class 4 has been perhaps the most prominent intervallic component of much of the music so far.

The phrase (bar 19) in its entirety, however, is not simply a transposition of its counterpart in bar 16. There the motion in thirds below the soprano followed the pattern half-step–whole-step. Here the corresponding motion is by half-step, with the result that two forms of tetrachord 4–7 interlock.

The chord at the end of the first gesture, on the third quaver of the bar, is of the same class in both cases, however – 4–19 – in consequence of the fact that the augmented triad is the core sonority in both instances (the two forms of 4–19 are inversionally equivalent).

A further difference is apparent when the semiquaver figure at the end of bar 16 is compared with that at the end of bar 19. The former prepares the ascending cadenza motion in bar 18, as discussed above; the latter also prepares the subsequent cadenza but at the same time embellishes the melodic note e♭′ by arpeggiation upwards to b♭′, a motion which, with the return to e♭′ via g′, expresses the motivic pitch-class set 4–17, which is now assuming a significant harmonic role. (See examples 7.3d and 7.4c and the discussion above.)

Notice that 4–17 occurs twice here: once starting from the tied e♭′ and again starting from g♭′, a motion that coincides with the beginning of the small phrase mark. The second form is thus syncopated by one semiquaver, a rhythmic subtlety that prepares the interlocking tetrachords of bar 21 (discussed below in connection with example 7.5a) and a motivic feature that relates directly to the symmetrical rhythmic figure in the left-hand part of bar 17, which was cited above in connection with examples 7.4b and c.

Beginning in bar 20, the chromatically moving thirds of the first subject descend underneath the sustained $e\flat'$ of the soprano. Here, as shown in example 7.5a, the whole-tone tetrachord 4–21 $d'–b\sharp–a\sharp–g\sharp$ emerges from the rhythmic pattern, and the last three of its members are enclosed in forms of tetrachord 4–19 until the final chord, 4–19, appears on the downbeat of bar 21. With respect to pitch-class, this final form of 4–19 is the same as 4–19 on the third quaver of bar 19 and the third quaver of bar 20 ($e–g\sharp–b\sharp–e\flat'$); in a more extended harmonic study, we might refer to this confluence of events as a prolongation of 4–19 in a specific pitch-class form.

In the left-hand part of bar 20 we hear the rhythmic motif from bar 17 (example 7.4b). Here, however, the figure plays a somewhat different role with respect to pitch structure. In addition to bringing in tetrachord 4–19, its second and third components form a third which, in each case, doubles the 'passing' third in the upper parts.

The continuous semiquaver pattern of bar 21 at first seems not to exhibit any differentiation that would provide a clue to the underlying pitch organization. However, with further examination this proves to be a misperception. First, phrasing provides an analytical clue that reveals something about the progression of longer range. The composer's careful slur from $f\sharp'$ up to $a\sharp''$ denotes the onset and terminal point of the gesture – an expanded major third.

This third, $f\sharp'–a\sharp''$, finds its 'resolution' in the third that begins with the climactic b'', namely $b''–g''$. Together these two thirds form tetrachord 4–7, which is identical with respect to pitch-class to the first four notes under the slur in the soprano of bar 21. (Indeed, the same tetrachord is also repeated just at the end of the bar.) Now, this slur begins with a semiquaver syncopation, just as did the figure at the end of bar 19, and it thus provides a rhythmic clue to the correct segmentation of the ensuing series of semiquavers. When we combine this analytically derived knowledge with what we know about the tetrachordal vocabulary of the piece that has already been presented, the analysis shown in example 7.5b results.

This example (7.5b) presents a re-beaming of the semiquavers of bar 20 and the beginning of bar 21 to show the interlocking tetrachords of classes 4–7 and 4–21 and the underlying syncopated rhythmic pattern determined by the onsets of each tetrachord. This pattern begins with a succession of two dotted quavers, exactly equivalent in duration to the slurred figure at the end of bar 19 which serves as preparation for this cadenza.

An acceleration follows, as represented by the quaver below the stave in example 7.5b, and the final tetrachord, 4–7, unfolds for the full value of a crotchet, without interruption by another onset.[7]

Example 7.5b Development, bars 21-2: rhythmic segmentation

Onsets:

Example 7.5c offers an alternative analysis of the passage, again starting with the syncopated $f\sharp'$ and segmenting by successive instead of interlocking tetrachords. Although this analysis is also convincing, in the sense that its tetrachordal organization corresponds to the harmonic vocabulary of the composition, and may even be more attractive than the analysis in example 7.5b because of the symmetrical harmonic arrangement 4–7/4–19/4–7, it lacks the correspondence between rhythm and performance slur of example 7.5b and does not show the development of the idiomatic syncopated figure represented by the duration dotted quaver. In this connection, it should be remarked that the segmentation into successive tetrachords beginning with the first semiquaver in bar 21 will produce a tetrachord that does not occur elsewhere in this piece, 4–11, and thus seems to contradict the developmental nature of this section as it pertains to the tetrachords idiomatic to the work.

Example 7.5c Development, bars 21-2: alternative segmentation

Onsets:

The symmetrical rhythmic figure semiquaver–quaver–semiquaver that enters at the beginning of bar 22 breaks up the succession of steady semiquavers and signals the end of the ascending progression shown both in example 7.5a and also in rhythmic detail in examples 7.5b and c. Its effect is to isolate $c\sharp''$, which, in this context, refers directly back to the head note of the soprano of the first subject (bar 1). Indeed, the music of bar 21 in its entirety comprises the large harmonic set 8–19, complement of the thematic tetrachord 4–19. The entrance of $c\sharp''$ in bar 22 not only breaks the pattern of continuous semiquavers, but also terminates that large harmony (8–19).

Example 7.6 Reprise

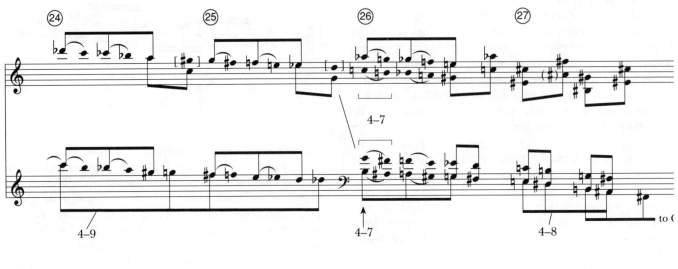

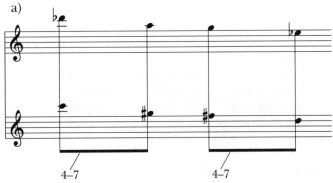

To sum up, this very free-sounding, improvisation-like passage derives from the first subject, and is also an elaborate and slightly concealed preparation for the return of that part in bar 24, where the succession of four semiquavers that replaced the original succession of four quavers now confirms the fact that the basic durational unit of the development, the semiquaver, as well as the successive groupings of four semiquavers in bar 18 and bar 21, derive by expansion from the durational succession introduced by the first subject.

The bracketed notation below bar 22 in example 7.5a shows the essential motion expressed by the single line in bars 22–3: a succession of ascending thirds comprising a retrograde of the first three thirds in the bass clef in the first subject (example 7.1). The final emphasized *b″* is carried in the rhythmic pattern quaver–quaver (tied semiquavers)–dotted quaver, exactly the 2 + 2 + 3 rhythm of bar 21 cited above (example 7.5b).

v   Reprise

Just as the listener understands the reprise in a traditional

sonata form not simply as a replica of the exposition, but in a different way because of the music that has transpired in the meantime, so the reprise of this short piece differs markedly from the exposition in its effect. In addition, the bagatelle character of the music is especially evident here: the composer avoids the obvious, the predictable, yet at the same time he brings the piece to a close in a way that links it firmly to the harmonic and rhythmic material of the opening music.

Example 7.6 summarizes the reprise, which begins with an attenuated version of bars 1–2 (now halved in value, but actually played faster) with the soprano now one octave and the 'tenor' two octaves higher, in the register of $d_\sharp‴$, the special pitch first activated in bar 3, regained in bar 13 and approached but not attained in the retransition, bars 21–3. Here soprano and tenor outline tetrachord 4–7, as shown in example 7.6 at a) below the main analytical sketch. In the exposition the corresponding structure presents tetrachord 4–20. Thus, the reprise brings into play the thematic harmony 4–7 formed by non-contiguous pitches, a harmony that is expressed by the durational succession crotchet (embracing the

Figure 7.1 Reprise bars 6-7

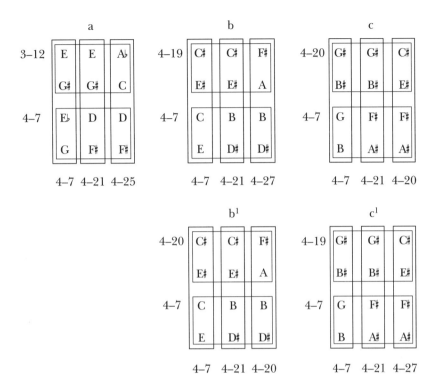

four semiquavers) followed by quaver, exactly the rhythm of the cadential gesture of bar 2 as abbreviated in bar 6 and elsewhere.

From the rhythmic view, each of the first two phrases of the reprise is the same as the first phrase of the exposition (bars 1–2). The cadential soprano motif crotchet–crotchet is now represented by the motif quaver–semiquaver–semiquaver rest, the two successive presentations of which in bar 27 clearly refer to the second part of the second subject in the exposition, even though the pitch parameter, including such surface features as contour, is radically changed. Thus, to state what is perhaps the most interesting generalization, rhythmic pattern preserves the association of components of the reprise with their counterparts in the exposition, so that rhythm, in this specific sense, is intimately allied with form in its traditional interpretation.

However, because bar 25 is a replica of bar 24, transposed down a tritone, the reprise introduces a new feature: pitch-class set 4–9 is now formed by the boundary pitches of each figure in the lower parts, as shown in example 7.6: c'''–g''–$f\sharp''$–$d\flat''$. This new set, which derives in such a natural way from the linear outline of the first subject, becomes the predominant sonority of the coda – to be discussed below.

The form of the first subject in the reprise differs from what it would have been had it followed the rhythm of the exposition

exactly. In the upper voice of the reprise the figure that ends each melodic phrase now consists of quaver–semiquaver, followed by semiquaver rest. This feature is emphasized in the foreground of bar 27, where the rhythm quaver–semiquaver–semiquaver rest against semiquaver–quaver–semiquaver rest emphasizes the retrograde relation of the two rhythms in counterpoint, with the lower component highlighted by the anticipation. The underlying triple grouping here, as 2 + 1 and 1 + 2, that is:

$$2 \quad 1 \quad (1)$$
$$1 \quad 2 \quad (1)$$

relates to the triple grouping in bar 21 of the development (example 7.5b).

Certainly more important than this somewhat remote connection is the complex pitch structure that the composite rhythmic pattern brings into play. This is illustrated in the grid format of figure 7.1, which begins at the end of bar 26 in order to include the three successive statements of the pattern, which correspond in number to the three statements of the pattern in part two of the second subject of the exposition (example 7.2a). In example 7.6 each pattern is divided into a two-dimensional pitch-class grid corresponding to the musical

Example 7.7a Coda normalized

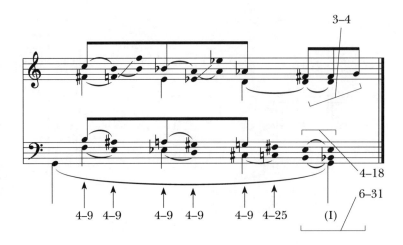

Example 7.7b Coda with rhythmic displacement

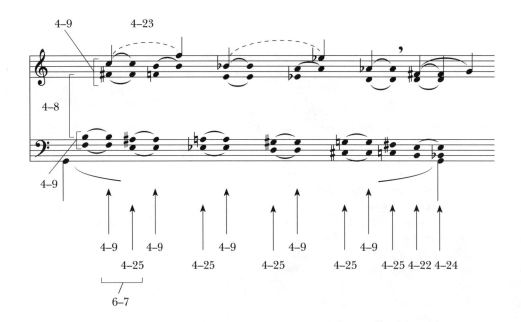

notation. Each grid has an identifying lower-case letter to facilitate reference.

Inspection of the grids (figure 7.1) considerably reduces the complexity of the total configuration. The basic unit is primarily the tetrachord – in both horizontal and vertical dimensions – and the tetrachords are mainly representatives of set classes familiar from the earlier music: 4–7, 4–19, 4–20, 4–21, 4–25 and 4–27. Of these, 4–27 (familiar as the dominant seventh chord or its inversion) seems totally out of place, while 4–25, although 'new', is closely related to its whole-tone cousin,

4–21. If a' in bar 27 is changed to $a_\sharp'$, as at y' in figure 7.1, 4–27 becomes 4–20, a major constituent of this work, especially in part two of the second subject of the exposition (example 7.2a). If, on the other hand, the second $e_\sharp'$ in bar 27 is changed to e' – as has been done in some editions – the result is again the maverick tetrachord 4–27, as shown at c' in figure 7.1. However this may be, the tetrachords in the horizontal strata remain members of the harmonic vocabulary of the piece, regardless of the change of $e_\sharp'$ to e' or a' to $a_\sharp'$, as figure 7.1 shows.

vi Coda

Pitch-class set 4–9 has only six distinct basic forms. Five of these appear in vertical succession over the pedal note *G* in the coda, ending on the downbeat of bar 31 with a_b' in the soprano (see example 7.7a). At that point the tenor continues downwards by half-step to B_b, the voice above the tenor continues by step to *e*, and the soprano executes the motion $f_\sharp$–*g*, presumably a cadential motion to Bartók's tonic note, *g*.[8] The vertical combinations at the cadence are not consistent with the atonal harmonies that appear throughout the piece in the foreground, but appear to result from this motion towards the quasi-tonal cadence. In the final stages, the trichord 3–4, *d'*–$f_\sharp$'–*g'*, formed between alto and soprano, is reminiscent of the first vertical. But the lower tetrachord at the cadence, 4–18: *G–B–B_b–e*, is heard only twice elsewhere in the composition, as the chord on the downbeat of the cadential bar 10 and as the chord in the left-hand part of bar 14, the transition between the exposition and the development.

As shown in example 7.7b, which reflects the actual temporal succession of the coda, as distinct from example 7.7a, which has normalized the coda to reveal the salient forms of 4–9, the rhythmic displacement represented on upper and lower staves has a significant effect upon the pitch structure. First, and perhaps most obviously, it renders the right- and left-hand strata separate, with the result that the lateral forms of 4–9 (bracketed on example 7.7b) are made apparent. This may be understood as an intensification of the opening music, where the left-hand part, also offset from the right-hand part, formed its series of interlocking forms of 4–7.

Although in terms of interval content 4–9 and 4–7 differ markedly, they share two interval classes: interval-class 1 and interval-class 5. It is the interval-class 1 they hold in common that links this coda in the most immediate way to the first subject of the exposition. However, interval-class 5 is represented in the coda as well. This set is formed by the inner voices, tenor and alto, in the horizontal stratum. Less direct, but nonetheless real, is the pattern of fifths formed in the soprano, as indicated by the dotted lines on example 7.7b. Note that the location of the upper note of the fifth is always on the second of the group of two quavers, creating the non-contiguous pattern dotted crotchet–quaver. This is then precisely the rhythm of the soprano in the final two bars, with a separate attack on $f_\sharp$' alone in the last bar. In terms of pitch content, as shown in example 7.7b, this secondary formation in the soprano of the coda expresses tetrachord 4–23, as a set that was in the foreground of the upper voice in the second part of the first subject (example 7.1). Now we understand that the upward leaps of a fourth in the soprano of bars 26 and 27 as well as the non-contiguous upward leaps of a fourth here in the coda refer back to the first subject.

The final effect of the rhythmic displacement in the coda (example 7.7b) that needs to be mentioned is the formation of the whole-tone tetrachord 4–25 on every other vertical. This

tetrachord, which we have not encountered before in the composition, serves as a passing chord in this context, a function well suited to its restricted interval content (ic2 and ic6 only). More important, however, is the fluctuation of intervals between the verticals 4–9 and 4–25 that the rhythmic pattern creates here. Both 4–9 and 4–25 contain two tritones, the most characteristic interval of this final passage, and no minor thirds, an interval that has played a limited and special role throughout – as in tetrachord 4–17. The two verticals therefore fluctuate with respect to the odd-interval classes 1 and 5 (minor second and fourth/fifth, respectively) and the even-interval classes 2 and 4 (major second and major third, respectively). The interval vectors below provide a concise picture of this situation:

$$4\text{–}9: \quad [200022]$$
$$4\text{–}25: \quad [020202]$$

These intervallic qualities, of course, are precisely those featured in the first subject, especially in part 2 of the first subject (example 7.1), where the soprano traverses a major third via major seconds, a progression that is interrupted by the open fifths ($c_\sharp$"–$g_\sharp$"–$d_\sharp$", etc.) accompanied in the left-hand part by the descending minor seconds. Totally absent from this context is the minor third; the tritone, however, is formed indirectly as a result of the underlying whole-tone progression. The coda in its thematic rhythmic configuration thus refer not only to the first subject through its general shape, the descending chromatic progression, and so on, but also and more artistically to the intervallic characteristics of the opening music, without literally replicating that music.

3 SUMMARY

Pitch and rhythm are inseparable, even though one or the other may be understood analytically as predominant in a particular context. While the rhythmic domain is expressed in linear successions of durations and in the interaction of such successions, the pitch domain is expressed most fundamentally as pitches in register, more generally as pitch-classes, reinterpreted relationally as interval and interval class, all within the fundamental harmonies we have designated pitch-class sets.

Rhythmic configurations associate and differentiate pitch-class sets and their intervallic constituents. These associative and differential processes, in turn, are intimately connected with the internal organization of the work, that complex of musical processes we think of as 'form'.

From the analytical standpoint, it seems essential to regard segmentation as the fundamental operation. Here we take into account not only the gross rhythmic pattern offered by the musical surface, but we also permit our reading to be influenced by the discovery of the basic harmonic components of the music – its idiomatic harmonies. This interaction of rhythmic pattern and harmonic structure leads in a natural way to an understanding of configurations formed by non-contiguous elements – the linear techniques mentioned at the beginning of this chapter.

Even though one might set out general guidelines and propose certain canons for research, such as those suggested in the foregoing summary, it is likely that further rhythmic-analytical studies of non-tonal works of the early twentieth century will also give appropriate attention to musical features that are of particular importance to the work of a given composer. In the model by Bartók chosen for this chapter, for example, we gave special attention to rhythm in its relation to contour and phrasing, and dealt, albeit briefly, with pro-portional aspects of rhythmic pattern that seem to be endemic to Bartók's music.

4 SUGGESTIONS FOR FURTHER STUDY

I have selected three complete short works and one excerpt from a larger work – all from the early twentieth century repertory – to suggest for analysis, each by a major composer of the period and each part of a significant composition. For each I provide a few comments below that are intended to help the reader get started. A caveat is in order, however: none of these pieces is easy to understand, either with respect to pitch or to rhythm. In general, I believe that a careful examination of pitch organization with due attention to rhyth-mic pattern is the best initial approach – that is, a pitch-to-rhythm analytical procedure. The works are listed below in chronological order.

Schoenberg, *Fünfzehn Gedichte aus 'Das Buch der hängenden Gärten' von Stefan George*, op. 15 (1909), no. 14: 'Sprich nicht immer von dem Laub'

This song, probably one of the last composed in this opus, is in Schoenberg's advanced atonal idiom; it relates closely in style to his *Three Piano Pieces*, op. 11. The pitch structure is very lucid, and there are many associations among pitch, pitch-class set and rhythm, as in the opening phrase, when $b\flat''-a''$ in the piano introduces the same rhythm crotchet–quaver, in the voice. The two-note figures combine to form tetrachord 4–9. Special attention should be given to the pitches and sets associated with particular rhythmic patterns, of which there is a limited number. Relations among rhythmic patterns are also of considerable interest with respect to continuity. And, of course, the link between rhythm and text requires attention, especially the connection between particular words, pitches and rhythms, as in the setting of 'Quitten' [quinces] in bar 5 and the other text syllables that are given the same pitches and similar rhythms. As in the model work of this chapter, due consideration should be given to register in relation to rhythm as well – for instance, to the peak notes of the three successive figures in bars 7–8 of the piano accompaniment.

Webern, *Six Bagatelles for String Quartet*, op. 9, no. 3 (1913)

In working out an analysis of this short composition, consider how each rhythmic component contributes to the pitch and interval structure. For example, in bar 2 the demisemiquavers effect an oscillation between two inversionally related trichords, which, in turn, are components of a symmetric tetrachord. With the entrance of c' in Violin I on the last quaver in the bar, the tetrachord class changes – in effect, an expansion.

Stravinsky, *Three Pieces for String Quartet*, no. 1 (1914)

This wonderful piece has an ostinato bass pattern – a fixed rhythm and pitch pattern – that continues throughout, except for the opening three bars and the closing three bars. Does this pattern cycle (group) in any special way? Although it remains constant, the parts above it change. What kinds of associations and differentiations occur and how does the pitch structure develop over this seemingly static component? How does rhythm contribute to form? In the pitch domain there is a strong octatonic element. How is this expressed in the rhythmic patterns formed between the melodic strands as well as within the separate strands?

Berg, *Wozzeck*, Act III, scene 3, bars 122–44 (1921)

This is the beginning of the famous invention on a rhythm, a remarkable movement in one of the masterworks of the early twentieth century. Here the fixed rhythmic pattern is easily ascertained (the eight-note succession in the upper part of bars 1–4). Note, however, that it is not an ostinato, since the pitch content of the pattern varies. In this instance adopting a rhythm-to-pitch approach may be the best strategy. What happens, for example, when the initial form of the fixed rhythmic pattern vanishes at bar 130? What changes occur in the pitch structure with respect to the fixed pattern at that point in the music? Some attention may be given to durations of larger scale in this excerpt, as well. For example, the first note in the bass, c, lasts for exactly four bars. Is a larger durational pattern created in the bass of the subsequent music?

NOTES

1 For analytical reasons that will become evident as we proceed, it is necessary to indicate unequivocally the octave in which a pitch occurs.

2 This description agrees in its essentials with that offered by Elliott Antokoletz in *The Music of Béla Bartók*. The analytical orientation and the analysis of the piece differ radically from those in the present essay, however.

3 The notion of interval class, to which reference is made throughout this chapter, is explained in chapter 6, Bryan R. Simms, 'The Theory of Pitch-Class Sets'.

4 With respect to a trichordal analysis of 5–21 here, it should be pointed out that of the four set classes represented by its ten distinct trichordal subsets, three account for all the pitches in the pentad:

trichords 3–3, 3–4 and 3–11. This suggests that a basic cell analysis in terms of a single trichord class might encounter difficulty determining a local trichord with structural priority.

5 In John Vinton's article 'Bartók on his own Music', the author extracts several excerpts from an unpublished document, Bartók's notes made in 1942–3 for a lecture entitled 'The New Hungarian Art Music'. There the composer provides a list of tonalities for the Bagatelles and states: 'This information is addressed especially to those who like to label all music they do not understand as *atonal* music' (his emphasis). Bagatelle No. 8 is assigned the tonality of G minor. Although this referential tonality is evident here at the end of bar 10 and at one or two places elsewhere in the bagatelle, notably at the final cadence, it seems clear that the harmonies of the piece at the foreground level are effectively approached analytically using what has been called 'the technology of pitch-class sets', without engaging the question of what constitutes tonality in highly chromatic works of the early twentieth century such as this.

6 See Lendvai, *The Workshop of Bartók and Kodály.*

7 The pattern dotted quaver–dotted quaver–quaver is equivalent to the durational pattern 3–3–2. Bartók found patterns such as this in his folk music research and used them often in his music. (See Suchoff, *Béla Bartók's Essays.*) For example, the last of the *Six Dances in Bulgarian Rhythm* in his *Mikrokosmos*, Vol. VI, is based precisely upon this pattern.

8 See note 5 above.

BIBLIOGRAPHY

This bibliography is restricted to writings that deal with rhythm in the non-tonal music of the earlier twentieth century, before the advent of the twelve-tone music of Schoenberg and his followers. Even with this relatively large time-range, the number of items in the bibliography is quite small. Nonetheless, I have tried to include all those that would be appropriate to the topic of this chapter and, in the process, may inadvertently have omitted significant entries – for which I apologize in advance. I have annotated some of the items below, but not all. This is not, however, intended to imply that the items not annotated are of less interest to the topic.

Antokoletz, Elliott, *The Music of Béla Bartók* (Berkeley, Los Angeles and London: University of California Press, 1984).

Contains frequent references to rhythmic-metric features as they relate to the symmetrical cell concept that is basic to this study of Bartók's music. See, for example, the discussion of the *Fourth String Quartet* on p. 109.

Berry, Wallace, *Structural Functions in Music* (Englewood Cliffs, NJ: Prentice-Hall, 1976).

Chapter 3 of this book is devoted to rhythm and meter. Of particular interest is the portion on Webern's *Four Pieces for Cello and Piano*, op. 11, and his *Five Pieces for String Quartet*, op. 5, pp. 397–408.

Forte, Allen, 'Aspects of Rhythm in Webern's Atonal Music', *Music Theory Spectrum*, 2 (1980), pp. 90–109.

——, 'Foreground Rhythm in Early Twentieth-Century Music', *Music Analysis*, 2 (1983), pp. 239–68.

Hasty, Christopher, 'Segmentation and Process in Post-Tonal Music', *Music Theory Spectrum*, 3 (1981), pp. 54–73.

This article develops important theoretical concepts of segmentation and has significant implications for rhythmic analysis. One of the three works analysed falls within the historical period relevant to this chapter: Schoenberg's *Five Piano Pieces*, op. 23.

Howat, Roy, 'Review-Article: Bartók, Lendvai and the Principles of Proportional Analysis', *Music Analysis*, 2, (1983), pp. 69–95.

An extensive critique of Lendvai's theoretical ideas, with emphasis upon the golden section as it relates to the Fibonacci sequence, and a thorough review of the relevant literature.

Kramer, Jonathan, 'Studies of Time and Music: A Bibliography', *Music Theory Spectrum*, 7, (1985), pp. 72–106.

Although this exceeds the scope of the present limited bibliography, I have included it here because it is a standard research reference for musical rhythm – a comprehensive and well-constructed compilation.

Lendvai, Erno, *The Workshop of Bartók and Kodály* (Budapest: Editio Musica, 1983).

The most recent version of Lendvai's theoretical work. Deals mainly with pitch organization.

Simms, Bryan R., *Music of the Twentieth Century; Style and Structure* (New York: Schirmer Books, 1986).

In chapter 5, 'Rhythm and Meter', the author surveys a number of important developments during the century, with reference to non-tonal early twentieth-century works by Ravel, Stravinsky, and Ives.

Suchoff, Benjamin, ed., *Béla Bartók Essays* (London: Faber and Faber, 1976).

This collection of Bartók's writings contains a number of interesting items, such as chapter 9, 'The So-Called Bulgarian Rhythm'. In chapter 42, entitled 'The Folk Songs of Hungary', Bartók writes of 'the quite incredible rhythmic variety inherent in our peasant melodies'. In none of his published writings does he touch upon the intricate relation of pitch and rhythm in his own music, however.

van den Toorn, Pieter, *The Music of Igor Stravinsky* (New Haven, CT, and London: Yale University Press, 1983).

A detailed study of the metric-rhythmic complexity of Stravinsky's music with considerable attention given to the relation between meter and rhythm and pitch. Among the works discussed is *L'Histoire du Soldat*.

Vinton, John, 'Bartók on his own Music', *Journal of the American Musicological Society*, XIX (1960), pp. 232–43.

An annotated compilation of Bartók's comments on his own music, drawn from published as well as unpublished materials.

Winold, Allen, 'Rhythm in Twentieth-Century Music', in *Aspects of Twentieth-Century Music*, ed. Gary Wittlich (Englewood Cliffs, NJ: Prentice-Hall, 1975).

Index

Note: In entries for composers, general references are placed first, followed by musical works, followed by theoretical writings. **Bold** page references indicate detailed analyses; *italic* page references are to musical examples.